Clouded Ambitions

The Trial and the Tower

Fiction by John Sailors

OffCide Gamer Mysteries

Flying the Coop: The Vide Game Mystery Novel

Clouded Ambitions: The Trial and the Tower

Other

Homeownership Disease: The Saga of Owen Cash

Clouded Ambitions

The Trial and the Tower

Another Video Game Mystery Novel

John Sailors

Story Crest Press

Published by Story Crest Press.

Visit us on the Web at www.StoryCrest.com.
Email us at info@storycrest.com.
And find John Sailors on Twitter at
@JSailors_Author.

Special thanks to Jessie, my wife, for putting up with
my endless writing sessions and my proofreading during
football games, and my son, JJ, for video game inspiration.

This is a work of fiction. All characters and
names are invented and the events
are purely make-believe.

Some of the activities described
should not be tried at home.
Or the office.
And certainly not in stairwells.

ISBN: 978-1-938688-12-6

Level 1

The Trial

It's all on video . . . sensors and video:

At a hundred and six degrees the spa burned at the skin but soothed muscles, warmed bones. Within minutes the week's anxieties slipped away, mind left to blissful oblivion . . . when—

The room quaked to the blast—the power of a jet engine firing up—as the building's super-cooling system thrust in a squall of ice-cold air . . . and fire sprinklers gushed freezing water . . . as the spa now scalded at a hundred and eleven . . . a hundred twelve . . .

The man jumped out, ran to the door—what was happening?—found it locked, banged at it with his fists, shouted vainly in the basement of an office tower he knew to be empty.

He grabbed his phone, tried to open the building-control app . . .

. . . got instead a screen that read, simply: "Time to die, Randolph," and within minutes he curled, wrapped in a towel, into fetal position, shivering, dizzy, his thoughts scattered farther, then farther . . . as the room froze the consciousness from his mind, squeezed the life from his veins . . .

1

Kelly.

Kelly Chambers emerges from her twelfth-story suite atop the historic Stanley Hotel, revealing briefly behind her a view of downtown Seattle and Elliot Bay through the windows inside.

A group of police officers watch video of her exit on a floor-to-ceiling "Video Wall," that divided into several large windows displaying her sleek figure from cameras along the ceiling, the walls, the floor . . .

Kelly enters the waiting century-old elevator, slams her shoulder hard against the outer glass door and inner gate, force needed to close them. A ceiling camera inside watches as she presses Lobby, and the car jolts, screeching downward—a clash of 1920s mechanics and twenty-first century security technology.

The elevator's progress pops up on a chart on the Video Wall.

Kelly looks down at the ashtray mounted on the car's wall, a leftover from the Stanley's heyday. Now the ornate brass dish holds a tray of jelly beans and black licorice, an idea Kelly herself came up with as chief executive officer at Cannecare Automation.

"As you can see," explains the executive demonstrating the Cannecare Video Wall, "we have comprehensive footage of Chambers' every movement. That video record is complemented and confirmed by data collected from audio and temperature sensors every few feet, measuring sound and body temperature and more—data you can see in waveform in these windows."

All eyes widen as this information sinks in: damning evidence, high-definition video and correlated sensor data, trial and conviction completed before the suspect is even arrested.

The surveillance continues as Kelly exits the Stanley and makes her way down Second Avenue, where at the other end of the block she enters Cannecare's high-tech headquarters.
The sky is cloudy and gray, typical for Seattle, but there is no rain, not even the pouting drizzle that is the norm.
The sparkling new Cannecare Tower presents a stark contrast to the historic hotel turned company residence that Kelly just left. The structure presents a modern architectural sensation, its spacious lobby adorned with marble floors and abstract sculptures the company never had been able to convince Kelly were, in fact, art.
With the lone security guard watching, Kelly crosses the lobby, glaring at a sculpture off to one side that resembles either an automobile or a duck, depending on which angle it is viewed from. Once across she is greeted by an elevator car that presents further contrast to the Stanley and its ancient lift.
Inside, a video screen plays Bloomberg TV just above where the previous elevator offered candy in an antique brass ashtray.

The Video Wall now shows Kelly from four angles, from cameras above and to the sides. She is dressed in a company uniform of sorts: a red polo shirt with a Cannecare logo, and jeans—part of a morale-building effort begun before she was hired, and one she had continuously failed to overturn.

An irritated expression builds on Kelly's face as she reluctantly offers her right eye to the car's iris scanner. At the same time she sets her right hand on its biometric hand scanner, and an automated computer voice lights up:
"Hello, Miss Chambers? Fine weather today! What floor, please?"
Kelly does not return the recorded voice's cheerful tone. "Penthouse!" she nearly shouts.

When the *vator opens at the top floor, the number of cameras*
covering Ke *ncreases fourfold as a symphony of Video Wall views*
follow he *wn the long hallway, where additional data from*
sensors *her movements in thorough detail.*

end of the hall she sighs and commits to another iris
scan before being admitted through a glass door.

police watch now as Kelly enters the room—a strange
her walking into the same room they now stand in. On
video she sits at the wide console desk where two built-in
mputer screens show schematics of Cannecare Tower.

As Kelly goes to work, a new window appears on the
Video Wall before the assembled police, this one showing an
animation of a computer monitor.

"What you are seeing in this window is a replica of
everything Chambers is doing at this point on the computer,
of everything she sees on that screen," the Cannecare executive
tells the group. "And, again, backed up by correlated sensor
data, and of course computer records of lo— loc— locking . . ."

Stuttering, the executive turns to the screen to hide his
emotion.

A detective speaks up: "Please continue the video segments."

All eyes watch as a menu pops up on the replica of Kelly
screen.

She clicks on Sensor Report, then Club Level, and a b
opens, showing:

Location: Club Level
Temperature: 82 Degrees
Temperature Program: Auto
Occupants: 1

Next she clicks on an icon labeled Security Lo
then Club Level. And a blueprint-like map appears,
readout:

Location: Club Level
Status: All doors locked
Occupants: 1

And in a small room labeled Spa on the map, a re
blinks, locating the lone occupant.

The police now see Kelly smiling for the first time.

She pulls up a new menu and on this one selects S
Temperature, and that she increases to 200 degrees Fahrenheit.
A readout underneath shows the temperature climbing: 104
. . . 105 . . . 106 . . .

On another menu Kelly selects Room Temperature and sets
it to a negative 10 degrees, and a second readout shows the
temperature quickly dropping: 78 . . . 77 . . . 76 . . .

And pulling up another menu she studies its map of the
'oor and selects the corner of the building where the spa is
·ated, then clicks Fire Sprinklers On.

t to make sure you're following," the executive says to
ified faces fixed on the Video Wall, "Chambers has just
building's experimental high-power cooling system
e air temperature down, that after raising the spa's
rature to a dangerous level. And then she drenched
h the fire sprinklers.

by this point, wearing only a swimsuit, has
ng heat to ice-cold temperatures.

of the spa, as well, but that is unnecessarily
demonstration. All the same, the audio
e is that of the victim, just as Chambers
e video before you."

ilent, concentrating on the Video Wall.
continues its descent: 24 . . . 23 . . .
nding on the door: "Open the hell
of here, for God's sake!"

ninutes before the shouting fades
e: "Please, someone, please . . ."

and the pounding gets quieter, as, a moment later, the room falls silent.

On the Video Wall map, the police see the red circle disappear and the readout above the blueprint changes . . . to:

Location: Club Level
Occupants: 0

The video windows freeze as a police detective steps forward.

"I think we've seen enough. Tate was found dead later yesterday evening, curled up next to the spa door. The autopsy's in the making, but it was pretty clear he . . . he froze to death."

Another of the detectives turns and walks to the engineering center's door.

He emerges into the outer hallway where Kelly Chambers sits in an office chair, surrounded on either side by uniformed officers.

"Kelly Chambers," the detective addresses her. "You are under arrest. We're charging you with the murder of Randolph Tate."

Eye makeup is running down one of Kelly's cheeks, as if she's been crying.

In fact she has not. She is, rather, suffering from a problem faced by many women after they move to the Pacific Northwest: how to keep your damn eye makeup from running out of control in the region's infernal nonstop drizzle.

🎮 🎮 🎮

Bernard.

A glob of marinara sauce baked under the early-morning sun that poured in the window, the last remnant of a meatball sandwich Bernard had devoured before fading to sleep the previous night—rather, early morning, as logs on various video games he'd stayed up playing would, on inspection, attest.

Now he awoke, eyes still closed, blissful in the scent of the ocean and the sound of waves rolling onto shore.

Founder and CEO of a video game startup, Bernard spent twelve to fourteen hours a day staring at video screens of one sort or another, and that wasn't counting TV time.

Beyond that, he decided, he needed something more spectacular for his eyes, not to mention some fresh air. So he bought the three-level beach house and on the top floor set up an office-slash-playroom that could have doubled as a video game parlor and a malt shop, not to mention a case study in obsessive behavior.

Oh, and also a sports bar given the TV screens, computer monitors, and laptops that were scattered pretty much everywhere, except that they were used for displaying not football and baseball but rather battles between soldiers and Nazi zombies, or spaceships fighting it out in orbit.

And of course video-capture gameplay of his company's first big video game, *Murder Mystery: The Case of the Cleavered Clerk.*

On this particular morning Bernard awoke also to a soft pounding, a foot tapping . . .

His eyes squinted open, took in light, his brain trying to focus.

He made out ... an egg shape, long, oval, kind of pointed on the bottom.

A face, yes, a face, with a long chin. And a presence that haunted, oppressed . . .

Warily Bernard edged his eyes open wider, identified the shape.

"Is it your intention to sleep all day, Walker?" the frowning egg wailed.

The shape was none other than Herbert Iggid, or *Egghead*, as the staff at OffCide Studios called him, and they were referring not just to the similarity in the sound of his name. Whether viewed straight on or in profile, Herbert Iggid's head was shaped entirely like an egg.

And in terms of personality, the nickname fit wonderfully, as well.

You see, Herbert Iggid was a cold-hearted *nag*, a condescending prude, a hateful rule-citer, and he was the new chief financial officer at OffCide Studios, meaning he was a constant, hounding thorn in the backside of every employee at the company, even Bernard, who, as chairman and CEO, was at least technically Herbert Iggid's boss.

Yes, the tag *egghead* fit Iggid very nicely.

"You were supposed to be at the office, ready to leave, at nine a.m., Walker!" he proclaimed.

Iggid lit into Bernard with a string of accusations, most of them true, about Bernard's unprofessional work behavior, his staying up all night playing video games, his insistence on working primarily at his oceanfront home-studio, and "let's not forget the humongous lunch bills" Bernard was including in his monthly expense accounts.

Iggid stood more than six feet in height, but seemed still to appear somehow short and plump, and in fact the egg shape of his balding head was pretty much emulated by his overall figure.

". . . and the IRS is going to get suspicious," he went on, "especially since most of these receipts are from a *minimart!* Not many people *I* know conduct business events at . . . minimarts!"

The image of the nearby store floated happily into Bernard's mind. 'Ah, MoMo's Minimart,' he sang silently, his brain still in sleep mode as he pictured the new Big Bad Breakfast Wrap that the local market recently began selling: bacon, scrambled eggs, Cheddar cheese, and jalapeño peppers, all wrapped conveniently in a corn tortilla and doused liberally with hot sauce and Parmesan . . .

Come to think of it, it was morning, and morning was the perfect time for Bernard to be thinking about Big Bad Breakfast Wraps . . .

Iggid noticed the empty fast-food wrappers and potato chip bags piled around the room, a sight that helped shed some of his suspicions about the lunch receipts.

As he took further stock of the studio, Bernard sat up slightly and, having not taken in a word the bothersome man had said—but irritated all the same—made a solemn vow to have the outside stairwell that led up to his windowed studio permanently removed. Or at least lethally booby-trapped.

Bernard was wondering sleepily where the nearest Pepsi might be found; he wasn't yet up to investors and time frames. In fact the bathroom, while noticeably in demand, seemed at an insurmountable distance just now.

Eggs, too, hung on his mind, and he wasn't sure whether the image was of a breakfast wrap or a bothersome CFO.

Bernard needed a Pepsi.

"Well, what do you have to say for yourself, Walker?" Iggid demanded.

Bernard sat the rest of the way up and fumbled about his vest pockets until he located a plastic bottle—of, Iggid noticed, *chilled* Pepsi. Bernard twisted it open and took a long draw.

"Sorry," he said, an earnest, innocent tone. "I have not heard a word you've said. Just waking up. Could you start over?"

And as Herbert Iggid the Egghead fumed, Bernard produced another bottle of Pepsi from his vest and held it out.

"Soda?" he offered.

🐾 🐾 🐾

Lester.

Lead Game Designer Lester Argyle studied the list of YouTube videos: screen captures of kids (and often adults) playing his company's first big video game hit: *Murder Mystery: The Case of the Cleavered Clerk*.

When the elevator opens at the top floor, the number of cameras covering Kelly increases fourfold as a symphony of Video Wall views follow her down the long hallway, where additional data from sensors chart her movements in thorough detail.

At the end of the hall she sighs and commits to another iris and hand scan before being admitted through a glass door.

The police watch now as Kelly enters the room—a strange sight, her walking into the same room they now stand in. On the video she sits at the wide console desk where two built-in computer screens show schematics of Cannecare Tower.

As Kelly goes to work, a new window appears on the Video Wall before the assembled police, this one showing an animation of a computer monitor.

"What you are seeing in this window is a replica of everything Chambers is doing at this point on the computer, of everything she sees on that screen," the Cannecare executive tells the group. "And, again, backed up by correlated sensor data, and of course computer records of lo— loc— locking . . ."

Stuttering, the executive turns to the screen to hide his emotion.

A detective speaks up: "Please continue the video segments."

All eyes watch as a menu pops up on the replica of Kelly's screen.

She clicks on Sensor Report, then Club Level, and a box opens, showing:

> **Location:** Club Level
> **Temperature:** 82 Degrees
> **Temperature Program:** Auto
> **Occupants:** 1

Next she clicks on an icon labeled Security Lockdown, then Club Level. And a blueprint-like map appears, with the readout:

Location: Club Level
Status: All doors locked
Occupants: 1

And in a small room labeled Spa on the map, a red circle blinks, locating the lone occupant.

The police now see Kelly smiling for the first time.

She pulls up a new menu and on this one selects Spa Temperature, and that she increases to 200 degrees Fahrenheit. A readout underneath shows the temperature climbing: 104 . . . 105 . . . 106 . . .

On another menu Kelly selects Room Temperature and sets it to a negative 10 degrees, and a second readout shows the temperature quickly dropping: 78 . . . 77 . . . 76 . . .

And pulling up another menu she studies its map of the floor and selects the corner of the building where the spa is located, then clicks Fire Sprinklers On.

"Just to make sure you're following," the executive says to the horrified faces fixed on the Video Wall, "Chambers has just used the building's experimental high-power cooling system to push the air temperature down, that after raising the spa's water temperature to a dangerous level. And then she drenched the room with the fire sprinklers.

"The victim by this point, wearing only a swimsuit, has gone from boiling heat to ice-cold temperatures.

"We have video of the spa, as well, but that is unnecessarily graphic for today's demonstration. All the same, the audio you are hearing here is that of the victim, just as Chambers is listening to it in the video before you."

Everyone remains silent, concentrating on the Video Wall.

The air temperature continues its descent: 24 . . . 23 . . .

The victim begins pounding on the door: "Open the hell up! Somebody get me out of here, for God's sake!"

This goes on for a few minutes before the shouting fades into a sobbing, begging voice: "Please, someone, please . . ."

and the pounding gets quieter, as, a moment later, the room falls silent.

On the Video Wall map, the police see the red circle disappear and the readout above the blueprint changes . . . to:

Location: Club Level
Occupants: 0

The video windows freeze as a police detective steps forward.

"I think we've seen enough. Tate was found dead later yesterday evening, curled up next to the spa door. The autopsy's in the making, but it was pretty clear he . . . he froze to death."

Another of the detectives turns and walks to the engineering center's door.

He emerges into the outer hallway where Kelly Chambers sits in an office chair, surrounded on either side by uniformed officers.

"Kelly Chambers," the detective addresses her. "You are under arrest. We're charging you with the murder of Randolph Tate."

Eye makeup is running down one of Kelly's cheeks, as if she's been crying.

In fact she has not. She is, rather, suffering from a problem faced by many women after they move to the Pacific Northwest: how to keep your damn eye makeup from running out of control in the region's infernal nonstop drizzle.

🎮 🎮 🎮

Bernard.

A glob of marinara sauce baked under the early-morning sun that poured in the window, the last remnant of a meatball sandwich Bernard had devoured before fading to sleep the previous night—rather, early morning, as logs on various video games he'd stayed up playing would, on inspection, attest.

Now he awoke, eyes still closed, blissful in the scent of the ocean and the sound of waves rolling onto shore.

Founder and CEO of a video game startup, Bernard spent twelve to fourteen hours a day staring at video screens of one sort or another, and that wasn't counting TV time.

Beyond that, he decided, he needed something more spectacular for his eyes, not to mention some fresh air. So he bought the three-level beach house and on the top floor set up an office-slash-playroom that could have doubled as a video game parlor and a malt shop, not to mention a case study in obsessive behavior.

Oh, and also a sports bar given the TV screens, computer monitors, and laptops that were scattered pretty much everywhere, except that they were used for displaying not football and baseball but rather battles between soldiers and Nazi zombies, or spaceships fighting it out in orbit.

And of course video-capture gameplay of his company's first big video game, *Murder Mystery: The Case of the Cleavered Clerk.*

On this particular morning Bernard awoke also to a soft pounding, a foot tapping . . .

His eyes squinted open, took in light, his brain trying to focus.

He made out . . . an egg shape, long, oval, kind of pointed on the bottom.

A face, yes, a face, with a long chin. And a presence that haunted, oppressed . . .

Warily Bernard edged his eyes open wider, identified the shape.

"Is it your intention to sleep all day, Walker?" the frowning egg wailed.

The shape was none other than Herbert Iggid, or *Egghead,* as the staff at OffCide Studios called him, and they were referring not just to the similarity in the sound of his name. Whether viewed straight on or in profile, Herbert Iggid's head was shaped entirely like an egg.

And in terms of personality, the nickname fit wonderfully, as well.

You see, Herbert Iggid was a cold-hearted *nag*, a condescending prude, a hateful rule-citer, and he was the new chief financial officer at OffCide Studios, meaning he was a constant, hounding thorn in the backside of every employee at the company, even Bernard, who, as chairman and CEO, was at least technically Herbert Iggid's boss.

Yes, the tag *egghead* fit Iggid very nicely.

"You were supposed to be at the office, ready to leave, at nine a.m., Walker!" he proclaimed.

Iggid lit into Bernard with a string of accusations, most of them true, about Bernard's unprofessional work behavior, his staying up all night playing video games, his insistence on working primarily at his oceanfront home-studio, and "let's not forget the humongous lunch bills" Bernard was including in his monthly expense accounts.

Iggid stood more than six feet in height, but seemed still to appear somehow short and plump, and in fact the egg shape of his balding head was pretty much emulated by his overall figure.

". . . and the IRS is going to get suspicious," he went on, "especially since most of these receipts are from a *minimart!* Not many people *I* know conduct business events at . . . minimarts!"

The image of the nearby store floated happily into Bernard's mind. 'Ah, MoMo's Minimart,' he sang silently, his brain still in sleep mode as he pictured the new Big Bad Breakfast Wrap that the local market recently began selling: bacon, scrambled eggs, Cheddar cheese, and jalapeño peppers, all wrapped conveniently in a corn tortilla and doused liberally with hot sauce and Parmesan . . .

Come to think of it, it was morning, and morning was the perfect time for Bernard to be thinking about Big Bad Breakfast Wraps . . .

Iggid noticed the empty fast-food wrappers and potato chip bags piled around the room, a sight that helped shed some of his suspicions about the lunch receipts.

As he took further stock of the studio, Bernard sat up slightly and, having not taken in a word the bothersome man had said—but irritated all the same—made a solemn vow to have the outside stairwell that led up to his windowed studio permanently removed. Or at least lethally booby-trapped.

Bernard was wondering sleepily where the nearest Pepsi might be found; he wasn't yet up to investors and time frames. In fact the bathroom, while noticeably in demand, seemed at an insurmountable distance just now.

Eggs, too, hung on his mind, and he wasn't sure whether the image was of a breakfast wrap or a bothersome CFO.

Bernard needed a Pepsi.

"Well, what do you have to say for yourself, Walker?" Iggid demanded.

Bernard sat the rest of the way up and fumbled about his vest pockets until he located a plastic bottle—of, Iggid noticed, *chilled* Pepsi. Bernard twisted it open and took a long draw.

"Sorry," he said, an earnest, innocent tone. "I have not heard a word you've said. Just waking up. Could you start over?"

And as Herbert Iggid the Egghead fumed, Bernard produced another bottle of Pepsi from his vest and held it out.

"Soda?" he offered.

🎮 🎮 🎮

Lester.

Lead Game Designer Lester Argyle studied the list of YouTube videos: screen captures of kids (and often adults) playing his company's first big video game hit: *Murder Mystery: The Case of the Cleavered Clerk.*

The game had been so popular that hundreds of the videos sprang up on sites like YouTube, often with voiceover explaining what was happening.

Lester put on thick-framed glasses that sat too large on his narrow face and clicked on one of the gameplay videos.

The Case of the Cleavered Clerk: A haunted bank building in the 1920s, from the point of view of a newly hired clerk who has arrived for his first day of work (on a spooky street in an eerie neighborhood) to discover this is no ordinary bank.

He reports to the bank manager's office to find an older, balding man seated at a desk, stuffing his mouth with what appears to be raw, bloody meat. Smiling, blood dripping down his chin, the manager emits a terrifying laugh, as other bank employees begin to surround the desk, each of them armed with a hunting knife—and a large fork.

"Save a leg for me!" the bank manager shouts, his evil laugh continuing to echo through the building.

Lester forwards the video.

Level 2: A detective strolls through the main office of the bank, his deerstalker detective cap shading the view through his large magnifying glass.

"Chopped pieces of flesh are all that remain of the victim," the detective states in an unidentifiable but captivating accent.

"Where were these morsels—um, chunks of flesh—found?" inquires the bank manager.

"In your office. Can you tell me what happened to the poor man?"

"Got his tie caught in the paper shredder?" ventures the bank manager, before turning briefly to conceal a burp.

Lester smiled.

How can you *better* that?

The game had been so popular ... and yet after two sequels, it had all dried up, and the company was having a hell of a time coming up with something new to match it. No, not match it. They were told to *better* it.

How can you *better* that?

All this left investors breathing down his and Bernard's necks, asking daily for time frames on new releases.

At twenty-six, Lester was the senior member of the design team, after Bernard, both in rank and age, and that meant it was up to him to produce ideas when Bernard had his mind on other things.

Lester stared at the screen. Who could match a murder like this?

🎮 🎮 🎮

Kelly.

Kelly Chambers sat thankfully alone in a tiny cell, staring out, her mind concentrating on a single thought.

She had not cried. She had not cried since she was nine, that after striking out in a youth baseball game, and she was not crying—*would not cry*—now.

Oddly, the fact that she had been arrested for murder, the fact that she was sitting in jail, the fact that she was facing more trouble than she could ever imagine, these were not what occupied the top portion of her mind.

The thing was, off in the distance, down a hall of sorts, Kelly could see a tiny window, and the color was . . . blue.

So not only was Kelly sitting in jail, but she happened to be sitting in jail on the first day in ninety-three consecutive days (*ninety-flipping-three—she had been counting them!*) that the sun had come out in the city, a glorious event that occurred just as the police were locking her in the oppressive cell.

And she now sat crouched on a cot viewing the miracle through a distant square of window in a Seattle jail.

Cold, gruesome murders, Kelly reflected, sure were a pain in the neck.

Kelly was still steaming on this thought when two officers escorted her out to a small cubicle where she was told she could make a phone call.

One of the officers waiting there offered support, asking if she needed help finding an attorney.

Kelly said, no, she did not; she would not be calling an attorney.

The comment lifted eyebrows among the group gathered to observe the now-quite-famous murder suspect. Not calling a lawyer?

This corporate-executive-gone-bad might be one real space case after all, it seemed.

Kelly picked up the receiver and dialed.

🦅 🦅 🦅

Bernard.

Bernard's phone rang, disturbing his concentration. He sat engrossed in a video game spread across three 32-inch monitors as he battled for dominance across the European continent: from the Lowlands, to France, then the Papal States, then Switzerland (yeah, they've always been neutral, but *have you tried the chocolate?*) . . .

A small meter top left showed that more than forty brick-and-mortar players were logged on, from who knew where around the world, competing to take over the virtual globe that existed both in the cloud and on all of their computer screens.

Bernard's avatar, named OffCide Gamer, was a large, terrifying figure commanding armies of mercenary zombies that sacked villages to gather supplies and spread their domination farther across the face of the globe.

In the brick-and-mortar world Bernard looked very much like the massive avatar: With his oversize frame hiding to some degree his rolls of body fat, he appeared larger somehow than humans are supposed to—a small giant walking among men.

The phone rang a second time as Bernard finished conquering Southern Germania and combined it with Gallia.

Then it rang again . . . then again. Bernard always wondered why it did that. He heard it the first time! Didn't Alexander Graham Bell have any sense?

After three more rings, the phone switched to voice mail, a useless function since it was full, allowing no new messages to be accepted.

Bernard made a mental note to have the low-tech device disconnected.

And as if the thought redirected the caller, his main smart-phone suddenly lit up to the classic *Mario Bros.* theme song that he set as its ring tone.

The song was well into the second verse before Bernard checked the device, trying to decide whether to silence the ringer, decline the call, or throw the stupid thing out the window—a fate suffered by at least three previous phones in the year and a half Bernard had been living at the beach house.

He eyed the screen, saw the area code: 206. Where the heck was that? He opened a new window and typed a search on the number. A robocall scam, perhaps?

The results spit back: "King County Adult Detention." What the heck was that?

Bernard looked back at the game. The Evil Iberian had just captured the rest of Northern Africa and appeared to be going after Southern France, a territory Bernard had just taken over. If this latest invasion continued, he soon would have more zombies on his doorstep than he was ready for.

The phone continued to beg for attention. Bernard bit his lip, took a long, hard draw of Pepsi, and—very reluctantly—tapped Answer.

Kelly glanced back, judged that none of the officers was standing close enough to hear.

"Bernard," she said, "this is Kelly, Kelly Chambers."

"Who?"

"Kelly *Chambers*, Bernard."

Silence.

Then: "Kelly Chambers? *Thee* Kelly Chambers? You mean that *Benedict Arnold* Kelly Chambers who *abandoned* my company, abandoned my staff, abandoned *me!*, all for a measly pay raise? *That* Kelly Chambers?"

"It was a pay raise of nearly twelve million dollars, Bernard."

"I offered to raise your transportation allowance."

"I worked at home."

"Which *I* allowed. In your current assignment you are living, where is it again? Seattle?" He checked the computer screen. "King County Adult Detention? I'm sorry, but I fail to identify the qualities of a promotion in all of this."

"I was *arrested*, Bernard."

"What? Hah! I'm sorry, but I have no sympathy. No, I have no sympathy at all. Rather I have something called a *Herbert Iggid*—the man *you* hired as your replacement. The man who is making my life and everyone else's life *miserable*. So I hope you're not calling to ask for a favor or something."

"I need your help, Bernard."

"Hah! My help! Hah! Do you have *any idea* what this *Iggid* is doing? He actually expects me to go in to the office."

"I'm sorry, Bernard, but I'm . . . this is serious." Kelly's voice broke as she said it.

Bernard squinted. What could be more serious than waking up to the shape of Herbert Iggid standing over you? He checked again the search result: King County Adult Detention. How could a county have a king?

But Bernard did not do well with breaking voices, particularly from someone strong, and he knew Kelly Chambers to be very strong.

"What does that mean, King County Adult Detention?"

"I've been *arrested*, Bernard. Didn't you hear me? I'm in jail." Kelly pleaded, knowing the personality she was dealing with.

"Arrested? Kelly Chambers *arrested*? That doesn't make any sense. For *what?*"

"For murder."

"What? Murder? *What* murder?" Bernard broke into a laugh, but it faded as his brain connected *arrested* with *adult detention*. "You said *murder?*"

"*First degree* murder, yes, thank you, and I've already been tried and convicted on a computer."

"They arrested *you* for *murder?*"

"Yeah, and I think this is my one phone call."

Bernard hesitated.

"Your *one* phone call?" he asked. "I am not an expert on such matters, but from what I've seen watching movies and TV, you're supposed to contact *a lawyer* with your one phone call."

"Yeah, I know, thanks."

"Yeah?"

"Yeah. But a lawyer can't help me, Bernard. It's *that* serious. I need *you*, Bernard. *You* and your engineers—Lester Argyle and Eric Lyle. I need you here in Seattle, now!"

"What?"

"You heard me, Bernard."

"And what would possess you to imagine I might just drop everything to fly to Seattle? *Seattle* of all places. To help *a former employee* who *betrayed* me, you Benedict Arnold. Hah!"

"You owe me, Bernard."

"I *owe* you? *How* do you figure that?"

"I got you out of a bind a while back, remember? You gotta help me."

"You did *no* such thing."

"Yeah, I did. Listen, I know—Iggid. I hear Iggid's a real pain in the ass to work with. Coming to Seattle would get you away, and as soon as this mess is figured out, I promise I'll find some way of getting rid of him for you . . ."

"I'm sorry, but what you suggest is simply *not* going to happen. I *happen* to have a particularly full schedule throughout this week. I am preparing for a major video game tournament, and I need both to practice and to prepare myself mentally. And *that* is not going to happen in . . . in *Seattle*."

"Bernard . . ." Kelly pleaded. "I could go to prison. For life."

" . . ."

"I need your help, Bernard . . . You're my only hope. You and your technology. That's all that can save me. You solved a murder once before, and now you have to do it again."

"Why do I have to?"

"Because I know you. I know you won't be able to concentrate on whatever video game it is. You'll have the image of me rotting away in jail burning in your mind."

"And if I help you, you'll make the egghead go away?"

"Iggid, you mean? Yeah. I promise I will. And I'll make it so you never again have someone forcing you to get up early and go to the office."

Kelly's voice broke as she said this.

"Please, Bernard . . ."

2

Iggid.

Herbert Iggid replaced Kelly Chambers as chief financial officer at OffCide Studios, the video game company Bernard founded.

Chambers hired him after taking the job of chief executive officer at Cannecare Automation in Seattle—fulfilling her long-held dream of heading a tech company. Moving on, she thought it prudent to leave OffCide with a financial chief who would provide a check and balance against an unconventional company culture that considered interdepartmental pool tournaments in the break room more important than scheduled meetings.

On Iggid's fourth day at OffCide he held a mandatory all-staff meeting at eight-thirty a.m., a work event announced with promises of retaliation for any staff who failed to attend, and also one scheduled so early it was unprecedented at OffCide Studios, where office hours typically began sometime around twelve.

And so on this morning, from engineering to marketing, employees wandered in laden with coffee, nutrition bars, and donuts, some horrified, others amused, at seeing what their colleagues looked like before noon—the hour when most of them would *normally* have begun stumbling in at.

But for those who smiled at the entertainment, their jubilance quickly evaporated at the sight of Chief Financial Officer Herbert Iggid as he marched to the front of the conference room, which now was jam-packed with forty people, most of them standing.

Producing notes, Iggid proceeded to explain at length how he had never encountered an office where no one observed any sort of "proper" work hours, and he went on to read a list of new policies for OffCide Studios that ranged from mandatory use of a punch clock and fines for failing to clock in and out on time, to a new dress code (that included having to wear actual shoes!), to even a rule against playing around on company time.

At a video game company!

Herbert Iggid, you see, had more than thirty years' experience running company finances at both major corporations and tech startups, but all in the Boston area, a stiffly cold region where companies enforced conservative business cultures, where people dressed in suits and ties and arrived at work by eight or nine—and where offices did *not* have foosball tables and bunk beds for post-lunch (dinner) naps.

Herbert Iggid never had any fun at work. He certainly didn't see why other people should.

The day after the "Egghead Event," as it became known, a delegation of staff from every department in the company—including the weekend security guards, who had been told they could no longer barbecue during their shifts—descended upon nearby Cliff Shores, where Bernard's home-studio was located. They went to demand something be done about the egghead.

But they arrived to find Bernard engrossed in a game of *League of Legends* on one computer while a game of *American Zombie Slicer* streamed on another.

Exasperated at the interruption, he paused briefly to hear their complaints, then side-stepped the issue by emailing Iggid to express heartfelt approval for the time-clock plan. He added that he had assigned several engineers to develop a system that would *force* employees to punch in using the GPS technology on mobile phones, which of course by proving they were actually *on* the premises would be far more reliable than traditional punch cards.

Reading the message, Iggid swelled with pride for having so reformed such a wreck of a company straight off the bat. In the days that followed, he was particularly elated to review the glittering attendance rolls that were automatically "pushed" to his own new smartphone each morning . . . until the following Friday, when the entire staff was present, or so his phone told him, but in fact the only person Iggid could find, on inspection, was the security guard on duty, and he was sitting on a balcony cleaning a barbecue grill.

It was only then that Iggid recalled seeing a requisition form for fifty smartphones, with a note at the bottom identifying the order as GPS phones for the employee time clock system.

And strolling about the office, he noticed that nearly every desk had an identical phone sitting on it—no doubt informing the system that the worker whose desk it was was present.

"I should have forced them to have GPS technology implanted in their *behinds*," Iggid growled at every unused smartphone within hearing distance, which was pretty far.

By Monday morning the main entryway had been redesigned to feature a punch clock beneath a menacingly visible security camera and a framed printout that read, in intimidatingly thick type:

> **I am watching!**
> **Always!**
> ~H. Iggid.

"Time clocks!" Iggid repeated over and over. "This is how IBM got started. This'll put our workforce on a reliable record that we can show to investors, banks, everyone."

🐾 🐾 🐾

Monday afternoon.

Bernard's expression projected gloom as he met with Lester Argyle, Eric Lyle, and the company's newest game designer,

Patricia Mayhelm, a girl all of about twenty who was known to walk the extra mile to show disrespect for any sort of authority, but who was brilliant at designing textures for video game modeling.

Bernard had planned to spend the week sequestered in his oceanfront studio preparing for the upcoming video game tournament . . . and now apparently he was going to Seattle to help someone he did not particularly like.

It was news he would keep to himself, though; there was no way he was going to bring Lester and Eric with him, and certainly not the sassy new girl.

If they came along, Bernard knew, he would get sucked even deeper into this mess that Kelly Chambers had gotten herself into.

No. He had a plan. He would fly to Seattle, meet with an arranged attorney, get Kelly out on bail, make a quick appearance, and immediately return to Cliff Shores to prepare for the video game tournament. He figured he could be there and back in two days, maybe faster.

He had only to get through this final meeting and he could go.

Before them now on one of six large TVs in his studio was the face of Chen Li, head of their production team in Beijing.

"These are the avatars we've been using in demonstrations," Chen said, as a second TV screen lit to show cartoon images of Bernard and Lester, avatars that featured neither detail nor imagination.

No one spoke for a moment. Then: "I would strive to make them more interesting, Chen." Bernard said. "Make them caricatures. Exaggerate certain features to make them . . . more appealing."

"Or at least less boring," Patricia added.

"I don't understand."

Bernard sipped his Pepsi. "Let me show you an example." On another TV he opened a shared window and a browser, clicked on Image Search and typed in "Brad Pitt"—and instantly the screen filled with thumbnails of the actor wearing an array of haircuts, from long to short, and looking irritatingly handsome regardless.

"Now which of his features, what parts of his face, could we exaggerate or change to make him look funny?"

"Maybe his nose, or lips?" Chen ventured.

"That would work. Let's see." Now Bernard added the word *caricature* to the search and the screen showed row after row of comical Brad Pitt faces with stretched features, many of them with emphasis on wide jaws.

"Let me show a better example," Patricia butted in. She pointed her cellphone camera at Bernard, snapped a picture, and then using a three-dollar app created a caricature that bloated Bernard's cheeks, gave him a fat, protruding chin, and turned his hair purple.

Texting the new image to the chat session they all were using, she smiled at her boss, whose brick-and-mortar face was also transforming.

For a brief instant the room was silent, all eyes on Bernard, until the tension was cut by the laughter of several people on Chen's end and then Chen himself, causing Lester and the others to join in.

And The Stare of Death fell helpless against the mischievous but somehow sisterly smirk of the girl who had been entertaining everyone recently by signing onto Internet games using the name The Girl Who Clobbers Bernard, and several times since starting at the company outplaying him in *Counter-Strike*.

Bernard vowed to spend any free time he had over the next few days hunting her down in whatever video game world he could find her in, and ambushing her.

"I understand," Chen said. "I'll make new avatars on the airplane."

"Good." Bernard took a gulp of soda. "We can discuss it more when you get here. You are ready to go?"

"Of course. I'm looking forward to the trip. It's my first time to go to the states, you know."

"I'll show you around *personally*," Patricia said. She had been working a lot with Chen over the past month.

Bernard eyed Chen, then the girl.

This, he figured, was not the ideal cultural ambassador for the first visit to the United States of their China manager, Chen Li.

🐾 🐾 🐾

Kelly Chambers lay alone in a cell of sorts, a space she judged to be the size of the closet in her tiny Manhattan apartment.

From her Manhattan apartment, which she was renting out while in Seattle, Kelly could see one corner of the Empire State Building, her meek claim to fame given that even her high salary and stock options had not amounted to more-substantial real estate in her beloved New York City.

And for the past eight months she'd been stuck living out of the historic Stanley Hotel suite that afforded, her company had promised, a "breathtaking view" of Elliot Bay, the stretch of water that downtown Seattle was built on.

But in fact for pretty much the entire eight months' time the windows showcased a grand view of drizzle and clouds and a city struggling against the soaking rain, and her superior vantage point served only to heighten the resulting depression.

And now she lay in jail on a cot sort of affair no doubt in-fested with bedbugs from God only knows who had slept there before, and . . . and . . . and, yes, far worse, off in the distance she could see the window, and a tiny square of clear-freakin'-blue sky and glorious sunshine.

Now, finally the day local residents had been promising would make up for the long gray winter, the first sunny day of spring, a day on which, she had been assured, everyone in the city would light up, would smile . . . the day had finally come.

Kelly eyed the distant window, then the woman across the way who threatened to kill every person who happened to walk by.

"Happy freakin' spring!" Kelly mumbled.

Monday evening, eight-fifty p.m.

Tired of waiting in traffic, Herbert Iggid got out of his limousine two blocks from the office to continue on foot, as much as he hated walking in this city.

Herbert Iggid had spent the majority of his life in Class A offices, country clubs, and gated communities, and the frightening mix of people he encountered on San Francisco streets scared him more than he admitted.

The city's South of Market area, where OffCide Studios had joined the host of startups flocking to the growing tech hub, was just blocks away from the financial district, the shopping district, and close behind them Chinatown, Japantown, and more . . .

And within a few-block radius he passed people ranging from global banking executives in three-piece suits, to hordes of tourists sporting cameras and shopping bags, to buskers playing saxophones or drums fashioned out of coffee cans.

So it was already with a bit of discomfort that he made his way into the office Monday evening, adding to the irritation he felt at having to come in at nine at night, just so he could meet with company staff—the design team included.

Iggid comforted himself by relishing his coming announcement: Most of them would see their pay docked, for violating company work rules.

Iggid got off the elevator on the fourth floor and swiped his ID in a reader, unlocking the giant glass door that led into the dark, empty lobby. As he entered, the automatic door squeaked closed behind him and locked with a startling *clang*.

Herbert scanned the lobby, so empty at night, focused on the floor-to-ceiling glass that offered—should have offered—a clear view into the production and design departments beyond . . . but everything was dark. No lights?

Had the entire staff decided *not* to attend the meeting after he had driven into the city?

But wait. A light *was* on, a *flickering* light toward the back. In the unfamiliar dark, Iggid ventured halfway across the lobby, darting his head back and forth but making out no detail through the glass.

Then from inside, a loud crash.

Iggid jumped, and inched behind a plant along one wall.

A shape appeared, a dark silhouette that began to glide across the glass wall that separated the lobby. As it neared, it took on more definition . . . it was a person . . . yes . . . *holding up a gun*—a pistol raised above the silhouette's head.

A blow of panic hitting his throat, Iggid glared back at the outer glass door that had just *locked* loudly behind him. He estimated the time it would take to swipe his ID to *unlock* it, and how much noise that would cause—and still he would be left to wait for the slow elevator. No escape.

The shape continued to stride across the glass wall.

Iggid squatted and crawled, careful to remain silent, to the reception desk and the stationery closet slash supply room behind it. He fumbled about to locate the doorknob, and found the thing locked! And he could see the figure nearing the glass door that opened into the lobby.

Herbert grabbed at his pockets, found his giant set of keys, began sifting through them frantically in search of the one he needed. As chief financial officer, Iggid insisted on having a key to everything, and while the key to the stationery closet suddenly seemed to be an item of grave importance, he was now finding less useful the key to the coffee-storage cupboard, the key to the small on-site data center, or for that matter the key to the women's rest room.

What did the key to the stationery closet look like? He glanced up at the lock, tried to make out its shape, then remembered it was that key with images of video game characters on the sides. He had been embarrassed more than once while using it.

Now he praised the silly, wonderful decorations, checked the dark shape in the glass before reaching up, and silently unlocked the door, breath held, and slipped inside.

Monday night, forty minutes earlier.

Lester Argyle came rushing into the office sporting a wide smile, his enthusiasm catching the attention of his co-workers, who turned from work stations to see what was happening.

"They came," he shouted to Patricia, who stood at a pool table at the far end of the space. "They're here!"

"Cool!"

Lester rushed over and set two packages on the table, disturbing the balls as he did so. Producing a utility knife from his pocket, he cut the tape on one box as Patricia began to open the other.

From the boxes, they each pulled out a black leather case, and opening them to the oohs and aahs of the others, revealed high-power airsoft BB pistols designed to resemble real handguns.

"The Prostman 2100 BB pistol," Lester proclaimed. "Check it out. It's semiautomatic, has a superaccurate red-dot sight, a flashlight on the side, Bluetooth, and it shoots different pellets."

"I got the Prostman X-Eagle," Patricia countered. "These things look seriously real, you got to admit. We're going to kill Eric with these."

"Oh, yeah," Lester agreed as he turned toward Eric Lyle's desk.

His smile faded when he saw it was empty—and worse, empty save for Eric's new oversize smartphone, the latest device to capture Eric's imagination.

All eyes followed and the room fell silent. Eric Lyle never set down whatever new device he had become fixated on, be it a handheld game console or a smartphone, never, unless . . . he had some . . . reason . . .

And in unison the entire group of about ten-plus software engineers and animators jumped to the floor as a barrage of plastic BBs came shooting out of the kitchenette and at the space Lester and Patricia just barely managed to vacate.

The two of them rolled behind the pool table, grabbing the gun cases along the way.

They quickly loaded their new weapons and opened fire as Eric dashed from the kitchenette toward the pinball machine.

And they now found themselves facing not only Eric but several other workers who had produced airsoft guns, and within minutes the entire office broke out into open warfare.

The situation degenerated as the engineers spread to the distant set of cubicles that held the Marketing Department, a well-armed group but one lacking the sophisticated weaponry and competitive mind-set of the attackers.

The marketing people retreated into Accounting, a department so dull and uninspired it could have been readily occupied by a janitor shooting rubber bands.

The quality control team then stole the leftover sandwiches from Marketing's afternoon staff meeting. The hardware research guy, who had rigged all the office's lights so he could control them from a tablet, plunged much of the floor into darkness.

And three of the animators introduced into the equation weapons of mass destruction—power squirt guns!—which added a whole new dimension to interdepartmental politics.

🎮 🎮 🎮

A bare trace of light slipped under the door of the otherwise-dark stationery closet.

Iggid took out his new smartphone—they forced him to junk his BlackBerry and switch to an iPhone.

But, boy, was that turning out to be a good thing. Yes, he could quietly call 911 from here. He wouldn't even have to speak; these things had GPS tracking on them, technology required by government mandate for this very reason, emergency calls *just like this*.

He pushed the power button and—flash, the screen lit up the room, causing him nearly to drop the device.

Covering it with his suit coat, Iggid froze and listened. He heard no sound, saw no change of light under the door.

He took a deep breath, dialed 911 . . . and nothing.

Studying the top of the screen, he located the connection status, and . . . no bars.

No bars!

In Boston, his BlackBerry never read no bars, but here in San Francisco they apparently had these "wireless dead zones" people talked about.

He never understood what that meant. Now he did.

No bars!

🦬 🦬 🦬

The glass door from the offices swung open as Lester and Patricia paraded out, triumphant smiles on their faces.

"We killed 'em," Patricia shouted.

"I shot Lyle right in the butt! You should have seen him jump," Lester added.

Shivering in the dark of the stationery closet, Herbert Iggid heard every word . . . Was this for real?

Patricia held her gun up. "We can kill everyone with these."

"Hey, hang on." Les reached into his pocket. "I need to get some batteries from the stationery room."

'Oh God,' Iggid moaned to himself.

"Better reload your gun," Patricia shouted, just as Les edged open the door. "There might be someone still hiding in there."

'Oh God, oh God!'

With the door opened just a bit, Lester turned back and proclaimed in a proud voice: "With this pistol, I can take out anyone who—"

He turned on the light to find himself in surprising and not altogether comfortable proximity to Herbert Iggid.

"Hey, Herbert," he said, trying to hide his astonishment. "How ya doin'? How can you see in here? Oh, looking forward to the meeting." He reached to a shelf on one side and helped himself to a large pack of double-A batteries.

He turned to leave, then as an afterthought turned back to Iggid. "Hey, check out the new BB gun." He held it up. "Packs the feel and the look of the real thing. Cool or what?"

Herbert sort of nodded.

Les thought about the planned meeting, which wound up turning into a companywide airsoft war, and realized perhaps this might be an ideal time *not* to be present in the office.

And without further conversation he and a wide-eyed Patricia hurried out the main door to the elevator, intent on making the fastest getaway possible.

Iggid shivered, then sighed as he walked out of the stationery room. "*BB gun*?" he asked aloud.

"I was dialing 911 to say I was being attacked by a toy *BB gun*?

"That's it. Those kids have gone too far. And I come in at nine o'clock and the entire company fails to show?"

It was only then that Iggid realized all the lights were now back on inside, and through the glass he could see what appeared to be the entire staff present in the building. Except of course for that damned Argyle and the upstart girl he hired.

🐾 🐾 🐾

"Please empty your pockets and put everything into this bin. And you need to take your shoes off and set them in here."

The man who spoke was well groomed, his hair cropped clean, his uniform lined with sharp creases from thorough pressing.

And yet he had not the slightest hint of manners, Bernard noted, appalled at the officer's rude tone.

Bernard pried off his loafers and put them in one bin, and, glancing behind, saw the entire line of waiting passengers staring. 'Why am I being picked on?' he asked himself.

But the general view among his fellow passengers was, yes, here indeed was a person worth checking very carefully in Airport Security.

His wrinkled photographer's vest, the bulging pockets, the messed-up hair and sleepy eyes . . . he looked as though he had just escaped from a mental institution. Or been kicked out.

But far scarier, the two laptop bags he carried were packed too tight to zip fully, leaving unexplained cords to protrude out the top and the side pockets.

"Those are five-thousand-dollar computers," Bernard cautioned as another officer fed his bags into an X-Ray machine. "Be careful with those."

And of course Bernard beeped as he stepped through the metal detector, and he was called aside for further inspection.

He now found himself facing the officer who took his shoes and a heavy-set woman wearing an expression that said she didn't need any help if there were trouble here.

The woman took a hand scanner and motioned it along the right side of Bernard's vest, causing it to ring at two different points. She frowned, then scanned the other side with much the same result.

"OK, this time *really* empty out your pockets," she said in a tone Bernard considered lacking completely in etiquette. "Everything."

"You can't be serious."

"Oh, yeah, I am very serious. Place everything right there on the table."

Bernard eyed the woman, eyed the other two officers, peered back at the very interested crowd that was working its way past him.

"Very well," he growled.

From a pocket on the lower right, he pulled out a submarine sandwich. Next came a bag of beef jerky . . . then two small bags of potato chips, a donut . . . and several candy bars.

And it was clear he was not finished.

And that this was already turning into an unpleasant trip.

🦬 🦬 🦬

Woeful WasteWorld: The year is 2417 and the planet has fallen victim to a plague that turns people into crazed zombies.

Only a few dozen survivors are left unaffected (twenty-three logged-in players currently, according to the meter top right), and these lucky few must attempt to round up armies of mutant animals, monsters, and zombies, and use them to reconquer the world.

One such leader gazes down from a cliff as her low-pitch laugh echoes across the valley below. Her name is Mainly Mayhem (Patricia in the brick-and-mortar world), and her opponents are unable to detect her sex, since the software has, by her settings, lowered her voice several octaves and added to it a deep, pounding echo.

In her path lies West Transylvania, and it appears to be hers for the taking. Viewing the undefended land before her, she relishes the prize: an army of vampires that will be brought under her command. And if she manages to move beyond and beat opponents into the dark forests of East Transylvania, she will be able to add an army of werewolves to the mix.

Off along the hills to the south, scattered AI (computer-generated) zombies can be seen roaming.

And, alas, it appears nothing can stop her. She will arrive well ahead of the AI zombies.

So it is without fear that Mainly Mayhem floats down into the valley to claim the valuable prize . . . and it is with a great deal of surprise that she finds herself facing the dreaded OffCide Gamer, who . . .

"Oh damn!"

. . . jumps from behind a rock and slices her in half with a sword.

And Mainly Mayhem is killed (by her brick-and-mortar boss) and left to respawn in her native Scandinavia, half a continent away.

"Damn it, Bernard," shouts Mainly Mayhem.

A message appears in the text window at the bottom of the screen. "Hah!" it reads.

🎮 🎮 🎮

The Pendrite Hotel in Seattle offered views in every direction: to the north the glittering downtown that spreads toward the distant Space Needle; to the south the ornate vintage high-rises and Pioneer Square; to the east the hospitals and red-brick apartments of Pill Hill across Interstate 5; and to the west the water of Elliot Bay that serves as a moist reminder that Seattle is a city built on water, both salt- and fresh-.

Bernard's suite faced northward, offering a view that would have left most travelers in awe.

But to Bernard it served merely as a backdrop to two laptops, their screens devoted to a massive Internet search for fast-food restaurants, delis, and minimarts—the three-hundred-dollar-per-night vantage point complementing his digital search.

"Minimart," he typed in both Google and Bing search boxes, and the results showed only two within walking distance, one an Asian foods market—possibly interesting—the other apparently a concession space at a local hospital.

"Fast food," he typed next, and his opinion of Seattle improved markedly as the maps filled with red (Google) and blue (Bing) circles denoting locations of McDonald's, Subway, Quiznos, Jack in the Box, and . . . Taco Del Mar . . .

Lastly, on a note of curiosity, he searched on "coffee shop"— this was Seattle, after all. And the number of dots on the maps tripled, marking the locations of countless Starbucks, as well as coffee bars, coffee houses, coffee roasters, coffee counters, and café this-and-thats.

Suddenly the aromatic ambiance brewing on the two screens was shattered by a Skype video window that popped up.

It was Wilbur Kendeff, the Seattle attorney Bernard's own lawyer hired to work on Kelly's case.

Clicking on Answer, Bernard found himself looking at a thin-faced man who did not appear at all comfortable at the idea of a videoconference.

"You happen to be late," Bernard started out.

"Hi . . . uh . . . You're Bernard Walker?"

"Yes, and I assume you are Wilbur Kendeff."

"Correct. Sorry, I'm late. I got my intern here to download Skype. It really would've been easier for me to visit you at your hotel."

"It would not have been easier for me. I do have priorities."

"Yeeaaah . . ."

"So where are we with Kelly Chambers?"

Kendeff collected himself and set out a legal pad before him.

"They're going to arraign Miss Chambers tomorrow morning," he said, a slow monotone.

Figuring it took the attorney four seconds to pass on this information, Bernard calculated that at four hundred and twenty-five dollars an hour in legal fees, he had just spent roughly forty-four cents to hear the news, then realized he had spent another forty-four cents figuring out how much it had cost.

Bernard arrived in Seattle that evening and checked into the plush suite. His hope was to get whatever business Kelly had gotten herself into, over with as quickly as possible.

"She is currently being held without bail," Kendeff said, not sure if Bernard was paying attention. "We can bring that up at the arraignment, though I am in no way optimistic."

Another forty-four cents to learn the man was not optimistic?

Bernard glared at Kendeff, fixing his Look on the man.

"You are . . . *not optimistic*?"

"No. Considering the circumstances, the odds of getting Miss Chambers released on bail are about the same as, say, my winning the Kentucky Derby. You see, the Seattle Police Department's CSI people went in to collect evidence while the homicide detectives questioned people at the company . . . and, basically, well, both groups left the murder scene about an hour later . . . *giggling*."

"Giggling?"

"Yes, giggling. *Visibly*; there were news cameras. You see, Miss Chambers' company makes these state-of-the-art building automation and security systems that employ heavy use of video surveillance, coupled with sensors in the ceilings and walls that detect every movement. They track heat, sound, and other data. And apparently all the data are instantly correlated with the video, then collected, analyzed, and stored.

"And in Miss Chambers' case, it was copied onto external hard drives that were given to the police, who saw quickly enough that they would not be required to work any overtime on this case."

"And you met with Kelly Chambers, correct?" Bernard asked. "Just what did she have to say?"

"She claims the entire thing is an elaborate setup. She says she never left her room Sunday night."

"Her *room*?"

"Uh . . . Apparently she's been living in a penthouse suite at some historic hotel that her company restored."

"Did anyone see her leaving this . . . hotel?"

"That's just it. The hotel is down the block from the company offices, and the whole block is on the same automation and security system. The police have video and sensor evidence recording Miss Chambers leaving her suite, walking up the street to the offices, and making her way to the engineering center where she quite clearly, on camera and in front of sensors, committed the murder, and committed it leaving behind full computer records of everything she did."

"What do you mean?"

"Well, the computer records and sensor data show that Miss Chambers logged on using her password, and then used the building's automated systems to kill Randolph Tate. Oh, and she entered the room after an iris and fingerprint scan. All recorded. With that much evidence, you won't find a judge anywhere who's going to let her out on bail."

"And how was this . . . *Randolph Tate* killed again?"

"As I understand it, she used the building-control system to lock him in a spa in the basement, then turned on the fire sprinklers to drench him, and then set the room's temperature to zero degrees."

"And so? I don't get it. It got cold?"

"It's an experimental, high-powered cooling system. The police believe Randolph Tate died from hypothermia."

"What?"

"Randolph Tate died from hypothermia. Miss Chambers basically froze him to death."

"Wait a minute. You're saying the man was killed by . . . an *air conditioner*?"

They call it a *hyper-cooling system*. Apparently, it can create freezing temperatures in minutes. And the building's walls are packed with insulation that holds in all temperature—part of the company's focus is on green building design.

"So, yes, incredible as it sounds . . . he was killed by air conditioning."

"That was cold," Bernard said, unable to resist. He paused for a good dollar-fifty of legal time before continuing.

"So if I were to make a video game mystery based on this case, it would be called, what, *Murder by Air Conditioner*? Sorry, but I cannot see that one selling."

Kendeff offered no reply. He simply did not understand.

"Well, Mr. Kendeff, I have two things to say. One, I just heard you say Miss Chambers *left her suite*, that *she used the building automation system* to do this and that. I don't ever want to hear you talk like she is guilty again."

Kendeff lifted an eyebrow.

"And, two, you have a very, very short time to figure out *how* to win the Kentucky Derby. I do hope you will be ready, because I expect you to get her out on bail tomorrow," he stated, electing not to calculate how much the statement had cost him in legal fees.

"I . . . I . . . I'm not sure you understand the gravity of her situation, of these charges."

"The gravity? The *gravity*? I'll have you know I have an extremely important video game tournament starting soon, and I do not have time for gravity. Find a solution to gravity. That is what I am paying you for."

Kelly lay on the dingy cot that served as a bed, willing with all her might that she could levitate so as not to actually touch the mattress-like thing beneath her, all the while wondering how many "detainees" had previously been disgusted at having to sleep on it—and, worse, how many had not.

Detainee was the word Kelly was using, rejecting terms like *prisoner* and *inmate* and especially *accused murderer*; Kelly had never been in trouble in her life. God!

She had been given a message late in the evening. Her "contact" had arrived in Seattle and would be in to see her, along with Kendeff, the attorney, first thing tomorrow morning.

The news seemed good, yet Kelly offered an icy stare to the officer who delivered it.

What the officer did not know was that for Bernard Walker, "first thing tomorrow morning" could well mean three in the afternoon.

Kelly closed her eyes and tried not to think.

3

O'Brian.

Nine-thirty a.m. and Ron O'Brian was hard at work.

Sure, he might be sitting on a lounge chair set on the white sand of Cliff Shores Main Beach, he might just be sipping hot coffee purchased at the donut shop down the way, and it was even possible that the phone in his pocket was playing a stomping Woody Herman number—but, damn it, the papers on his lap were, in fact, work.

A former police chief in Cliff Shores, Ron O'Brian was now chief executive officer of SimCide Investigations, a high-tech startup that was adapting OffCide Studios' video game technology for use in criminal investigations.

A spinoff from OffCide, it was an independent company, though the two firms shared several investors and board members, and, tragically in the eyes of both, a chief financial officer by the name of Herbert Iggid.

That was an arrangement Kelly Chambers made before she left the CFO post at OffCide, and O'Brian swore that someday he would have a word with her about it.

Spread out on his lap and threatening to blow down the beach were the outlines of several criminal cases, a few solved and a few unsolved, that area police departments had shared with SimCide. O'Brian was in the process of choosing two to use in case studies for his company's new forensics technology.

SimCide's systems would create virtual crime scenes for the cases, digital worlds that police could interact in and study—much like the virtual worlds that OffCide Studios created for its video games. The company was targeting police agencies, district and state attorneys' offices, and law firms as customers for its forensics modeling software.

And as chief executive, O'Brian had the luxury of working at home from time to time, and while his home was a good ten minutes' drive down the peaceful beach, he figured he was at least *close* to home at the moment.

A seagull the shape of a beach ball waddled past in search of food, presumably french fries judging by its shape, while down the way a couple of surfers clad in wetsuits were largely failing to stand on their boards.

More essential, the smells of the sea calmed O'Brian's soul as Woody Herman and band stomped a modern beat into swing on the phone.

So it was like a record player suddenly jolting into reverse when O'Brian's irritating new smartphone blared out a ringtone that sounded too much like an alarm clock for a telephone call—one of the unending *wonders* these modern devices provided.

"And they call these things smartphones?" he growled to the air around him. "*Smartphone*s and *dumb* people is how I'd put it."

And his mood was further disturbed when he saw on the phone's screen the egg-shaped profile image of Herbert Iggid as the caller ID.

O'Brian slid his finger on the screen to ignore the call—the one function of this space-age device that he enjoyed—but seconds later the thing rang again.

Again he choose Ignore, recalling as he did a kinder day, not so long ago, when cellphones were something from science fiction and you could go to the beach without some egghead having free access to disturb you.

After a brief pause the phone made another sound, an alert O'Brian vaguely recalled was a text message.

He turned it on and pressed the messaging icon.

"*Text messages!*" His mood was failing completely now. "We have landlines, answering machines, personal and company email, cellphones, cellphone voice mail, instant messaging, Skype . . . and now they expect us to read *text messages*, too. What the hell happened to the good old-fashioned *secretary*?"

He pressed the icon for text messages and saw a new one from, no surprise, Herbert Iggid. And the beachfront mood he cultivated earlier now simply up and flowed out to sea when he read it: "I just figured out how to send a text message," it said. "Turn around."

O'Brian glanced over and saw there on the sidewalk just beyond the beach none other than Herbert Iggid in person, clad in suit and tie as usual, and looking on with—and though it was too distant to say for certain, but O'Brian had no doubt—with an expression of utter disgust on his face.

And it was in this position, the upper half of his body twisted about, that O'Brian failed to secure the papers on his lap from the waterfront wind and he found himself chasing down the beach the details of two unsolved murders, an armed bank robbery, and a dastardly case of walking an elephant without a leash down San Francisco's Market Street (apparently the police officers he was working with had a sense of humor).

"Ron, I have to tell you what happened last night at the OffCide offices."

Iggid stood over O'Brian, the latter on his knees trying to reorganize the papers on the lounge chair.

O'Brian cussed silently. A veteran police officer and former police chief, he had dealt with mobsters, drug dealers, and city politicians . . . It said something about the personality of this Herbert Iggid that the man could so easily get under his skin.

"You won't be*lieve* what those *kids* at OffCide are doing now."

O'Brian growled. "I don't work at OffCide, Herbert, remember?"

"Yes, I know, but I need to talk to you, because this time it's a police matter."

"And I am also no longer a police officer," O'Brian shot back.

"That's why I came to you. I can't go to the *actual* police. That would be unthinkable. It has to do with the company. You wouldn't believe what those smart-aleck *kids* are doing now."

"Those *smart-aleck kids* have made your company tens of millions of dollars, Herbert."

O'Brian had worked with Bernard and his engineers and he wasn't crazy about them.

But he knew they had talent that people of his own generation could not quite comprehend—though to be fair, due largely to a complete lack of interest in trying.

And O'Brian's own company was using technology that those "smart-aleck kids" had put together.

"This time they've gone too far," Iggid insisted.

"OK, Herb, what did they do?"

"They brought guns in to work," Iggid proclaimed, and he looked as if he expected lightning to shoot out of the sky.

"Guns? Seriously?"

"Yes, well, guns of a sort. Something called *airsoft* guns."

"*Airsoft* guns? Herbert, those are toys."

"These were no toys. They looked just like real guns."

"But they're toys, Herb. They're *made* to look like real guns, but they're toys."

"Yeah, well, these *looked* real! And if I'd been armed, I could have shot one of the kids."

O'Brian narrowed his eyes. "Are you *often* armed, Herbert?"

"No, but that's beside the point. The point is I could have killed one of them."

How many times over the years had O'Brian heard people who didn't own guns say that about a trespasser? It was the ones *with* guns you worried about.

O'Brian reflected on how just moments earlier he'd been at total peace, and now no doubt his coffee would be cold and probably flavored with a good deal of sand.

As Iggid continued his rant, his face blurred in O'Brian's vision, and it became clear just how dangerous a gun could be around the man, since people would be very tempted to shoot him with it.

'Egghead,' O'Brian muttered to himself.

Bernard stared at the laptop, a blank expression on his face, as he sipped at his morning Pepsi.

This business with Kelly Chambers was turning out to be a lot worse than he had reckoned.

He figured there would be some simple explanation and he'd be able to return immediately to Cliff Shores, where he would cut himself off from the world and prepare for the *Woeful WasteWorld* tournament.

He planned, needed, to play at his oceanfront studio, where he would stock his freezer with microwavable burritos and frozen pizzas, then lock all doors, close all blinds, and cut off all contact with work, for probably a very enjoyable couple of weeks.

But now the attorney was saying they might not even get Kelly out on bail.

Bernard was stewing on the thought, sipping Pepsi, when a video call appeared on the laptop, flashing the username Mainly Mayhem. That of course was Patricia Meyheim, who delighted in the misspelling of her surname.

"Damn," Bernard muttered.

The alert rang a second time, then a third.

"Damn," Bernard repeated, "just like the telephone."

Finally, he clicked Answer With Video, figuring it could be worse. It could be Herbert Iggid calling.

"What is it, Patricia?" he asked straight away.

"Herbert Iggid," she shot back.

"Damn." It *was* Herbert Iggid, if not directly so. "What happened now?"

"The egghead is all up in arms over our airsoft guns. He sent out a companywide email late last night saying all guns are banned at the office. Completely. Can you believe the nerve of that guy?"

"What? Why?"

"He claims they're dangerous." Patricia sounded like a child reporting details of some mischief a sibling just committed. "Said he even talked to that O'Brian guy—you know, the ex-cop guy. Said O'Brian agreed. They both say the guns could be mistaken for real weapons and someone could get hurt. He even called an all-staff meeting for this afternoon, said everyone has to be there to go over the new policies. You gotta do something, Bernard."

"No, I do not have to do something. I am currently involved in extremely important business, and I have to get it over with and get on a plane and get home. I do not have any time at present for Herbert Iggid."

"Get on a plane from where?"

"Seattle," Bernard replied without thinking.

"You're in Seattle?"

"Yes, but not for long. I plan to finish my business here and return home immediately."

"You're in a hotel?"

"Yes." Bernard replied, not seeing the relevance of the question.

"Wow, it looks like a nice hotel, from what I can see in the background. It looks like you have a nice view."

"Not as nice as my studio, where I would far rather be right at the moment," Bernard snapped back.

"What's the name?"

"What's the name of what?"

"What's the name of your hotel?"

"It happens to be the Pendrite Hotel. Why in God's name are you asking me the name of my hotel?"

"Wait just a minute." The video went blank.

"Just what is that girl up to?" Bernard asked aloud.

As if to answer, the screen lit back up showing a different angle, this one catching Patricia with Lester Argyle and Eric Lyle, the latter two with laptops of their own.

"We're booked to fly out in two hours, dude," Eric reported to Bernard, who stared back in bewilderment.

"What? Fly where?"

"To Seattle, of course."

"Yeah," Lester added, "I just booked us reservations at the Pendrite, too. I requested rooms next to yours. Seems like a good hotel, judging by the website."

"What?" Bernard gasped, not understanding.

"No, you can't . . . I'm leaving, I mean, I am only staying as long as—"

"And we're going to be there to help, whatever it is you're doing, dude," Eric said.

"No, you can't, I—wait. You can't. That's right, you can't. Herbert Iggid called an all-staff meeting for this afternoon. Patricia just told me."

Patricia shot him a mischievous smile. "Well, if we're busy helping our CEO on some *important project* in Seattle, I guess we'll just have to miss the all-staff meeting." She spoke with a strong hint of *I got you* in her tone. "Pretty good excuse if you ask me."

"See you in a few hours, Bernard," Lester said.

"Later, dude," Eric added, and their video disappeared, leaving Bernard glaring at a blank window. And steaming.

If his design team came to town, he'd be stuck even longer. "Damn, damn, damn, damn . . ." he hissed.

🎮 🎮 🎮

Herbert Iggid fumed as he stormed out of the packed (though not quite packed enough) conference room to track down—who was it that failed to attend the all-staff meeting?— *the Design Team*, the very group responsible for his calling the meeting in the first place.

The security guard in the lobby watched as Iggid marched by. A young man in his early twenties, the guard sat at a desk, clipboard and pencil in hand, and began adding a fast caricature of the stressed-out executive to the other talented doodling he had accumulated through the day.

Iggid heard the sound of his own thumping feet, made them thump louder as he headed for the "Design Department"—a name he insisted on (everyone else in the company called it the "Argyle Area," which was fair considering it resembled more Lester Argyle's small bachelor pad in Daly City than it did a "design department" or an office).

The guard was a college student, an art major, who spent his free time sitting in a park or a downtown café doing pretty much exactly what he was doing now at work—figuring out clever ways to draw people around him.

For Iggid he drew a tall oval shape with traces of hair on either side of the head, and from there heat rising, illustrated by three wavy lines that highlighted the down-turned eyebrows and hard-set frown.

As Iggid walked he prepared to make an entrance that would impress, would instill fear throughout the Design Department— a horrid combination of cubicles with wiring running over the partitions, surrounding stand-up arcade gaming consoles, flat screen TVs, and a pool table.

A pool table!

Pool tables were not allowed in offices where Herbert Iggid came from.

He halted just outside the cubicle that marked the Argyle Area entrance, straightened his back, adjusted his tie knot, and pulled the ends of his shirt cuffs to the correct distance beyond the pinstripe coat sleeves.

And marched forward ready to send a jolt of terror into every employee within.

"The entire company is gathered in the conference room waiting for you," he proclaimed, trying to sound commanding to . . . to a lone stranger sitting by a desk and looking completely out of place.

Chen Li stared back in fright, his self-consciousness spiraling as he eyed the empty room about him.

"Uh, they told me to wait here," he put out, hoping he wasn't in trouble already. Chen had arrived in San Francisco from Beijing several hours earlier and made his way directly to the company office where the design team was supposed to meet him.

"Who— wha—" Iggid muttered, shocked to find himself facing a roomful of empty desks, save for this apparent tourist, who sat surrounded by a set of luggage.

"Where is everyone?" Iggid demanded. "We have an all-staff meeting in progress!"

"I . . . I . . ." was all Chen Li could come up with. Though already an employee of OffCide Studios for some time, Chen had been hired in Beijing, where he and his own team worked. This was his first visit to the headquarter office and his first visit to the United States, where, it was turning out, big hospitable welcomes apparently were not the going custom.

"I will not tolerate this kind of behavior, including from you, young man," Iggid declared to a wide-eyed Chen, who didn't consider himself all that young but suddenly felt entirely so.

And with that Iggid stormed out, thumping his feet in a zealous trek back to the conference room where he would report to the company's entire staff how *the Design Department* had again let everyone down, and the company's entire staff would shake their heads in disapproval (focused actually over how they themselves failed to find excuses for not attending).

Back in the Argyle Area Chen Li stood by a window wondering what to do, wondering what just happened.

That was the company's CFO; Chen had studied the executive bios on the OffCide website before coming.

He hadn't been at the San Francisco office for half an hour and already he had been badly scolded by one of the company's top executives.

And what was that about a meeting? What meeting? None of the email or conference calls had said anything about a meeting—just that he should find Lester in the office.

Timidly, Chen made his way back to the lobby. He peered out at first, saw it empty save for the security guard.

He walked to the guard desk.

"Excuse me. You are sure I should wait there?" he asked, indicating the Design Department. "I just arrive from Beijing.

I came here to meet Lester Argyle." Chen's voice broke as he talked.

"You said you just arrived from Beijing, right?"

"Yes," Chen said, his head going back and forth between the Design Department and where Iggid had walked. "But that man . . . He talked about a *meeting* . . ."

"Yeah," the guard said. "You don't want to go to the meeting. I recommend you wait in the Argyle—uh, *Design Department*."

Chen remained uncertain, his head bobbling about.

The guard widened his right eye at Chen, gestured downward, then lifted an empty clipboard from the report forms he had been doodling on.

At the top of four or five caricatures was one Chen Li recognized instantly: an egg-shaped cartoon figure with little hair and with heat emanating from the top of its head.

The two smiled at each other.

"OK, thank you." Chen walked back toward the Design Department.

"Xiang Beijing yiyang (Just like Beijing)," he said aloud.

🎮 🎮 🎮

The King County Correctional Facility, as the county jail is called, sits among a cluster of law-enforcement and administrative offices on the southern edge of Seattle's high-rise district.

When Bernard learned it was only a short walk from his hotel, he suggested to Kendeff that they walk to visit Kelly, though the recommendation was less about avoiding parking difficulties than it was about locating interesting nearby delis or restaurants.

But his hopes of finding an area bustling with homey family-run eateries and small exotic markets were quashed in the newer section of the downtown, where decades earlier city planners specified that high-rises be set back from the street, with their retail and restaurants secluded inside plazas.

Still, he counted something like six Starbucks between his hotel and the jail. If only Starbucks sold Pepsi and hot dogs.

And if he needed coffee, Bernard reasoned, this being Seattle there would probably be a Starbucks at the jail, possibly in the cellblocks themselves.

Once inside, he and Kendeff were led to a room where they would be able to meet with Kelly to prepare for the arraignment.

A short while later the door opened and two officers squeezed in, leading Kelly and a fourth into the room.

Kelly appeared a different woman than the one Bernard knew. Her brown hair was ragged, a shade darker than normal, and void of luster, and her face seemed pale and empty.

The impression was showcased by her bright orange prison jumpsuit.

Kendeff stood, while Bernard looked on from his seat.

"Miss Chambers."

"Kelly?" Bernard said.

"Yes. Bernard, thank you for coming." Kelly for once was not trying to hide her New York accent.

"You look, um . . ." Bernard decided not to finish the comment.

"I believe what you mean to say is, 'My God, you look like hell.'"

Bernard smiled. "It's just, you look different without any makeup on."

"Bernard, this is Seattle. Given the constant rain in this city, I look quite a bit different *with makeup on.*"

The officers stepped out. "We'll be waiting just outside," the last said as he closed the door behind them.

Kelly sat down. "Thank you, Bernard. I can't thank you enough for coming."

Bernard's expression turned to irritation. "I'm not sure why you want me here."

Kelly rolled her eyeballs. This was the card she had to pull out of her sleeve? Bernard Walker, a selfish, self-absorbed, immature, video game fanatic? This was the cavalry she had coming over the hill to rescue her?

Bernard went on. "But never mind. I am here. I'll do what I can do for the next day or so. But I am scheduled to compete in a highly prestigious video game tournament, so you'll have to plead insanity or whatever you're going to do before then."

"A *video game*? You can't be serious."

"Not *any* video game. It is the annual *Woeful WasteWorld* tournament, and I happen to be the defending champion," Bernard corrected her.

"A video game tournament? Really?"

"Defending champion three years in a row."

"Bernard, listen. Mr. Kendeff here in fact suggested when we talked yesterday that I *do* plead insanity, considering the evidence they have."

"And so, in what way is it that I can help you do that?"

" . . ."

"Seriously. Why me?"

Kelly lost what little color remained in her face.

"Bernard . . ."

"Yes?"

"They're talking about ironclad evidence for first-degree murder."

"And that has *what* to do with *me*?" Bernard asked, but it was clear from his voice that his resistance was breaking down.

"Because you know I didn't commit a murder."

Bernard made an exaggerated frown, and said, defeated, "Yes, I suppose I do."

"What do you mean?" Kendeff butted in.

Bernard glared at the attorney. "This, Wilbur, is Kelly Chambers. Unless you're trying to steal her sandwich, which I would not recommend, I fully believe she is completely incapable of murder."

"Oookaay . . ."

"But tell me again," Bernard pressed, "how it is that I am somehow your only hope."

"I'm sure Wilbur told you—they have enough evidence that it'll take all of about ten minutes to convince a jury I committed the crime."

"What *evidence*? So they have some video or something."

"It's a hell of a lot worse than that, Bernard. I know! I was CEO of the company. Cannecare's technology is good, and I mean *really* good."

"Is that so?"

"Bernard, believe me, these guys know what they're doing. They've combined building automation technology with building security systems, data networks, utilities—everything. And it's all networked together.

"Then they added high-quality video cameras, audio sensors that can pick up people's heartbeats, and temperature sensors that can identify people with fevers . . .

"And all this data is recorded and stored and archived, so that any person's movements through one of their buildings, maybe months before, can be intricately retraced and rendered into high-definition video segments with matching sensor data."

"This sounds like a sales pitch."

Kelly smiled. "Yeah, that's how I learned it. Only I'm no longer quite as enthusiastic as I was only a few days ago."

"So they have several types of monitoring," Bernard said. "So what?"

"They have several types of monitoring that they collected together with video segments and gave to the police. And it is now being used by the prosecution as damning evidence."

"I could create that over a weekend," Bernard said.

Kendeff butted in: "What do you mean, you could *create* that?"

"Simple reverse engineering."

Kelly and Kendeff both showed confusion.

"Listen," Bernard explained, "OffCide Studios has created best-selling video games with tens of millions of registered users, games that have you crawling around in the jungle shooting giant spiders and Mayan ghosts, but of course being careful *not* to shoot environmentalists and jungle researchers . . . or walking through a detailed 3-D post-apocalyptic world clubbing zombies with giant chicken legs."

The imagery failed to clear the confusion.

"Not to mention our flagship Murder Mystery franchise, in which players plot crimes, commit murders, and then solve them in fully animated virtual worlds. So I am certainly unimpressed by video simulations. We create these things in the office every day."

Kelly took on deadly serious stare. "Well, the prosecution it turns out *is* impressed. And I'm in a lot of trouble."

"Then I suppose I'll have to come up with something that will *un*impress them."

4

Bernard's T-shirt, photographer's vest, and shorts stood out among the formal dress in the King County arraignment court nearly as loudly as Kelly's bright orange jumpsuit.

The room resembled more a post office, Bernard thought. The judge sat in one corner behind two clerks with computers, and before them all was a counter that would have served well for selling stamps and posting packages.

Facing this in the rear was a glassed-in seating area where spectators could view the proceedings.

"Arnold Merlson, Judge," read the plaque on the back bench. The judge appeared to be in his sixties and had a face that even without expression looked as if he had just bitten into a lime.

Two uniformed officers led Kelly in, and Kendeff got up to stand beside her, leaving Bernard at a table facing the bench.

Surveying the room, the judge appraised those in attendance. An eyebrow lifted, a pause of the head, as his gaze fell on Kelly, but it was the sight of Bernard that held his attention the longest, and demonstrated just how much more sour his face could become.

Bernard turned around to see just who the judge was glaring at, then realized he was the attraction. The discovery sent him to checking nervously his vest pockets; he needed a game console, a snack, or something.

Fortunately for Kelly, Kendeff's reproachful eye reminded Bernard of the long lecture on how a game console or a snack in the arraignment court could get him kicked out and possibly even jailed for contempt.

Once the case was introduced and the formalities completed, the hearing began without trouble.

The charges were presented: aggravated first-degree murder and a list of crimes that went along with it.

Bernard wondered briefly if he could sneak out. The officer posted at the door made the prospect unlikely.

He hated this, hated being stuck in this room. He had to sit still with no device, no phone, nothing to do.

So he tried to focus his mind on the *Woeful Waste World* tournament, how wonderful it would be to face his annual rivals once again, how sweet it would be to wipe them out yet again. If he didn't wind up sitting in a courtroom.

The thought brought his mind back to the business at hand:

". . . clearly the vileness of this crime . . ." the voice of the prosecuting attorney rang out.

But, no, they'd get Kelly out and the overpriced attorney would clean up the rest of the mess . . . While Bernard flew back to San Francisco to get ready . . .

". . . and given the clear evidence of premeditation . . ."

Yes, and then Bernard could forget all about this Kelly Chambers business and could concentrate on the video game tournament—

"We've decided to seek the death penalty."

"What?" Bernard shouted out.

"Order!" the judge warned, shooting Bernard a Look of Death that rivaled Bernard's own.

Not surprisingly, Kelly appeared more shocked than Bernard. The prospect of being convicted was not one she had allowed herself to entertain; possible execution hadn't entered her mind.

🎮 🎮 🎮

Sitting alone in OffCide's Design Department, still somewhat bewildered, Chen was relieved finally when a young woman came in to find him.

"Are you Chen Li?"

"Yes. I'm here to see Lester Argyle."

"Right. Hi. My name's Gina."

"Hi."

"Listen, Lester had to fly to Seattle this afternoon, and he wants you to fly there tomorrow."

"Seattle?" Chen had no idea what a Seattle was.

"Yeah. They have some sort of an emergency up there. I booked a room for you at a hotel near here for tonight, and I'll book a flight to Seattle for you too."

"Seattle?"

"Yeah. It's not far—only, I think, about a two-hour flight. But you must be exhausted. So you should spend the night here in San Francisco and fly out tomorrow. Sorry I made you wait here. We had this horrible all-staff meeting."

"Oh, was I supposed to attend the meeting? I didn't know."

"God, no. You don't have a gun, do you?"

"A gun? No." The question seemed an odd one. What do they do at meetings in America?

"Then, no, you're fine. But listen, I need about five minutes, and then I'll walk you to your hotel. It's right up Market Street. That'll give you a chance to rest up."

"OK."

"So make yourself comfortable a minute."

"Uh . . . Can I get Wi-Fi here. I need to check my email. I have a laptop."

"Sure. The network is called OffCide and the password is jalapeno, all lowercase."

"Hala . . . I'm sorry. Can you repeat?"

"Here, I'll write it down for you."

A moment later Chen again was alone in the Argyle Area, which, he noted, was probably a pretty fun place to work. His office in Beijing didn't have a pool table or a lot of the other stuff he saw here.

Another moment later, checking his email, he found a message from Lester:

Hey Chen,

We had to fly to Seattle for an emergency. Please fly up tomorrow. Gina (a co-worker) will take you to a hotel down there for tonight and book a flight for you. We'll arrange for a limo to pick you up at the airport when you get here. I'll call you tonight at your hotel.

Les

Seattle?

Chen opened a Web browser and searched on Seattle. Of course—Seattle, or Xiyatu in Chinese. He had certainly heard of it.

Opening a new tab, he did a Baidu search, then chose a top result, a page on the Baidu site.

It began with statistics, then went into an introduction of the city. Scanning it he saw Seattle was known as the Emerald City, the Jet City and . . . the Rainy City?

The Rainy City?

Chen had been dreaming of sightseeing in San Francisco, one of the best-known U.S. cities in China, or Asia for that matter. And San Francisco's many attractions were widely known: Chinatown, that prison island, and so many things.

Seattle?

🐾 🐾 🐾

Kelly was stunned, gutted; she felt her knees ready to melt.

The death penalty?

This couldn't be possible.

". . . first-degree murder . . . the death penalty . . ." The words echoed in her mind.

Nervous, Bernard let his hand feel the shape of a Hostess Ding Dong in a vest pocket as he watched in disbelief.

Kendeff stood before the judge, pale and ineffective.

"And how does your client plead?" Judge Merlson asked.

"Uh, Miss Chambers pleads, uh, not guilty, your honor."

This prompted a stern stare, first at Kendeff, then Kelly.

"You do both understand the thorough nature of the evidence, don't you?"

"Yes, your honor," Kendeff said, his eyes on the floor.

"And you, Miss Chambers, do you understand the weight of the evidence the prosecution is presenting against you in this case? It's . . . it's . . . technological evidence apparently on an unprecedented scale, I'm told. Do you understand that?"

"Yes sir."

The judge frowned. "Very well. Now—"

"Your honor," Kendeff interrupted. "We'd like to ask the court to consider releasing Miss Chambers on bail."

"Pardon me?"

"We'd like to request that Miss Chambers be released on bail."

Shaking his head, the judge said, almost in disbelief, "I'm afraid I can't see that. Given the seriousness of the crime, the extent of the evidence . . . I certainly cannot see the possibility of bail."

"But on substantial bail, the court—"

"Substantial bail? Bail for first-degree murder is usually one or two million dollars in this state. I have a report showing Miss Chambers' wealth, and I'm not sure . . ."

"But, your honor, we have reason to believe Miss Chambers will be in danger if she's kept in jail."

"In danger from what?"

"From fellow prisoners. She's a high-profile detainee. The case has been all over the news."

"Thank you, Mr. Kendeff, but I trust our detention system will be able to protect Miss Chambers adequately."

Kendeff glanced about nervously, wondering what else to try. Behind him he caught an angry stare from Bernard. And another thought struck him.

"There's one more thing, your honor."

"Yes?"

"The evidence. Though it appears foolproof, it will almost certainly be struck down and deemed unusable in the long run. I would argue that it therefore should not be used as reason to deny Miss Chambers bail."

Kendeff now found himself facing a completely new, redefined and improved version of sourness in the lines on the judge's face.

"And how do you figure that?" Judge Merlson demanded.

"Why, your honor, first, while parts of it such as the video are tried and tested as evidence, the combination of components is *un*tested in courts. Remember the number of trials that were dismissed and convictions that were overturned when video and audio alone, and other new technologies, were first introduced in courts?"

"Phooey."

"Pardon me?"

"Phooey."

"Your honor, this type of evidence could easily be faked."

"Faked?"

"Yes, this new combination of evidence has not yet been put to the test."

"Frankly I don't see how it could be faked. And I would thank you to focus your arguments on the case at hand and *not* suggest I make decisions based on *your future appeals,* Mr. Kendeff. Is there anything else?"

Kelly began to panic. Was this it? Was it back to the cell for another night, left to stew on thoughts of being tried for first-degree murder and then executed? Really? No, *really*?

How the hell do they execute people in the state of Washington anyhow?

🐦 🐦 🐦

"Imagine a world that is completely filmed," says the voiceover. On the screen, families are strolling about at a street fair.

"Add to that, sensor data, facial-recognition software, and the power of high-performance computing . . ."

Many of the children in the video have their faces painted, many are eating cotton candy and snow cones. Some of the adults carry wine glasses from tasting booths; others hold coffee cups.

"Now you have a world that is finally safe, a world where you can bring your families and your children out without fearing criminals or terrorists or gangs. It is a world that is fully policed, and the hero is . . . technology."

The video freezes as arrows appear at numerous points in the scene, and the shot zooms in on one to show a video camera station.

"Each of these video stations has cameras shooting continuous video wherever sensors show motion, thus keeping track of every person who passes. And this is networked, with data streamed instantly to a central processing point.

"And everywhere, sensors track movement, as well as change of temperature, humidity, sound, and more.

"This is a world where there can be no crime, where people can't break the law without getting caught.

"This is a world where you and your children can be safe and secure.

"Welcome to Cannecare Automation . . ."

🐾 🐾 🐾

Kendeff stood at the front of the courtroom defeated, knowing he dare not push bail any further. A bad relationship with the arraignment judge would not help Kelly's case.

Bernard, however, was nowhere near as prudent.

"In fact such evidence *can* be faked, and I can prove it!" he proclaimed, standing up, in what proved to be a successful experiment in pushing the limits of sourness this particular judge's face could take on.

"And just *who* may I ask are you?"

Kendeff jumped in. "This is Bernard Walker, your honor. He's, uh—"

"I asked him." Judge Merlson's eyes fixed on Bernard.

"I happen to be Bernard Walker, founder and chief executive officer of OffCide Studios, a leading—and cutting-edge—video game maker."

"And you are somehow an expert on how evidence of this sort can be faked?"

Kendeff jumped in. "Your honor, this man has expertise that is of direct relevance to this case."

Sour lips bittered yet further. "Very well, then. I suppose with a case like this, we have to listen to everything." The impression of fairness was soured by the tone of voice.

His nervousness mounting, Bernard let slip from his mind the prohibition on food in a courtroom and the packet of Ding Dongs magically appeared. He took one out, put the other back in a pocket.

"And just what is that?" the judge demanded.

Bernard returned an equally annoyed stare. "I should like to think that as a key official in this state's judiciary, that you would be able to recognize a Hostess Ding Dong."

Judge Merlson gasped for air. Then: "A *Ding Dong*? Bailiff! Remove the Ding Dong from the courtroom."

All eyes watched as a clean-cut officer marched from the door and set a hand on Bernard's shoulder.

"Sir, you'll come with me."

"Not the *human* ding dong," the judge moaned. "The *Hostess* Ding Dong."

"Oh, I'm sorry, your honor." And to Bernard: "Sir, I'll have to confiscate your Ding Dong."

The dignity of the courtroom, an essential ingredient in the imposition of justice, slid several definite levels with each mention of the word *ding dong*.

And hanging on intently to every word, and watching as Bernard clearly was considering a fast bite before handing over the Ding Dong, Kelly really wished she could remember how to cry.

This was the cavalry coming over the hill?

🎮 🎮 🎮

"*Here we see a clean-cut man carrying a backpack.*

"*To the people around him, this is just another tourist out enjoying a little wine tasting at the street fair.*

"*The man passes three police officers on patrol. Notice that even they fail to detect anything out of the ordinary as he passes.*

"*But Cannecare's security system is alert on a much higher level. As the man passes the camera station above, he is filmed and his movements are recorded, and by the time he's out of range, the next station has picked him up and continues to record his journey.*

"*Meanwhile, when he first entered the event area, still images of his face were cropped from video and sent through Cannecare's supercomputing system, to process facial-recognition software and try to ID the man's face using databases of known terrorists, criminals, and others that society needs to keep an eye on.*

"*Well before he passed the police officers, the stills were processed; it took only seconds for the system to identify the man as a known terrorist with connections in the Middle East.*

"*And when the man enters a restaurant and sets down the backpack, an all-out police lockdown of the area is executed; and the man is apprehended before he gets two feet from the suspicious backpack . . .*"

🎮 🎮 🎮

Once the Ding Dong was removed from the courtroom, justice was permitted to continue.

"I'll try again, Mr. Walker. Tell me: What is the source of your expertise?"

Bernard puzzled at the need for such a question.

"I am the founder and chief executive officer of OffCide Studios. We happen to make a few of the most cutting-edge video game titles on the market now."

He might as well have claimed to be a Peruvian banjo repairman for all the confidence his answer instilled in the judge.

"And in what way does that make you an expert in a murder case?"

Here Bernard perked up. He felt for certain he had the perfect answer to the question. Kelly appeared less sure.

"Our company makes the hugely popular video game *Murder Mystery: The Case of the Cleavered Clerk.*"

"This is a video game?"

"Yes."

"And it's called *what*?"

"The franchise is called Murder Mystery. You see, we've already released three titles: *The Case of the Cleavered Clerk, The Story of the Strewed Starlet,* and—"

"Seriously," the judge blurted out, and it was not posed as a question. "And this, this, video game, it somehow qualifies you as an expert in a murder case?"

Bernard patted his vest nervously, and, watching, Kelly sincerely hoped he was not going after the second Ding Dong.

But luckily: "That is correct," Bernard explained. "The thing is, I personally design and oversee production of video game modeling that is far more complex than the technology described in this case. We are talking about modeling with complex correlation of everything from weapon depletion to health."

A worried brow swelled across the judge's (and Kelly's) face. "Weapon depletion?"

Kendeff broke in: "This same technology, your honor, is currently being developed with Mr. Walker's help for use in forensics investigations. In fact the very technology he is talking about helped solve a murder case in California last year."

"I . . . I still fail to see how this evidence could be faked."

"Reverse engineering?" Bernard offered—a term he'd made up, but one that made sense.

"What?"

"Look at it as reverse engineering, or reverse production. It's simple. You begin with a video track, or an animation track in the case of games, and then you systematically add back the needed sensor data that appears to correlate with it."

"And where do you get this . . . data?"

Bernard shuddered. "I should think from a keyboard. Series of ones and zeros, most simply put. Lots and lots, to be sure, but still, data."

His sensible analysis spread confusion throughout the courtroom.

"But what about the video? Certainly that's not ones and zeros."

"When stored, yes. It is a matter of ones, zeros, man hours, and frozen microwavable burritos—don't forget those. And the ones and zeros can be cut up, rearranged to substantially alter and enhance what the viewer sees."

"Your honor," the prosecuting attorney jumped in, "we have real video, unquestionably of Miss Chambers, and mounds of sensor data that could not have been faked."

Bernard shot back: "Video, as I understand, of Kelly Chambers wearing the same clothes, the same uniform that she wore daily, on a route she took to work, also daily."

"She wears the same clothes in the video that she did every day?" the judge asked.

Kendeff answered. "Yes, your honor. A red polo shirt and jeans. It's sort of a company uniform."

Judge Merlson turned to the prosecutor. "Is this true? The defendant wore the same uniform and took the same route as in the video every day?"

"Just a moment." Biting his lip, the prosecutor walked over to his assistant, a young woman in a smart business suit. They conferred in whispers before he turned back.

"Yes, that's . . . uh, correct. Your honor."

"And could video of her on her way into the office be . . . I don't know, reused or changed?"

"It certainly can," Bernard insisted, not pleasing the judge with continued interruption. "If I can show you a demonstration on my phone."

"I *do not care* to look at your *phone*, Mr. Walker."

"But, I, I have here a two-minute animated clip that will *prove* just how sophisticated and yet simple this modeling can be."

Bernard held up his phone.

Sour here blended into heartburn. "Oh, very well. Let's be done with this quickly. Bailiff, please bring me Mr. Walker's cellphone."

Bernard opened an application on his phone, a modeling sequence he created on his laptop while waiting for the arraignment to begin. He launched the sequence and handed the device to the officer.

As the bailiff approached the bench, the judge put on a pair of glasses.

Taking the phone, he held it up, focused, tried again to focus, then finally let himself believe what he was seeing.

A moment later: "What is it that I am looking at, Mr. Walker?"

"This is a demonstration of how quickly modeling and video can be constructed. I began creating this as they walked to the courthouse today."

Judge Merlson squinted again at the screen, then at the prosecuting attorney. "It's him . . . and her . . ." he ventured, indicating the prosecutor's assistant.

In fact the judge was looking at two caricature avatars, one with the prosecutor's head and one with the assistant's. They were walking along outside, incredibly, a 3-D model of the courthouse.

"For all I know, Mr. Walker, you made this weeks ago and spent days working on it."

"Yes, well, except that Kelly Chambers was not arrested weeks ago. Oh, and if you will notice the clothes on the two avatars."

The judge wasn't sure what an avatar was, but he did notice the two figures on the screen were wearing more or less the same clothes, the same colors, as the prosecutor and his assistant.

"I filmed the two of them walking and then created this animation—in about half an hour."

"Your honor, this is nonsense. I can't see what's on that phone, but if it is video or . . . whatever . . . it's just a trick. The video sequencing from Cannecare . . ."

The judge was about to agree when the scene on the phone changed.

Suddenly Judge Merlson was looking at the official portrait of himself hanging on the wall outside the courtroom. And slowly, right before his eyes, the face in the portrait, *his* face, began to morph into a caricature: The ears grew larger than the head, the nose protruded into a long, pointy snout, and the chin shot down and outward.

And here the brick-and-mortar judge's eyes popped open to nearly the size of his ears and nose on the screen.

And so focused was he that he jumped when the device began blaring music, an instantly recognizable melody to people of all ages: the theme to Loony Tunes.

And after four bars it faded, and the judge avatar shook its head and blurted out in a Porky Pig voice: "Th— th— th— that's all, folks."

The judge squinted at the phone, squinted at the prosecutor, then at Kendeff, and finally at Bernard.

"I don't like any of you, and I certainly don't like any of this," he said. Why was he on a cellphone? Why was the courthouse on it?

Judge Merlson held the phone out to the bailiff, found himself longing for a simpler day.

And now he spoke to the prosecutor and his assistant. "We're going to take a break so I can have another look at the evidence. But unless I can be convinced this evidence *can't* be doctored, I'm going to grant the request for bail."

"Your honor," the prosecutor protested, "come on, this is a high-profile case. The nature of the crime—"

"The nature of the crime means we cannot make mistakes, and that we cannot overestimate the value of evidence. Now, I have one more question for Mr. Walker."

Bernard, unthinkably, was peeking down at a different cellphone held at his side, and took a second to react.

"Uh, yes?"

The judge experimented with new flavors of sourness in his cheeks, chin, and mouth.

But ignoring Bernard's disrespect and having given up on the concept of dignity in the courtroom, he asked: "Do you *really* make a living creating video games?"

"Yes."

"*Why?*"

Bernard squinted. "I'm sorry. I don't understand."

"Oh, never mind." Judge Merlson took to scribbling on a legal pad; the court appeared to be finished with Bernard Walker.

But Bernard was not finished with the court: "Wait, I have a question, your honor."

The judge grimaced (picture a lime being squeezed under a tank); everyone in the entire courtroom gawked, including Kelly, whose face showed a confused mix of relief and of horror over what he might say now.

"*You* have a question?" the judge roared.

"Yes."

". . . *Well*? What is it?"

"Where do I go to get my Ding Dong back?"

5

The bellhop at the Pendrite Hotel struggled with the packed baggage cart as he led Lester, Eric, and Patricia to their suite.

Along the cart's rails hung six bulging laptop cases, and those were in addition to suitcases and two trunks, the sort used to haul audio and video equipment.

The group explained excitedly how they had to buy an extra airline ticket and pay fees to carry their equipment on board, then joked about company expense accounts.

The excitement increased as they entered the suite. "Awesome, dude, there's an actual *kitchen*." "Great TVs. They got premium cable, you know." "Wow, look at the view out this window."

The reaction was warranted. The deluxe suites on the upper floors featured teak furnishings, plush carpeting, and artwork people might actually want to take home—unlike pictures at many hotels, whose artistic value lay in their never being stolen.

Les had booked a corner suite that had three individual bedrooms, a small but elegant dining area, and a living room complete with a leather sofa set and a 50-inch TV. To the wings were a kitchenette and a work area.

There's nothing like a company credit card, Lester figured when he made the reservation.

And now, as the bellhop watched, the three of them froze and eyed one another briefly before shooting in different directions, running room to room.

Patricia moved fastest, scouting all three of the individual guest rooms and running back to one to scream: "This room's mine!"

This met an immediate "It is not!" from Eric.

"Hey, if I'm sharing a suite with two *male* colleagues, *I* get to choose my room."

Eric countered: "Why, does that room somehow have better security?"

"No. It has a better view, so I won't have to spend so much of my day looking at you two."

And as she dashed to grab her bags, Eric and Les raced for the one remaining room that had a good view, with Eric winning out and leaving Les to accept that he'd been beat.

"Hah!" Eric shouted and disappeared inside.

Les picked up a suitcase and walked sullenly to the room with the inferior view, stopping briefly to hand the bellhop a tip—a hundred-dollar bill.

"Thank you," the latter replied.

"My name's Lester. Listen, we've got a work project going here, and we may need a little extra help from time to time."

"No problem, sir. My name's Paul. Would you like an introduction to the room's amenities or the hotel's services?"

"No, thanks, Paul. I gotta go unpack."

"Oh, by the way, sir. Sorry you lost the competition for the best view. But you did get the only room with a spa."

"Oh, I know." Lester grinned. "It was *me* who booked the suite. I have all the view I want right here in the living room. But *I'm* the only one with a *spa.*"

His smile broadened.

🎮 🎮 🎮

After reconsidering the arguments and checking the Cannecare video segments—and frankly being unnerved by Bernard—the judge decided the evidence was in fact insufficient to deny bail, though given the circumstances and the possibility that the evidence *was* real, he did not make things easy for Kelly.

He set bail at a whopping ten million dollars, and Kelly would still be under house arrest, her movements monitored via ankle bracelet.

But it was a start, Bernard reflected as he and Kendeff walked to a bench in the small park that faced the courthouse entrance.

With Kelly out on bail, maybe, just maybe, he could ditch the whole mess for a few days, fly back to San Francisco . . . leaving Lester and the others to explain things to Iggid . . .

Off to one corner of the park a news truck monitored the front of the courthouse, its antenna raised and ready to broadcast anything its cameras shot to the entire world.

Sitting down, Bernard eyed the truck.

"I cannot believe they threw my Ding Dong away. Hey, can I sue them for that?"

Kendeff smiled. "For what I charge, I'd say write it off."

That earned him an unhappy "Really?" face.

"Hopefully we can get Miss Chambers out in a couple of hours," Kendeff said. "I have our staff already arranging things."

"What happens next?" he asked.

"We've arranged for her house arrest to be in a suite at the Pendrite, since going back to her own room at that Cannecare . . . hotel—that would be out of the question."

"Not on my floor, I hope." Kelly on his floor? That would make an escape even more difficult; he'd have a lot more explaining to do.

"Well, we've set up security plans that include booking all the suites on the floor. We need to keep the public and the press far away from Miss Chambers. A few were occupied but the Pendrite will make the necessary arrangements and move those guests."

"But I can go to another floor, right?"

"No. For security reasons, we're being advised to keep everyone involved in the case together on one floor. Access to the floor will be restricted and monitored."

The prospect of having to room near the engineers and now Kelly, as well, that was the first disturbing thought. But it lost out when Bernard calculated the cost of a full floor of suites at the five-star Pendrite Hotel, then thought about having to explain that to Herbert Iggid.

"Who, may I ask, put you in charge?"

"I apologize, but securing Miss Chambers' release was only the first step in actually *getting* her released. There was security to consider, and then there was the matter of arranging ten million dollars' bail."

Kendeff paused to let this sink in, but the reaction was minimal.

"I am guessing they do not accept PayPal."

". . . no."

"I get two percent cash back on my American Express card."

"Yeah . . . Anyway, our staff has been working with your attorney in San Francisco. We didn't expect bail to be that high, but we'll work it out."

A lack of sleep setting in, Bernard tilted his head to one side, as a childish smile crossed his face. In his hands he held an imaginary video game controller, and letting the sight of Kendeff before him morph into a cartoon, he began to imagine a new video game where you would drive . . . a news truck around a park chasing bothersome attorneys . . . and that antenna raised way up in the air, that would hold weapons . . .

🎮 🎮 🎮

An hour after Lester and team checked in, their accommodations at the Pendrite no longer resembled a suite in a five-star hotel, or a hotel room of any sort, for that matter.

The dining table had been moved into the living room and set next to a window, which now served as a backdrop for several laptop computers and other devices. The sofa had been pulled to one side of that and an armchair set on the other, with Eric lying on the sofa and Patricia draped across the chair.

Lester, meanwhile, had dragged the desk from the wall and parked it where the sofa had been, with his two laptops leaving just enough space for a coffee pitcher and a cup.

Next to that was a nightstand from his bedroom, now holding a four-hundred-and-fifty-dollar espresso machine he had carried onto the airplane.

Lester texted several times asking for information, and finally a reply came, announced by a vibration alert.

Lester held his phone up. "Maybe we'll finally find out what the heck he's doing up here."

"If it turns out it isn't that big," Patricia ventured, "he's gonna be pretty pissed. This suite isn't cheap. And we have Chen Li flying up too."

"We'd better hope it *is* big, then," Lester said, as he began silently reading the text:

> Kelly Chambers charged with murder, soon out on bail. Get modeling software, map templates sent up from SF. Time to build a new virtual murder scene.

Patricia looked on. "Is it big?"

"Uh, yeah."

Ten minutes later, the three sat sulking in silence, the nagging image of a nagging Herbert Iggid now no longer at the top of their minds.

"Murder? Kelly Chambers?" Eric mused. "I kinda don't think so. Did you find anything on bail?"

"Yeah, here, I found something." Lester stared at the screen before him. "I found something called the King County Felony Bail Schedule."

"Cool!"

"Let's see . . . Treason, no bail. Legislator receiving bribe, one hundred thousand dollars . . . Gotta scroll down . . . Vehicular manslaughter for financial gain? What the heck is that?"

"Wow."

"What's next? Kidnapping, a hundred thousand dollars, mayhem, two hundred and fifty thousand, torture, five hundred thousand . . ."

"What if it's kidnapping, mayhem, and torture together?" Eric asked.

"I suppose you could get a bundle deal, like with cable and Internet. What else do we have? Train robbery? Do people still rob trains? Next is train wrecking, throwing missiles at a bus, bigamy, marrying spouse of another . . . Then there's lynching . . . looting, forgery, counterfeiting . . . and, oh, here it is, murder."

"What's the bail?" Eric asked.

"No bail's listed."

"Does Washington State have the death penalty?"

"Good question." Lester did a new search on his laptop, and a moment later: "Yeah, they do," he said quietly.

They eyed one another briefly until Patricia asked: "What's the method of execution?"

"Let's see. Washington's death penalty . . . was reenacted in 1975, and they've only executed five people since. Maybe not so bad. In Texas, let's see . . . in Texas they've put to death five hundred thirty people in less time. Oh, and look, there are five inmates on death row now in Washington, none of them women."

Patricia bit her lip. "So what's the method of execution?"

Lester hesitated a moment before answering. Then: "Choice of lethal injection or hanging."

"Choice?" Patricia asked in disbelief.

Downtown Seattle stretches along a narrow north-south strip between Interstate 5 and Elliot Bay. Walking east or west from the courthouse would have meant treading up or down a steep grade, a prospect that prompted Bernard to walk north, until he found a coffee shop that advertised free Wi-Fi and did not appear so trendy that a beret and an acoustic guitar would be required to gain entry.

After setting his laptop on a table in the back, as far as possible from other customers, he ordered a cup of coffee and an empty cup, and, back at his seat, set the coffee out of reach and filled the cup with Pepsi from his vest.

His mind was fuming. This business with Kelly had turned out to be a lot more than he had bargained for.

There was no question: Kelly didn't commit any murder, and yet here these crazy people were talking about the death penalty and ten million dollars' bail.

Bernard was supposed to be playing *Woeful WasteWorld*, not Sherlock in Seattle.

And with these thoughts boiling deep in his stomach, he logged onto *Woeful WasteWorld* and sought to cheer himself up by taking a journey into a post-apocalyptic wasteland dominated by Fascist zombies and mutant pigeons.

Woeful WasteWorld: OffCide Gamer floats southward over the Jutland peninsula from his home base of Oslo.

Seeing no signs of invading armies, he touches down in Hamburg to inspect the bottom of the peninsula firsthand. Along the streets of the burned-out city he finds scattered zombies, but they appear to be moving randomly, meaning they have not yet been captured and controlled by an enemy.

If they get close enough, of course, they will rip him to pieces, eating chunks of his flesh and chewing on bones as he screams in agony . . .

So he pulls out an automatic rifle and begins shooting.

Now, an undead doesn't go down with one shot. No, you have to shoot them into pieces—it's best to start with the legs—to keep them away.

And taking a chance, OffCide orders his starting army to descend on Hamburg. Taking the city will give him control of Jutland and he can go on to possess all the zombies it holds.

But just as his unsuspecting army enters the city, waves of organized enemy zombies pour out the doors of buildings in far superior numbers, armed with knives and axes and forks, and quickly OffCide is surrounded.

"Ha-ha-hah!" a voice cracks in the sky.

OffCide looks up to see, incredibly—Nnnooo!—the Evil Iberian Emperor, his archenemy, staring down from the sky above.

This is the rival that nearly beat him in the previous year's tournament and the player he is most worried about in the one to come.

"I beat you," the voice says with a low echo—the game lets players filter their voices and add effects. "And I am going to beat you again in the tournament! Ha-ha-ha-ha!" the voice bellows.

6

Kelly Chambers was far from the picture of happiness sitting in the back of the police cruiser heading to the Pendrite. Fidgeting beside her was Kendeff, who appeared in no way comfortable in such close quarters—not really the show of confidence the average murder suspect wants from her attorney.

Kelly studied the bulky ankle bracelet that stuck out plainly above her shoe. There would be no hiding the monstrous thing, that was for sure.

Ankle bracelets were supposed to make women sexy, yet the one locked on her leg presented a very different sort of luster. This was an ankle adornment that identified the wearer not as a sex object but rather, possibly, a sex offender—or in Kelly's case, an accused murderer.

And yet that was not what Kelly was concerned about; what concerned Kelly more was the teasing she was going to receive from Bernard, and now, as Kendeff just informed her, the design team that had come up from San Francisco, as well.

"Fates worse than death," she cursed as she leaned forward to speak to the sheriff's deputy driving the car.

"Hey, any chance we could stop at a deli on the way?" she asked.

Her sudden change in voice and accent stunned Kendeff. Until now Kelly talked with a somewhat stuffy Midwestern flavor. And yet all the sudden she sounded like a showgirl in a Broadway play, one whose trip to Broadway was her first outside of Brooklyn.

"No offense to your fine detention facility back there, officer, but the food, frankly, sucks. I'd kill for a decent sandwich right now."

The deputy glared back by way of the rear-view mirror. "I'm afraid my orders are to drive you directly to your hotel and escort you to your room, ma'am. This is part of the house arrest."

"Yeah, yeah. Gotta follow orders. Always. But, hey, what would it hurt to stop off at a deli real quick?"

The officer frowned. "I'm afraid you are, technically, in custody, ma'am. We need to stick to the planned route."

"What planned route? We're going to the hotel. No one specified any *particular road* we gotta take, did they? Look, if you turn right at that light, there's a coffee shop that puts together a mean pastrami on rye. Mr. Kendeff here will run in, and I'll stay in the backseat. What difference would it make?"

Kelly received no reply, but the deputy pulled into the right lane, all the same, and moments later they were pulling over next to a sign that read Berry Avenue Coffee & Sandwiches.

As the car stopped, Kelly leaned over to Kendeff. "Get me four sandwiches, two pastrami on rye and two ham and cheese. Oh, and don't forget potato chips. *Several bags.*"

"And thank *you*," Kelly said to the officer, depriving Kendeff of a chance to protest. He stared a moment, then climbed out on a mission that turned him into a very highly paid sandwich-delivery boy.

"After this we go straight to the hotel," the deputy made clear.

"Fine, fine, thank you so much."

Nervously, the deputy twisted to face Kelly from the driver's seat. He hesitated, unsure what to say. Finally, weakly: "So, you're from New York, is that right?"

"What, you can tell from my accent?"

"Well, uh, no. I, uh, I read your police file . . ." he stuttered, embarrassed. "You know, I, uh, I'd better wait outside the car." With that he got out and stood on alert next to the driver's side door.

Kelly smiled for the first time in days.

🐾 🐾 🐾

Back in Cliff Shores, Ron O'Brian was jogging along the path that lined the beach, an evening health regimen he maintained just often enough that he could boast having it.

He reached the aquarium still feeling enough energy to complete the run home, but just as he passed the T-shirt shop down the way, he spotted Iggid in the distance.

On this pleasant spring evening when the sun showed plans of projecting glorious rays of color across the sky, Herbert Iggid was standing next to a trashcan in a suit and tie (as always) with a face that seemed searching for an oncoming tsunami—and was disappointed not to find it.

"Shit," O'Brian said with at least intended silence, as he ditched for cover behind two women and a T-shirt rack.

He hadn't been spotted—a piece of luck he was more than thankful for.

O'Brian hadn't planned on making the evening run tonight, had made a point of complaining to his wife of some mysterious back pain he'd been experiencing. But his mind changed at the sight of four voice messages on the answering machine in his home office, all of them from Herbert Iggid.

"I better not let myself get distracted by more work," he shouted moments later to his wife as he ran out the *back* door, clad in jogging suit, and began running the long way down the beach. He had already received several emails from Iggid. The subject of the most recent read "Need Your Advice!" and the message was a tirade about the "insolent" staff at OffCide Studios and a plea for help from O'Brian.

Another detailed how Bernard had disappeared suddenly on some unexplained emergency, and now a group of his staff had followed, missing a *mandatory* all-staff meeting . . .

Glaring now at Iggid in the flesh, O'Brian cursed Bernard and the kids, cursed their work behavior that was again upsetting a day on the beach.

He stepped back to ensure he wouldn't be seen.

From the more-secure vantage point he relaxed enough to gaze out at the ocean, a sight that always brought him a sense of depth, a spirit of reckoning.

And after a moment of focus: "I *will* find you, Bernard Walker," he said, his voice startling one of the women outside the T-shirt shop.

"And when I do . . ." the woman heard him groan.

"And when I do . . . there had better be a pretty damned good lounge and some decent restaurants nearby."

And as O'Brian glanced out at the ocean, he paused to appreciate how easy his police background would make it to find just where Bernard and his staff had disappeared to.

🐾 🐾 🐾

Bernard knocked on the door to suite 2217, which opened to the face of Wilbur Kendeff.

"Mr. Walker, come in."

And there at the entry of the kitchenette stood Kelly, hair still ragged, face devoid of makeup, but at least her clothes, though wrinkled, were a step above the glimmering orange prison jumpsuit.

Bernard inspected her for a second time in one day. "Kelly. You look, um . . ." And for a second time he decided not to say how she looked, but he failed to keep in check the smile that blossomed on his cheeks when his gaze caught her left ankle.

Kelly responded with a pitying air.

"Yeah, yeah, ankle bracelet, ha-ha! Go ahead, get it out of your system. I'm *not* going anywhere, obviously. I can't! So get it over with now."

She turned and walked back into the kitchenette. Bernard followed, smiling at Kendeff.

Standing at the kitchen counter Kelly began unwrapping one of the sandwiches.

"I take it prison fare was not to your liking?" Bernard asked.

Kelly took a bite, then said, chewing, "It's a *jail*, not a prison. *Suspects* go to *jail*, not prison. And, no, suffice to say, the place did not exactly make the Zagat guide."

"So, how'd you get this if you're under house arrest?"

"Ah! Mr. Kendeff here didn't much approve of my methods, but it turns out the officer driving us over was pretty easy to charm. Either that or he found my efforts pitiful enough to pretend. Anyway, he stopped at a deli. Wilbur ran in."

"Nice."

"Now if I just had some clothes."

"You do," Kendeff said. "The boxes in the bedroom. One of my aides bought some for you. We'll send someone over to get your own things tomorrow."

"You think of everything," Kelly responded, not sounding entirely genuine. "Hey, how about you two giving me an hour to unwind. And eat."

Bernard took out his phone. "OK, but let me get a picture of that ankle bracelet first. Lester's going to want to see this."

"Point that thing at me and I break it. And if you do get a shot and are in any way considering posting it on the Internet, I'll ask you to remember that I *am* an accused murderer and there *aren't* any high-tech security systems in this hotel to keep an eye on me."

Bernard's smile grew in direct proportion to Kendeff's wary frown.

Chen Li had been up for more hours than he cared to think about, his long flight from Beijing followed by the added wait at the office. And there his confrontation with CFO Herbert Iggid proved more stressful than hurling across the Pacific Ocean in a 600,000-pound 747 at 600 miles an hour.

He needed desperately to get back to the hotel and *sleep*, since it turned out he had to return to the airport the following morning to fly to Seattle.

But now he was told to go back to the OffCide office and pick up some hard drives to take with him. He waited outside the building's entrance, as instructed, leaning on a wall for needed support.

Around him scattered pedestrians made their way along the narrow street, and after a few minutes he spotted a man down the way staring intently in his direction.

Suddenly the stranger walked over, and Chen, spooked, was about to head into the lobby when the man called out: "Mr. Chen, isn't it?"

"Yes," he answered. How dumb. This was probably the person delivering the hard drives.

The man held out his hand. "I'm Ron O'Brian. We've met in videoconferences."

"Oh, yes," Chen said. "I'm sorry. It's nice to see you."

"Are you here visiting OffCide Studios?"

"Yes, but—"

Before he could speak, the two were joined by Gina, the woman who booked Chen's room—and now was delivering the hard drives.

"Here you go, Mr. Chen. These are the drives." She handed him a leather bag. Then: "Mr. O'Brian. How are you?"

"Fine," he said, smiling.

Chen looked confused.

"Lester said these hard drives are important," Gina told Chen. "They need the content and software in Seattle right away. He said to make sure you carry them on the plane."

"I certainly will," Chen replied.

"Seattle?" O'Brian asked, his smile growing.

"Yeah. Bernard, Lester, and a few others are working on some project up there." She realized as she spoke that she probably shouldn't be divulging that much information.

"And you're going to Seattle, too?" O'Brian asked Chen.

"Yes."

"Wonderful. I love Seattle. I started my police career up there. Have you been there?"

"This is my first trip to the States."

"Well, you're going to love Seattle. Make sure someone takes you around to see all the lakes in the area."

"The lakes?"

"Yeah. I tell you what: I'll send you an email with a list of sights. I have your email address. When do you fly out?"

"Tomorrow," Chen said.

"Oh, very soon. Where are you staying?"

"I'm . . . I don't know." Chen looked at Gina.

"They're all staying at a hotel downtown. It's called the Pendrite or something like that," she said, again worried she might be saying too much.

"Oh, yeah. I know the Pendrite. An excellent hotel, in walking distance to all sorts of places. You're going to love it."

"Oh, uh, good."

"Well, have a nice flight, and enjoy your stay in Seattle."

"I will," he said.

Moments later as they were parting, O'Brian said to himself, "Maybe it'll be *me* who shows you the lakes of Seattle, Mr. Chen. Better than trying to work with Herbert Iggid around."

🐾 🐾 🐾

Patricia's smiley-face headphones were the least expensive in the room, though at a hundred ninety-nine dollars they were nothing to scoff at.

And though she was listening to something between grunge and hop-hop, at the same time that Lester was blowing up Nazi zombies and Eric was playing *Fruit Ninja*—thanks to headphones, the room was largely silent, save for the occasional laugh, cheer, or curse.

Luckily those occasional outbursts let Bernard know that someone was, in fact, in the room despite a complete lack of response to his knocking.

Sighing at the sound of Lester yelling "you die," Bernard thought again about the added complications the three of them were causing by coming up to Seattle. Their presence made a quick escape back to San Francisco more and more unlikely.

Especially Patricia: With her around, he'd never hear the end of it if he left town while Kelly was still in trouble, and Patricia was the only one of them who had never met Kelly.

Bernard took out a phone and recorded video, first of the room number, then of his face, then of his right fist pounding on the door. This he texted to all three of them and then counted to nearly thirty before he heard the latch.

Patricia opened the door to reveal the rearranged suite.

"Hey, Bernard," Lester said, looking up from a laptop on the desk. "Welcome."

"Dude," came a greeting from Eric.

"I will have you all know I am in no way happy to see you here," Bernard stated to the room in general. "I was hoping to be back in San Francisco already."

"Hey," Lester said, "we *needed* to escape the egghead, and it turns out you need our help here."

"Kelly Chambers needs help. What *I* need is fewer complications. Anyhow, did you send for the modeling? It appears we may have some work to do."

"Chen Li is going to hand-carry it. We have him flying up tomorrow morning."

"Oh, God, Chen Li's coming too? I'm supposed to be preparing for a game tournament, not opening a Seattle branch office."

"At least we're together," Patricia consoled in a loving tone she knew would further rattle him.

Bernard sighed. "I may as well fill you in on Kelly."

Eric Lyle, not unexpectedly, continued to play *Fruit Ninja*, though with the headphones off, so he could hear.

As quickly as he could Bernard filled them in and did so, surprisingly, without Patricia making a single wisecrack.

Then he laid out a plan.

"We are going to examine these Cannecare video and sensor sequences. They had to have been faked, and we need to prove it. We're also going to make our own modeling and our own sequences for the murder. That may show us how the Cannecare evidence was done."

"Maybe this is the inspiration we need for a new Murder Mystery title," Lester offered.

"Frankly, I am tired of inspiration for Murder Mystery titles. What I *am* lacking is inspiration for my video game tournament."

Ten minutes later Bernard walked to his own suite down the hall. He looked about as he walked. Kendeff had arranged to book every room on the floor.

'The whole damned floor is ours,' he pouted. 'So much for a quick trip and a quick exit. Damn you, Kelly Chambers.'

🎮 🎮 🎮

O'Brian sat at the small desk in his hotel room staring at a laptop. After seeing Herbert Iggid on the beach, he had run back home, packed a suitcase, and told his wife he had to leave town on sudden business. He then hightailed it to San Francisco, where he checked into a hotel not far from the OffCide office.

Next he rushed over to the office to do the necessary snooping to find Bernard, and accomplished the mission, talking to Chen Li, without even going inside.

Now back in his room, O'Brian was going to find out just what it was that Bernard and the others were up to in Seattle.

He did an Internet search on *OffCide* and *Seattle*, then tried a news search on the same, as well as on *Bernard Walker* and *Seattle*. He found nothing.

Finally he remembered Kelly Chambers had gone to work for a company up there and he tried a news search on her name with *Seattle*. And he was stunned by the long list of results.

"Murder Suspect Kelly Chambers Released on Bail," read one. "Tate Widow Furious over Chambers' Bail," read another.

"Holy Christ," O'Brian said aloud, scanning further headlines to get a gist of the situation. Finally he clicked on one to get details:

Cannecare Murder Suspect Out on Bail

Cannecare CEO Kelly Chambers, charged with the murder of company co-founder Randolph Tate, was released today on $10 million bail.

Chambers had been held since Monday at the King County jail in Seattle facing first-degree murder charges.

At her arraignment this afternoon, Chambers pled not guilty. Prosecutors are seeking the death penalty in the case.

Prosecuting Attorney Albert Estivich called the decision to release Chambers "unwise," saying his office had substantial evidence that included video and sensor records.

Chambers was arrested after video traced her on Sunday walking through the offices of Cannecare Automation in downtown Seattle, where she allegedly used the automated building-control system to kill Tate, who police found dead Sunday evening.

Chambers remains under house arrest in a Seattle hotel.

"I don't goddamn believe it," O'Brian marveled aloud. "Kelly Chambers?"

As he spoke, he felt a set of emotions that had hit him off and on over the past year, since he left his last post as a police officer. It was a combination of longing for a job he had grown used to and powerlessness over no longer being a cop, or in his case, a police chief. And the feeling stung him harder than ever after he saw the news.

He pulled up another browser window and checked the weather forecast for Seattle. It was expected to be sunny with highs in the eighties throughout the week.

7

Pride swelled in Mira Martin's chest as she inspected the morning breakfast buffet, *her* morning creation.

The Pendrite positioned itself as a high-end hotel catering to wealthy business travelers, people who expected a higher class of amenities, from the rooms to the fitness center to the restaurant and lounge.

And Mira's job was to set up the Pendrite's *complimentary* breakfast, a feature American hotels had to offer to stay competitive.

On the lower end, this meant large plastic bins of bargain-brand breakfast cereals, along with industrial toaster units and trays of day-old bread—the entire display highlighted by browning bananas, dispensers of watery orange juice, and large pitchers of bad coffee.

Better hotels had to go further and offer hot breakfasts. But to feed in a cost-efficient manner the hordes of suddenly starving guests (most of whom would not yet be out of bed if the meal weren't free), those buffets typically were produced using military mess hall tactics of mass heating in tubs to serve fatty sausages, puffy scrambled eggs, soggy hash browns, and other horrors.

Mira Martin was going to do much better, was going to show off her five years in culinary school in New York and two more in an internship at a five-star hotel in her hometown of Stockholm. It was her third week at the Pendrite and she had the chance to prove herself by outdoing those crass breakfasts.

And so using her small kitchen staff, Mira found efficient alternatives to cooking in cafeteria tubs, by setting up production processes for nearly greaseless grilling, and careful treatment of every dish.

Now she inspected her work. The center rack in the buffet held platters of thick-cut hickory-smoked bacon; grilled sausage patties; country-style potatoes, spiced and mixed with diced onions and green peppers; and omelets cut into square portions and garnished.

This was lined on one side with freshly cut pineapple, honeydew, and watermelon, on plates that rested on ice . . . and on the other side two toasters were surrounded by an elaborate selection of breads.

And the setup was laid out with an artful mix of colors and textures, and highlighted with the aroma of freshly brewed coffee. Presentation is *not* everything, Mira was taught: Olfactory background is equally important.

Yes, this was artistic culinary expression, Mira said to herself, moved with emotion.

Ah, the first customer, a few minutes early, though that was fine, Mira thought proudly as the man stopped at the center of the breakfast area, stood, and took in the display.

He walked to the left, then the center, then to the right, then back to the center.

And turned to Mira. "What, no Frosted Flakes?"

"Pardon me?" she asked, not understanding.

"You mean to tell me you don't have Frosted Flakes? You can't have a breakfast buffet without Frosted Flakes."

"Seriously?" was all Mira could come up with in reply.

She stood speechless.

"And *shredded* hash browns would be better. And those sausage patties should be more crispy—just to prove they weren't cooked in a microwave, if nothing else."

Mira felt strange sensations in her stomach, felt dizzy as she stood watching.

"Well, when you travel, I suppose you have to put up with the less-than-ideal."

Stepping to the left, Bernard picked up a tray, several plates, and silverware, then filled a toaster with bread, and while that cooked slopped piles of food onto the plates.

Moments later he was seated and buttering his toast, watching a video on an iPad.

Incensed, Mira tidied up the mess Bernard left just as the next few customers entered. As the new guests inspected the buffet, she walked over to Bernard's table.

"My staff and I spent hours this morning preparing the best breakfast buffet of any hotel in this city. We carefully hand-prepared everything and used only the freshest of ingredients. Why, the cost of the coffee we put out this morning alone was more than some hotels spend on their entire buffets."

"Oh, that reminds me," Bernard said, not looking up from his video. "You need to stock Pepsi, preferably in bottles—*glass* bottles."

Fuming, and searching for something to say, Mira turned to the boisterous noise of the three guests now at the buffet, who were competing to pile food onto plates, two each, and in the process slopping globs of egg and hash browns all over the counter and onto the fruit plates.

One of them then piled an additional two plates with breads, unplugged one of the toasters, and carried it over next to Bernard.

"Morning," Lester said as he searched for a place to plug the toaster in.

By the time Mira managed to take this in, the other two were coming over to join him, leaving behind a largely depleted buffet that now resembled more a school cafeteria after a food fight than a fine buffet in a high-class hotel.

"Americans!" she cursed under her breath as she stormed out of the room.

🐾 🐾 🐾

With the plan of getting started on Kelly's case first thing in the morning, Bernard had called the front desk before going to bed and left a wake-up call for noon.

But Kelly caught him minutes after and demanded they get moving earlier, persuading him only when she mentioned the free breakfast buffet beginning at 7 a.m.—and of course Bernard knew that any good breakfast buffet must in fact be hit the moment it opens, before the other guests mess it up.

And now with breakfast under his belt, he got Patricia to help drag a dining table from an unused suite down the hall to theirs, where he set up two laptops of his own.

By the time Kelly arrived twenty minutes later, the room was packed overly tight. The sight startled her as she entered.

"Kelly, great to see you," Lester said, then added, remembering the circumstances, "or not so great, actually."

"Nifty ankle bracelet," Eric added without looking in her direction, his attention glued to a double banana event in *Fruit Ninja*.

Patricia cleared her a space.

"Here, sit down. I'm Patricia, by the way. I'm the new kid."

"Nice to meet you, Patricia." And to Bernard: "I'm glad to see you heeded my advice and added some diversity in your hiring."

"He didn't hire me because I'm a girl," Patricia said.

"No?"

"We don't need to discuss that now," Bernard interrupted.

"No. In my job interview, I beat him at a game of *Counter-Strike*. That's why he hired me."

"You *beat* him?"

"Yeah, and he didn't hire me because of my skills. He hired me because he wanted a chance to play again and *try* to beat *me*."

"What I did *not* hire her for was this constant chatter."

"Anyhow," Kelly said, "I'm sure the company's products will be improved vastly just having a female designer involved."

"Thank you."

Bernard eyed the two, thought how easy it would be simply to walk out, hop in a cab, head to the airport, and catch the first flight back home . . . but, no, he was stuck in an overcrowded hotel room with *these* two. *These four!*

The architects who designed Cannecare Tower envisioned a building that would stand out among the assortment of high-rises that adorned Seattle's skyline. This they achieved by putting a pointed crown at the top of the twenty-story building and lining its sides with blackish-red glass that shined brightly even on the cloudiest of days.

Though the building was far from the city's tallest, its Halloween-like luster and swordlike top made it a focal point along the skyline.

Other buildings in the area proclaimed grandness or history or modern architecture; Cannecare Tower, rather, portrayed something sinister, something that spooked the onlooker and made a lot of passersby cross the street rather than walk in front of it.

And that was without even knowing the true character of the building, a high-rise that was alive and smart and constantly watching . . .

🐾 🐾 🐾

Multitasking.

Bernard was using one laptop to compile a to-do list for the planned modeling scenes and another to watch screen capture of his time on *Woeful WasteWorld* the previous night.

For the modeling he listed places they needed to film and photograph, questions he would need Kelly to answer, measurements they would require of the Cannecare building, and so on.

He was planning to build a complete virtual replica of Cannecare Tower and, if necessary, the entire block, the old hotel included.

As he checked over his list, a window appeared at the bottom right of the screen, an email alert whose subject read: "Notice of OffCide Studios Board Meeting," and the sender was, no big surprise, Herbert Iggid.

Angry, Bernard grabbed his iPad and made a video call to Iggid.

The call rang five times before it was answered, and then what Bernard got was a video window of a confused Herbert Iggid, who apparently had never before received a video call on his new iPhone. His elongated face and forehead could be seen studying the device as he tried to locate the camera.

"Herbert Iggid," Bernard demanded.

"I, uh, oh boy. How did you . . . Hi. Hey, I can see you. Can you see me?"

"I would like to ask, what is this business about a board meeting?"

"Can you see me?" Iggid was trying to figure out how to position the phone—phones for him previously being something one held to one's ear. "Can you hear me?"

"*I* can see and hear you and I know perfectly well you can hear me. Now, what is this business about a board meeting?"

Iggid finally settled on holding the phone in front of him, then straightened his tie and quickly composed his thoughts, stoking his own anger in the process.

"Well, what's this about disappearing with the design team?" Iggid countered.

"That would be none of *your* business, I'll have you know."

"Your engineers missed my all-staff meeting."

"On my orders. My engineers work for me. Hence the *my.* And they happen to be right here with me. Working, or at least we are supposed to be working. Instead we are watching you learn how to operate a smartphone."

"And just where are you?"

"Top secret. Research, company research."

This sent Iggid into a new tirade: "I demand an expense account of everything that you are spending. I want every detail: travel, hotels. I assume you are on the road somewhere, since you are *not* in the office or at your home . . ."

Bernard studied the *Woeful WasteWorld* video again, trying his best not to listen.

". . . a board meeting if I don't get it by the end of the day. That's *today.*"

🐾 🐾 🐾

"I need to get the room number of a Bernard Walker," O'Brian told the clerk at the Pendrite's front desk.

It was a smart-looking woman, about thirty, wearing her hair tied back and a uniform that at once said "hotel" and "expensive hotel" at that.

Her reply was not welcoming: "I'm sorry, sir, I am not allowed to give that information out."

"What do you mean?"

"For security purposes we do not give out the room numbers of our guests. In fact, I cannot confirm that we have a guest by that name staying at our hotel."

A second clerk appeared beside them.

O'Brian took out his wallet and produced his work ID, flashed it as if it were a badge, a habit he had trouble breaking.

He leaned toward the desk and spoke quietly to the woman, glancing about as if to make sure no one could hear, even though save for the three of them, the lobby was empty.

"I'm working with Bernard Walker on the Chambers case," he confided. "I have some very important papers here."

"Perhaps I can deliver them for you."

"Sorry. They're legal documents, and I have a court order to deliver them personally."

Now the second clerk spoke. "If I may, sir. Do you know the name of any of Mr. Walker's staff?"

"Probably a Lester Argyle, and another kid who's permanently attached to a device at any one time."

"Oh, yes, just one moment, sir." The clerk took out a phone, snapped a picture of O'Brian, then began typing.

O'Brian flinched as the photo was taken, but watched, intrigued.

A moment later, the clerk smiled and said, "Welcome to the Pendrite, sir. My name is Paul." He had just texted O'Brian's picture to Lester Argyle and received the OK.

🍖 🍖 🍖

". . . am contacting each member of the board . . . I can't even schedule a staff meeting, I've been shot at . . . and as chief financial officer *my job is . . .*"

In the background the doorbell rang.

". . . need to know *everything* about every project and that is final. Either that or I go to the board."

Bernard stared in disbelief as a voice interrupted from behind "No, you do *not*, Herbert."

"Who's that?" Iggid asked.

"Ron O'Brian," came the answer, as O'Brian leaned down behind Bernard to be seen.

"I've been looking everywhere for you, Ron. What's going on?"

"I'm working, and so is Bernard and his team. This is *not* an OffCide Studios project; it is *my* company's project, a test case you do in fact already know we were planning, a test case that Bernard and team have committed to helping us with. And also one that we have set aside money for."

Lester, Patricia, and even Eric fell silent, quieted their devices to listen. They crowded behind Bernard and O'Brian to get a glance of a stunned Iggid.

O'Brian continued, sounding like the no-nonsense police chief he once was. "You've been informed and the boards of both companies have been informed about the test projects. As for the details, Herb, you're *not* being informed of them because you have *not* demonstrated the ability to be trusted. Now go back to your office and do financial things and leave us to do our work. Any further interference from you, and Bernard and I will convene the boards of both companies."

And with that O'Brian reached across to the iPad and ended the call, setting off a silent Holy Crap moment in the room.

With the call ended, the hardened former police chief turned his expression on Bernard, leaned so that his face was just inches away. "I swear to you, Walker, if you ever, ever

decide to run away with everyone from Iggid like this again
. . ."

Bernard lifted an eyebrow in defiance. "Then what?"

". . . then you had *damn* well better remember to bring
me with you, damn it."

🐃 🐃 🐃

"Test project? And just what might that be?"

O'Brian stared Bernard in the eyes. "I'm guessing you
four are about to build a virtual murder scene, one for Kelly's
case." He eyed Kelly across the room. OffCide Studios had
produced three murder mystery video games, one of them a
year earlier based on a real murder.

O'Brian had been the police chief in Cliff Shores where
the crime had taken place.

"Yes, that is correct."

"Well, I need a test case for the SimCide software. Funds
have already been budgeted, which means Herbert will be off
your back—*and mine*. And besides, testing the software on a
forgotten police case just wouldn't be as good as testing it on a
real crime."

"Glad I could be of service, Ron," Kelly put in, a dead
smile on her face.

"Ah, sorry." O'Brian leaned to one side to get a better
view of the ankle bracelet.

"Kelly, I'm glad to see you're, uh, well. I don't know
anything more than what I've read in the news, but we're
going to figure this thing out."

"Thanks, Ron." Kelly had been largely responsible for arranging SimCide's funding and installing O'Brian as CEO.

"Anyhow," O'Brian said, turning back to Bernard, "frankly,
you need my help. And so does Kelly. This is no video game;
the murder victim won't just be reborn and get to start over.
And for Kelly, this is not really—"

"For Kelly it's not exactly a bowl of, what is that game? A bowl of *Fruit Ninja*," Kelly said. Then to Patricia, "Hey, what the hell is this *Fruit Ninja* thing, anyway?"

"Oh, you're gonna love it. Oh, and, Mr. O'Brian, it's called *being spawned*."

"What?" O'Brian sort of growled. Patricia was the only one in the room he didn't know.

"When a player is reborn in a game, it's called being *spawned*."

Bernard eyed Kelly, then Patricia and Ron O'Brian, and lastly the laptop that still showed a *Woeful WasteWorld* video.

More people! This whole mess kept getting worse, and the likelihood of his getting back to San Francisco for the tournament was becoming more and more remote.

🎮 🎮 🎮

An hour and a half later, Chen Li was riding an elevator up to the twenty-second floor of the Pendrite, where, he was told, his room awaited.

The elevator door opened to reveal marble walls, lush carpeting, and someone shooting a gun—

Chen jumped back into the corner of the elevator. That had certainly looked like a gun.

Another figure to the left jumped around a corner for cover, and just as Chen was about to panic, he recognized it as Patricia, the new girl he had talked with many times in videoconferences.

It was then that he remembered Lester and Eric talking about getting new airsoft guns, and he breathed a sigh of relief.

"Hey," he shouted, but the sound was drowned out by a much louder *hey* in the distance. And stepping out of the elevator, he saw, amazingly, Ron O'Brian, whom he'd just seen in San Francisco, storming down the hall.

"Give me that," O'Brian moaned at Lester.

"It's an airsoft gun."

"A realistic one, too. And this a replica of what?"

"A Desert Eagle?"

O'Brian took out a revolver from his shoulder holster. "This is a Smith & Wesson Six-Eighty-Six Plus. A real one. This is the sort of gun police carry, and what's *not* safe about your gun is that it *looks* real."

"Oh." Lester's enthusiasm for his airsoft gun was fading.

"I'll tell you what. I'm going to hang on to this while we *work on Kelly's case*, a murder investigation that a good friend of ours is at the center of. I hope you guys realize this isn't a vacation."

O'Brian was met with three blank stares, and a confused one from Chen Li.

"Mr. Chen," he said. "You made it. Welcome to Seattle."

"How did you . . ."

"Yeah. I decided to fly up today too. I just got in a while ago." O'Brian noticed Chen's suitcases. "Do you have a suite?"

Chen pulled a key card from his front pocket. "Yes."

"Well, you must be tired, too. Lester, why don't you guys show Mr. Chen to his suite?"

Down the hall, Bernard stuck his head out to find out what all the noise was. Seeing the group, seeing Chen Li among them, he wondered who else might show up in Seattle to help keep him from getting back to his life.

Kendeff.

For Wilbur Kendeff, this was a case that could change his life, could push his career to new heights.

Randolph Tate made headlines a few years earlier developing software and automation systems that could do amazing things, technology that scored venture funding and some sizable early contracts.

Now the media was having a field day. The bizarre murder instantly became the lead story in every local TV and radio news broadcast, and it was being closely followed on national television as well.

That was the sort of exposure Kendeff could benefit from. He'd be up there with the attorneys who defended the O.J. Simpsons and the Bernie Madoffs, lawyers who made small fortunes and weren't even expected to get their clients off.

Just being involved translated into future brand recognition for Wilbur Kendeff.

So he intended to use the afternoon meeting to establish personal control over the case and how it was handled. He was already uncomfortable defending Chambers and yet somehow reporting also to Walker, and now he was told there was a former police chief involved too, who was going to run a forensic investigation to help present their case in court.

But his hopes of a perfect meeting were quickly dashed as the group entered and began plugging in devices, moving furniture, and fussing over beverages. They turned down the coffee offered by Kendeff's two assistants, and one set up an espresso machine and began passing out cups.

"It might be advisable to move beyond the refreshments and get down to business," he told the group, irritated at the sudden preoccupation with beverages, and then by the realization that he had a dry throat and was the only person present *without* one.

🐾 🐾 🐾

Chen Li struggled to keep pace with Patricia as they crossed the parking lot at Seattle's Northgate Mall. Chen found himself dragging from a combination of two days' travel, jet lag, and the wonders of everything he was seeing here in the States.

Still, his exhaustion was matched by enthusiasm just to be out and exploring. He had seen pictures and video of American malls and he was excited now to be visiting one. They had borrowed O'Brian's rental car and come to buy phones and computers.

As for Patricia, she seemed to have no end of energy as she led the way, studying a GPS map on her phone as they walked.

"We'll get phones for you and Kelly here at the mall," she shouted through hurried breaths.

Chen was touched by Patricia's enthusiasm at getting him a phone to use while in the country. What he didn't know was that a big part of Patricia's vigor emanated not from her youth but from a company credit card, one which, very cool, had her name on it, along with a gigantic credit limit. Oh, that and a long shopping list from Bernard that would be fun to fill.

"So Chen's your family name, right?" she asked as they entered the mall.

"Yes."

"So I should call you Li?"

"You can. But I usually go by Chen. I know . . . it's complicated. How about you? How do you say your surname? May—"

"May*helm*."

"What country is that name from?"

"No one knows. The family story is that our first ancestors in America couldn't spell very well."

"Hah! How about Pat? Isn't Pat short for Patricia?"

"Yeah . . . but don't call me that. My older brother used to call me Pat; he said it was because I looked like a boy."

They continued getting acquainted as they shopped. Thirty minutes later she was loading him with a new iPhone and a large bag of accessories—a Bluetooth device, a two-hundred-dollar pair of headphones, a hundred-dollar waterproof case, and an extra charger cord.

She bought the same set of items for Kelly, who had been left deviceless by the police investigation.

Next they left the mall and crossed a tree-lined boulevard to a Comp City store, also a bit of a marvel for Chen. It was crowded with all manner of electronics and other products, but it was somehow *so clean and neat.*

Insisting they talk to a manager, they were led to a customer service desk, where very quickly a man in his fifties appeared.

Patricia sounded annoyed as she spoke. "I need to buy a bunch of computer equipment for a company project."

"I can set you up with someone in our computer department."

"No, it's a large order, and I want to work directly with a manager. You'll do," she stated, examining his badge.

Patricia was twenty-two, but was skinny, wore short hair, and had a baby face—features that together made her look all of about fifteen.

"I'll be happy to help you, but if I bring you to one of our associates, you'll be able to get the best of advice on what items to choose. Buying a computer can be very complicated. Especially for a young lady, who might not be so computer-savvy."

Young lady? "I'm not interested in advice, thank you."

"Are you sure? Our associates know all the best brands. They'll find you a computer that can run your favorite chat programs and games. I know you kids love to chat."

"I'm going to be doing a bit more than chatting, thank you."

"OK, then tell me what you're looking for, young lady."

"You might want to write it down?"

"That won't be necessary."

"OK." Young lady? Really? "I need three Dell XPS or Alienware machines, each with an EVGA GeForce Titan X graphics card and twelve gigabytes of dedicated video RAM, along with thirty-two gigabytes of DDR3 SDRAM for memory, two terabytes of standard hard drive space, a solid-state drive, and a second optical drive, one of them Blue-ray, for each system."

"Wha—"

"And to go with each system I'll need the largest Dell monitors you have in stock, one Cyborg STRIKE gaming keyboard, and a Cyborg MMO gaming mouse—they're listed on your website; see what models you have in stock."

"You're talking about thousands of dollars of equipment. This is a joke, right?"

"No. Here's my company credit card. And here's my list, since you didn't want to write it all down. Check to make sure the card's good, then put together an invoice. I need all of this delivered to the Pendrite Hotel downtown by tomorrow at the latest."

Biting his lower lip, the manager glanced at the list.

"Will there be anything else?"

"Yeah, throw in this Hello Kitty flash drive. I found it at the entrance. Isn't it cute?"

"So if everybody has their refreshments, we can get started," Kendeff repeated. "Since Mr. O'Brian has just arrived, I'm going to start from the top to make sure everyone is up to speed on the situation."

"Good," O'Brian said, a notepad and pen set out before him.

"Let's go over the basic facts. On Sunday afternoon, Randolph Tate was murdered. He was found dead, apparently from hypothermia, after being . . . attacked, I guess, by Cannecare Tower's automated building systems."

O'Brian squinted. "I read something like that, but I don't get it. What do you mean *attacked*? How do you get attacked by building systems?"

"The tower's automation system has been identified as the murder weapon."

"Humpth."

"The victim was dressed in only a bathing suit, was locked in a room, and apparently died from hypothermia after the air cooling system was run at full."

"So basically," Bernard jumped in with a sarcastic tone, "he was killed by an air conditioner."

"Hah!" Kelly blurted out.

O'Brian eyed her.

"Well, think about it." Here, Kelly's expression took on a philosophical seriousness. "I wake up one morning and find I'm being arrested for murder, right? Well, then they say I did it with *an air conditioner*. It's like Kafka with a sense of humor."

"Who?" Lester asked.

"I'll tell you later."

"If we can continue," Kendeff pushed, "Tate stepped down as CEO of Cannecare six months ago when Miss Chambers joined the company."

"You took *his* job as CEO?" O'Brian asked Kelly. "Was there a conflict?"

"Oh, God no. Randolph *hated* the job. He's the one who wanted to be replaced. He hired me himself."

Kendeff eyed her, calculating, then continued: "Now, Cannecare Automation makes systems that link video with sensors that keep track of everything that happens in an area, indoors and out.

"Immediately following the murder, the company turned over to police indisputable evidence—video and sensor animations—from its systems showing Miss Chambers walking into the Cannecare offices, going to the top floor, and using a computer there to lock all doors leading in and out of the health club . . . and then . . . well, committing the other acts that led to Tate's death."

Kelly stared fiercely now, an unhappy expression on her face.

"The evidence in fact is so damning that the police concluded there was no reason to further investigate."

O'Brian broke in: "And what was the supposed motive?" he asked.

"Ah, I was getting to that. I just learned from the prosecution, it is widely believed around the company that Miss Chambers and Randolph Tate were having an affair."

"What?" Kelly demanded.

"Several executives at Cannecare told police that Miss Chambers and Tate often held clandestine meetings, and other staff confirmed the reports. What's more, the Cannecare technology tracked their moves, and the company provided police with additional data and video showing visits by Kelly to Tate's office, and frequent trips by Tate to Kelly's office or . . . or to her suite in the old Stanley Hotel."

"We were *not* having an affair," Kelly growled, a command, not a denial, and one backed up by a visible readiness to pounce and attack.

Kendeff stepped back and slid a chair between himself and Kelly.

"So the question is, are we sure we don't want to change our plea to guilty and argue that Miss Chambers was . . . *distracted* . . . at the time of the murder?"

The expression that spread now across Kelly's face would have proved the existence of a "distraction" to any jury.

But Bernard beat her to the punch. "I'll have you know, we shall *not* be pleading guilty or insanity. If that is the best you can come up with, then we shall be seeking a new attorney. A *competent* one."

Kendeff frowned.

"I'm sorry, Miss Chambers. First of all, I have to offer you what I believe to be the best counsel. Second," he said, turning to Bernard, "I believe I am representing *Miss Chambers*, and it must be Miss Chambers' decision what her plea will be. The fact is, Miss Chambers, given the amount and seriousness of the evidence, the prosecution will have little trouble showing guilt, and premeditation to go with it. And I remind you, the prosecution is seeking the death penalty."

Kelly's stare remained fixed.

"If, however, you can show mental instability at the time of the murder, you may wind up with only twenty years or so in prison, as opposed to death row. So, as I said, it is *you* who must decide, not Mr. Walker."

The room had fallen silent, all eyes staring in disbelief at the discussion.

Her head perfectly still, Kelly spoke in a low voice: "It wasn't *me* who called you into this case, Wilbur. When they offered me my one phone call, I called Bernard. Now, if you suggest one more time that I plead guilty, or if you suggest one more time that I actually committed the murder, then I swear to whoever it was who created a universe with you in it, that I will rip your tongue out."

Kendeff turned an odd shade of pink.

"Les," Kelly said with a crazed grin, "gimme another cup of espresso, please."

It was getting late as Patricia and Chen made their way out of the mall, but Patricia had promised to find some sightseeing for Chen.

Walking to their rental car, she took out a list of sights O'Brian had given her, hoping to find somewhere worth stopping on the way back to the Pendrite.

"So, Chen, sightseeing time. What sounds like fun?"

"Really?"

"Yeah." She compared the list with a city map on her phone. "We could check out the Space Needle. You want to go?"

"I guess." Chen appeared less than enthusiastic.

"You choose. We'll go wherever you want to go."

"Really? I can choose?"

"Yeah? Anything you want to do."

"Really?"

"Yeah. You know, I bet you can learn a lot about a person by what sightseeing they pick."

"OK." Chen took out his wallet, pulled out a card with a name scribbled on the back, and handed it to her.

Patricia held it up and read: "Round One"?

Fifteen minutes later the two of them stood in a Radio Shack, where Chen quickly found his way to a display on one side.

"So you're looking for a drone, is that it?" Patricia asked.

"Yeah, a quadcopter drone."

"One with a camera on it, right?"

"Right," Chen confirmed. "And there's a model I really want. I read that the store called Radio Shack may sell it."

"Well, if they don't, I'll help you find someplace that does."

"Great. Then maybe you can help me find a place to fly it."

"I'm sure I'll be able to come up with something, or somewhere where we can try it."

Patricia was impressed. If the first sight a person picks to see while traveling in a country for the first time, if that tells you something about the person's character, then Patricia knew she was going to like Chen Li, who had just chosen a video game arcade.

🎮 🎮 🎮

"I should like to speak with Kelly alone," Bernard said as the group filed out of the conference room.

O'Brian insisted on staying, insisted he needed to be in on this particular conversation, and reluctantly, Bernard agreed.

The three sat facing one another.

"I believe it is time to open a whole new can of worms," Bernard said, opening a pack of gummi worms. "I should like to hear about these meetings with Tate."

Kelly frowned, then said, wearily, "We *weren't* having an affair, Bernard."

"No?"

"No . . . at least not . . . not in the normal sense."

"At least not in the normal sense? And that means what?" The possibility that his video game tournament was being put further at risk because of an affair did not please him. Murder was bad enough.

"As in . . . as in there was no sex?" This Kelly offered knowing it was a weak defense.

O'Brian chimed in: "I vaguely remember hearing that somewhere before . . . wasn't it a president who said that?"

"There was no sex, and no romance."

"Then why the clandestine meetings?" Bernard pushed.

"We were . . . we were . . ."

"Yes?"

"We were eating."

That drew silence, a good thirty seconds of silence.

"Eating?" Bernard said finally, his frustration turning to disbelief, but with a smile ready to take over.

"Yes. It was about food," Kelly stated flatly, turning red.

"Would you mind explaining?" O'Brian asked.

"OK . . . You see, Randolph's cholesterol was high, and he was . . . a little overweight. And his wife's a control freak—the witch. The woman also happens to be an SVP at Cannecare and she watches—*watched*—everything the poor man did. Including and especially what he ate.

"And she only allowed him to eat at the company cafeteria, where the staff had strict orders as to what they could serve him and . . . I can tell you it was not a particularly appetizing menu. Salads mostly."

"So you had, a . . . um, *food affair* with Tate?" Bernard asked, clearly more interested in posing the question than getting an answer.

He and O'Brian stared in disbelief. Kelly responded with a stern face, but one that gradually deteriorated into a smile.

"Yeah," she said, suddenly sounding cute. "I guess you could say Randolph was cheating on his wife . . . not in the *carnal* sense, but in the *culinary* sense?"

Bernard's hint of a grin morphed into a Stare of Death. "I should be collecting supplies needed to repel a zombie invasion of Germania right now, and you're making jokes about . . . *culinary* relations."

The phrase caused him to smile again. "Which allegedly compelled you to use the cooling systems to murder Tate in . . . in . . . cold blood."

The expressions he received in response would also have been well described as cold.

"It sounds like she cared very much about Randolph," O'Brian put in to change the subject, "if she was trying that hard to watch his health."

"It wasn't *Randolph* she cared about. Not in any way. You see, Randolph had a big inheritance, money she had plans for. But without her permission, he invested it in Cannecare, and Brenda—that's his wife—Brenda figured if he died, the company was doomed to fail. The investment would be lost, and she'd be left a middle-aged woman, broke and without prospects."

"How do you know all this?" O'Brian asked.

"Everybody knew it. She talked about little else. She'd say things like 'I don't want you dying until I have an inheritance freed up.' She said stuff like that all the time. And she meant it. She wasn't joking."

"How did you get involved?"

"Hey, I was CEO, I was working eighty-hour weeks. I was new in town, didn't have time to explore, make friends, or even find a decent sausage grinder. But Randolph was a real foodie. One day he gave me a list of places to eat at and then looked real sad, said he wasn't allowed to have any of that stuff himself."

"And so you offered to get some for him?"

"Correct. Pretty soon we got into a habit. We developed a code. When one of us got hungry, we'd either send an email or say out loud in front of others that we wanted to discuss marketing strategy. It was a signal. And when we'd meet I'd have a meal waiting."

"The code apparently did not work very well," Bernard suggested.

"And it sounds like it went a bit further than eating," O'Brian added.

"We became friends, if that's what you mean. I repeat: I didn't know anyone in Seattle. But I would never consider getting involved with a married man, and even if I did, Randolph was far from my type."

"How's that?" O'Brian pressed.

Kelly responded without thinking. "To begin with he was about an inch shorter than me, and he was nearly bald," she said, realizing only afterward that the description would also have fit O'Brian, who now glared through narrowed eyes.

But he continued his questioning. "What about the other co-founder?"

"Oh, Hazly. Ned Hazly."

"Is he a possible suspect?"

Kelly thought a moment. "I don't think Ned has it in him. The guy's a schmuck."

"How so?"

"Well, he starts following the dumbest ideas, things the technology might be used for. And you can't trust him. He's always got a hidden agenda."

"What is this Stanley Hotel you were living in?"

"Oh, God, the building that even Hell wouldn't claim. It was built in the twenties and I'm sure it was falling apart by the forties at least. And it was *never* renovated before Cannecare bought it.

"See, Randolph had this grand notion that a tech startup had to have exotic or romantic surroundings—a lot like you see in Manhattan or San Francisco, where they take decrepit warehouses and turn them into space-age tech campuses. That's an old Seattle thing, too."

"I would say they failed in this case," Bernard commented.

"Miserably. Randolph, it turned out, wound up loving the building. And he was planning to build a cutting-edge campus right up the street—Cannecare Tower—so he decided to preserve the Stanley, right down to the rickety old elevator . . . Oh, and the rats! And a wooden fuse box that uses screw-in glass fuses in the basement. Living in that hole was driving me crazy."

"Crazy enough to commit murder?" Bernard asked.

"Damn near."

The three sat in silence a moment before O'Brian stood up.

"Well, we have Tate's wife, and maybe this Hazly. That's two suspects we can put on our list. That's a start."

Kelly shuddered at the prospect. Being arrested and framed for murder, that was daunting, but far more oppressive was the knowledge that someone out there did it to her. Someone had tried to get her locked up and left facing capital punishment.

The same someone, presumably, who killed Randolph.

🐾 🐾 🐾

Carl Bessite, the Pendrite's evening shift manager, knocked on the door of suite 2221, his mind raging over complaints from the maids. Apparently the guests on the twenty-second floor were disrupting the furnishings and refusing to allow the rooms to be cleaned.

Carl spent four years in Paris studying hotel management, had chosen the Pendrite as the next step in his career. He was not going to tolerate inappropriate, low-class behavior in *his* establishment.

He gasped when the door opened to reveal a sight far worse than what the maids described. Through squinted eyes he surveyed the room: the disarranged furniture, electronics and cords everywhere, empty fast-food bags and other garbage.

"What, might I ask, is going on here?" he demanded of Patricia, who opened the door.

"We're working. Who the heck are you?" she answered with a challenging grin.

"I am the evening manager, young lady, and you are in violation of several of our hotel's guest policies. For instance, we prohibit the rearranging of furniture."

Patricia smiled. "*Young lady*? Seriously?"

"You do not realize how much trouble you're in," Bessite snapped back.

"Yeah? You haven't met my boss." Patricia's eyes glared behind him, where Bernard now suddenly appeared.

"Yes?" Bernard inquired, startling Bessite.

"And you are?"

"Bernard Walker, CEO of OffCide Studios, the company that is renting this floor. And what, may I ask, is the problem?"

"What's the problem? Just look at this suite."

Bernard eyed the room, nodded. "Yes, you are quite correct."

"It's a disgrace!"

"I totally agree."

"You agree? Good."

"Yes. The colors are horrid, the carpet has a rough feel to it, and the cable TV package leaves much to be desired. You do not even have Cartoon Network. This place is practically a youth hostel."

"Sir!" the manager blurted out. "This room is a shambles, the furniture has been moved around, and the maids are refusing to even come up to this floor."

"For the prices you charge, your guests should be allowed to take the furniture home if they want. Speaking of which, my company is paying a fortune to use this floor for a special work project, and for the money we're paying, I expect full cooperation from the hotel in all matters."

O'Brian watched Bernard handle the night manager, watched with a mixture of disdain and respect. Bernard was self-absorbed and insensitive, and yet impressively effective.

He waited beside Bernard and Patricia as the poor man retreated to the elevator, and then he pulled Bernard aside.

"Walk me to my suite," he said.

At the door to O'Brian's suite, they stopped.

"So you're going to do it?" O'Brian asked.

"Do what?"

"Make it into a video game."

"By *it* I am guessing you mean the murder."

"Yeah."

"I'm planning to put it into development, yes. But we may very well find the answers to our questions before it is finished."

"OK, well . . . I assume your next step is filming?"

"That is correct. We will have to do a full photo and video shoot, from Kelly's suite in that old hotel to that fancy computer room where she supposedly committed the murder. Oh, and the spa, as well. In fact, the entire spa floor. The rest of the building we can handle on spec."

"I think I can arrange that. I have two former colleagues, two officers who are involved in the investigation. If the police ask in cases like this, they can usually get people to cooperate. I think they can get Cannecare to let us do what you need."

"Excellent. That is a necessary first step."

"Anything else you'll need?"

"Yes. I will need a full sample of the so-called sensor data from their systems for all day Sunday, midnight to midnight, and the entire weekend if possible. And the software to display it—ideally whatever software they're using."

"I'll try."

"Good, because I have other things to do."

"What's that?"

Bernard didn't answer, but O'Brian guessed it had to do with his tournament.

🎮 🎮 🎮

"Introducing the Cannecare Video Wall, a floor-to-ceiling high-definition screen that serves as the centerpiece of Cannecare's Building Automation and Security System, or CBASS.

"Here engineers can create an infinite combination of windows in different sizes and shapes to display output from CBASS.

"For example, you see in this window a simplified schematic of the fire alarm system at Cannecare's futuristic headquarter building in downtown Seattle. And in this window is a blueprint map of the tower, showing how many people are present and where.

"And while we're at it, let's pull up another window, this one showing the Seahawks game; they're on their way to the playoffs, after all."

The figure at the console paused the marketing sequence on the Video Wall.

The thing sickened him, not only the tacky marketing but the content itself. Here the company had a revolutionary concept combining cutting-edge technology from numerous fields, and all this video was pushing was a building automation system similar to ones that had been in use since the seventies, save of course for the wonderful Video Wall.

The figure did a little mousework and pulled up instead windows that were more interesting.

The first showed a section of office with five-foot-high cubicles seating some ten employees, each apparently at work at his or her desks.

Apparently, that is, for another few clicks opened a series of smaller windows, one for each worker, displaying what was on their monitors. Four were marked in red.

"And when they're marked in red," the figure said, mimicking the cheesy voice of the promotional video's narrator, "when they're marked red, it means the employees are doing things they should not be doing at the office, on company time."

And indeed, one employee was shopping on eBay, another was downloading unlicensed music, and two others were chatting with each other, complaining, it turned out on closer inspection, about how hard they were forced to work.

Now the video showed a window labeled Employee Productivity Analysis.

This displayed a picture of an employee, a young woman, punching in that morning.

Readout at the top provided details:

> **Employee:** Jennifer Mills
> **Age:** 28 yrs., 5 mos.
> **Tenure:** 2 yrs., 7 mos.
> **Today's Arrival:** 13 min. late
> **Average Arrival:** 7 min. late
> Click to run daily analysis.

A cursor appeared and clicked on the last line, causing the window to speed up and show the woman's every move in fast motion—trips across the office to the kitchenette, to the bathroom, to the stairwell where she and other staff broke company rules and smoked cigarettes . . . to the coffee shop in the lobby . . .

The figure continued to mimic the promo video voice: "And every trip was filmed from numerous angles and coupled with sensor data confirming her movements."

The surveillance stopped only at the rest room door—"yet another wimpy limitation at a company with weak vision," the figure complained as a new readout appeared at the top of the screen:

Time of Apparent Work: 40%
Time in Rest Room: 12%
Time in Stairwell: 17%
Time in Kitchenette: 6%
Time off Floor: 6%
Time Idle at Desk: 19%

"Now this is technology at work," the figure concluded, smiling.

9

Hazly.

Ned Hazly, co-founder and now interim CEO of Cannecare Automation, sat on this Thursday morning facing the Cannecare Video Wall in the Prototype Engineering Center, or P-E-C as the company branded it. The room was really more of a demonstration center, with a computer console to one side and a row of conference chairs to the other that seated small groups for marketing presentations.

The console desk housed two built-in monitors and keyboards. Though it was connected to the building's automation systems and could operate everything from air temperature to fire sprinklers to lights, this was not where day-to-day building operation was carried out.

The computers that normally ran the building were on the ground floor, where they could be accessed in case of a fire or other emergency. The room they were in was manned by security guards, and building engineers and others were in and out during the day. It had a much smaller version of the Cannecare Video Wall, a six-square-foot screen along the back.

But the PEC . . . This was a wondrous place. The PEC served as the showroom for Cannecare's systems, and it was where Ned Hazly loved to sit and bask in the marvelous technology.

It was also where, all evidence attested, Kelly Chambers had murdered Randolph Tate.

And now it was where Ned Hazly tracked, on the Cannecare Video Wall, the Chambers defense team as it progressed through the lobby, into the elevator, and up to the nineteenth floor.

Hazly fumed at the interruption: He did not have time for things like this. As interim chief executive he needed to put every effort into smoothing company operations following the rather unexpected but thorough management shakeup, not to mention work at making the *interim* CEO title permanent.

Even more galling, the group had requested to photograph and film the offices and even the Stanley. There was nothing to hide; photos and video of the high-tech building could be downloaded from the company website, were in fact used by Cannecare's marketing staff to showcase the company's technology. Still, it seemed an offensive intrusion considering that Chambers' guilt had been perfectly well established.

Hazly reluctantly agreed to the meeting, and then only after warnings that a lack of cooperation could jeopardize the case against Chambers.

But his own participation would be brief, very brief. The first half of the meeting he was leaving to Mr. Smiles, as Hazly secretly called the man.

This was Rainer Holstenbeck, an investor in Cannecare and an unofficial product adviser who possessed an enthusiasm for technology that far outpaced his actual understanding of it. This was a man known for getting confused when trying to distinguish between files and folders, or trying to remember how to carry out such complicated tasks as copying and pasting.

But it didn't matter to Hazly if Chambers' defense team was completely misinformed by the man, so long that they received the friendly, heartfelt cooperation the police were expecting, and that they would get from Mr. Smiles.

Yes, *friendly* was the best adjective you could use to describe Rainer Holstenbeck. The man would latch onto people and charm them until they were on a best-friend basis—a useful tool when trying to sell a new client or get a positive write-up out of a reporter, even if the man's irritating affability proved a tiresome trait to be around day after day.

Hazly clicked a couple of icons and a new window opened on the Video Wall, this one showing the conference room that the defense team was now entering, and sure enough, Holstenbeck was at his best playing host.

"We have several kinds of coffee," he announced excitedly, his Austrian accent tempered by eloquent enunciation. "Seattle has wonderful coffees, wonderful, as I'm sure you know. I understand you are visiting from San Francisco. Is that correct?

"Oh, here, these muffins my wife baked herself," he said, indicating a tray on the table. "They are a specialty in my country."

"Really?" O'Brian asked with sudden interest. "Where is that?"

"Lessenberg, in Eastern Europe. Are you familiar?"

"Ah . . . a little," O'Brian lied.

"It was one of the only countries in the area to remain neutral during the Cold War. Since the nineteenth century we have had a sizable textile industry."

Holstenbeck stood a good six-foot-two, was somewhere in his mid-fifties, and had a large head and pronounced features that somehow worked to put people around him at ease.

"Ah, yes," O'Brian said to be polite. O'Brian spent a lot of time reading biographies and books about World War II; he considered his geography to be excellent. Yet he had never heard of Lessenberg. "Is it a nice place to live?"

"Yes, yes. Mountains, wonderful mountains, if you don't mind cold. But, ah, how do you say it, a *hearty* country, yes, hearty, and a hearty people—very much like here in Seattle. We have a rich culture and a wonderful cuisine. The frigid winters make us stay indoors, and we spend our time inventing new methods with which to prepare dishes and foods."

"Fascinating."

(In the background, Bernard cased out the wife's muffins, viewed them from different angles, finally picked one up and chanced a small bite. A moment later he snatched another, which by the time he turned around had disappeared into a vest pocket.)

"Oh, and here," Holstenbeck continued his banter, "let me introduce Phil Gradee, our lead building manager."

"Howdy," Gradee said, shaking O'Brian's hand. He was tall and thin and had a seriousness built into his face that directly contrasted with Holstenbeck's jovial character. In fact his voice was as cold as his handshake was firm, and his expression revealed a feeling of distrust.

"The name's Ron O'Brian. And you're the *lead* building manager? Is that it?"

"Yeah."

Holstenbeck jumped in. "We have so-called building managers on duty every day. They're all talented, *super*-talented electrical engineering people. And they all report to Phil here."

"Well, pleased to meet you," O'Brian said. "And this is Bernard Walker, CEO of OffCide Studios, and these two are Lester Argyle and Eric Lyle, both OffCide engineers."

"Phil here also designed several pioneering safety features that are part of our automation systems," Holstenbeck said. "Features such as the self-drive door regulator."

"Really?" O'Brian asked, trying his best to sound impressed. "How does that work?"

"Fire doors throughout a building can be remotely opened and closed. Push of a button, yes. It's brilliant."

"It is *not* brilliant," Gradee said. "In fact, it's a simple mechanical arm. It's the same hydraulic regulator that keeps heavy doors from slamming, but ours has an elbow that pulls or pushes a door's weight. It's something we should have been doing decades ago."

"Simple, but brilliant for the added safety to a stairwell in a high-rise or large building," Holstenbeck insisted.

Bernard butted in, still chewing. "I would think stairwell doors would be best kept closed and locked," he commented, the image of Herbert Iggid climbing his beach house stairs etched in his mind.

"Fire safety, I am guessing." O'Brian ventured. He could see a clear splash of unease on the building manager's part, normal for a first impression of Bernard.

"Yes, correct." Gradee wasn't interested in taking credit for the self-drive regulator, but he lit up some at the chance to talk about building systems.

"In a smart building," he went on, "your doors are all fire doors. And remote control is part of your fire-safety system."

"In fact, all doors are automatically unlocked during a fire alarm," Gradee added. "But Cannecare's doors can be held in an open position just by pulling on them. That way people don't use doorstops—or folded-up newspapers—to keep them open."

"Yes, yes," Holstenbeck said, "and then we know we can remotely close them if we need to contain a fire."

Bernard did not look totally convinced.

"So, if I want to get into a building, or, say, from a stairwell into hallway, I don't need a key. All I have to do is set off a fire alarm?"

From the PEC Hazly watched the whole thing—via cameras—with a feeling of disgust growing in his stomach. Here these people were trying to get Chambers off and Holstenbeck was feeding them muffins and teaching them about fire safety.

The small talk went on for a good ten minutes before the meeting got started. As they were sitting down, Holstenbeck connected a laptop to a projector.

"I do apologize for not having this ready. I bought this computer just this afternoon so I could show you this video."

Bernard eyed the Alienware logo on the back of the screen—not bad, a couple-thousand-dollar gaming computer just to show a video.

"Ah, yes, here we go," Holstenbeck announced.

As the screen on the wall lit up, O'Brian took on a serious face, while Bernard got comfortable in the cushy conference room chair, muffin in hand, as if he were in a cinema.

The vague glow of a man sitting alone at a desk. He starts out in a low voice: "Cannecare Automation . . ,

"This is the company that will define innovation for the next several decades.

"It will be the next IBM, the next General Electric, the next Microsoft, Google, and Facebook . . . It will be the tech company everyone is talking about, the one changing lives.

"Excuse me," he says, breaking the serious tone, "it's kind of hard to see in here." He types on a keyboard and the room lights up.

The man smiles at the camera. "Other people in the building might be thinking it's a little dark, too. So . . ." The video divides into two windows, the one on the left showing the speaker and the one on the right showing the outside of a glass skyscraper, completely dark in the night.

He hits another key and the building flashes to life, brighter than anything around.

"Whoops, that might be a tad too bright."

The man hits another key and a piano piece, Für Elise, begins playing in the background, and as it does, lights on various floors of the building begin to blink and flash to create a fifty-story light show.

For the first time, Bernard realized it was Randolph Tate in the video, filmed, presumably, before the murder. He glanced at O'Brian, guessed by the stone face that O'Brian, too, had caught that point.

The video flashes back to the man, who is now more serious.

"We are developing technologies that manage environments, buildings, and soon, entire cities.

"Let's begin with building automation. The so-called Smart Building has been around for decades. But the building you just saw me play musical lights on is the fifty-story First Credential Bank Building in downtown Seattle. Built in the early nineteen-eighties, it featured what was at the time state-of-the-art building automation using Honeywell computers.

"Sitting in a little room on the ground floor next to the loading dock, a building engineer could turn on and off every light in the building, lock and unlock every door, and ignite the boilers and air-conditioning systems to control air temperature across all fifty stories. Not to mention stop and control the tower's fifteen elevators and set off fire sprinklers if needed.

"Now imagine adding to all this the cutting-edge technologies of today, including infrastructures for networks, for power, for data, for different types and levels of data . . .

"More recently with society pushing for more-energy-efficient buildings, we have turned our lighting systems into networks that collect data from each light fixture, and from sensors that detect a space's temperature, whether people are present, and the amount of sunlight pouring in through the windows.

"To conserve energy the systems adjust heating and cooling, shut off lights, and even dim the window glass to hold out the sun's rays.

"So the Smart Building has also become a Green Building.

"Of course, all that data is worthless on its own. To make use of it Cannecare has built complex content-management software that correlates sensor and video databases to present custom reports that can re-create any moment or day on record . . ."

O'Brian shot Bernard an uneasy look, though only to find Bernard's large figure snuggled well into the office chair, occasionally putting bits of muffin into his mouth, his attention lost in the video.

"Cannecare's automation systems are already at work operating state-of-the-art tech campuses with green building systems that maintain healthy work environments.

"Energy efficiency is a market we see as driving our technology faster than any other.

"In fact we are now aligning our systems to make it easy for property developers to attain the exalted LEED—or Leadership in Energy and Environmental Design—certification from the nonprofit Green Building Council.

"In the near future you will see our systems used at hospitals, schools, sports venues, and other sectors we are targeting.

"And we at Cannecare envision a day not too far off when our technology will be running regional infrastructure, traffic-control systems, and more . . .

"For a further glimpse of the future, be sure to visit our website—"

Holstenbeck stopped the video. "Yes, yes, imagine all of this installed in our schools. Brilliant, brilliant," he raved.

"Imagine it in the hands of a murderer," O'Brian said just loud enough to be heard.

Kelly stared out a window at the brilliant blue (*now* it's blue!) sky and the sparkling metropolitan cityscape where months of incessant drizzle had finally evaporated to provide a glorious scene. Kelly believed fully well she could detect the scent of moisture being baked out of everything—wood, glass, earthen, and carbon-based, as well.

This from the twenty-second floor of the Pendrite, behind thick, locked windows that eliminated any hope of actually inhaling that longed-for scented air.

Kelly felt herself drawn to the outside world of downtown Seattle, but the impulse trickled down her body to the weight pulling at her slim ankle, the hideous-looking ankle bracelet that allowed God knew who to see her every movement, whether she was walking into the kitchen or into the bathroom.

Yes, the ankle bracelet, the thick dark windows, and the carefully controlled atmosphere made for an impressively oppressive prison for Kelly Chambers' house arrest after all.

Ned Hazly's appearance could best be described as *pointy*. The man had a long, narrow chin and combed his hair so as to cover early signs of thinning—the effect being an arrow of bangs pointing down his forehead.

His bony cheeks and chin then provided the backdrop for a long, thin nose and eyes that even wide open seemed still to squint.

And they were wide-open squinty with emotion as he entered the conference room, an impression that even the jovial ravings of Rainer Holstenbeck could not overcome.

"Ned, Ned," the latter cried out, stepping over to pat Hazly on the shoulder. "Welcome, we've been waiting for you, welcome.

"Everyone, this is Ned Hazly, the genius who, along with dear Randolph, made all of this happen. Ned is Cannecare's co-founder, and now its interim CEO."

The compliments failed to lighten Hazly's mood.

"Oh, and speaking of which, I have no doubt that Ned is a busy, busy man, what with the murder just days behind us, and much, much work to be done.

"Ned, let me introduce to you Bernard Walker, who is CEO of a video game company called OffCide Studios. And this is Ron O'Brian, who heads a related software company."

Ignoring them, Hazly replied: "And they're here to *help* Kelly Chambers? And they want *me* to help, too?"

"Well, yes and no," Holstenbeck shot back. Here was a man who wanted everyone to be happy, wanted everything to run smoothly. A single unhappy camper threw his constant joy into a panic.

"It's not so much trying to help Kelly Chambers, really, as helping the police. And they're helping Cannecare, too, you know. Yes, yes, our technology is so new and so revolutionary, the police and the district attorney's office need more analysis. And that is going to shine well on us, yes, it will.

"We've just watched Randolph's marketing video, and now that you're here, maybe everyone would like to ask some questions."

Hazly faced the group, tried to fake a cooperative face, but failed to succeed.

"OK," he said. "I'll answer your questions. Who has a question?"

Bernard raised a hand. "I do."

"Yes?"

"Who made that awful video? It was rather melodramatic."

Hazly somehow made his eyes squint further.

"It happens that it was made by the late Randolph Tate, and it happens to have been instrumental in selling our systems to several clients including the city of Seattle. I am a very busy man, as Rainer just noted. I have a company to try to hold together. Perhaps one of you has a *more-intelligent* question."

"OK," Bernard continued, undeterred. "How is it this technology of yours is supposed to be, somehow . . . 'impressive?'"

Hazly's face twisted. "Pardon me?"

Bernard took a final bite of the muffin. Chewing, he repeated the question: "How is all of this supposed to be . . . *revolutionary*? I mean, I am sure technology of this sort has been in use by the military, at airports . . . And it so happens, we use cooler stuff than this at my company to make video games."

Hazly staggered, looked like he had just had the wind knocked out of him.

Then, "Mr. Walker, is it? Your *video games* don't contain a fraction of the technological sophistication that we are employing in Cannecare's systems. In a fifty-story building, our systems are correlating hundreds of millions of sensor readings per hour with ongoing video from thousands of cameras."

Bernard's expression grew blander. "Well, we work with software platforms and tools that allow ten-year-olds to build virtual worlds with just as many variables."

Hazly jumped at the challenge, a competitive grin building across his face.

"*Virtual!* Playthings. Like a little girl playing house? Hah! Cannecare Automation's systems operate in the real world, do real-world things. And we have built applications far beyond anything you could imagine. Follow me and I'll show you some *real* technology." He appeared at once inconvenienced and yet eager to prove his point.

"Rainer, escort these people to the PEC for a demonstration."

And with that he walked out, turning back briefly to urge his new rival to dare follow.

Ten minutes later the group stood along the back of the PEC, facing the attention-grabbing Video Wall that now was blank and dark.

"No need to sit," Hazly told them as they entered. "This will take only a moment. What you see before you is the Cannecare Video Wall, basically a twelve-square-foot computer screen run by software custom-designed to display our building data. Oh, and let's not forget, this is the computer console over here that Kelly Chambers used to kill my dear friend Randolph."

Delivered in Hazly's high-pitch voice, the *dear friend* bit seemed more like a gibe at Bernard than a tribute to a lost companion.

"Now watch this." Hazly turned to the console for effect.

"C-Command. Power up," he said and the entire wall came to life, displaying eight-foot-high live video of Cannecare Tower, surrounded by probably a hundred boxes offering information about different spots, and on either side were graphs and charts showing everything from weather conditions to lists of people present on various floors. Much of it was easy to figure out but there was so much there. Hazly let them study the information and take in all it represented.

Then: "This is just a display monitoring building operations. Sort of a high-tech screen saver when nothing else is being done on the system."

Even Bernard stared somewhat in awe at the sight.

"C-Command. Open project, Kelly Chambers Zero-Seven." With that the display was replaced by eight ornately framed windows showing a hallway from different angles.

Hazly threw a slightly crazed stare at Bernard.

"Pay attention, Mr. Walker. What you are seeing is video of the hallway leading to Kelly Chambers' suite at the Stanley.

Watch and you'll see just how thoroughly our systems track a person's movements."

As he said this, a door to the left opened and Kelly could be seen, from eight different angles, emerging into the hallway.

The windows then tracked her progress as seen from above and along the floor, with the eight windows rotating among different cameras in a grand and somewhat dizzying re-creation of her journey.

After a few seconds, Hazly brought three new windows to life.

"This," he said pointing at one, "is a map of the hallway as measured by audio sensors, and on this one is a map measuring temperature fluctuations."

And sure enough, the two maps tracked Kelly's progress, as measured by sound and movement of body temperature, as she made her way down the hall—confirming her movements in the video footage. The third window required no explanation. It read:

Area Occupants: 1
Weight: 124 lbs.
Body Temperature: Normal
Face Search: Underway

And seconds later:

Face Search: ID Positive
Subject: Kelly Chambers, Cannecare CEO

It was no wonder, O'Brian reflected, that the police were impressed by the Cannecare sequences, that the prosecution tried to fight allowing Kelly out on bail.

For Bernard, though, it was the room that held his attention. Anything, he said to himself, shown in this room, on this "video wall," would be impressive.

The video sequences went on to document Kelly's progress out of the Stanley and up the street to the Cannecare building, where she made her way, as viewed from different angles, to the top floor, to the engineering center, where they now stood—an eerie experience, to watch the multicamera journey to a door that opens to show the room you're in.

"C-Command, pause. It gets pretty gruesome from here. You want to see more?"

"Absolutely," O'Brian responded with a cutting, stone face.

Hazly smiled, then asked Bernard. "And you?"

"What, no popcorn?"

"Very well. C-Command, resume."

As the video and related sensor graphs and boxes restarted, they showed Kelly sitting down to commit a cold-blooded murder.

Watching, Bernard did his best to take in the feeling of this odd room, where the murder had supposedly been committed, and where, he was told, the police had been shown the evidence.

O'Brian eyed the myriad details that tracked Kelly's movements as she worked on the computer. How in hell did they let her out on bail after seeing this?

Next to him Lester also watched closely, all the while making a mental list of the spots they needed to film.

Only Eric Lyle had his attention elsewhere—as usual on a device. But not his eyes. His eyes were on the video wall, but his attention was focused rather on the phone he held casually before him, on which a wide-angle lens was capturing video of everything that was happening.

The room remained silent a moment after the video sequences finished.

Hazly turned to the visitors, his face entirely too cheerful for what they had just witnessed.

"So as you can see," he said, confident he would receive no further challenge, "there is no question. Kelly Chambers murdered Randolph Tate."

And now he looked directly at Bernard. "A bit more than a video game, wouldn't you say, Mr. Walker?"

Bernard took out a container of Tic Tacs, loudly shook a few out and popped them into his mouth. And crunching: "Cheesy entertainment at best."

"Excuse me?" Hazly asked, not understanding.

"Easily tailored video footage."

"*With*, don't forget, correlated sensor data proving it is not *tailored*, as you say."

"And very similar to virtual-world aspects we add to our video games, and like them, your sensor data could be easily tailored as well."

"Hah!"

"And with that much data and that much detail, I am quite certain we shall be able to prove in very little time that the whole thing *is* tailored, *is* doctored."

The two faced each other intently, challenge presented, challenge accepted.

Hazly knew he would prove this cretin, this kid, wrong. He knew they would find no problems with his data.

Bernard knew he would, and he would show this pointy little man for what he was.

Bernard knew Kelly Chambers was not a murderer, and that the technology therefore had to be wrong, the sequences had to have been faked.

It was like knowing the outcome of a video game before you played it. You knew what you needed to do to win; you just had to figure out how to do it.

🎮 🎮 🎮

While the rest of the group was at Cannecare, Patricia and Chen Li went to Kelly's former suite at the Stanley, just down the block, to pick up items she needed.

"What a cool apartment," Patricia commented as they checked the place out. The suite featured white art deco paneling, antique furniture, and large windows on the east side that looked out onto the bay. Strangely, all the pictures had been taken off the walls. Nails showed where they had once hung; the pictures themselves sat stacked along one wall, covered by towels.

Patricia walked over and leaned one back. It was a framed black-and-white photo of the Stanley when the building was new, in the 1920s, when it towered above the rest of the city both in height and splendor.

Patricia checked another, then a few more, and found they were all historical photos of the building. Blown up and framed, they presented the history of the Stanley in the twenties, the thirties, and beyond.

"Looks like Kelly didn't care for the artwork," she said to Chen. "Here, do some historical sightseeing while I pack some clothes. This is what this building used to look like."

Moments later Patricia had located Kelly's suitcases and was filling them with clothes from the bedroom closet. Patricia's own interest in clothes was typically limited to T-shirts and jeans, and Kelly's preferred fashion was at a glance too old for her.

But Patricia's tastes were quickly transformed as she sifted through the expensive silk blouses, the Armani business coats and skirts, suits from Saks Fifth Avenue . . .

"Jesus, some of these probably cost more than my whole freakin' wardrobe," she said under her breath.

She came across a cashmere coat in the closet that nearly made her melt, and before she knew it she had tried it on and was modeling before the mirror—not noticing that Chen had wandered to the bedroom door.

"Is that Kelly's coat?" he asked.

"Hey!" Patricia moaned, deflated, and slid out of the garment—which she knew probably cost a couple thousand dollars. "I just wanted to see it in full light."

Ten minutes later, two suitcases loaded, Patricia scoured the suite for other things Kelly might want.

Lastly she checked Kelly's desk. There she found three books stacked in the center, two with bookmarks sticking out. One was *Jack Welch: Straight from the Gut*, written by the iconic CEO of General Electric, and the other was a biography of IBM founder Tom Watson.

The third was a cookbook titled *Cooking When You're Not in New York.*

"Wow." Patricia glanced around the room. She remembered hearing about Kelly's twelve- and fourteen-hour days, seven days per week, pictured Kelly spending what little free time she had in this suite reading these books.

"She must have been so lonely. I'd go crazy enough to want to murder someone, living like this."

🐾 🐾 🐾

Sitting in the PEC, Ned Hazly watched the Video Wall with disdain as Lester and Eric walked freely through the two upper floors of the building, filming and taking stills of everything in sight, including the security cameras, the sensor stations, and the light fixtures.

How did they identify the sensor stations? The things looked like overgrown electrical outlets, nothing more. And why the light fixtures? Did they know somehow that the fixtures were loaded with sensors and networking boxes?

Bernard and O'Brian walked a ways behind them taking notes. The group filmed their way down to the lobby, which they shot from several angles, and then down Second Avenue to the Stanley, at the entrance of which they were joined by a young man and a young woman carrying suitcases.

His temper building, Hazly called the lobby, where a guard on duty answered the reception desk phone.

"This is Ned Hazly," he said.

"Yes sir."

"That group that just went through the lobby with cameras?"

"Yes?"

"If they come back, I want you to hold them there and call the police. They are no longer allowed in this building."

"Yes sir."

"Right now they're at the Stanley, and that's fine. For one hour. But write it in the log book and make sure every shift knows that if any of them is seen again anywhere on the block, you are to call the police immediately and then call me. Got that?"

"Yes sir."

Phil Gradee sat in the real engineering center, the small ground-floor room which, while its video wall was only six feet by six feet, was the center that actually ran the building day to day. Ned Hazly, Rainer Holstenbeck, and, previously, Randolph—they were in love with the PEC. They loved just to sit there and test software and play with the Video Wall. You could see they felt power, being in that room.

But the ground-floor engineering center, this was Phil's place, where he spent his spare time. This was where the actual day-to-day work was done. And while it wasn't anywhere near as fancy as the PEC, Phil always secretly enjoyed the fact that from here, he could override anything done upstairs, could grab control of the entire tower.

On this day, Gradee didn't bother turning on the small video wall, but sat staring at a small monitor as a security program flashed through images from the thousands of cameras that constantly watched the building, the block, and the Stanley.

Occasionally he stopped the program when a stairwell shot came up, so he could test the door. Watching on video, he'd click on a pop-up box, hit Open, and the door would slowly slide open, pulled along by a mechanical elbow in its hydraulic regulator. Then once it reached the open position, he would hit Close, and the door would slowly slide shut.

This was his doing, his innovation, and while he didn't think it was that ingenious, Phil was quietly proud that the arms had been installed in Cannecare Tower.

More important for the minute, testing the doors helped him get his mind off something ugly, something scary, something causing stress to settle deep into his stomach.

For when he stared at a monitor for too long, or gazed at a window for a time, he could begin to make out the dim image of Randolph Tate staring back, with sad, questioning eyes, a forlorn face that asked, no, *begged*, "Why?"

🐘 🐘 🐘

Sitting near the base of the Space Needle gives the figure a picture of power. Looming above, the round space capsule perched high on the tower begs the imagination; what a PEC it would be.

Around the bench, evening tourists stroll and gawk and exert a chatty, festive air, this as the sun gets ready to close a rare but stellar appearance with a clear blue sky over Elliot Bay.

Reaching into a lower coat pocket, the figure discreetly pulls out a bottle of Schnapps and spikes the coffee he holds in his other hand, making it sort of a mocha à la peppermint, a personal favorite. A little of home mixed with a little of Seattle.

The figure smiles.

Imagine the PEC Video Wall up there, at the top of the Space Needle, its control boards at your fingertips, overlooking the city as it unfolds to the south.

Imagine the power.

10

Friday morning.

The group was to gather in Suite 2202, the room chosen as their new meeting room slash office—a move necessitated by the deteriorating condition of the design team's suite. O'Brian now simply refused to enter, and Kelly eagerly voiced her support for a change of venue, as well.

Lester had gotten key cards to the several remaining suites on the floor and he and Eric went room to room commandeering various furniture: two dining tables, a couple of desks, extra dining chairs, an extra sofa, and two additional TVs.

If they had to set up a new meeting room, it would be one of their liking.

The suite opened up to a dining area with a living room beyond.

Along one wall, they arranged the three TVs on low dressers and wired them to laptops, which they set up on a dining table in the room's center.

Next they transformed the dining area into a sort of lounge, with a table serving as a food-and-beverage bar. This they stocked with snacks ranging from chips to cookies to fruit (Patricia's insistence), along of course with Lester's espresso machine and a regular coffeemaker.

The rest of the area was given over to two sofas, arm chairs, and end tables.

It was, all in all, an office space they could be proud of, one they could text images of to their friends.

Their pride did them little good, though, when Kendeff showed up, the first to arrive. After a cursory inspection, the attorney launched into a lecture about how this was a murder investigation, not a party, about how a person's future and even life was on the line.

The tirade was broken a minute later when Kelly and O'Brian arrived. Patricia held the door as they entered.

Kendeff turned to Kelly. "Can you believe this?"

Kelly checked out the dining room and the kitchenette, then the living room—one wall of windows and one wall of TVs.

O'Brian followed. "I don't believe it," he said.

"I know!" Kendeff agreed.

Kelly walked over to the TVs, reached out and ran an index finger along the top of one, deep in thought.

The others looked on.

To her right, the windows offered the brilliance of clear blue skies, the world beyond—and freedom.

While before her the TVs represented her only hope for salvation, her only chance to re-enter that world.

O'Brian repeated his comment: "I don't goddamn believe it."

"Me either," Kelly agreed.

"Right!" Kendeff insisted, trying to gain command. "It is totally inappropriate."

"It's beautiful," Kelly muttered, smiling slightly at O'Brian.

He smiled back. "It looks like a miniature version of Bernard's studio back home."

"Who— wha—" Kendeff stuttered.

"Even the view," Kelly added.

"And do you think somehow that this is an appropriate room in which to plot a trial strategy? For a murder trial?"

Kelly let the smile grow. "Perfect," she said.

O'Brian glanced briefly at the man, then at Lester. "Hey, any chance you've got some *normal* coffee brewed?"

🐾 🐾 🐾

Woeful WasteWorld: *Within a hundred miles of Transylvania, the zombies were replaced by vampires and occasional werewolves. These monsters didn't come in the numbers the* zombies had, but if Bernard hadn't been ready (he had already been killed and had respawned several times), he wouldn't have made it.

You see, vampires, being dead, after all, were not easy to kill—until you learned to buy silver bullets.

And while werewolves were far and few between, when one did attack, it could do a lot of damage before you got off the four or five rounds needed to kill the thing.

But Bernard discovered a trick, and it was a delightful one: Among the various supplies players could buy with their "coffers"—the virtual money they collected in the game—he noticed among such things as dynamite, bazookas, and shoulder-fired missiles were inexpensive bags of live kittens.

And sure enough, even if a werewolf was already pouncing at you at full speed, even if the beast could taste your blood in the back of its throat, all you had to do was press a few buttons on your controller and your avatar would throw a cute, furry kitten in the air—and the werewolf would go nuts chasing after the poor thing, and never return to attack you.

This was the sort of feature Patricia would complain about. She would say it was cruel to throw innocent kittens about as weapons.

But on this morning Patricia couldn't complain. On this morning his cellphones were silenced and his door was bolted and blocked by a dresser, so no one could interrupt. And his virtual pockets were loaded with silver bullets and adorable yet tasty kittens.

Tragically, neither would be ample weaponry to handle the first avatar he came across, not an AI but one controlled by a real person, or so the game indicated.

"Stay out of the way or die!" Bernard challenged.

"Log off and come to room 2202," the avatar responded in a voice that clearly was Patricia's. "Or I'll shoot you. You wouldn't want to lose all this progress you made, would you?"

How the hell had she gotten this far? How did she find him?

Most of the group were bleary-eyed even at noon, having stayed up much of the night to begin animation and modeling based on the photos and video they shot.

"How far along are we?" O'Brian asked as Lester poured him coffee.

"We sent several orders to our China studio and we have them working overtime. We'll get portions back as they're completed. By Saturday night we should have basic maps to work with. It'll be crude, but we'll be able to get started."

"Excellent."

As they were speaking, Bernard arrived. He came in and sat at an unused laptop next to Lester, avoiding all eye contact with Patricia. It was only after he sat down that he appraised the setup—the TVs, the tables and lounge area, the view.

"Nice."

"You approve?" Kelly asked.

"Certainly."

"We were just going over everyone's progress," Lester said. "Let's hear from Chen. What have you completed?"

"We finished several avatars." Chen took out a thumb drive and plugged it into his laptop.

He pulled up the first image, a Randolph Tate avatar. The GIF had a big head with an image of Tate's face, that on top of a nearly naked body, and it continually shivered.

The impression drew morbid smiles out on the engineers' faces, but expressions of horror on Kelly's and O'Brian's.

O'Brian glared at Chen. "Is the shivering absolutely necessary?"

"Yeah. Bernard told me to make caricatures for avatars, to make them more appealing."

"I hardly think we need the murder victim's avatar to be *appealing*."

Chen Li continued, undeterred. He was proud of his work.

"This next one is an avatar for Mr. Hazly. Lester and I made it together."

The image showed an avatar with a giant face, beady eyes, a pointed nose and chin, and a pointy hair arrangement at the top of its forehead.

Now O'Brian smiled too. In his brief time with Ned Hazly, he developed a distaste for the man similar to Kelly's.

"The next one Lester did. It's Mr. . . . . Holstenbeck. Am I saying that right?"

Holstenbeck's avatar was about a foot taller than the others and had an oval head and a smile that stretched, literally, from ear to ear.

"How about Kelly's?" Patricia asked. "Did you make one for Kelly yet?"

"Yes, Miss Chambers' avatar is next."

When the next image appeared, you could have heard a pin fall through the air. It showed Kelly Chambers, tall, thin, her straight hair hanging to her shoulders, all with little distortion from her true form. But the eyes, the cheeks . . .

Her eyes were smeared in black makeup like an emo punk rock star, and that ran down her face on both sides.

Everyone stared in silence for a good fifteen seconds, before they all—well, with the exception of Kelly—began to chuckle.

"What the hell is that?" Kelly insisted, but only to hear Bernard commend Chen Li on his work.

Chen was eager to explain. "Well, I just studied the pictures we got at Miss Chambers' apartment. The pictures of Miss Chambers in Seattle. And in almost every one, her eye makeup was . . . on her cheeks . . . was, how do you say . . ."

"Running?" Eric offered. "Like water, going down her cheeks?"

"Yeah."

"That's called *running*."

"Chen, that's terrible," Patricia protested, surprising everyone; *she* was the person usually making irrelevant jokes.

"Yee-aah," Kelly said. "That's OK, Chen. Seattle's damn rain."

She turned away as everyone leaned in to see the photos Chen held out.

"Ooh, look at that one," Lester commented.

"My God, she looks like a vampire," Eric said, giggling. "Pretty scary."

"Yeah, runny makeup and an ankle bracelet; Seattle's been real good to me. So what of it?"

"What's next?" O'Brian asked Bernard.

"What I am planning is for us to put together our own modeling, and at the same time examine Cannecare's video and sensor data, and we're going to search for holes in both."

"Holes?"

"Yes. The video and data have to be faked, and so there will be holes. That's one of the last things you do with video game modeling, search for holes."

Lester joined in. "In video games you have virtual worlds you can walk through. But let's say you're walking along and suddenly a tree disappears or a car is replaced by a—I don't know—a white square. Those are things you've got to weed out before a game title can be released."

"News of holes like that would go viral on the Internet within hours," Eric added, without looking up from his 3DS. "There'd be YouTube uploads, screen shots on Twitter . . ."

"And everyone would be laughing at us, and *not* buying our games," Les said.

"And you expect to find these holes in Cannecare's . . . sequences?" O'Brian asked.

Bernard stood. "Given the amount of sensor detail the sequences contain, yes. And, given that huge amount of sensor detail, if we do not find holes, it can mean only one thing."

"What's that?"

"That Kelly is the murderer."

🎮 🎮 🎮

An hour after their meeting, O'Brian came out to find Kelly by a window at the far end of the hall, curled up in an armchair pulled from a suite.

"Kelly," he said softly as he walked up.

"Yeah."

"Listen, whoever faked the data and murdered Tate had to have access to the—what's it called? The room with the wall."

"The Prototype Engineering Center, or P-E-C, and not many people had access."

"Like how many?"

"Fewer still with the ability to . . . do that."

"Let's go through names."

Kelly glanced out the window, then turned back. "OK. There was Randolph, and of course me. Then there was Ned Hazly, and Brenda, Randolph's wife . . ."

"Brenda Tate? His wife had access to the room?"

"That woman had to have her hands on everything, had to *control* everything—product planning, the interface, the color of paint in the lobby . . . She was chief product officer; she did a lot of demos in the PEC.

"Then there was Phil Gradee, the senior building manager. You said you met him, right?"

"Yeah. Would he have had a motive?"

"No. Gradee's a Boy Scout. He's always talking about best practices and industry standards. The only hidden agenda that man has is wanting to show off his work to the fire department when they come to inspect."

"How about Holstenbeck? He's an odd sort. Is he allowed into that . . . PEC?"

"Oh, you met Rainer yesterday, didn't you? No. God. Rainer goes in, but there's no security risk there."

"Why?"

"Rainer . . . he's sweet, but he's got the technical capability of a four-year-old."

"What do you mean?"

"Rainer's one of those people who's constantly asking for help with anything. A copy machine, a water fountain."

"So what's he do in there?"

"Oh, Rainer's a major investor in Cannecare, and he's great in sales presentations."

"An investor?" O'Brian asked.

"Yeah, Rainer's a senior partner at this firm called Lessenberg Capital. They're a main investor in Cannecare."

"That's the country he's from? What's it called?"

"Lessenberg. I've seen photos. Looks beautiful. The firm is sort of a government investment arm."

"Hmm . . . OK, let's think about who might have had something to gain. Who had reason to want to do this? To Tate, and to you?"

"God, I don't know." Kelly thought a moment, then: "Hazly. He certainly had something to gain if he could become the permanent CEO of Cannecare. That is, if the company doesn't fold because of the murder."

"Power? A bigger compensation package?"

"It's more than pay," she said. "Hazly's co-founder and already owns a big stake. What Hazly would be more interested in is controlling the product."

"What do you mean?" O'Brian asked.

"How do I put this? . . . Cannecare's technology can do some wonderful things, but . . ."

"But what?"

"It could also be abused."

"Abused?"

"Yeah. Think about it. Right now, if a Cannecare employee wants to, say, sneak out into a stairwell and smoke a cigarette, his or her every move is noted, recorded, and archived, right down to the number of drags taken off the cigarette."

"So there are . . . privacy issues?"

"Oh, there are definitely privacy issues. And it could get a lot worse than that."

"What do you mean?"

"Well, if this sort of system was installed in your home, it could collect data on everything you do—how often you eat, go to the bathroom, whether you wash the dishes, or brush your teeth. We're talking Big Brother big time."

The explanation earned a stern silence from O'Brian, whose scowl said clearly enough what he was thinking.

"So, anyway, Randolph called the board together, along with the senior staff—*but not* Ned—and they put together a privacy and security policy that built safeguards into every deployment of the company's systems. A policy that prevented us from even compiling technology for such uses."

"And Hazly didn't like that?"

"He ignored it. You see, he had staff working on a secret project, something he called Project X."

"Project X?"

"Yeah, only Ned Hazly would come up with a name like that. The X came from *ex*tra security."

"Tell me about this project."

"Well, it was a Cannecare system on a mass scale, big enough to deploy citywide, or over even larger areas."

"I thought municipalities and such were a target business for Cannecare."

"Sure, for operating traffic lights and fire and safety systems. But Ned's Project X had cameras and sensors everywhere: every street and every sidewalk, in schools, parks, public buildings. And it had plug-ins for police and military use, too."

"Military?"

"Yeah, along with . . . what you might call a customer-management system for riots."

"A what?"

"It had, basically, an interactive riot-control guide. The system would know exactly how many people were gathered and where, and it would offer a series of solutions to break them up. I mean water cannons, tear gas bombs, pepper-spray guns, all automatically deployed from a computer. Ned's Project X was built to control people, not aid them."

"My God."

"Yeah. Randolph only found out about it a month ago. And he was furious. So were the board members."

"So what happened?"

"Randolph got the board to launch an investigation. The aim was to see how extensive the wasted investment was, and also identify every bit of code and hardware involved in the project, so it could be destroyed."

"Was it?"

"No. This wasn't long before the murder."

"So there was quite a rift with Hazly then. With Randolph."

"God, yes. I mean, they were college roommates, they shared an apartment before Randolph got married. They did everything together, never had a bone of contention. Then suddenly they couldn't be in the same room together. And Ned's job was on the line."

"But surely, Cannecare couldn't sell a system like that. Not in this country. It wouldn't get past city councils and state legislatures. Hell, I couldn't get red-light cameras installed in Cliff Shores."

"Hah! But remember, after 9/11, Americans suddenly weren't so interested in privacy. Even when the NSA spying program got exposed, a lot of people—people in Congress, too—were quick to defend it.

"And remember, we already have cameras recording our every movement in stores, malls, public parking lots . . . Ned did market research, used focus groups. People are getting used to giving up privacy to technology."

"You mean like the NSA checking their email."

"Hah! Forget the NSA. People already had Google and other Internet companies reading their email to serve ads. And people have their Internet activity tracked by cookies, their movements tracked by cellphones. Hell, people *check in* to show where they're at nowadays."

"Right . . ."

"Yeah. So even if Ned had nothing to do with the murder, I bet that is exactly the sort of product he'll use to try to save Cannecare."

A few hours earlier, just before midnight Friday in Beijing, Guo Shangzhen walked into OffCide Studios' China office.

Their boss, Chen Li, he had been told, wanted his team working sixteen-hour days, nonstop, with the promise of a prolonged paid vacation when this "special project" was completed.

Guo had been out of town and hadn't yet heard details of the job.

As he crossed the office, he spoke to the room in general. "Na, zheci you shenme huor gan ah? (So what are we supposed to do this time?)"

"You shi tongyi zhong sharen an, (It's another murder case,)" explained a colleague as Guo fetched a cup of tea from a large metal dispenser by the door.

"Wa, you laile, (Wow, here we go again,)" Guo commented. "Zheici shi shenme qingxing? (What's the situation this time?)"

Guo's colleague explained that the story involved a rich company executive who is killed in a spa by a super-powerful air-conditioning system—information that prompted a conversation among the staff about just what kinds of games were popular among Americans, and *why.*

Still, they looked forward to working on the modeling. They were given the best in software and powerful machines to work on, and the results were always impressive, even if they were sometimes strange.

"Zhende shi kongtiao sharen ma? (Really it's an air conditioner that killed someone?)" Guo mumbled as he sat down to begin work.

11

Herbert Iggid rose to his position, a sought-after C-level executive, by sticking to his principles, by never giving up. And it was in this spirit that he had spent the past two days grilling employees to find out where Bernard and the others had disappeared to, but with little luck.

But late Thursday evening he was watching Bloomberg TV and caught a report on Kelly and Cannecare. Kelly Chambers, the woman who had arranged his hiring at OffCide Studios, Kelly Chambers apparently had committed a horrific murder.

Murder.

SimCide was founded after a murder investigation in Cliff Shores.

And O'Brian was talking about a test case. Was this the test case, this murder apparently committed by Kelly Chambers?

But what were they doing? Were they helping the police? Were they making animation for the prosecution—that's what O'Brian's company was focused on, just the sort of thing he needed a test case for.

But would they want to do that when they would be proving a former colleague committed murder?

So could they be trying to show Chambers *had not* committed the murder?

Iggid flipped through the immediate news stations until he found another report showing a picture of Kelly Chambers, and he turned up the sound to find an analyst speaking with a female anchor.

. . . course. It will affect the company in a big way.

How so?

> Oh, come on. Chambers allegedly used the company's technology to commit the murder. I think *that's* going to make it pretty weird for customers. And Chambers was CEO. Both current and potential customers will have met her.

Now a second expert joined in, this one in a video window.

> Let's not forget about funding, John. Cannecare's been around a few years, has set roots, but the company's still in growth stage. It's been expected for a while they would be trying to put together a third round of funding. And I don't think investors are going to be quick to put money into Cannecare after this, not for a while.

Iggid had no idea what to make of it all, but he felt certain he knew where Bernard and the others had run off to.

They were in Seattle.

By Saturday Iggid was packed and ready to fly out, with a reservation made for Monday afternoon.

And he had discovered exactly where to find his delinquent employees. One not-so-minor detail Bernard had overlooked in his plans to escape was that it wound up being Iggid's office that was contacted by the law firm of Teller Kendeff & Riley to arrange payment *for an entire floor* at some plush hotel in Seattle.

And Iggid figured if they couldn't punch in at the office, he'd bring a punch clock to them.

He inspected his suitcase and carry-on proudly. The suitcase was more of a trunk, with one half built for hanging suits. In the other half, each piece of clothing was neatly folded and inventoried on a list Iggid stored in the outside pocket, so he could keep careful track of when he would need to send out for dry cleaning.

Oh, and there was that one other piece of baggage: the time clock. It was symbolic, it was for show; he didn't really entertain the notion that anyone was going to start using it. But wrapped neatly in a box that stood about knee-high next to his suitcase was a brand-new time clock Iggid had bought.

Policy was policy, that was the message: All employees were required to punch in and punch out and to do so at the appropriate times. Or be fined.

Let Bernard and O'Brian move staff away from the time clock; he would bring a time clock to them.

Even if the box were never opened, the move would sit like a rock on a report to board members about how OffCide Studios was being mismanaged.

🎮 🎮 🎮

Friday night dragged agonizingly into Saturday, leaving Kelly to feel increasingly helpless, her time running out with very little being done.

What she couldn't see was a sizable staff in Beijing working around the clock on modeling, modeling that would be sent soon.

What she could see was the design team playing video games, watching movies, and having target practice with airsoft guns in the hall.

Kelly tried reading, tried watching the news, tried researching the local criminal justice system . . . until the whole thing depressed her so much she was left staring out a window in silence.

For time that was running out uncomfortably fast, it was ticking along at a dreadful crawl.

🎮 🎮 🎮

YouTube on a laptop:

> *The Keyline Ultra UAV Quadcopter Drone comes ready to shoot video and stills using a mounted camera . . .*

"Wow, look," Chen said to Patricia.

> *Controlled using a full-feature remote that feeds video to mounted mobile devices, the Keyline Ultra flies with a four-prop system that is easy to navigate with its stabilization, autopilot, and GPS capabilities.*

As Patricia watched, Chen opened the box and began taking the drone out. Unable to find the model he wanted, they got a store to order it for him with a promise of two-day delivery. And now he was showing Patricia videos of what it could do.

> *What's more, should something go wrong, should the drone fly out of range, the autopilot system kicks in, steadies the craft, and returns the drone to where it took off . . .*

"Wow!" Patricia agreed. "Come on, we can try it in the hall."

The Pendrite Hotel featured ceilings whose heights were designed to impress, not just on the lower few floors but throughout. Built in the 1970s, the building was intended to be a modern-day version of a Victorian era hotel. That included vaulted ceilings and wide hallways joined by expanded nooks at their ends.

And in the 1970s when the hot new technology of the day was the cassette tape player and people took pictures with Kodak Instamatics, it is unlikely the architects ever envisioned how the added space would aid free flight of a twelve-hundred-dollar remote-control quadcopter drone equipped with a high-resolution camera that streamed video to an iPad.

"I feel this is not . . . really very safe," Chen protested as Patricia set the drone at the end of the hall farthest from the elevators.

"Every suite on this floor is ours. Who's it going to hit? Bernard?" Patricia asked. "That'd be *good*."

"What I'm worried about is not Bernard," Chen said. "It's the drone."

"Hah! Don't worry. Try it."

The drone took off and held steady in the air on its own, and Chen needed only a little practice to learn to maneuver it. Within an hour, he had learned to fly it up and down the hallway—helped by its ability to suddenly stop and hover.

Chen went about it slowly, carefully, teaching himself first how to land—to ongoing complaints from Patricia that he was far too timid.

This was a girl, he figured, who was a little young to understand the value of things.

A short while later he was able to fly it down the hall at a fairly fast speed, then lift the front to make a short stop before it hit the wall above the elevators—and the drone, amazingly, would stabilize and just hang there awaiting new instructions.

And eyeing the device from the far end of the hall, Chen smiled with appreciation for the high-tech toy.

Patricia smiled along with him, though her appreciation was not for the drone so much as the mischief she could imagine causing with it.

🐾 🐾 🐾

The rest of the weekend for Kelly inched along like rush-hour traffic on Interstate 5. O'Brian was out, Bernard presumably was preparing for the damn video game tournament, Lester and Eric were in and out and never completely present even when they were there, and Kelly had absolutely nothing to do but sit about and stew over her predicament.

It hadn't seemed real, it hadn't seemed scary, not until now, when she was sitting helpless in this oppressive hotel, whose monotonous bland colorings were becoming as horrific as the county jail; it was in fact a jail itself, the house arrest was real, the colors and restrictions as limiting, the bars having been miniaturized to a bracelet on her ankle, one that was not, incidentally in any way comfortable.

Bernard finally appeared about two p.m. Sunday and headed for the elevator. Kelly had to stop him to ask if anyone had made any progress.

He said yes, the first modeling was coming in from Beijing as they spoke, though the huge file transfers would take several hours to complete.

And so the waiting dragged on.

Just after six, Lester sent a group email telling everyone to come to his suite right away.

Kelly jumped at the possibility of news. Maybe they'd discovered something, maybe some sort of progress had been made. O'Brian was back and he perked up at the possibility, too.

Bernard, however, took his time. He knew perfectly well why Lester had summoned everyone: There was a *Doctor Who* marathon starting on TV. They'd be able to spend the entire evening watching the Doctor battle the Daleks as they began work with the modeling.

As Bernard finally reached the suite, Kelly was just hustling out, looking flush, unhappy.

Apparently, Bernard guessed, Kelly had less enthusiasm under the circumstances for the newest incarnation of the Doctor than did the members of the design team.

🐾 🐾 🐾

Sunday night at the Pendrite.

Kelly knew she should be relieved at least to be free—or something *like* free—to be somewhere safe, sleeping on a clean bed that was not previously home to murderers, robbers, and drug dealers.

She knew she should be thankful for a refrigerator full of groceries, knew she should be grateful for the six bottles of Chardonnay stacked on top.

But she sank deeper and deeper into depression, and rather than drinking found herself instead gazing into an untouched glass of musty white wine that blurred the eyesight in her mindless stare.

The waiting was too much, the waiting for this modeling that was supposed to form a video game that was supposed to convince a court of her innocence; the more she thought about it, the more absurd it seemed.

And now as the sun dipped in its late-evening descent, Kelly sat in near dark in silence, trying to not think at all.

She didn't cry. Kelly never cried; that was important. Somehow she knew that was important, something deep inside insisted it was.

Kelly had nearly fallen asleep when she heard laughing down the hall, then a series of loud clicks, then more laughing.

She listened a few minutes and then stood, took a hefty gulp from the now quite warm Chardonnay, and strode, sleepily, out to see what was going on.

Down the hall she found the lot of them gathered, O'Brian included, watching Eric aim an airsoft gun at a target ten yards beyond.

The target—a bull's-eye and a series of red circles printed on paper—was taped onto an empty shoe box, that placed on a nightstand they dragged from a room.

Kelly watched as Eric fired a shot, piercing the paper just outside the bull's-eye, drawing a cheer from Lester and Patricia as it missed the target's center.

Eric corrected his aim, closed one eye, focused, then fired again. This time he put a hole at the very edge of the bull's-eye.

"Hah!" he exclaimed. "That counts. It broke red."

"He is right, it does," Bernard confirmed. "That is two bull's-eyes out of ten shots for Eric. Now it is Ron's turn."

Kelly nodded at Patricia as she walked up. She was shocked to see O'Brian taking part in this.

It was O'Brian who had been moaning about the dangers of BB guns, and yet here the guy was joining a target-shooting competition.

She watched as O'Brian selected one of the weapons Bernard offered, a transparent plastic pistol with a red tip on the barrel.

"This one looks good enough," he said.

Taking the gun, he walked to the line they had laid down with duct tape, turned to one side, aimed, and fired, hitting the edge of the bull's-eye on his first shot.

"That's one," he proclaimed with an air of confidence that said here was a man who couldn't be challenged at this particular sport. O'Brian had spent a considerable amount of time over the past three decades at shooting ranges.

His hand held steady, he adjusted his aim inward slightly and fired off a second round, this one striking a centimeter inside the red circle. "That's two."

By his tenth shot O'Brian had racked up eight bull's-eyes and widened the eyes of the design team.

"That ties Bernard," Lester reported. It was newsworthy whenever someone presented a serious challenge to Bernard in pretty much any game. That it was O'Brian, the normally stiff former police chief, made it all the more fun.

As Lester walked down to tape a fresh target on the box and empty out the BBs inside, Bernard turned to O'Brian. "I believe it is time that you and I had a tiebreaker."

"Wait," Patricia interrupted. "Kelly's here. Kelly gets a turn."

"Ha!" Eric muttered. "I don't think *Miss Master Fruit Ninja* is going to beat eight bull's-eyes."

Bernard agreed. "I am afraid I fail to see Kelly as the sharp-shooter type."

O'Brian noted a cold stare in Kelly's eyes. "You all right?"

"Yeah, sure." Kelly's New York tone was coming through as strong as ever. She approached Bernard and pointed at the airsoft gun in his left hand. "I'll take that one."

Silently he handed it over.

"It's loaded?"

"Of course. And try to avoid pointing it at me, if you do not mind."

"I'll do my best," she responded. "Now everyone stay behind me."

With that Kelly turned and walked an additional five yards back from the duct tape, then spun around and aimed at the now-much-farther target, leaving everyone to scramble to get behind her before she began shooting—the memory of her aim in *Fruit Ninja* etched deeply into their minds.

Kelly stretched her right arm in line with her sight, her left hand steadying the wrist, aimed . . . turned her head briefly, eyed the now-silent group, and smiled, sort of . . .

Then eyed again the target and fired one shot, liked it, then let off nine more, one right after another, each hitting a tiny black hole near the center of the bull's-eye.

And, turning to Bernard, she returned the gun before walking silently back to her room and disappearing inside.

In shock, the group edged toward the target, not sure what they just witnessed. Lester held it up; there was a single tiny hole near the center of the bull's-eye.

He slipped the target off and held the box out for everyone to see. And sure enough, there inside the box were ten plastic BBs.

Bernard squinted at Kelly's door. This was the woman he knew so well he was certain she could not commit murder?

O'Brian was thinking much the same.

Back in her room, Kelly turned on a light, freshened her Chardonnay, and sat back on the sofa. Smiling. This was as good as she had felt all week.

🐼 🐼 🐼

"Wo zhende buliaojie tade zhao ben, (I really don't understand the story,)" Guo Shangzhen complained, and judging by the agreeing murmur echoing through the room, his colleagues were equally confused.

Oh, the project was intriguing. They were creating rooms and halls, as they would for any video game project, but these plans called for novel features—audio and temperature sensors, as well as cameras built into the ceilings, the walls, and even the floors in some places.

Still the problem wasn't the futuristic virtual world they were building; the part they could not quite grasp was the main murder scenario this game was being built on, the central premise.

Namely a woman walking from the top of one building to the top of another, knowing all those cameras and sensors were recording her journey in minute detail—and then killing a nearly naked man in a spa using fire sprinklers and a high-power air conditioning system.

And cameras and sensors and machines watching, recording one's every movement, this for people in the Chinese capital, where Internet and other communication was monitored, and their working at the Beijing branch of an American tech firm . . . worse, a video game studio!

Guo smiled briefly as he imagined some government official sitting up late at night, monitoring their communications to see what sorts of dissident activities might be taking place . . . and intercepting their modeling files, and sitting down to watch this crazy panda-eyed woman deliberately killing a naked man using . . . an air conditioner.

One of his colleagues shook his attention back.

"Na, ni youmeiyou wen Chen Li . . . zheige xiaojie weishenmo yao sha ta ne? (Did you ask Chen Li . . . why this woman wanted to kill him?)"

"You, (I did,)" Guo answered.

"Ta shuo shenmo? (What did he say?)"

Guo let a look of confusion build on his face, then answered in a thoughtful voice.

"Ta shuo keneng shi yinwei . . . yinwei yu xiade tai duo le . . . (He said maybe it's because . . . because it rained too much . . .)"

12

Monday morning.

Monday morning took on a decidedly different pace and rhythm on the twenty-second floor of the Pendrite.

Even Bernard made the scheduled morning meeting, arriving at Suite 2202 just before ten.

O'Brian followed him in and sat down next to Kelly. "Where the hell did you learn to shoot like that, anyway?" he asked.

"Hah! My father. He was a state trooper in New York. He used to take me to the range all the time."

"Jesus," O'Brian groaned.

Biting on a donut, Bernard spoke up to get everyone's attention.

"I have to remind you, my video game tournament begins tonight, so that gives us today to get this thing off the ground."

Kelly turned a pale shade of red. "You mean to say we've been sitting around doing nothing all weekend, and now because of your stupid tournament we have only one day?"

"A day will be more than sufficient to get things started."

The group sat facing the three TVs where they were about to watch the eagerly awaited virtual-world city block just digitally imported from China, while off to the right the windows showed the brick-and-mortar city, a view in, coincidentally, the very direction of the brick-and-mortar block they were about to visit, *virtually*.

Lester went to work at the computer that controlled the TVs, and two of the screens lit up to show the basic outline of Kelly's door and the hallway at the Stanley.

"We don't have much color or texture yet, but it's enough to begin working with."

"Let's take her for a spin," Bernard said.

A menu popped up. "Choose Your Avatar," it read, and offered a choice of Kelly Chambers, Ned Hazly, Brenda Tate, Phil Gradee, and an unnamed avatar that was a two-dimensional picture of Humpty Dumpty.

"You made a Herbert Iggid avatar?" O'Brian asked, annoyed.

"Yeah," Eric answered, "though I think he'll be more popular as the victim than as the murderer."

"Choose Kelly and give it a run-through," Bernard said.

Lester clicked on Kelly's name and the Kelly avatar appeared in the hallway, runny makeup and all. She wore jeans and a red polo shirt with the Cannecare logo on the breast.

"Everyone wore those uniforms?" O'Brian asked Kelly. "Red polo shirts and jeans?"

"Yeah . . . It was Randolph's idea before I got there. It drove me nuts initially, but I didn't want to step on Randolph's toes on something so . . . high-profile. So I learned to live with it. Actually, in time I got used to not having to take clothes in to the dry cleaner and not having to iron. Turned out to be kind of nice."

The comment caught Patricia's attention. Seated behind them, she was picturing the expensive wardrobe at Kelly's apartment. Patricia had never worn much other than jeans and T-shirts, but if she had a closet full of clothes from Armani and Saks Fifth Avenue, she wouldn't be wearing a tacky polo shirt.

"I take it the policy was supposed to build *team spirit?*" Bernard asked, showing disgust at the idea.

"Yeah."

"How *dis*piriting."

"Yeah."

"OK, here we go," Lester put in, and using his arrow keys began navigating the avatar down the hall toward the elevator.

Bernard motioned to the TV and looked at Kelly. "I want you to spend some time with Les and Eric explaining anything special about any part of the buildings—the doors, the windows, the hallways, anything you can think of."

The Kelly avatar was entering the elevator as he spoke.

"Well, there's one for you right there," Kelly said. "I got to tell you, that elevator was built in the Middle Ages, and the damn door hasn't been oiled since."

"That is exactly the type of thing we are looking for," Bernard said.

"What do you mean?"

"If it was loud, then the audio sensors would have picked up the sound. And if the Cannecare sequencing was faked, then we should find instances where a loud noise, or a temperature change, *should* have registered in places but did not."

He paused to watch the screens. The Kelly avatar was walking through the Stanley's lobby and out onto the street under a cloudy but rainless sky.

"Was it raining that day?"

"After this much time in Seattle, I'm afraid I am not a reliable source of information for such a question. Seems to me like it is always raining here. Except of course when I'm under house arrest and can't go out."

"I didn't see rain in the Cannecare video segments," Lester put in.

"Get some weather bureau data and find out for sure. Next, Kelly, we'll need a list of how many employees would be in the building on weekends, and how many at night."

"Got it."

"Then make a list of names. If you don't know the name, call them Security Guard One, IT Guy Two, Soda Machine Guy Three . . ."

"You think we have three soda machine guys?"

"In a perfect world, you would. Next, for each of them, assign a number, one to five, for how dangerous each might be to a would-be murderer, with one meaning no problem and five meaning they could arrest the murderer or testify against him."

"Or *her*," Kelly added. "So a security guard would probably be, like, a four or a five?"

"Yes. Unless they are barbecuing, as they usually are at our office. Next, Les will work with you to figure out what departments are where, and how many people would be in each and when."

Kelly pictured the whole Cannecare building, the arrangement of the different floors, the people who worked there. It was too bizarre, what they were doing now, creating a virtual world out of it all.

But it was also a source of strength. Kelly hadn't faced it yet, but somewhere there really was a murderer, and she was a victim too.

Somewhere there was a person who had framed her, and that person was about to have his or her world turned into a *virtual* world, a video game.

And they were going to use the game to hunt that person down. Like a zombie. Or a fruit.

Bernard stood. "So this is the plan of action. Lester, I would like you to time each part of Kelly's journey on the Cannecare segments. Film and time her as she really walks—so we're using actual measurements in the modeling, instead of just averages, which is what's programmed into the modeling now.

"Next, Chen Li, review the modeling sent from China so far and work with Eric to see what improvements are needed. Set priorities. We probably want the textures and details of the Cannecare offices first. The Stanley can wait."

"What about the sidewalk between?" Chen asked.

"That might be useful. Let's get them working on that. And, Eric, work with Chen to see what we can get the San Francisco office doing."

"Sure thing," Eric said, his attention focused otherwise completely on his phone.

"That leaves me," O'Brian said. "I'm off in a minute to pay another visit to Mr. Hazly."

"You're going back?" Bernard asked. "I got the distinct impression that Mr. Hazly was not going to cooperate anymore."

"Yeah, well, this time I'll be going not to question him about the company. I'm going there to question him as a suspect. You see, he tried to tell me he was too busy for us, but then I told him I wanted to discuss his *secret project.*"

"Ah. Well, I think I need to come along with you on that."

🪶 🪶 🪶

Thirteen-year-old Kelly Chambers tensed up to the point of stumbling as she waddled down the "runway," which in this case was a narrow space between two rows of foldable chairs.

She felt her head bobbing up and down—she was supposed to be able to balance a book on it—and the frilly dress they gave her to model didn't fit right at all.

"That was too fast, Kelly," her modeling instructor whined. "And you're bobbing like a fish. Is it a fish you want to look like in front of your parents and everyone's parents next week, Kelly?"

"No, Miss Jenkins," Kelly answered.

"You need to steady yourself, you need to float *down the runway. Do you understand, Kelly?"*

Now, more than two decades later, Patricia's snide remarks were not helping as Kelly tried to do a similar walk for Les, this one being filmed at varying speeds along the twenty-second floor hallway at the Pendrite.

"That *was* faster," Kelly insisted.

"Faster than what?" Patricia asked.

Les checked the time on the video. "It actually was four seconds *slower.*"

"Can I call you Miss Jenkins?" Kelly asked Patricia.

"That depends. Who's Miss Jenkins?"

"My modeling instructor when I was a kid."

"You took modeling lessons? Oh God."

"Hey, come on, when I was a kid, things were a lot different."

"*That* different?"

"Yeah. For one, we didn't have all manner of video games. And the ones we did have mainly interested boys."

Kelly met a blank stare on that remark, remembered that the bloody first-person shoot-'em-up games Patricia and the others played were far more male-centric than the old arcade games.

"We didn't have a lot of things you did, like . . . parents smart enough to put us into soccer instead of modeling."

"Uh-huh."

"OK, I hated it. It got so it was worse than being dragged to church on Sunday morning. OK?"

"OK," Patricia said, smiling. Patricia had been dragged to church a lot, so that part she understood.

"Yeah, so what'd you get into when you were a kid, lacrosse?" Kelly asked.

"No, karate."

"What, seriously?"

"Yep. Until high school, when I discovered other things."

"Ah, same here," Kelly agreed. "Yep, forget modeling, forget softball. In high school, suddenly, it's all about *boys*."

"Boys?" Patricia gasped with a tone that dismissed the notion. "God, no, not with me. With me, it was the PlayStation 2, the Xbox . . . Who had time for *boys*?"

". . . uh, right. Well, as I said, things were a lot different when I was a kid."

"Please walk back and start again," Les pleaded. He had pulled out his phone as they talked, checked for messages and posts, and even played a sixty-second game of *Fruit Ninja*, but he had run out of distractions and was getting bored.

"Mindless talking," he added. "Now there's an obstacle we should add to our game: the possibility that the murderer when walking down the hall might get caught up in a senseless conversation about the pros and cons of modeling versus karate. Water cooler talk."

"Yeah?" Patricia challenged. "What did you take when you were a kid?"

Lester walked back to begin filming again, ignoring the question completely.

Lester's father had been a professional baseball player when Les was young, and had forced him to play baseball for years. The sport terrified Les to no end, and it was only when his father bought him a PlayStation baseball video game, which they played together, that the two began to get along.

Of course, Les had to let his father win a lot.

"Let's start again," he said.

🎮 🎮 🎮

Hazly had a crazed expression on his face as he entered the conference room where O'Brian and Bernard waited, the same room they met Holstenbeck in during their last visit.

"What is it you people want now?" Hazly demanded. "I've talked with the police, the *actual* police, several times, and now you want me to talk to the video game police?"

Bernard returned the stare, though his was watered down by the red Twizzler he was shoving into his mouth. It's hard to scare someone when you're eating red licorice.

O'Brian responded: "This is an open investigation."

Hazly was fuming. "How is it an open investigation when the murder was recorded in every detail?"

"Our video game modeling is going to show that it was not," Bernard asserted.

"Your *video game modeling*," Hazly moaned in disbelief. "This is a serious matter. A man was murdered, cruelly murdered. And this company has been falling apart since. And now you two come along with some video game . . . I think it's offensive. And I don't have time for it. Or you."

Bernard took another bite and said, chewing, "You're just afraid you'll lose."

Hazly's head jerked. His voice trembling, he said: "It so happens that I have a Ph.D. and two masters degrees. I am involved in an array of university research, and I sit on the boards of Cannecare and two other companies. I see things on a level well above what you can understand."

Bernard's expression molded into his gaming face, stern and focused, interrupted only by another bite of licorice.

Then: "I, sir, will have you know I have been the reigning champion of *Woeful WasteWorld* for three years in a row, I reached Level Seven of *Furious Frank 2* in only twelve hours, and I run a video game design studio that has attracted more funding than your company has, and we have substantially more revenue, too.

"Oh, yes, and I fully intend to prove that your *technology* is about as reliable and as impressive as a floppy disk."

Hazly let out a high-pitch sound that was somewhere between laughter and a cry: "Huuuuhhhh . . . And how's that?"

O'Brian stepped in, worried the interview was going to end prematurely. He promised himself this was the last interrogation he would take Bernard on.

"This same software solved a murder case once before, and that's why we're working on this case. And we have every reason to believe the Cannecare sequencing *was* faked."

"That's impossible. The system's far too complex for sequences to be faked. Do you know how many sensors and cameras were involved, all working together?"

"And where were you that evening?" O'Brian asked.

"As a matter of fact, the *real* police asked me that question more than once."

"And what was your answer?"

Hazly hesitated briefly. "I was visiting a friend in Tacoma."

"OK. What time did you leave this friend's house?" O'Brian asked.

"About three-thirty or four, I think. We were watching a basketball game. I remember leaving shortly after it finished."

"Then you would have had plenty of time to get back to Cannecare before the murder occurred." O'Brian knew Tacoma was about a forty-five-minute drive.

"I went over this with the police. I would have had time, except there was an accident on I-5 that afternoon. I have the unpleasant memory of being stuck in traffic for something like three hours."

"You were driving alone?" O'Brian asked with interest.

"Yes, alone."

"You drove home?"

"Yeah. I was home a little while when I got a call about Randolph. And if you're seriously suggesting I was involved in his murder, you *are* crazy. Randolph and I were best friends."

"Until you began suggesting that Cannecare get into the business of invading people's privacy."

"I never suggested anything of the sort."

"Kelly Chambers said otherwise."

"Oh, so *that's* it. Well, I expect Kelly Chambers will say anything she can think of to save her neck. The woman's crazy. She murdered Randolph, for God's sake, and now she's grasping at straws."

"Yeah," O'Brian said, "she told us about your Project X."

Hazly's stone-cold face turned icier. "*That* happens to be confidential. Top secret."

"It's my understanding that you and Tate were not getting along, not after the Project X business. And I'm guessing your employees will be able to substantiate that."

"As I said, that's confidential company business. And if Chambers is talking about stuff like this, I'll have her in court for divulging company secrets, too."

"You *will* be seeing her in court, Mr. Hazly, and you'll be seeing a whole lot of confidential information exposed in the process."

"You're not the police. I don't have to stand here and take this."

"You're right. I'm not the police, and you don't have to answer my questions. But the questions you don't answer now will be asked at Kelly's trial, and that is one event that's promising to be very public. Who knows, it might just get aired live on CNN. It's just bizarre enough, it'll get the ratings."

The exchange left O'Brian and Hazly staring at each other intently, their silence broken only when Bernard held out a Twizzler pack.

"Licorice?" he asked.

* * *

Monday afternoon found Kelly comparatively upbeat. It was a scary thought that possibly the only thing standing between her and capital punishment was a video game—a mock video game at that—but the fact that the design team finally had some of it up and running made her feel a lot better.

But if there was anything that could rain down on her hope, it was a visit from Wilbur Kendeff.

"Good afternoon, Miss Chambers," he said as he entered her suite. "How are you?"

"OK, all things considered."

"I need to check in with you. The prosecution's pushing to get your trial started as soon as the court will allow."

"Oh God."

"Let's sit down," he said, motioning her to the dining chairs. "Have Mr. Walker and the others come up with anything?" His tone did nothing to suggest optimism in the question.

"They have the basis of a video game."

"Well, I hope they're having fun. I'm afraid, though, that the prosecution has filed a . . . they've asked to get the Cannecare evidence admitted, once and for all."

"What does that mean?"

"It means we will be very limited in how we can get it *un*admitted, video game or no video game. They're already scheduling jury selection. Once the trial starts, the Cannecare sequences will be shown and that's all the jury will—"

"But we'll still be able to show that the sequences are faked, correct?"

"No. We'll be able to *argue* that they're faked, but we'll be arguing to a jury that has just seen the video sequences, along with expert testimony about how they *could not* have been faked."

"Well, we'll have our own expert testimony, right?"

"Yes, but by the time we're arguing about the first sequences, the prosecution will be presenting further Cannecare sequences showing your clandestine meetings with Tate."

"We were eating!"

"And those clandestine sequences presumably were *not* faked."

"We were eating!"

"I'm afraid after seeing the murder sequences, the jury is going to have a hard time accepting that the two of you were . . . eating."

"Oh God . . . OK, how long do we have?"

"How long before the judge rules on the evidence?"

"Yeah."

"It's not scheduled yet, but two days, maybe. And we'll need a lot more than a video game to stop it."

"We told you, this type of mock video game was used successfully—"

"Yeeaaah . . . Listen, while I'm talking to you alone . . ."

"Yeah?"

Kendeff stood and stepped behind his chair.

"Well, as your attorney, it's my duty to inform you of all your options."

"And they would be?"

"For one, you could change your plea."

"You mean claim insanity, like you suggested before?"

"That, or . . ."

"Or what?"

"Possibly a plea bargain."

"A plea bargain? What, like involuntary manslaughter or something? That's crazy."

"I'm afraid it's also not possible, since they have the whole thing on video. There's no question of intent, or lack of premeditation."

"Then what?"

"Well, and remember, it's my duty to present you with *all* options."

"Yeah?"

"We might be able to swing life."

"Life what?"

"Life . . . A life sentence. No capital punishment."

"Are you serious?"

"I certainly wouldn't be joking about something like this. The prosecution might take a deal."

Kelly glanced out the window, saw the crystal blue skies above Seattle, skies she could only watch from the vantage point of the twenty-second floor and the ankle bracelet. She remembered the jail, the tiny square window of light. A life sentence?

"Listen, Miss Chambers, take a day, take two days. Think about what you want to do. Don't get pushed into any decision you don't think is best."

"Let me ask you, Wilbur—I never did ask you—do *you* think I killed Randolph?"

"I . . . I don't think either way. That's not my job. My job is to do my best to defend the client under the law, to make sure that you get a fair trial."

That tiny square window of light burned its way into Kelly's mind. The thought of one like it down the hall every day for the rest of her life . . . a tiny, distant square . . . of Pacific Northwest drizzle . . .

13

"Make a legal U-turn at the next convenient location," insisted a female voice that O'Brian swore to God sounded like his wife.

Had his wife been moonlighting, had she been working on the side without telling him? he mused as he continued to ignore the GPS device while navigating a shortcut and wondering just how lost he was about to get after so many years.

He had crossed the narrow east-west span of Seattle on Madison Street, but rather than driving the additional stretch to Lake Washington and turning south, he cut east early, opting for residential streets with less traffic and a straight line to his destination: the home of Brenda Tate and until a week ago the late Randolph Tate.

O'Brian remembered this odd section of town from years earlier. The blocks from Madison eastward to the lake varied from delightful old houses to long-neglected ancient ones, a low-income neighborhood that suddenly gives in to hills filled with multimillion-dollar homes, those overlooking lakefront mansions beyond.

It was here among the homes near the top of the hill that O'Brian found the address he was looking for.

The Tates' home was not grand enough in size or location to be termed "the Tate Estate," but it sported every pretense it could to usurp the name.

Round mahogany posts framing the entryway offered a wooden equivalent of imposing Roman columns, those set up to highlight the polished dark panels that covered the two-story home's front. The natural wooded impression was distorted by a white palatial gate and six-foot walls, and more so by a tennis court whose placement seemed aimed not at creating a convenient sports facility so much as making it easily visible to people driving by.

O'Brian pulled into the driveway and parked a short distance from the door, so he could inspect the surroundings as he climbed out of his rental car and walked up.

He rang the bell, and when the door was finally answered, he found himself talking to a uniformed maid.

"What can I do for you?" she asked.

"I'm looking for Mrs. Brenda Tate."

"May I ask what it is about? I'm afraid now may not be a good time."

"I understand," O'Brian said. "But I have some further questions about her husband."

"Are you with the police?"

"I'm a consultant working along with the police on their investigation." He handed her a laminated ID card that identified him as CEO of SimCide Investigations.

"Very well," the woman said after a moment.

As she led him through the house, O'Brian couldn't help but notice a stack of shopping bags in the living room, two of which read Coach on the outside, and next to them a box of Michael Kors shoes and a small bag from Tiffany's.

Someone had been spending some money.

The maid brought him to a balcony where through the trees the lake was visible, but only off in the distance.

"Ma'am, a Mr. O'Brian, who is working with the police."

Seated on the balcony was a woman who appeared to be in her late forties, which would make her a bit older than her late husband.

Her makeup and clothes painted a picture of a wealthy businesswoman, a glamorous look but in a 1960s sort of way; in fact she was wearing a dress and a hairstyle that would have fit right into the decade.

"Mrs. Tate?"

"Yes."

"My name's Ron O'Brian. I'm a consultant working alongside the Seattle Police Department." He flashed his ID and handed her a name card to back the exaggerated assertion.

"Oh, God, not more questions about this . . . now."

"I'm afraid so, ma'am. It is an unfortunate part of a major investigation—the more we study things, the more questions we come up with."

"OK." The woman sounded like a teenager committing to turning off the TV and cleaning a long-neglected bedroom. "Please, sit down then if we must. Would you like some tea?" she asked. Before her on the table was a silver teapot and tray, along with several cups.

"Yeah, that would be nice, thank you."

Sitting, he waited until she poured the tea, and then, taking out a notepad, he began.

"I'm afraid I have to begin with a less-than-delicate question. We're asking everyone who had access to the main computers in the engineering center at Cannecare where they were on Sunday afternoon and evening."

"Are you serious?" Brenda Tate asked, offended.

"As I said, we're asking everyone. It's a matter of procedure."

"And you don't think the police already asked me that? Also, as I understand it, you already have all the evidence you need on that tart Chambers."

"Ma'am?"

"I said *tart*. You heard me. That tramp was fooling around with my husband."

"Is that right?"

"Yes. They were meeting secretly in Randolph's office and later at Chambers' suite in that Stanley dump."

"Did you tell this to the police?"

"Don't you have their notes? Yeah, I told them. They need to lock that woman up. I don't know why they let her out, anyway."

"You say your husband and Miss Chambers were *meeting*?"

"Yes. I was monitoring them, how often they met, how long . . . Cannecare makes security systems designed for just such purposes. For Christ's sake, I can't imagine how they thought they could get away with it."

"I understand your husband was implementing privacy policies for Cannecare systems."

"Again that tramp Chambers. It was *her* doing. But again, what was she thinking? That's just the sort of thing we were building our systems to do. They're *security* systems; they were built to *watch* people. Hell, shackling the system with privacy policies is like building a gun and then forbidding anyone to put bullets in it."

"Interesting analogy. I notice you said *built*."

"Pardon me?"

"You just said *built*, past tense. Is the company doing something different now?"

"I have no idea what the company's doing now. I was, rather, *let go* the day after Randolph's death."

"Let go?"

"Fired, if you must. And even though I own a good portion of the now-worthless company, my attorney assures me there's nothing I can do."

"Who . . . let you go? Ned Hazly?"

"The little twerp, yeah. And he's all that's left to try to pick the company back up. I'll never see a dime of it. God! Randolph invested everything we had."

"Everything?"

"He even stopped paying his life insurance, just let the policy expire. And with the way the real estate market's been going, this house is now worth about half of what we owe on it."

"It's a very nice house," O'Brian commented.

"It's a dump. This is *not* the sort of home I envisioned living in when I decided to marry Randolph."

O'Brian scribbled something in his notebook. "I understand your husband was on a special diet."

"His cholesterol was high. So was his blood pressure."

"How was he doing on the diet?"

"Fine—as soon as he found Chambers. Then he had something else to do other than eat. He suddenly stopped sneaking hot dogs into the building."

O'Brian fought back a smile, remembered Kelly's comment that Tate was cheating on his wife—in the *culinary* sense.

"If I can get back to my original question, where were you on the afternoon of the murder?"

"Do you really think I had something to do with it? Look around you, Mr. . . ." She glanced at his card on the table before her. "Mr. O'Brian. Look down the hill at those houses along the lake. *That's* where I should be living, where I *would* be living if Randolph hadn't squandered away all of his inheritance. Look at those homes. They have personal docks on the lake, they have boat houses and guest houses and servants' quarters. And I got stuck in this," she said, indicating the house, which was about four times the size of O'Brian's—and probably its price, too, he guessed.

"And now with Randolph gone and his inheritance sitting in the hands of that bastard Ned Hazly, soon I'll be living about fifteen blocks *west* of here."

O'Brian thought about the old homes he had driven past on his way.

"No, Mr. O'Brian, I did *not* kill my husband."

"As I said, we're asking everyone who had access. We aren't thinking about motives. It's standard procedure."

"I was here at the time, if you must know."

"Were you home alone?"

"Yes."

"What about the maid?"

"She was here, too, of course."

"So you weren't alone?"

"Well, I was except of course for the maid. But she's always here."

O'Brian scribbled a note.

"She's lives here?"

"Yes. We have a maid's room. It's small, but her needs are simple." Brenda Tate said this with confidence, fully willing to decide what another person's needs and wants were.

"Do you have any other household staff?"

"Well, we have gardeners, of course. And a pool man comes once a week."

"I see." He didn't, but he decided not to dwell on the subject, not to show his sudden interest in her finances. "Do you swim a lot?"

"In Seattle?"

"Yeah."

"You must be joking."

Brenda Tate did not act like a woman who was broke, not in terms of shopping habits, of household staff, or of maintaining a swimming pool that she apparently did not use.

O'Brian took a final sip of tea and moved to stand. "One more question?"

"If you must."

"Did you approach your husband about his meetings with Miss Chambers?"

"That was between my husband and me, Mr. O'Brian, entirely between the two of us."

"I was just wondering, because police would normally place suspicion on a spouse if he or she thought the victim was having an extramarital affair."

"No. No, I didn't tell Randolph. I was waiting, waiting for the right moment to . . . to do something. My husband was a brilliant man, Mr. O'Brian, but in the end, he deserved what that tart did to him."

🐦 🐦 🐦

Herbert Iggid was an East Coast man, a Boston man, a man of culture, and the West Coast was not an easy concept for him.

San Francisco didn't even exist a hundred and sixty years ago; no one lived in the region except Indians and Spanish missionaries. You can't build a world-class city in a century and a half.

Boston, New York, Philadelphia, on the other hand, those were world-class cities with centuries of history. They were financial and political centers that pioneered modern commerce, democracy, and capitalism.

Now Iggid was going to have to suffer a visit to this . . . *Seattle*. It was sure to be awful.

And if the flight was to serve as an omen, it was going to be an uncomfortable visit. The plane fought hard turbulence the entire way, and he spent much of the time eyeing his air-sickness bag.

And so it was with a heavy heart that Herbert Iggid peered out the window on his first aerial approach to Seattle, what he was sure would be a dreadful sight. And saw instead rich green spreading into the distance . . .

The plane coasted smoothly down, bounced just a tad as the wheels came to grips with the runway.

And looking around, left and right, Iggid was amazed to see . . . trees . . . beautiful trees under . . . clear blue skies.

🐾 🐾 🐾

In need of a break from the mess that was the engineers' suite, Kelly and O'Brian opted to go to Kelly's room to discuss the day's events over scotch and Chardonnay.

"It seems there's plenty of motive going around," O'Brian started out, shaking the ice in his glass to chill the scotch.

"What do you mean?"

"Well, Hazly for one. I'm sure Bernard told you."

"Yeah." She smiled. "I understand Bernard and Hazly don't get along real well."

"You could say that. And I certainly *can* see Hazly having sufficient motive to kill Randolph Tate."

"You think?"

"Yeah, I think. And Brenda Tate, too. There's something funny going on there."

"What do you mean?"

"The woman claims she's broke."

"She is. I went over Randolph's finances to help him cut expenses. He had several high-interest loans and wasn't doing things correctly for taxes at all. And credit card bills. All hers."

"Loans?"

"Yeah, a big mortgage, a couple of car loans, and a couple of loans he made to pump more funds into the company."

"Hmm . . . Anyway, the woman talks like she's about to wind up on the street, and yet she's been doing some serious shopping. We're talking Coach, Tiffany's . . ."

"Wow."

"And that's not all. If she's worried about losing her house, then why does she still have a full-time maid, who apparently is a live-in? And gardeners and pool maintenance."

And here O'Brian gave Kelly a consoling look.

"Oh, and there's something else."

"What?"

"She knew about you and Randolph meeting secretly. She thinks you really were having an affair."

"No!"

"Apparently her interest in following her husband's movements was stronger than his privacy policies."

"Oh God."

"Yeah, and there's motive enough to commit murder right there: jealousy. So anyway, I had coffee with my buddy who's involved in the investigation. It turns out the police knew about that. They know a lot more than they've let on so far. But they still think . . . think the Cannecare evidence is enough to get a guilty verdict."

"You mean they believe I did it."

O'Brian hesitated. "Yeah."

Kelly thought about the upcoming hearing, thought about the time she'd spent in orange.

"I'll tell you one thing," O'Brian said. "I'd sure like to get a look at the Tates' finances."

"I'll show you."

"What? How?"

"I just told you, I went over them. I had copies of bank statements, everything."

"But the police confiscated all your documents, your computers and everything"

"Yeah, so?" Kelly said with a wry smile. "They thought they were pretty slick, too."

"What does that mean?"

"They didn't touch my Web mail accounts."

"Your Web mail accounts?"

"Yeah, I have two different emails I use for work—Yahoo and Gmail. I email stuff to myself all the time just as a quick way to get files from my laptop to my desktop, or from the office to home."

"Wow."

"So I not only transferred files. I also built up one heck of an archive of documents, an archive that sits on a server somewhere and that's available to me anywhere, on any computer or device that does email."

An hour later they rejoined the engineers and were surprised to find Bernard still present. Everyone expected he would have disappeared by late afternoon to get ready for his tournament's kickoff event, which went live at midnight in New York.

But for some reason he stuck around, checking the early work from China and appearing generally far more organized and ambitious than the self-obsessed Bernard Walker they all knew—especially right before a major tournament.

Had they examined his mood and gestures closely, they might have detected just a hint of mystery in his eyes, as if there were something deeper there, something watching, something thinking. Some secret plan.

They did not have time to sense it, though, as Bernard had his attention hijacked by lofty opportunities he could not resist.

"I figured out how to fly it," Chen said, holding out a drone remote with a tablet attached. "Check it out. The camera works great. You fly it watching the camera's video."

Minutes later they stood in the hallway as Chen demonstrated how to fly it up and down the hall.

Bernard took over. After a few trips, he left it hovering down near the elevator when suddenly a loud *ding* rang out.

🐾 🐾 🐾

It was with a sense of triumph that Herbert Iggid paraded from the Pendrite's front desk, where he left his luggage, and into the elevator. The front-desk clerks initially refused to tell him the engineers' room number, but when they saw the name on his driver's license matched the name listed as paying the bill for the entire floor of suites, they became more cooperative.

And now, the time clock under one arm, Herbert was ready, he had arrived. Here was a man on a crusade; now was the moment.

When the elevator door opened, though, his focus was quickly shattered by . . . by something hanging in the air.

It was white and surrounded by tiny propellers, and it just hovered there in an otherworldly manner.

Nervous, Iggid cleared his throat, started forward, and just as he moved, the thing fell to chest height, blocking his path.

Iggid halted, perplexed. Was this some kind of security device? He'd never seen anything like it.

He tried to sidestep the thing, but it followed his movement and continued to block his path.

Now he stepped back and straightened his tie.

And watching, he cautiously tried to move to the left— and again it followed. Next it began moving up and down in a menacing way, its high-pitched whining offering further threat.

But Herbert Iggid being Herbert Iggid would not be beat. Determined, he stepped forward, moved closer . . . and it moved back. Hah!

It appeared he had the upper hand, so he continued forward, forcing it to retreat.

But the feeling of victory was short-lived. The thing suddenly lifted to a foot beneath the ceiling, turned, and zipped halfway down the hall, where it stopped and turned back.

And with Iggid staring in disbelief it charged, darting straight down the hall toward him, faster and faster, lowering itself along the way to the height of Iggid's head . . .

When it got within about five feet, Iggid finally panicked and jumped back to the elevators—whose doors were closed— and ducked . . .

To see the thing turn upward in a last-minute attempt to halt. But the momentum was too much: It dinged the wall above Iggid's head and bounced back a few feet before its autopilot kicked in and steadied the thing, leaving it to hover, albeit pride injured, in the air.

Iggid looked up, saw the camera rotate downward to face him, heard laughter down the hall, recognized voices, including Bernard's.

🎮 🎮 🎮

Had city inspectors staged a surprise visit to the engineers' suite, crowded with furniture, computers, people, and piles of food, the hotel could well have been cited for violating a long list of fire, safety, and sanitation codes.

It was in fact just enough of a sight to leave Iggid speechless, even if briefly, despite his anger.

"Herbert!" O'Brian exclaimed cheerfully, holding up his scotch in a welcoming gesture.

That O'Brian, normally the serious one, was enjoying the moment . . . that put a smile on everyone's face.

Iggid inventoried the room. "What happened in here?"

"Terrible maid service," Bernard said. "Now, what are you doing here, Herbert?"

"What was that in the hallway? You could have hurt somebody with that thing! What did you think you were doing?"

O'Brian chuckled into his drink. "I'm sorry, Herb, but you should have seen the look on your face. We saw it all in HD on Chen Li's tablet."

Iggid fumed. "Well, it's a good, good thing that I find you all together here. Now, I want everybody's attention."

He opened the top of the cardboard box and pulled out the time clock, removing its packaging as he lifted it out.

"Listen up. You may be able to hide away on some special project with Bernard here, but you will still punch in and punch out like employees at a responsible company. That is our policy and that is what you are going to do."

"You got to be kidding," Eric said.

"This punch clock runs on batteries," Iggid went on, "so you can bring it with you if you wind up going to Alaska, for all I care. I have punch cards right here. Each of you will fill one out and punch in when you begin work and punch out when you finish. All work time will be fully recorded or you will not be paid."

The entire room stared in disbelief.

Only now did Iggid notice Kelly sitting on the sofa.

"Kelly," he said, a bit of fright in his eyes. "I heard that you were . . . uh . . ."

"Having trouble, Herbert?"

"Yeah . . ."

"Well, I'm not now."

"Yeah, I see. I'm, uh, I'm glad to see that you are . . . uh . . . well."

"Really, Herbert?" Kelly opened her eyes in a crazed manner, mixed with a forced smile.

Iggid gave in to nervousness, began blabbering. "I, uh, I told you that, that when I was being hired, that I would turn OffCide Studios into a . . . a responsibly managed company, a company with full accounting for everything. I told you, didn't I? When I say I'm going to do something, I do it."

Kelly tilted her head. "You bought a battery-powered time clock and flew all the way to Seattle just to get a few employees to punch in, Herbert? How much did all that cost the company?"

"Uh . . ."

"Yeah, 'uh'—'uh' is about the right thing to say."

Now Bernard jumped in.

"Yes, Herb, you are correct. I fully believe the design team *should* be punching in and out. Excellent idea." He stood and grabbed the blank time cards, and opening the packet began passing them around the room.

"I want you all to fill out the top of the card very carefully. Write neatly."

Iggid was speechless.

"Yeah, I'll be sure to tell the board all about this the next time we meet, Herb." Bernard turned back to the engineers: "And as soon as you finish filling in the top, come on over and punch in."

"I can't tell you how surprised I—" Iggid stopped short. "Wait, what do you mean *punch in*? It's eight o'clock at night."

"I realize that," Bernard said. "And in about two hours they will begin receiving a new round of modeling from Beijing, and an hour after that the team will be holding a videoconference with our people there. And of course, it's only fair that our engineers be paid *all* the overtime they deserve—what do you guys get for overtime, Lester, is it time and a half?"

"No, double time."

Bernard narrowed his eyes. "I had them willing to work on all this extra stuff just because they like me. But you happen to be correct: They should be *properly* paid for their efforts. And I am sure the board will applaud your efforts to ensure they get paid all that extra overtime."

Moments later, Iggid was heading back to the lobby, completely unsure of what had just happened. As soon as he left, Bernard picked up the hotel telephone and dialed zero.

"Front desk, may I help you?"

"Yes, this is Bernard Walker. I'm staying in room 2221."

"Yes, Mr. Walker, what can I do for you? Are you expecting another pizza delivery?"

"No, but one of my colleagues, a Mr. Herbert Iggid, is coming down to check in."

"OK, would you like me to set him up in one of the suites on your floor?"

"No, no, God no. Keep him as far away as possible. Put him in the basement if you have one. And give him the worst room you can find—something with a broken air conditioner, or undergoing repairs. Tell him it is the only room you have left."

"Really?"

"Yes, really, and once he leaves, call me. I'll run down and give you a sizable tip."

"Oh, well, thank you, Mr. Walker."

14

Game time.

Nine p.m. Monday, room 143.

The Fourth Annual Woeful WasteWorld Tournament officially begins, midnight Eastern Time. Many players will log on for only an hour or less, just to check out this year's maps; the real competition will spread out over weeks.

Bernard studies the screen, takes note of his opponents and their locations.

He managed to get Jutland as a starting region, a good one since it puts him in easy striking distance of the rich resources of northern Germania and the Lowlands.

He scouts the continent for the Evil Iberian, checks the Iberian Peninsula, and is surprised to find instead an avatar there named Queen Izzie.

Queen Izzie?

The Evil Iberian, his main rival, was the only player to give him a run for his money in the previous year's tournament, and had been constantly turning up and ambushing him in regular games over the twelve months since.

Where is he? Or *she*?—there's no way to tell the sex, since the game allows players to filter their voices with a variety of effects.

The varmint must be using a pseudonym. You can do that in *Woeful WasteWorld*, you can change your handle at any time.

This is going to take study and analysis, is going to require time and focus and *no* interruptions from employees, murder suspects, or eggheads bearing time clocks.

But Bernard is up to the task. The challenge is no problem. This is why he got into gaming, why he made it his life.

The focus is also not a problem, for Bernard Walker has an uncanny ability to tune out the world around him, whatever catastrophes might be unfolding.

Oh, that and the fact that he has checked into another hotel without telling anyone.

🐾 🐾 🐾

Game time.

Tuesday morning, suite 2202, their new meeting room.

Nearly everyone was present.

"Where the heck's Bernard?" O'Brian asked, causing Les and Eric to turn their heads, avoiding the question.

"The game's ready for full testing," Lester said. He was seated on the floor in front of the three TVs.

"Yeah? Has it found me innocent yet?" Kelly asked.

"Not quite yet."

Patricia sat down next to Kelly. "But we mapped out a bunch of scenarios. Show her."

"OK, first, the cast of characters." Les hit a key to pull up three rows of avatars on the left TV: Kelly, Randolph Tate, Brenda Tate, Hazly, Holstenbeck, and Gradee. Also included were generic avatars marked things like IT Staff 1, 2, and 3, Janitor 1, 2, and 3, and one marked Weird Guy Who Hangs Out at the Water Cooler All Day.

The Humpty Dumpty avatar they had to scrap, much to their disappointment, to keep the peace with O'Brian.

"Each of these can be operated by a person or can work as an AI—that is, an artificial intelligence, operated by the computer," Les explained.

The middle screen now came to life. "What you are about to see is Cannecare Tower's lobby, crowded with morning traffic as employees make their way in to work. And here, we choose our avatars—the characters we want to play. Patricia, you first."

"Always the girl first? No, wait, in this case, that's good. OK. And because I'm a girl, I'll choose Brenda Tate."

"And I'll be Randolph Tate, the victim," Lester said. "In Level 1, I try not to get murdered. Ron, what's your choice?"

"I think I'll just watch, thanks."

"No, no. You have to play to really understand."

"All right . . ." It was more of a grunt. "I'll choose Holsten-beck, then."

"Eric?"

"I choose the Mail Guy."

"Chen?"

"I'll be a security guard."

Lester smiled. "Kelly?"

"This is totally warped—you guys understand that, right?"

"Choose your character," Les pressed her.

"I mean it: This is warped."

Patricia interrupted with a slight smile. "You know what's really warped? What's really warped is you're going to wind up getting into it and trying to win."

Kelly relaxed a little.

"Yeah, tell ya what, then, I'll be Ned Hazly. The twerp."

🎮 🎮 🎮

Walk time.

Early Tuesday morning, a Seattle sidewalk.

The sky was blue and the air carried a refreshing chill—needed refreshment for Herbert.

Traveling, leaving his beloved Boston, that was bad enough, but . . .

Herbert awoke at five-thirty, as he was accustomed, no alarm clock needed, but he awoke with no schedule, no plan, and worse, without a *Wall Street Journal* or a decent cup of tea. As he was accustomed.

Moreover, they gave him a "room" whose space defied the term's very definition. Fortunately, the resulting claustrophobia was quickly put out of mind by the damp carpet, the broken toilet, the dim lights, and the constant passing of emergency vehicles—the room, by the sound of things, must have been across the street from a fire station, a hospital, and possibly an airport, as well.

Herbert certainly hoped this wasn't the best hospitality Seattle had to offer.

He had protested, to be sure, insisted that his company had booked an entire floor, but the clerk, an apologetic expression on his face, said no one else was allowed to stay on that floor for security reasons. And remembering the crazed look on Kelly Chambers' face, not to mention the aerial dangers, Herbert chose to accept the assertion.

But now on this glorious morning, Herbert found himself strolling through Seattle's financial district in search of a paper and breakfast, and everything seemed so clean and so fresh as the early-morning sunlight baked warmth into the buildings, the buses, the sidewalks, the people.

Also soothing his soul as he walked, here was a city business district getting ready for a day's work. Trucks delivered supplies to loading docks, coffee shops opened their doors, and at six-fifteen already people were making their way along the sidewalks to their offices and jobs. Women in smartly pressed coats, men in suits, up and hustling to be the first into work, the first to get the ball rolling on this quite pleasant Tuesday morning.

This was the sort of person Herbert liked and respected. This was the sort of person he preferred to be around. Early birds, go-getters.

After some initial searching and doubling back, he settled for an expensive-looking coffee shop, not a chain location, but one he found in the ground-level plaza of a high-rise. There he ordered a cup of tea and a Danish to go with the paper he picked up down the road, and sitting down he felt comfortable for the first time since he had arrived in this . . . this . . . suddenly pleasant city.

🐾 🐾 🐾

"It's time to choose motives now," Lester said. "Go ahead, Patricia. I mean, Brenda Tate."

"All right." She hit the M key on her laptop and a pop-up menu appeared atop the middle TV screen. Patricia read aloud:

"Motive number one: Kill Randolph Tate in a fit of jealousy because (a) you *think* he is having an affair with Kelly Chambers, and (b) Kelly can be framed, so she will suffer, too."

Kelly glared at Patricia.

"Motive number two: I am having an affair with the chief financial officer, and together we have been embezzling money from the company. We plan to run away together to a South American country where they do not . . . impose a recycle tax on glass bottles?" she read in wonder.

"Shouldn't that be 'where they don't have an *extradition treaty*'?" O'Brian grunted.

Lester smiled. "Got to keep things fun. Your turn, Eric."

"OK. I'm the Mail Guy." He hit the M key on his laptop and read aloud from the middle screen.

"Motive number one: I am the Mail Guy, a holdover position from an earlier day when companies actually had mail—God, I can't imagine that. Now I deliver coffee and sandwiches or flowers or birthday balloons. Everyone treats me like a servant, so I'm about to—heh-heh—go *postal*."

"All right, who wrote this?" O'Brian demanded.

"Hey, it's the Mail Guy," Lester argued. "*Going postal* was a given."

"Motive number two," Eric continued, "I am madly in love with Brenda Tate, but she won't even acknowledge my existence. So I will kill her husband to get him out of the picture," he added, drawing gasps of air and strained expressions from Kelly and O'Brian.

"Your turn, Mr. O'Brian," Patricia said. "You're that Holstenbeck guy. Here, I'll pull up your motives."

O'Brian squinted, cleared his throat, and read aloud: "Motive number one: Randolph Tate continuously refused to eat my wife's muffins. Time to kill him . . ."

Patricia chuckled. "A little weak, wouldn't you say, Lester?"

"I don't know . . . Bernard said those muffins were pretty tasty."

O'Brian pressed on, sounding none too pleased: "Motive number two: My cousin the dictator wants to buy Cannecare software to automate his palace's kitchen, but Randolph Tate wouldn't give him a discount." O'Brian glared at Les. "Come on, where did you guys come up with this stuff?"

"Listen," Lester said, "from what we've learned, the guy's the model of dull. Outside of Cannecare, he spends his time counseling exchange students from his country and coaching kids' soccer."

Kelly frowned. "What, so this is my defense? We sit around talking about ridiculous motives?"

"Kelly's right," O'Brian said. "This is not a game."

The group responded with blank stares. Of course it was a game.

"Never mind. Come on," Kelly said. "It's my turn, right?"

Patricia pushed her laptop over to Kelly and hit the M key. "There, there're your possible motives."

"OK. Let's see . . . I am Ned Hazly, and I am a pinhead. Yeah, I like that one."

"That's not what it says," Patricia complained.

"Well, it's true."

"Read!"

"Motive number one: I am Ned Hazly, and I believe Randolph Tate is ruining this company. He believes the only future for our technology is to create energy-efficient buildings, and so I am going to use our technology to kill him in the most-unpleasant way I can think of, and he will die slowly knowing not only that I was right, but that I was the one who killed him."

No one laughed or commented.

"Yeah, I like it," Kelly said with a hint of malice in the smile she shot at Patricia. "Now that's focus. No need to read the other motives."

Ned Hazly stared across his desk at Wilbur Kendeff and Lisa Jenkins, Cannecare's chief counsel.

"Lisa here tells me I don't have to give you squat," Hazly said to Kendeff.

"She is correct, quite correct. And I can only praise the manner in which you've cooperated with the police—and our team—so far."

One thing Wilbur Kendeff had learned in his work was the need for diplomacy.

"And I *em*pathize, not just *sym*pathize, fully with your complaints about Mr. Walker—who is, shall we say, a character."

"He's a clown is what he is."

"I understand your frustration. But here's the problem. Cannecare's technology is too . . . how do I say it? Too good."

"What?"

"What I'm saying is Cannecare's technology isn't just effective; it's going to change the way trials are run."

"What do you mean?"

"Think about it. The very process of presenting evidence and moving forward with cases is going to be forever altered whenever a Cannecare or similar security system is involved.

"But we're not there yet—as a society. We're there in technology; your system has shown that. But our courts, our legal system—it'll take time. Right now, Cannecare's technology, especially this sensor-video correlation, it's too revolutionary. It takes the *oomph* out of *right to a fair trial by a jury of peers* and all that stuff."

Hazly was confused.

"The problem is it's just too ironclad. That creeps people out—juries and judges alike. But it's cases like Chambers' that have the power to bring on change."

"I think I see what you're getting at," Hazly said.

"But something they teach in law school is that the cases that can set precedents are often cases that can go awry. To make sure that doesn't happen, our team must be allowed to examine the evidence in full, to challenge it openly in court, to pick it apart and criticize its every facet."

"And just what will be accomplished by that, other than a big waste of taxpayer money and court time?"

"Actually, one of two possible things."

"And they are?"

"One, it could prove that Miss Chambers is innocent."

"Not likely. And two?"

"Two, Mr. Hazly, it may prove before a court and before the press in a high-profile murder case that Cannecare's technology is in fact impeccable."

Minutes later, alone in his office, Hazly had Phil Gradee on the phone.

"Yeah, they want the whole thing, all the data for all four days, Friday through Monday."

"That could take some time to extract," Gradee explained.

"I'll tell you what: Make contact with them and say you're putting it all together. Then take your goddamn time about it."

Hazly knew he tended to look gullible, but knew also that he had spent as many years in classrooms as Wilbur Kendeff. No, Ned Hazly was not so easily fooled.

"Take my time?"

"Yeah. If we get the case back on track, it'll be settled, Chambers will be locked back up, and we won't have to bother with Walker anymore, either."

🐾 🐾 🐾

Late in the afternoon, Patricia declared she needed a break and that Chen Li was overdue for more sightseeing, and she vowed to take him somewhere more touristy than a Round One arcade.

The two of them headed out on foot, northward with the plan of checking out the famous Pike Place Market.

They walked up Third Avenue, navigating with Patricia's phone. At Pike Street they turned left and began walking downhill toward the famous tourist attraction when Patricia suddenly stopped and pulled Chen into a doorway.

"That's Iggid up there," she said.

They peered around the corner, and sure enough, there stood Herbert Iggid, wearing suit and tie, but somehow appearing . . . *comfortable* for a change. That stiff, about-to-explode look was absent.

Iggid was strolling along, checking out a vegetable stand with an expression of wonder.

"Let's follow," Patricia said, a note of adventure in her voice.

They trailed Iggid as he paused at the market's entry, his attention caught by a fish stand where two attendants chanted while playing catch with a two-foot trout—to the delight of several tourists. A moment later one of them picked up a large octopus and walked it out toward a group of women, who screamed and ran back.

Patricia swore she saw Iggid smile at that.

Next, they followed him inside the market's waterfront building, where moments later he slipped into a shop that sold all manner of comic books and related merchandise, then another that sold magic kits and magicians' props.

Here Iggid suddenly appeared suspicious, darting his head back and forth, before taking a magic kit off a shelf and bringing it to the cashier.

Forty minutes later he was at the far end of the market, where a stretch of outdoor booths faded into park along the water. Patricia and Chen had watched as he bought several T-shirts and a Chinese scroll that spelled out his name in colorful brush strokes.

And now he sat on a bench eating ice cream and gazing out at the bay. This was not the Herbert Iggid the company had come to know.

The design team spent Tuesday evening and night in Suite 2202 working on the game and deciding what new orders to send to Beijing.

Kelly grew tired of watching a cartoon version of the murder she was supposed to have committed, though she stopped back every hour or so to see if anyone had learned anything.

They had not.

Instead they seemed to be having too much fun, not so much with the game as with seeing how to improve it. They were running video and slideshows of Cannecare Tower from their shoot the previous week and seeing how their virtual world could be made more like the real one.

As for Bernard, he was nowhere to be seen. Again Kelly felt haunted by the notion that time was slipping away faster and faster and that the people who were supposed to be helping her . . . really were not. It was like one of those dreams where you need to escape, need to run away, but your legs fail to move.

15

Wednesday morning started off with what were fast becoming rituals: preparing coffee, opening laptops, and trying not to appear uncomfortable after living in such close quarters with colleagues for so many days.

It's tough enough with families, worse with co-workers, stranger still when one present is about to be tried for murder.

No one asked or spoke about the missing Bernard, but instead everyone concentrated on the next phase of the Cannecare game simulation, which was downloaded overnight.

Game time.

Brenda Tate appears on the corner of Second Avenue where across a narrow street is the block that is "Cannecare territory," that is, the area under the Cannecare umbrella.

The umbrella notion in fact is more than a metaphor in this virtual world; it exists in the form of a reddish oblong dome that covers an entire city block, along with the accompanying stretch of Second Avenue and some airspace above.

That red dome meets the ground just in front of Brenda as she waits.

In preparing for play, she (Lester) has collected several items that may come in handy: a handgun, hidden away in her purse; a hat and sunglasses so she will not be recognized; an umbrella, though it is closed since there is no rain; and a flask of brandy and two Valiums, should she get the shakes.

Murder is a high-tension undertaking, after all.

When the light changes to Walk, Brenda moves swiftly and with determination. The second she enters the red umbrella, a series of tiny windows open in the sky, showing her progress as seen from *different cameras, most of them mounted aboveground and aiming downward . . . where they record only hat, sunglasses, and the tacky overcoat the engineers in Beijing chose for the avatar.*

The distance to Cannecare's main entrance she quickly covers.

And as a co-founder's wife and a senior executive, Brenda freely makes her way to the PEC, careful to attract as little notice as possible along the way, and once there she sits down to murder her husband.

And here a second window comes to life to show the spa, glassed in next to a lap pool.

Seated at the PEC console Brenda the avatar has at her fingertips the controls for the entire block, the entire red umbrella, and her cheating husband, Randolph, sits helpless in the basement twenty floors below.

And now her head turns a hundred and eighty degrees, like an owl's, so that she is facing the players. Her mouth opens and lets out a horrifying laugh, Wicked Witch of the West–like:

"Eeeaahhh ha-ha-ha-ha-ha-ha!"

🎮 🎮 🎮

Phil Gradee's expression was one of worry as he handed the two drives to Ned Hazly and sat down across the desk.

"What's this all about, Ned?" Gradee asked.

"What the hell are those?"

"External hard drives."

"Why are you giving me external hard drives? These are the data sets?"

"Yeah."

"You said it would take a while. Phil, I want you to sit on it. Say you're getting the data ready, but sit on it. It's just good business sense to *not* give in to distractions. We're a business, and one that doesn't have a lot of second chances right now."

"What's all this about?"

"I got a call from the prosecutor's office. It seems they've pushed for a final ruling on whether our video segments will be admissible as evidence."

"What does that mean?"

"What it means is that the trial will proceed and Chambers' defense team won't be able to stall anymore. Once the evidence is formally admitted, I am told, it'll be an open-and-shut case."

"When will this happen?"

"The judge scheduled a hearing for Friday afternoon. And that, possibly, will be Kelly Chambers' last day in the outside world."

Moments later, Hazly watched with interest as Gradee stood and left.

Gradee was a good engineer, the best. That Ned knew. But he was too good, and the time to get rid of him was coming soon—paperwork for Gradee's layoff, detailing made-up charges of incompetence and a meager severance package, sat in Ned's top drawer.

You see, for Ned Hazly, Phil Gradee was the boy scout you didn't want around. Ned had his own engineers, men more interested in seeing how much they could do than how ethical they could make it.

For Gradee, great invention lay in self-opening stairwell doors. Ned's men, conversely, had proved capable of far more-interesting feats.

And with Phil Gradee gone, Ned would not have to go to so much trouble to hide some of the things they were working on, like the extracurricular fixtures on the thirteenth floor.

Count them off: Randolph gone, Kelly Chambers gone, Brenda gone. Once Phil was gone, Ned would be free to do with Cannecare and Cannecare Tower whatsoever he pleased.

🐦 🐦 🐦

A very pointy Ned Hazly avatar exits a taxi just up Second Avenue from Cannecare Tower and strides along, clad in a leather coat, a fedora, and sunglasses.

He came by cab so his car wouldn't be filmed by the scattered cameras along the way, whether Cannecare's, or city traffic cameras, or video cams at businesses.

Hazly walks to a bookstore window and pretends to browse until a group of tourists comes along. Falling in among them he crosses the street and walks to the Cannecare entrance—unseen.

The cameras again spy downward and catch only a field of heads passing by. It would take a keen eye to pick out the sudden decrease in number of a single head as the group passes the Cannecare door.

There, Pointy Ned ducks inside, makes his way through the lobby. A security guard moves to question him, but Hazly turns, draws a ray gun as large as his upper body, and fires. The guard blows up, leaving only a trace of flame on the ground where he once stood.

"Damn it, Eric, I told you no guns."

"Aaaawww!" the fast dropping tone of disappointment.

Now Pointy Hazly enters the elevator and faces the biometric scanner, which will record his entry and keep that data for the police to find. This is a dilemma in their game so far.

But Pointy Hazly has a solution. He produces a hand, its fingers stretched out. This he places on the hand scanner.

"What floor would you like to go to today, Mrs. Tate?" the elevator asks in a perky computer voice.

"What the hell did you just do?" Lester asks.

Eric giggles as he turns to Patricia, who leers back.

"Well, check out *my* avatar," she says.

On the rightmost screen they see the Brenda Tate avatar. It is holding up its right arm, but in place of the hand that should rightfully be attached, is spurting blood.

🐾 🐾 🐾

To Kelly, waiting for Wilbur Kendeff Wednesday afternoon was like waiting for a case of the shingles.

It was two p.m. and still no sign of Bernard. They had pounded on his door, called, emailed, texted, but nothing.

O'Brian returned from another meeting with the police, bringing further bad news: They were not going to extend their investigation and in fact told O'Brian to stop his snooping. Apparently both Brenda Tate and Ned Hazly had complained.

And that was what Kelly had going for her as she waited for Kendeff. O'Brian waited with her, at her request. She wasn't up to dealing with Kendeff alone just now.

"Miss Chambers," the attorney said gently as Kelly opened the door to let him in.

"Hi, Wilbur." Her greeting was a question. "Come in."

Kendeff nodded to O'Brian. Then to Kelly: "You might want to sit down."

"I'll stand if that's OK."

"All right. I'll get straight to the point. The judge scheduled the hearing for Friday afternoon, and I don't see any reason to think he *won't* admit the evidence."

"But it was faked," Kelly pleaded.

"The segments show you . . ." Kendeff hesitated, decided to rephrase it. "Listen, at the center of these segments is video. Video footage is used all the time in court. There's no reason to think this footage will be deemed inadmissible."

O'Brian interrupted. "Video footage is sometimes thrown out as evidence."

"This time it won't be. And once a jury sees it, the image of Miss Chambers . . ." Again he paused to choose his words carefully. "Once a jury sees Miss Chambers *at that computer* . . . there isn't going to be any argument that either I or Bernard Walker with his video games can offer that's going to make any difference. Once that evidence is admitted, you're as good as convicted. You won't be able to overcome it."

Her knees beginning to tremble, Kelly sat down.

"We still have two days if the hearing's Friday," O'Brian insisted. This was no time to quit.

"Right. Has Mr. Walker come up with anything?"

"We, uh . . . we think he's working on it."

Kendeff turned to Kelly, then back to O'Brian. "Very well. I'm going to leave it at that for now, then. Miss Chambers still has one or two options, not pleasant options necessarily, but we've discussed them. Perhaps you can advise her some, too."

"What do you mean?"

"I'm not sure she's getting the best of advice from Bernard Walker."

To this last remark neither Kelly nor O'Brian could muster a reply, since in fact she was currently getting none.

Wednesday had so far been one of the best days Herbert had had in a very long time.

He awoke at five-thirty, as he did always, anywhere, but today he had a plan. Today he returned to the coffee shop he found the previous morning and once seated, instead of opening the *Wall Street Journal* he'd bought along the way, he took out the iPhone the company forced on him.

Before going to bed, Herbert had downloaded an app from OffCide Studios' bank, and exploring briefly he was instantly impressed. The amazing things he suddenly could do on his phone!

Herbert had been without a computer now for more than a day (he was probably the only employee in the company who didn't use a laptop—or two), and that meant he couldn't keep watch on what Bernard and his horde were spending, since he couldn't access the bank website to monitor accounts.

But now this wondrous phone! Going through the banking app, Herbert learned he could monitor all the different accounts as transactions registered—in real time. What's more, he could instantly shut down any company credit card, he could move funds from account to account, he could even make deposits. All from this little device.

Oh, how he had hated the dreadful thing when they forced it on him, and, oh, how he now had a new best friend.

Turning it over in his hand, he examined the sleek device. The dignity and prestige he saw in the BlackBerry, he now saw the same in this. This phone was power.

And once he surveyed the banking app's features, Iggid went into company accounts and his spirits jumped up yet another notch. For he instantly discovered the past day and a half of charges from the Pendrite had registered at the bank, and, boy, Ron O'Brian, no, you *don't* have *that* much money set aside for your test case.

And now Herbert was smiling.

And, oh boy, are the boards *of both* companies going to flip out over these charges.

An hour later Iggid was walking north on his way to the Space Needle. He decided he needed to hang around for a few days and keep an eye on things as much as he could, but with little else to do, he figured he might as well take in the sights, maybe buy a souvenir or two to send back to his mother in Boston.

"Seattle?" his mother would ask. "Where on earth is *that*? How quaint!"

But she would have seen the Space Needle. You can't see a movie filmed in Seattle without the landmark being prominently featured.

It was a bit of a walk. The front-desk clerk told him it would take about half an hour, but the mix of architecture along the way, the fine, clean morning air—it all made for an enjoyable morning trek.

And within five minutes at Seattle Center, the parklike area that is home to the Space Needle and more, Herbert began to see the attraction was, yes, very impressive.

Exploring the area, he saw there was a science museum, a music museum, a children's museum, and something about gardens and glass. There were venues for exhibits and festivals, there were rides for children, and there were elaborate fountains.

And best of all the Space Needle itself, an immense white tower that all this was centered around. Standing before it, Herbert took out his travel guide and read:

> Once the tallest structure west of the Mississippi River, the Space Needle has become an internationally recognized icon of the Pacific Northwest. The 605-foot tower, with an observation deck at 520 feet, was built for the 1962 World's Fair, which attracted more than 2.3 million . . .

Herbert raised his head to take in the towering sight. At the top was a round . . . "spaceship," featuring, he saw as he glanced down at the page, a restaurant that rotated 360 degrees, allowing diners to take in the views in every direction as they enjoyed their meals.

As Herbert read, it dawned on him that without his normal regimen of dinner meetings and company events, he really had an open schedule for the evening, and, well, it had been years since he had taken a vacation. So tonight it would be dinner at this phenomenal rotating restaurant, at a window seat affording gorgeous night views of the entire city.

🐘 🐘 🐘

Woeful WasteWorld: Something's wrong; this is too easy.

OffCide Gamer was able to sweep through Germania, then Rome, and even take Gaul, all no problem.

It should have been more difficult, there should have been more challenges.

In his conquests OffCide amassed a growing army of zombies and a cache of weapons. And once in Gaul he even took a chance by launching a naval attack on Britannia—and won, hands down.

A naval invasion of Britain? Not supposed to happen.

And all the while he has been searching the globe, scouring the maps to try to locate the Evil Iberian. But his archrival is nowhere to be seen, is, apparently, hiding under cover of a new avatar and a different name.

Where will he—or she—suddenly pop up?

🎮 🎮 🎮

Ned Hazly left the Video Wall dark, but watched at the PEC console as Holstenbeck made his way through the Cannecare lobby and up to the top floor.

As he watched, Ned pictured in his mind the systems that were going to save Cannecare, that were going to turn it into a technology giant.

You see, Ned had a concept behind the name Project X, one more brilliant than the lame X as in "*Ex*tra Security," the excuse he usually offered people. Project X got its name by being the first of *three* layers of security that Ned envisioned.

You see, Ned had also been planning a Project Y and a Project Z, each a little more sinister than the last according to *late* Randolph's *late* privacy policy. And Project Z was one he made sure would erase any need for further letters. Z was complete control of entire populations.

Ned smiled at the screen as Holstenbeck exited the elevator and came down the hall. Ned pictured some of the things hallways could be ('were being') packed with, on top of sensors and cameras.

Toxic gasses, for instance. And sniper guns he could aim and fire from this very seat.

And he imagined using these weapons now as he monitored Holstenbeck's progress down the hall.

"Simpleton," he said aloud.

Ned resented this man, resented his wealth. Ned had worked hard, very hard, to get to where he was; and now he was preparing to beg Holstenbeck for help—a man born into wealth and who had never had to work for anything.

The idea infuriated Hazly.

Holstenbeck crossed the final section of hallway unaware that he was, in Ned's imagination, being shot at, gassed, and toasted with flames as he walked.

No, it wasn't fair to Ned, but money was money, so Hazly's attitude changed as Holstenbeck entered the PEC.

"Ned, how are you?"

"Rainer. Thank you for coming."

"Yes, yes. Always glad to do anything I can to help."

"Yeah, well, please have a seat."

"How are you?"

"Not so great, and I'm afraid we may be asking for a little help."

"Oh?"

"Yeah."

"Business not going so well? It is so sad, first what happened with Randolph, and now the company, how do you say . . . dragging along."

"Yeah. As you know, things are . . . yes, dragging along. We've lost two major customers since Randolph's murder. Two *revenue-generating* customers."

"I knew that was happening, but I have confidence you are on top of things."

"Yeah, but it's worse than that. Some *potential* customers we were working with, spending money on, now they won't talk to us until the company's stable again. 'Come back in six months or a year down the line,' they say."

"Oh my. That sounds not good at all, not at all."

"No. And it's a bottom-line sort of *not good*. You see, we don't have operational funds for six months or a year."

"Ah, but I know you, Ned. You always have a plan. So, tell me, what is it you're going to do?"

"Right. Well, my friend, what I'm going to do is what we should have been doing all along."

"You will begin planning again on your Project X?"

"More than just planning."

"Really? You're working on prototype systems?" Holstenbeck nodded his head in his normally friendly manner, always happy to agree with whatever was being said.

"I told you a month ago we were considering it. You know Randolph wasn't completely on board."

"I rather had that feeling, yes."

"But we had already invested in the research, as you know. And we're still a young company. We can't afford waste. As an investor, you should appreciate that."

"Oh, certainly, yes."

"And our research was ninety percent complete. The remaining ten percent was systems testing."

"Testing?"

"Yes, proof of concept, so too speak. And we had the ideal testing ground right here at Cannecare."

"Really?"

"In fact, you've seen the interface several times right here on the PEC console. You just didn't understand what was in front of you."

Hazly's hidden contempt for this man who never had to work get his wealth, it stung all the more knowing Holstenbeck could stare right at a well-designed computer menu that operated live weapons system . . . and think he was viewing a spreadsheet.

"Oh my," Holstenbeck said.

Hazly remembered once coming in to find Holstenbeck after the fool stumbled his way into the Project X weapons interface. The imbecile could have made Randolph's murder appear more like a misdemeanor in comparison, if he had continued fiddling. That very afternoon Ned wasted no time in building what he called "childproofing" for the overall system, to ensure it did not happen again.

"Our people met with security experts, government, academic, and private sector. Heck, you connected us with a few people."

"Of course, I remember."

"But fortunately, I had the vision not to throw away what we already had. And it is near ready for . . . for demonstration."

"Demonstration? Interesting. But quite a jump from Randolph's privacy policy."

"A policy you agreed was short-sighted."

"But now so soon after the murder, to make such a change . . . Of course, we have to consider what is right, and not to forget what the full board will support."

"Rainer, I don't want to seem insensitive. But I know more than anyone that Randolph would want to see Cannecare march on. And we have the assets."

"So you think?"

"Randolph's murderer is about to be tried and convicted, open and shut like no high-profile murder case you can imagine . . . and it's going to have Cannecare written all over it. It's our evidence. It's our technology, our patents."

"I see, I see. Yes."

"And that's the way we can turn this thing in our favor, can make it work for us. I can get potential customers in and demonstrate building security like they've never seen."

"Building security that can go *beyond* the building, like you said before?"

"Precisely. Security that stretches around the block, around the neighborhood, even citywide."

"Yes, yes. I remember telling you how intrigued I was. I mean, there are global markets. I think *any* technology company these days *has* to have a world view, and a long-term global perspective."

"Right." Getting Holstenbeck to agree was just too easy. "See, we can have a *light* version, if you will, a version that people concerned with privacy can use. But what we have is a *platform*, and we can plug a lot of *additional* applications into it. That creates different layers."

"*Platform! Additional!* I like the sound of this, yes."

"Security, surveillance, the ability to ID and catalogue faces of anyone who enters an area. Our platform could change society, it could keep people safe from terrorism, from crime . . . My God, think about airports, border crossings . . . You made several suggestions that we put into our system."

"I see, I see. Yes."

"Here." Hazly turned to the console and pulled up a menu. "Let me show you a few of the things we are already installing to test."

"Yes, yes."

"In fact," Hazly added, "We can bill the new products as the *New* Cannecare, a company set out on a *new* path with *new* leadership."

"Yes, yes, I like it, I'm sure that can work."

"But there's the problem. To fully demonstrate the platform's potential, we need further funding."

"Yes?"

"That's why I asked you here today. I was hoping you could offer some additional support."

"Ah, I get it, I get it. Yes. And how much support are you talking about?"

"Five, maybe six million dollars."

"Ah-hah. Yes."

"But before you think any more about it, let me show you a demonstration of some of the stuff I'm talking about."

"Ah."

Hazly hit a couple of keys and the Video Wall lit up . . .

"I . . . I don't understand what use this is," Chen said.

Patricia didn't either and she fixed her stare at Les.

On the TVs before them, again a dangerous madman was on the move.

Les had chosen to be the murderer and selected the Ned Hazly avatar; Eric was playing Randolph Tate.

"He has a point," Patricia complained. "How does any of this help Kelly?"

Les ignored her for a moment. "Wanna go for a swim, Eric? Check out that cool, refreshing swimming pool. Wouldn't it feel good to swim a few laps and stretch out? Then you could have a nice relaxing soak in the spa. I'll make it real warm for you. It'll be the spa to end all spas."

"Yeah, one that'll make a new man out of me," Eric shot back, "or a dead one, anyway. Is there a cafeteria in this place? How about I buy you a coffee instead?"

Lester paused the game and turned to face Patricia. "This is the thing: There's no algorithm, no program, that solves the murder. We're searching for holes, remember?"

Chen nodded. "You know, we need that sensor data, the whole set. Our game by itself can only teach us . . . what should we look for."

Eric agreed. "Yeah. That's the only sure way to find holes."

A text alert sounded on Les' phone, effectively silencing the room. Could it be from Bernard?

All eyes fell onto the table where Les sat, where the phone sat. They hadn't heard from Bernard in a day and a half now, and with the hearing scheduled, Lester's explanation of what they were doing failed to instill optimism, even for him.

Les picked up the device and read the message.

"Wow, he says he found a hole. He found a hole!"

"Where? Where is it?" Patricia pleaded.

Les looked back at his phone, then drooped his head.

"What does he say?"

"He says, quote: 'Your head's in the clouds if you don't see it.'"

"That's it?"

"Well, no . . ."

"What else does he say?"

"He says: 'The clouds, the clouds!' And that's all."

🐾 🐾 🐾

O'Brian sat with Kelly for half an hour after Kendeff left, and there was little he could do to calm her. She had fallen into a sort of silent rage. Her hands shook, her body trembled, and there was a fierceness in her eyes that was unlike anything O'Brian had seen in her.

"What are these *options* Kendeff was talking about?" he asked finally.

She didn't answer at first.

"What, was he talking about pleading insanity again?"

"Yeah," she responded almost silently. "That or . . ."

"Or what?"

"Or a plea bargain."

"A plea bargain? With the evidence they have? What would be the bargain?"

"Life in prison with no possibility of parole."

"No!"

"Yeah . . ."

"Well, listen. None of this is going to happen, not while I'm here. Bernard may have disappeared on us, but the kids are going over their modeling, and I'm going back out and continue doing what *the police* should be doing—what they *would* be doing if it weren't for that damned evidence."

"You mean *damning* evidence."

"Yeah, same thing, it turns out."

O'Brian stood.

"Where are you going?"

"To talk to Phil Gradee."

"I thought the police told you no more involvement."

"Yeah. Funny, some of the things police tell you."

🎮 🎮 🎮

Woeful WasteWorld: Iberia fell as easily as Gaul had and from there it was a quick sweep across North Africa, and Bernard saw that he was wiping out pretty much everyone in the hemisphere.

But still no sign of the Evil Iberian.

How could there not be? This far into a tournament, if you hadn't already begun amassing huge armies, you couldn't catch up, you couldn't win.

The Evil Iberian knew that. The Iberian was a shrewd player, yes. This was no novice.

Bernard again studied the map. A couple of players in North America and a few more in Asia had some armies built up, but with limited territory, their supplies would be weak.

None of them could be the Iberian, not a chance.

So where?

🎮 🎮 🎮

Kelly did not speak after Patricia came in. She just opened the door, then walked back to the window, where she stood staring out in silence.

"I'm sure Bernard's onto something. Lester and Eric are trying to figure out what he was talking about in that text."

Kelly didn't stir.

"They'll figure it out. We might even have holes identified as early as tonight."

Still, Kelly did not move.

Patricia took out her phone and texted Bernard:

> Damn it Bernard, Kelly is hysterical! What is this hole? Answer me or I'm coming to hurt you.

She hit send, sat in silence a moment, when to her surprise, she got a reply:

Look to the clouds, the clouds!

"That was something more from Bernard," she said. "I'm going to go tell Les."

Patricia hurried out the door, only she didn't stop to talk to Lester, but rather hurried down to the front desk, where she got a key card for Bernard's suite.

Moments later, she burst through the door, to find . . . silence.

The suite was empty, save for a pile of dirty clothes, a few pizza boxes, and some empty fast-food bags.

🎮 🎮 🎮

Kelly is bold, she doesn't need a hat and sunglasses to commit murder, she just walks out of the Stanley and heads up Second Avenue to Cannecare Tower in plain view of all the cameras.

In the lobby she sees Randolph Tate walking in a jogging suit with a towel over his shoulder.

"Hah!" Tate says. "Now you're Kelly?"

"Yeah," Kelly replies, though in the voice of Lester Argyle. "I had to wait till Patricia left before I could be Kelly."

"Yeah, she's kind of freaked out," Randolph replies, in the voice of Eric Lyle. "Well, I'll be in the spa if anyone wants to murder me."

"Very good," Kelly replies. "Have a nice time."

Randolph stops at the stairwell door. "What does he mean, the clouds?"

The Kelly avatar walks back out onto Second Avenue and Randolph follows. "There are clouds," she says, "but what do they mean? The real Kelly says there are always clouds in Seattle."

"Yeah, but have you noticed something?" Randolph asks.
"What?"
"There hasn't been a cloud in the sky since we got here."

By Wednesday night, Kelly had calmed down somewhat, had gone from terror to simple resignation. Life had suddenly turned very ugly, and as clever as Kelly was, as educated and capable as she was, it appeared there wasn't a damn thing she could do about it.

The kids continued their "work," and O'Brian returned with no answers. He had talked to Gradee, but only briefly as the building engineer refused to discuss the case.

And Bernard was lost in "Video Game Land," as Kelly had come to call it (in virtual actuality at that moment he was caught in an epic battle against Zombie-laden Trojan horses just south of Byzantium).

Thursday went a lot like Wednesday, except that it dragged along even more painfully. No new modeling was coming in from China, since no one could think of anything to add.

And the expanded data from Cannecare had yet to arrive, despite repeated calls by Kendeff and O'Brian.

So the group took to running through the existing models and through the Cannecare segments, studying every detail, but learning nothing.

Patricia texted Bernard every hour, but received a reply only twice. The first was "How dark the clouds . . ." and the second was "Does Kelly like clouds? Why not?"

Finally, at five in the afternoon, O'Brian called everyone together in Suite 2202.

"Time to take stock," he said. "Where are we at? What do we know?"

The group sat scattered about the suite.

"We know we're not ready for tomorrow," Kelly replied.

"Look," Lester said, "just the fact that we can produce full modeling of the entire thing, that should show the Cannecare segments could have been faked."

"No. We're going to need a lot more than that, I'm afraid," O'Brian said.

Everyone stared blankly, eyes showing they were there, were listening, but mutually not wanting to make contact.

"Listen," O'Brian said, "we have to prepare to put on our best show. Lester, can you prepare to demonstrate what we do have, and while you're demonstrating it, explain how the production is done and . . . and . . . and how the Cannecare segments could have been similarly produced?"

"No problem."

"Next, I want you guys to make a list of the specific things a person would have to know how to do in order to fake segments like these."

"A list?"

"I met with Wilbur Kendeff earlier. He'll present a similar list at the hearing, along with a list of people who had such skills. And if the judge gives him the chance, he'll throw in the fact that at least two of those people had solid motives to kill Tate, and to frame Kelly."

"I'll do that," Chen said. "I've edited video a lot before. And the sensor technology, I think I understand."

"Good."

"Patricia and Eric, you two keep stabbing at that . . . video game. Try to find this hole. And, Patricia, keep trying to contact Bernard, for Christ's sake."

"I will."

O'Brian sighed, tried to offer a reassuring expression.

Silence a moment, then from Kelly: "What do I do?"

O'Brian looked her square in the eye. "Join me for a drink?"

"Can we make it two?"

"Yeah."

🐘 🐘 🐘

Across town, Ned Hazly was also preparing for the hearing. He had lined up two of his top product managers, as well as a city engineer Cannecare had worked with—an outside expert to testify on the integrity of the company's systems.

Between them they would satisfy any questions or doubts the judge might have, and the Cannecare segments would be admitted, the trial of Kelly Chambers would proceed, and Ned Hazly could get on with his grander Cannecare plans.

And more good news came in an afternoon meeting with Holstenbeck, who stopped in to say he'd discussed the funding request with his people back home, and he might have approval to arrange it in just a few weeks, once terms were worked out.

🐘 🐘 🐘

Lake Washington, the state's second-largest lake, was given its name in 1854 at the suggestion of Thomas Mercer, a year after the Washington territory received its name.

Herbert Iggid glared out the window in wonder at the yachting facilities lining the shore as his listened intently to the voice over the tour boat's loudspeaker.

Off in the distance you can see Seattle's famous floating bridges, which carry Interstate 90 across the lake.

'Truly wonderful,' Herbert said to himself. Seattle turned out to be *surrounded* by water, with the bay on one side, Lake Washington spanning the east, and other, smaller lakes to the north.

Herbert was captivated by the houseboats on Lake Union, which the tour boat had just passed. Some were absolute luxury, others simply . . . cute, but adorably so.

And now as they headed south they were passing rows and rows of boats on the right—sailboats, ski boats, cabin cruisers . . .

And as they passed the last of these Herbert's face truly lit up. Here began a stretch of shoreline that was given to luxury homes—*true* luxury homes—of a type he had never seen before.

These were stately mansions, each with its own dock out on the lake. Their narrow but long backyards held spas, pools, pool houses, boat houses, guest houses, all decorated with lush artistic gardens. One even had a seaplane parked at its dock.

These were certainly the equal of the mansions Herbert knew in the Boston area. But here from the lake, you could see right in on the lives of the very rich and famous, lives that by proximity to the water could not be walled off, as they would be back home.

This was the sort of home he longed to live in one day, this was the reason Herbert Iggid worked as hard as he did. It wouldn't be long, he knew in his heart, before he would be one of the elite crowd living in such a mansion, overseeing investments and businesses during the day, and then spending evenings with wealthy neighbors, trading stock tips and secrets on better ways to wax your yacht.

In fact, it was entirely possible Herbert Iggid might be heading a company very soon, after a promotion that would make his current six-figure salary look weak in comparison.

With that thought in mind, Herbert took out his iPhone and checked the banking app, and again added up in his mind the company credit card charges being registered.

It appeared OffCide Studios needed not just a change in office hours, but a complete shakeup of senior and middle management. And those credit card charges were continually adding ammunition Herbert could use in coming weeks when he met with OffCide's board of directors.

🎮 🎮 🎮

'OffCide Gamer. What a stupid name. He uses the name of a lame game company? Really?

'OffCide's the company that makes those lame Murder Mystery games. What's that? A game your aunt plays, that's what it is.

'And watch him now, all confident, playing the way Woeful WasteWorld's always been played.

'Clearly, he did not read the rules. The rules are pretty plain; that is, they state there pretty much aren't any rules.

'And Greece? Really? What are you going to win in Greece, squads of zombie philosophers? Ready, aim, think? No, I don't see it.

'And so shall end the Woeful WasteWorld championship reign of the OffCide Gamer.

'Yes, your time has come.' Typing in the chat box:

Mr. OffCide Gamer: I. am. going. to. get. you!
(: <)

16

For the second time in two weeks Kelly was outdoors, was on the move, even if it was only covering the same few blocks she traveled from the jail to the Pendrite ten days earlier.

Just soaking in the movement of cars around her, of people on the sidewalks, the blue sky . . . the world grabbed her attention, held it tight. But her thoughts hung low, were sunk into the tasks ahead.

Was this about to become a daily routine? A morning drive from the Pendrite Hotel to the King County Courthouse?

And would it then be one morning—probably the day the verdict was to be read, she guessed—would she one morning be making this drive knowing it would likely be her last on an open street? Ever.

'Hell, the sun's out, it's dry, and I'm still depressed in Seattle,' she said to herself.

Kelly rode beside O'Brian in the backseat of a limo; in front were the driver and a police officer on the right, *riding shotgun*, as it were, she mused.

And they were heading to court with no real defense, no way to prove the Cannecare segments were faked. They had learned nothing new and hadn't heard from Bernard, despite their barrage of pleading emails and texts about the hearing.

Well, they heard nothing except occasional text references to Seattle's clouds.

After only a few minutes on the road, Kelly caught sight of the courthouse, just downhill from the towering Columbia Center, the sleek seventy-six-story black skyscraper that stands tallest on Seattle's skyline—and second tallest on the West Coast.

And seconds later she saw the "sky bridge" that several stories above the street connects the courthouse to the county jail, a lonely walkway Kelly had crossed before, and one that could very soon be the path for her final journey from the world, a journey into prison, to Death Row, to . . .

Seattle's own Bridge of Sighs.

And here Kelly simply shut her mind down.

🐾 🐾 🐾

For Ned Hazly the journey from his office crossed the better part of downtown Seattle, north to south.

For him the trip was also a bit of a parade, his being the first of three limousines making their way through town for everyone to see.

It was a statement. The front of the courthouse would be packed with camera crews and news trucks, and that was opportunity.

With plans to exploit it, Hazly had spoken with his company's attorneys and public relations people, and honed the best-possible image to present.

This wasn't going to be a couple of Cannecare executives coming in to court to be questioned, to testify; this was going to be a Cannecare panel of experts arriving to advise the court in a murder trial.

And it wasn't the tragic co-founder of the just-murdered CEO who was in the first car; it was Co-Founder and Interim Chief Executive Ned Hazly in the lead, firmly in charge and accompanied by a hand-picked team to back him up.

And the line of three limos parading in together would make for quite the show.

Hazly would testify, the other executives would testify . . . and apparently Chambers' defense team was going to demonstrate a video game of some sort.

They'd be in and out in an hour or two, and Hazly would be back to his office by five, where he would watch coverage on the evening news.

It would be the parade of limos arriving together that TV stations would cover over and over: ". . . experts from Cannecare arrived to advise the court . . ."

Chambers would be on the road to certain conviction, and Ned would be getting credit, since it was his—oh, and also *the dearly departed victim's*, of course—technology that made it happen.

Yes, this was going to be a good day for Ned Hazly, he said to himself as he again pictured the parade of limos crossing town.

🐗 🐗 🐗

"Oh, God, Chen, tell me you didn't let Les pick the rental car," Patricia moaned, shaking her head as the Toyota Prius pulled up to the Pendrite.

She turned, compared the grandiose hotel entrance behind her with the tiny white Prius, and heard, echoing in her mind, her mother's words about why she *should not* seek a career as a video game designer.

"You know there are going to be TV cameras at the courthouse, right?" Patricia shouted as Les climbed out.

"Yeah, so?" he responded.

"A murder trial, Les. Maybe on national television. And we're showing up in a Prius? Really?!"

"Hey, model citizens, driving a hybrid because we're concerned about the environment."

"Yeah, a car you chose because you want to try a newer model."

"Hey, I wanted to compare the hills of Seattle with the hills of San Francisco." Lester drove a Prius at home.

"They're smaller. What else do you want to know?"

"Hills are different in a Prius. You wouldn't understand."

"Yeah, right. Well, never mind. Come load the car . . . Oh no, where are we going to fit everything?"

The two of them were still arguing five minutes later when Les jolted out onto Third Avenue behind a Lincoln Town Car, the Prius crawling along at a speed of about ten miles per hour, pretty much crippling traffic behind them.

"Hey, don't drive too fast now," Patricia warned with pronounced sarcasm.

"Gimme a break," Les answered. "I've never driven in Seattle before."

"You drive in San Francisco; you should survive here."

"Hey, check it out," Eric said from the backseat. "There's a car behind us that's just like the one in front. Oh, wait, no, there are *two* of them behind us. Identical models."

The car in front slowed somewhat. Through the darkened rear window Les could see a face bobbing around, but he couldn't make out details.

Then he saw the head pop out the left-side rear window.

"Oh my God. It's that Hazly guy."

"Where?" Patricia asked.

"In front of us, on my side, looking out the window."

Chen, seated directly behind, leaned forward. "That man looks angry."

"What do I do?" Les asked.

"Slow down further, put a distance between us," Patricia said.

"But there're cars behind us."

"Screw 'em."

"Wait, watch this." As the car in front passed through an intersection, Les slowed to nearly a halt, forcing traffic behind him to do so also. And just as they reached the intersection, the light turned yellow, and Les came to a stop, forcing the two trailing limos to do so also.

And they watched as the car in front—with an apparently cursing Hazly, head out the window—drove off into the distance and out of sight.

The arraignment court was crowded with press and court watchers in the outer area, and people directly involved in the glassed-in inner courtroom.

Kelly stood off to one side, surrounded by a bailiff and the officer who accompanied her, while Kendeff and the prosecutor stood at the front counter before Judge Merlson and two assistants.

Off to the other side sat, menacingly, a giant monitor on a stand, the type of demonstration screen designed for classrooms and meetings.

The prosecution spoke briefly before the judge called Hazly and his team forward. Once a sample of the Cannecare segments was played on the screen, Hazly's experts explained again how hundreds of sensors had collected the data, and how their software tools correlated and verified it.

Their argument was rock solid: Using this sort of built-in security and data management guaranteed that all parts of the segments were genuine.

By the end of the presentation, the judge appeared relaxed for the first time while presiding over the case, and for the first time something resembling a smile budded along his mouth, as if he had just developed a fondness for citrus fruit.

"Interesting presentation, Mr. Hazly. It very much confirms what I've been reading in my briefs."

"Yes sir."

'Damn,' Kelly said to herself.

"Now, normally we want to move cases along as quickly as possible, and after hearing from these gentlemen today, and following up with our own research, I am inclined to go ahead and admit the evidence and move on to trial."

"Thank you, your honor," the prosecutor said.

"We have a backlog of cases right now, but a high-profile one like this has to be made a priority. We'll get things rolling as quickly as possible. Both sides should now be thinking about jury selection."

"Your honor," Kendeff squeaked. "We have a presentation of our own."

"Really?" Judge Merlson turned from Hazly and his "experts," decked out in tailor-made suits, to Kendeff and the kids standing next to him, dressed in jeans and T-shirts. "And this presentation will somehow add light to this case?"

"Yes sir. We've created a demo of our own to show how the Cannecare evidence could be faked."

"Oh, very well. Please make it quick."

Moments later Les and Eric had set up a laptop on the counter. It was a high-end gaming machine, but it paled sadly in comparison with the giant presentation screen Hazly's people had used.

"We have a Mr. Chen Li," Les said, "who is production chief at our China office. If it's OK, he'll explain how the Cannecare evidence could have been faked."

"If you say so. Proceed."

Les began the animation from their game, which showed the Kelly avatar exit her suite and walk down the hallway at the Stanley.

"I'll speed this up," he said, his eye briefly catching a cold stare from Hazly, the face in the limo.

As the presentation continued, Chen explained that once they created the animation of Kelly Chambers walking, going back and adding sensor data to match her journey would be a simple matter, tedious, but simple.

The judge looked doubtful, both of the explanation and of his own ability to understand it.

"It would be troublesome, but my staff could do it in a day," Chen stated as the Kelly avatar exited the Cannecare elevator.

The judge was silent a moment, his eyes going back and forth from Chen to the laptop.

Finally he focused again on the animation, and what he wound up seeing was the caricature of Kelly, complete with elongated face and smeared eye makeup, sitting at a computer and cruelly murdering a cartoonlike Randolph Tate.

'Nice effect,' Kelly said to herself. From her vantage point she could just see the animation.

The judge shook his head, more of a spasm trying to shake off the image, like a dog just drenched with a hose.

"I'm sorry," he complained, a little anger in his voice. "But I don't see anything *new* here. This is pretty much the same argument we had last week."

Kendeff jumped in. "We would have more, your honor, but we're still waiting for the full data sets from Cannecare."

"The what?"

"The full data sets. Their sensor and video data. We're entitled to see it, but they haven't given it to us yet."

"Oh, yes, I see that here in my notes. But honestly, I believe Cannecare has given you more than adequate materials to allow us to proceed . . . and . . ." Here the judge's head went back and forth between Lester and Chen. "And I just don't see how these . . . *cartoons* of yours, can aid the court. We need to get this case to trial."

"But—"

"Miss Chambers, please step forward."

Kelly was in a daze and failed to comprehend. Watching Lester and Chen's weak presentation on the laptop, as opposed to Hazly's giant screen, a presentation that ended, incidentally, with her avatar murdering the Randolph Tate avatar—brilliant job, Lester!—watching all this, she had sunk lower and lower into depression.

The bailiff put a hand on Kelly's arm to get her attention.

"Miss Chambers? Please step forward."

Along with the bailiff, she did so, but there was something mournful in her step, making her seem to float to the bench.

The judge spoke as Kendeff moved beside her. "Miss Chambers, last week you entered a plea of not guilty. Do you want to change your plea?"

Kelly stared into his eyes, *pleading* a lot more than not guilty. Her expression kept even the judge silent for a moment, before she answered, finally, in a broken tone, "No, sir, I do not."

Merlson frowned. "All right. Does anyone have anything more to add today?"

"Yes," Kendeff said quickly. "If we can get the full data—"

"This court, Mr. Kendeff, cannot wait for you to produce more cartoons. Mr. Hazly. These data sets, whatever they are, is there some reason why these things have not been given to the defense?"

"Yes, your honor. It takes time to extract the mounds of data they've asked for, then verify that it is correct, and then put it into some form that they can make sense of."

"Once again," the judge said to Kendeff, "I am inclined to think the segments provided are adequate to proceed, at least for now."

Kendeff leaned over to whisper to Kelly.

"I think it's pretty clear that your Mr. Walker is *not* going to help. Later this afternoon, you and I can talk again about your options."

Kelly maintained her forward stare, a fierce anger etched into her face.

The judge continued:

"Very well then, I am hereby ruling to admit the Cannecare video segments as evidence, and that they are more than sufficient to bring the case to full trial. We should be able to get underway immediately."

The statement left the courtroom silent. Judge Merlson surveyed those in attendance, slowly took note of everyone present in the glassed-in inner area.

Then:

"Well, there's nothing more to be said. And so, *as* I said, I am ruling to admit the Cannecare evidence. The trial will get started immediately. And so, this hearing is hereby adjo—"

Twenty minutes earlier, Bernard showed up at the courthouse entrance, but only to be exasperated for the third time in the past ten days by a full-blown security check.

"Empty your pockets and put everything in this bin," a woman told him. She was middle-aged, about four feet tall but built like a linebacker.

Bernard guessed she could probably wrestle him to the ground and break both his arms in about five seconds.

"Is this really necessary?" he complained. "I'm late for a hearing."

"You're going to be a lot *later* if you don't cooperate. This is a secure courthouse. Please empty your pockets, sir."

"Seriously? Everything?"

"Everything, yes. Everybody who enters this courthouse gets checked."

"Oh God," he said, and slowly began pulling items one by one from his pockets, much to the increasing amusement of the security personnel and the people in line behind him.

And he continued to complain. "It so happens that I was up nearly all night, and this hearing, I have to say, was scheduled for an unreasonably early hour."

"It's one-thirty in the afternoon."

"Exactly."

Moments later, his vest pockets apparently emptied, his keys and change added also to the bin, Bernard proceeded through the metal detector.

Which of course beeped.

"Sir, step over here, please," the woman moaned, and clearly she was not happy.

🐾 🐾 🐾

Time seemed to freeze for Kelly. Her mind was transfixed now on the image of the sky bridge—Seattle's Bridge of Sighs, wasn't that what they called the one in Venice?—that narrow above-ground crossover where one day soon she might be left to take that final journey from the free world and into permanent incarceration, where she would wait in misery for . . .

And now for the first time, Kelly let her mind approach the subject head on: What, what would it be, the electric chair, lethal injection, hanging? What?

The judge was speaking, but his words only echoed in her mind; they made no sense.

And what if she were given a choice? Lethal injection? Hanging? Oh God. How do you choose? Whatever happened to *no cruel and unusual punishment*? What could be more cruel and unusual than telling someone you were going to kill them? And then *offering them a choice* of which horrifying way they would be put to death?

Kelly's eyes went back to pleading with the judge as she pondered these thoughts, and as she did, a few of his words slipped in through the haze:

". . . nothing more to be said. And so, *as* I said, I am ruling to admit the Cannecare evidence."

'Oh God no.'

"The trial will get started immediately."

'Oh God, oh God, oh God . . .'

She eyed the judge.

"And so, this hearing is hereby aaaadddjjjou—"

'God . . .'

"Yes," came a loud voice from the door.

Kelly flinched. '*God* sounds like Bernard?'

"You?" Judge Merlson blurted out, and it was more an accusation than a question. Bernard stood at the door with a bailiff.

"Correct. Bernard Walker. And I am here to prove the Cannecare evidence *was* faked."

"Oh, nonsense. We've already heard from *these kids*. And we've wasted more of this court's time than we should have. I was just adjourning this—"

"Give me sixty seconds, *just* sixty seconds. I was just *un-reasonably* delayed by your *tedious* security personnel out there, whom, I must complain, were entirely rude. But in sixty seconds, I can prove completely that the Cannecare evidence *was* faked. Sixty measly seconds."

Blankly examining the texture of his desk, Judge Merlson remembered how his law professors had told him there would be days like this. He also remembered their advice: (1) Don't get angry, and (2) give everyone the benefit of a doubt, however painful.

Fire already raging in his brain, there was no adhering to the first half, but to the second half . . .

"Sixty seconds then, Mr. Walker. Please step forward."

Bernard's stare fell onto Hazly's as he walked—renewed challenge from both sides.

"I mean it, sixty seconds."

"That shall be more than sufficient," Bernard promised, and went on to waste a good five seconds, head held high, staring Hazly straight in the eye.

Then he stepped to the laptop on the counter and moved the progress bar back halfway, to show Kelly walking on Second Avenue.

"I promise you, that cartoon will get you nowhere," Judge Merlson warned.

Bernard ignored him, turned to Lester instead, and pleaded, with frustration, "I told you: It's in the clouds. *What color* are the clouds?"

"Gray," Les answered.

"Yes, gray. But not *dark*, correct?"

Lester studied the screen. "Yeah."

"And do you see any rain?"

"No."

"But notice Kelly's eye makeup! It's smeared on both cheeks."

"Bernard," Kelly shouted. "Now is *not* the time to talk about eye makeup. Damn it!"

"I am merely pointing out that your eye makeup is *smeared*, and yet it is not raining."

"What are you talking about?" Kelly asked.

"And you don't cry—you've mentioned that, what, how many times now?"

"Bernard, this is a video game. That's the way Chen made the caricature."

Bernard turned to Les. "But that's the clue. It was sitting there in front of you *every time* you looked at the Kelly avatar."

"Mr. Walker," the judge commanded, "what *is* this all about?"

"It happens to be about clouds, your honor, clouds and rain—or the lack thereof."

Fumbling about his vest pockets in search of a Twinkie—a nervous habit—Bernard remembered how poorly Hostess treats had gone over with the judge the last time, and so he forced himself to behave. Though not without wondering briefly if it'd be OK to have a Twinkie if he offered one to the judge, too.

But instead he walked over to Hazly's giant screen, where the video segment was frozen on the image of Kelly in the Cannecare lobby. Now he was pointing at video, not cartoon modeling.

"Look," he declared, "smeared makeup in the Cannecare video, too."

Kelly looked. Thought about it. Looked again.

"Oh my God!" she shouted, suddenly elated, her normally subdued New York accent completely uncontrolled. "You're right. My eye makeup is running. Oh my God, how wonderful! My makeup is smeared! Check it out," she urged Kendeff, "it's running right onto my cheek."

"Your honor," the prosecutor interrupted, "this has no bearing. I fail to see—"

"No?" Bernard said. "How do I control this?"

One of Hazly's team weakly held out a tablet.

Bernard grabbed it, studied the screen briefly, then reversed the video until Kelly was back out on the sidewalk in front of Cannecare Tower.

"And this is the Cannecare video, not animation. There, see?" Bernard said, eyeing Hazly, then the judge. "No rain.

And look closely at Miss Chambers' eyes. *No* smeared makeup when she's out on the sidewalk."

"Your honor—" the prosecutor tried to interrupt.

"Now look again." Bernard forwarded the video to the lobby. "As soon as she's inside, she has smeared eye makeup."

"Yes!" Kelly shouted in the background.

"So, she started crying!" Hazly shot out. "She was on her way to murder the man she had been having an affair with. I *don't* think it would be unnatural for her to be crying under those circumstances."

"I do *not* cry!" Kelly insisted.

"So you say!"

"Please!" the judge interrupted.

Bernard raised his voice above everyone's. "It so happens it does not matter if she cries or not. That's the beauty of all this wonderful data. Watch!"

"What the hell do you mean?" Hazly asked.

Bernard reversed the video back to the street.

"The video now shows Kelly as shot from cameras outside. No rain, no smeared makeup. And, ooh, here we go, right here: The very second she turns into the building, she's picked up by the cameras inside. And watch: *Suddenly* her makeup is smeared, *already* smeared."

Reversing the video again, he repeated his findings: "Look, no smeared makeup." And forwarding again: "Look: smeared! Suddenly, out of nowhere."

Merlson thought about makeup, recalled for some reason how his mother disapproved of it, never wore it, viewed it as a sign of loose morals. Now he was beginning to dislike it as well.

Bernard continued. "As you see, the smeared makeup appears *out of nowhere*—suddenly, not gradually, as makeup typically smears, and at no point do we see Kelly Chambers cry. At no point do we see tears."

Hazly stared at the screen for a good thirty seconds before responding.

When he did, his voice was nervous, defensive. "Your honor, I'll look into this and find an explanation. But this really means nothing. It proves nothing."

The judge appeared totally confused, leaving Bernard to continue. A broad smile grew across his face as he eyed Hazly and prepared to imitate TV shopping commercials: "But wait, there's more!"

He reversed the video back onto the sidewalk.

"Look again. Light gray clouds, no rain, correct?" He forwarded back to the lobby. "But look at the glass doors behind Kelly now."

Everyone studied the video. The glass doors were spattered, lightly so but spattered, with what appeared to be rain.

"Raindrops. Inside, suddenly, the cameras show rain.

"And notice the clouds. They are much darker suddenly when shot from *inside* the lobby. And that happens to be *clear*, not *tinted*, glass. And so it is beyond doubt that the video footage of Kelly crossing the lobby is from some other time than the video of Kelly out on the sidewalk. That is an obvious sign that the overall segments *have* been doctored."

"That's a lie," Hazly protested, but his intent stare at the screen made the assertion seem a pretty void statement.

The judge looked on, his head wobbling back and forth, really wishing society could go back to a simpler day, a day when there weren't sensors and video and smart buildings, a day when there weren't people like this making justice really, really . . . *murky*.

The exalted technology that promised to make justice so black and white was now making it more of a mud-brown, the color of a slushy Seattle sidewalk half a day into a snow melt.

Kelly turned to face Kendeff, her nose set less than an inch from his.

"Yeah," she growled, "you and I *are* going to have a talk later this afternoon; you can count on that."

Guo Shangzhen awoke early Saturday morning with big plans for the day. He'd learned of a lake about two hours north of Beijing that was said to have great fishing, but was not so widely known. And after working long days (and nights) through the previous weekend, he was looking forward to some time off.

So it was with a great deal of disappointment that he read the email from Chen Li, his boss.

Sitting by the computer in their bedroom, he turned to his wife, who still lay in bed.

"Aiyou! You laile. You yao jiaban. (Oh no! Here we go again. Got to work overtime again.)"

And again it had something to do with this murder modeling the Americans wanted.

Guo rose to his feet, thinking about long days (and nights) at the office, thinking about driving far away from the city, thinking about fish.

"Aiyou!" he complained.

17

Back at the Pendrite Kelly waited in the lobby with O'Brian and the officer assigned to her, and as soon as the others entered she rushed forward.

"Bernard," she called out. "I owe you big." Her voice sounded grateful, emotional, though somehow flat.

"Forget it. I was glad—"

"I'm not *forgettin'* anything," she said as she lurched forward.

Now, Kelly stood about five-eight, a good six inches shorter than Bernard, and weighed about a hundred pounds less. But her thin body lit into him like it was shot out of a cannon.

She smashed him back against the inner lobby door, causing a thud that was felt as well as heard, then threw a hard underhand punch to the lower stomach, forcing a pained grunt.

"What the *hell* did you think you were doing? You *knew* all the time and you didn't tell us? You jackass!"

"I . . . I . . ."

The police officer moved to intervene, but O'Brian stopped him.

"It's all right. Let her go," he said with a smile just light enough to make the reluctant officer agree.

"Do you have any idea how damn scared I was? And you knew all the time?"

"I . . ."

"Don't *I* me, you *jerk*. We were up day and night running through your stupid modeling. And you knew."

"I am sorry, but I had to see whether Lester would figure it out. Didn't you see my text?"

"Well, he *didn't* figure it out! So I went in there today wondering whether it would be better to be hanged or shot by a firing squad."

"I am quite certain they no longer have firing squads. I believe many states now use lethal injection. It is much more humane. Besides, didn't you see my text?"

"You want to talk lethal injection?" Kelly asked as she again pounded him in the belly. "There's a lethal injection for you."

Bernard nearly doubled over. "Isn't anyone going to help?"

"Not me," Patricia said.

Bernard pleaded. "Let me explain."

Kelly stepped back. "OK, go ahead. This I'd like to hear."

"Let's go sit down somewhere."

"No. Talk, or brace for another lethal injection."

"It happens to be personal."

"I promise you my next lethal injection will be *quite* personal. Possibly about ten-inches-lower more personal."

Bernard eyed Kelly, then the design team on one side, and O'Brian and the officer on the other.

"Go ahead. Explain. You were playing in that stupid tournament, right?"

"But . . ."

"But what?"

Bernard spoke without looking up. "I . . . I . . ."

"What?"

"I was losing."

"You were *what*?"

"I . . . I am a three-time world champion. And I was losing." He eyed her squarely. Clearly he felt this predicament explained his behavior, would explain any behavior.

Kelly relaxed and recomposed herself somewhat. "Listen, Bernard, I'm grateful, very grateful for your help. But do you have any idea how much agony you caused me?"

"Didn't you see my texts?"

"Oh, your stupid texts to Lester about the rain and the clouds, huh? Big goddamn help they were."

"But the texts I sent *you* . . ."

"What?"

"The texts I sent you."

"You didn't send *me* any texts."

"I did too. Check your phone."

"My phone?"

"Yes, the phone Patricia bought you."

"The what?"

"*Check your phone*," Bernard said.

Kelly reached into her pocket and pulled the device out, handling it as if it were known to bite. She examined the screen, confused. "Text?" she asked. "I've hardly used this since Patricia gave it to me. I'm a BlackBerry person—or at least I was back when BlackBerry people ruled."

Bernard edged over and from as far a distance as possible, gingerly stuck out a finger and pointed to the messaging icon. At the top was a little red circle with the number 3 in it.

Kelly squinted, eyed Bernard, then tapped the screen to read what was billed as the oldest of three text messages:

> I found two obvious holes. In the Cannecare lobby your makeup is smeared, but there is no rain. Also see the raindrops on the lobby windows. Tell Lester if he doesn't figure it out.

The newest read:

> Can't talk now, Paris being eaten by Zombies (French cuisine!). Funny thing is, Chen was trying to make funny caricatures, like we told him. It was Chen's creativity with the running makeup that showed me where to look.

🐾 🐾 🐾

At the hearing, Judge Merlson had sat in silence for a good two minutes while everyone stared, wondering what he would rule. But it wasn't so much the evidence or the testimony he was thinking about.

What he was thinking about was a Mark Twain novel called *Pudd'nhead Wilson*. The book tells the story of a lawyer who everyone thinks of as a "pudd'nhead," partly because of his odd hobby of studying fingerprints.

Ah, to be a judge in the 1890s, how much better that would be. There wouldn't be all this, this . . . *technology* messing up trials. There wouldn't be technological evidence that supposedly *couldn't* be faked. There wouldn't be video games that somehow proved it *could be, was* faked. The hardest thing a judge might have to deal with would be deciding whether or not *fingerprints* proved anything.

Yes, that would be a much-better time to be a judge.

But after two minutes of reflecting on this idyllic picture, he rejoined the twenty-first century and he was not a happy judge.

He ordered Hazly to get the full data sets to Bernard by the end of the day, and he told both sides to return on Monday morning ready to show conclusively whether the Cannecare segments were real or not.

And he told the prosecution that if they were not shown to be trustworthy, the entire case would be thrown out and Kelly Chambers would be set free.

🐦 🐦 🐦

"I think I just found maps of the sensors, floor by floor," Bernard told Lester.

The data sets arrived about seven p.m., and the group was trying to make sense of them.

"It appears each one is identified by a floor number . . . and I believe the letters refer to the sensor type. See, A is for audio, T is for temperature . . ."

"That makes sense."

"So what we need to do is go through the databases and find the sensor ID numbers."

"But we still don't have the content-management system they used to make sense of all this."

"No, but we have our game. Send orders off to Beijing. Get them to put identifiers on all the sensors in our modeling. Next, have them run the Kelly avatar through the modeling at the same pace she does in the video. Then they can plug in the sensor data and see if or how much it matches."

"I think I get it. That should work."

"I fully believe it will. Get Chen to go online so he can explain everything. In the meantime, I plan to take the Cannecare video and study it some more."

"Got it. What about your tournament?"

"And I suppose you have never been forced to multitask."

"You're really losing?"

"Yes, I am."

"How?"

"I don't know. This guy—or girl—is . . . different, the way he plays. He does things he shouldn't, and somehow it winds up helping. Now I can't even find him."

"Ooh."

"And that is why I needed space, why I needed to be uninterrupted. If I did not have the luxury of being in my studio back home, I could at least be cut off from the world."

"Where'd you go, anyhow?"

"Don't ask."

"Where?"

"Oh . . . I checked into a motel near the airport."

"Whoa, dude! Here we have a whole floor of suites that go for several hundred bucks a night, and you were staying in a forty-dollar-per-night motel?"

"Suites and Kelly and murder investigations. And Patricia the practical joker. No. A dedicated gamer *must* make sacrifices. And it wasn't so bad, actually. Nearby was a Taco Bell, a Subway, a Jack in the Box, a Denny's . . . oh, and a reasonably decent pizza place that delivered. I had to advise them on how much tomato sauce to use, but otherwise, not bad."

"Oh, well, there it is, then."

"Anyhow, we need to get orders to Beijing immediately. We have until Monday morning. Our time."

"Yeah. I feel a lot better, though. I was pretty worried."

"You were not thinking."

"Yeah . . . I'm *still* worried, though. There's one thing we've been overlooking."

"And just what is that?"

"Well, all this time our focus has been on proving Kelly did not commit the murder."

"And?"

"Well, there's still a murderer out there, one that could kill again."

"That, I am afraid, is *not* our problem. We came here to help Kelly, which we have done, and as soon as we get her out on Monday, I, for one, plan to disappear, so that I can concentrate on the tournament."

🎮 🎮 🎮

The brick-and-mortar Evil Iberian watched the YouTube video of the previous night's gameplay with a wide, wide smile.

OffCide Gamer had taken most of Europe, all the good parts, anyway.

He thought he was winning, though clearly he was scared.

He was scared because no one had risen to challenge him, and that was unexpected.

He found himself sitting securely, with armies holding the Iberian and Italian peninsulas, as well as Greece and other spots where an invasion could be launched.

Oh, sure, there were some small players who could give him trouble, but with their small armies they would be minor irritations at best.

Like Joe the Muscovite in Russia and The Terracotta Terror in China.

And as soon as OffCide Gamer signed off for an apparent break, the Iberian went into action. Suddenly the small players in Russia and China joined to become one, and their names changed to Evil Iberian.

And as they traveled westward toward Europe, numerous other small players joined them: the Huns, the Vandals, the Ostrogoths . . .

And in no time at all, massive armies of barbarian zombies were piling up on Eastern Europe's doorstep, ready to invade.

And when the OffCide guy signed back on, a big surprise awaited him.

And later, when OffCide signed off, he would do so knowing that this year he might not be the world champion.

Yeah, this was a video clip worth saving, one worth streaming online, as well.

🎮 🎮 🎮

The weekend that followed was as weird for Kelly as the previous one, her being the only person with nothing to do—but a main difference now being the huge smile that simply refused to leave her face.

Bernard disappeared much earlier than Monday, was in fact not seen beyond dinner Friday evening. O'Brian, meanwhile, spent most of Saturday and Sunday at the police station talking with detectives whose interest in investigating the case had suddenly grown quite strong.

And the design team remained absorbed in sorting through the sensor data, so the China team could create a content-management system of sorts, to illustrate what all the data meant.

This left Kelly to wander the hallway, going back and forth between her suite and suite 2202, where she would run the Cannecare video sequences—over and over. She particularly enjoyed the part that showed the sequences had been doctored.

🐾 🐾 🐾

Herbert Iggid sat on the balcony of his 700-square-foot suite, complete with gas fireplace, pine furnishings, and minibar, and smiled at the view of Elliot Bay and the Olympic Mountains that "no other hotel in Seattle afforded," or so a Web page he found on his phone attested.

Unable to tolerate any longer the dinky room he was given at the Pendrite, Herbert had checked out and upgraded. If his low-level employees—that girl looked fresh out of high school—were staying in expensive suites, the company's chief financial officer would surely not be accommodated in a dark, musty dump of a room on the second floor of a hotel with a rude desk clerk.

A little angry (and a little jealous) over the liberal spending of company money, Herbert searched on his iPhone for Seattle hotels with a view—oh, what a wonder it was to be able to search for hotels *right on your phone*—and he learned of . . . of . . . this wonderful establishment.

With the evening air of the bay now all around him on the balcony, he reread the introduction he'd found on his phone:

> Built along with the Space Needle in 1962 for the World's Fair, the Edgewater Inn has become a landmark of the city and the bay. Standing actually over the water at Pier 67, it boasts a Pacific Northwest resort-like experience with unequaled views of . . .

At first, Herbert cringed at the thought of such extravagant spending. He was a man of principle, after all. How could he attack his CEO and staff for burning through money if he, too, were staying in a luxury suite?

> Situated a short walk from the Space Needle, Pike Place Market, and Olympic Sculpture Park, the hotel is perfect for explorers, not to mention museumgoers, shoppers, diners, students . . .

But the gorgeous suites shown in photos on the Edgewater's website were just too alluring. More and more Herbert pictured himself relaxing in one of those gorgeous rooms, and the more he thought about Bernard and the others in the Pendrite suites, the more he pictured himself as a victim in this whole mess, an innocent player who had been wronged and yet who still trudged forth loyally to save the day for the company . . .

Yes, he was a person for whom perhaps a little extra comfort was warranted.

And so it was that he now sat watching the sun set and checking again the bank app to see how much new trouble Bernard and the others were in. He smiled as he imagined presenting a report to the board. Maybe he'd be named to replace Bernard as CEO, and he would put the company back together and make it run properly, the way companies were meant to be run.

And, and this was a little naughty, Herbert also took pleasure in knowing that he'd managed to find far greater luxury than Bernard Walker had.

🐾 🐾 🐾

One floor up, one balcony over.

Yes, this was the way to get one's mind off murder investigations, condemned friends, and pesky employees, Bernard figured.

A view.

This was the way to get one's brain in proper condition for a video game tournament.

This was why Bernard had bought his oceanfront home-studio in Cliff Shores: It had a breathtaking view of water, beach, and cliff in three directions, and green hills behind. It was a place where he could truly relax, truly get his mind off irritating matters of business. It was the open space where his vision could find contrast to the constant staring at screens.

Lester was right: Bernard should not be staying at a motel while everyone else was enjoying expensive luxury suites twenty stories up at the Pendrite.

And now he sat on his suite's balcony, comparing the real-life view to famous photos on his laptop showing the Beatles fishing out the Edgewater's windows.

> It has been said that these 1964 photos of the Beatles fishing out their windows helped save the Edgewater, which was slated to be closed . . .

Ah, now this was a hotel, and it would be one worth owning. Tate had fallen in love with and bought the horrible Stanley dump. But this was the sort of hotel Bernard would buy if his company needed . . .

Yes, this would be the perfect hotel for OffCide Studios, Bernard figured. Guests would fish out their windows, and . . . and . . . they could earn bonus points for a future stay based on the number of fish they caught. And of course when they caught something worth eating, the hotel would pick it up, clean it, and cook it in any way they liked.

On the laptop next to him, he eyed mobs of zombies descending on North Germania. Yes, Bernard was in a much-better mood now for *Woeful WasteWorld*.

🎮 🎮 🎮

Sunday night.

Kelly sat next to two other women clad in orange prison jumpsuits in some sort of waiting room.

The one with her head shaved would sit in silence for a spell, then suddenly burst out laughing, then threaten to kill Kelly and the other woman, then fall back into silence. Kelly wasn't sure what she was doing here.

A guard walked by, as one did every so often, and Kelly asked when she would be able to go home. But each time the guards ignored her, causing the woman with the buzzcut to burst out laughing.

"I get to go home," Kelly pleaded. "Really, I do. There are holes. We found holes."

"I'll kill you, I *am going to* kill you!" the crazy woman shouted.

Kelly wanted to run, but they were in this room; there was nowhere to go. And she couldn't stand; she was stuck on this bench, stuck to wait . . .

When a feeling of relief settled in at the sound of a text alert. Kelly rolled over, found her phone under one of the pillows.

'Wow, what an awful dream,' she thought.

She picked up the phone and saw a message from Les:

> We did it. We found holes. Lots and lots and lots. I'll contact Bernard.

18

"So let me get this straight, Pudd'nhead. You say there are *holes* in the evidence?"

"That is correct," Bernard answered, not knowing why the judge kept calling him . . . *Pudd'nhead*? "We have identified numerous holes in both the sensor data and the video."

"OK, let's start with the, uh, sensor data."

"Our China head, Chen Li, will explain. Go ahead."

"Yes, go ahead, Mr. Li."

"Um . . . Chen."

"What's that, Mr. Li?"

"My name's not Mr. Li."

"Mr. Walker just said your name was Li."

"Yes, but my family name is Chen."

"But he . . . oh, never mind." Frustration was clear on Judge Merlson's face. "OK, tell me, what are these holes?"

"They are just . . . a database . . . a group of databases. And then they have readings from many hundreds of sensors. And then each sensor takes a reading each second. The result is the databases each minute collect tens of thousands of readings."

"Sorry I asked."

"I can show you." Chen walked to the laptop Lester set up on the outer bench and turned it to face the judge. "This animation is the hallway on the top floor of the Cannecare building. There are audio sensors in the wall every two feet." He pushed a button and red lights appeared to show the sensors' locations.

"Now," Chen continued, "when Miss Chambers walks down the hall, as we see here, the sensors indicate a person with her size and weight, and wearing sneakers like hers, is walking down the hall."

"OK . . ."

Trying to explain this was hard enough on its own; explaining it in English was even harder. Chen pointed to a sensor in the middle.

"Na, when Kelly Chambers walks by this sensor, it reads nine—that is on a scale from one to ten. Then the three sensors before and the three after, they also pick up her sound. But the sound is farther, so it is not so loud. The readings are lower. This one reads eight and this one reads six."

"So?"

"For Cannecare's data, only three sensors in each direction hear her sound. But when other people walk down this hall, five or six sensors in each direction record sound."

The judge appeared confused. "And this data you're using came from the Cannecare sensors?"

"Yes."

"And you are using it with your . . . cartoons here."

"Yes."

Bernard jumped in to help. "Whoever doctored these started with video of Kelly Chambers and then added or changed sensor data to match it."

Merlson at this point defined sourness with his eyes alone. "And?"

"Well, the person was lazy. At times, he or she changed only a few numbers in the database to show Kelly Chambers walking down a hall. If she had really walked down the hall at this time, more sensors would have picked her up. We found similar holes throughout the data sets that Cannecare provided."

Merlson squinted further sourness.

"And there are other problems." Bernard pulled up another window. "This is the Cannecare video. Here we see Kelly exiting the Stanley, supposedly on her way to murder Randolph Tate. When we see her from cameras in the Stanley's lobby, we see a bus outside in the middle of the block. See? And the audio sensors do record a bus passing by."

"Uh-huh . . ."

"But the second Kelly arrives on the sidewalk, the second she goes out into the outside cameras' view, there is no bus. Somehow the bus just bleeped out of existence, according to both the video and the audio sensors."

"Uh-huh . . ." How nice it would be to be a legal official in a world where things did not *bleep in and out of existence.*

Judge Merlson turned to the prosecutor. "And you went over all of this?"

"Yes, your honor."

"And Mr. Hazly?"

"Uh, Mr. Hazly declined to participate. But we brought in . . . outside experts."

"Experts *you hired* to testify?"

". . . Experts we paid, yes."

"And what is their opinion of the evidence now?"

"Uh, they . . . uh . . ."

"Yes?"

"They said there is no question."

"They said there is no question of *what*?"

"They said there is no question that the evidence was heavily doctored . . . that it . . . cannot be trusted."

". . . And, so, two weeks down the line, we have learned *what* about Randolph Tate's killing? You've pursued first-degree murder charges against a woman based on doctored evidence that someone handed you on a silver platter. I have to tell you," the judge said, still talking to the prosecutor but scanning all the faces in the room, "the amount of trouble you have caused a possibly innocent woman, and this court, and everyone involved, it is a . . . a crime."

His gaze rested at last on Bernard, as, somehow, people's gazes tended to.

Bernard took that as a cue to respond:

"Tell me about it," he complained, thrusting out his chest, and torso also in the process. "I just lost all of Croatia to mutant fanged farm animals. That *would not* have occurred if

I had *not* been forced to spend the better part of the weekend examining this stupid data."

Life in the arraignment court stood still and silent for a good thirty seconds after he said this, before Judge Merlson lurched his upper body forward and shouted, yet somehow in a whisper: "Pudd'nhead!"

It was an accusation, not an address.

"Pardon me?" Bernard asked, his hands nervously seeking out pockets that might hold a snack.

"Pudd'nhead!"

🐾 🐾 🐾

A dark figure sat before the Cannecare Video Wall—a dark room, dark thoughts. How had they done it? Worse, how much trouble had Walker and the others caused? And how much money was it all going to cost?

A window playing cable TV news in the center of the wall shed a dim light across the room, and its reports made that shine ever gloomier.

> . . . after determining the evidence had been doctored. In addition, all charges against Kelly Chambers were dropped, ending her house arrest.

> Meanwhile, police are reopening the investigation and returning to Cannecare Tower to search for more evidence, and to again question employees.

> And in a bizarre twist, rumors have it the police may be hiring the consultants who helped Chambers, to help *them* find Tate's murderer. We return now to—

A mouse click silenced and darkened the room.

Things were definitely not going as planned, not at all. The case against Kelly Chambers should have been open and shut, leaving her to grasp at appeals and try to delay as long as possible the inevitable—a last meal, a final walk.

But then those kids showed up. *Kids!* And they ruined the plan, using toys. Toys!

But a good master plan is one that has contingencies, can be adjusted to handle the unexpected; and, yes, can in fact convert an unpleasant turn of events to its advantage.

The figure hit a couple of buttons to pull up building schematics on the Video Wall, maps gleaming now an eerie blue light through the room and bringing a smile to the lips.

Those kids made Cannecare technology look bad and look bad in public.

But soon, very soon, they would gain a definite, even grave, respect for it. Yes, they would learn a whole new regard for Cannecare technology if it was the last thing they ever did.

Heh-heh, which in fact it might well be.

Level 2
The Tower

1

Kelly.

Kelly Chambers emerged from her room atop the prominent Pendrite Hotel in downtown Seattle, revealing briefly behind her a plush luxury suite that had served as a drab dungeon, a closed-in habitat which, along with the ankle bracelet that guarded her house arrest, had grown nearly as oppressive as the cell she was locked up in briefly at the King County Jail.

Kelly was a talented business executive, had never been in trouble, had succeeded in nearly everything she'd done. Then out of the clear gray Seattle sky she found herself arrested for murder, framed with evidence so technologically clad that ten million dollars' bail and a fake video game was all that stood between Kelly and Death Row.

Then the video game, played by the impossible Bernard Walker who built it, up and tilted Death Row like it was a tawdry pinball machine, one built with shoddy bells, limp bumpers, and a broken score reel.

Flash—Kelly was free now, could go where she would, and did, into a waiting elevator and down to the lobby, where she slipped unseen out a side entrance to a bright Seattle afternoon and—and this was novel—a clear blue sky.

🎮 🎮 🎮

Bernard.

Bernard Walker finally was packing his bags.

He'd been dragged against his will to Seattle to help Kelly. He then was followed by an exodus of employees running from the eternal egghead named CFO Herbert Iggid, and finally even by Iggid himself. Escape became impossible, and the situation continued to blow more and more out of control.

Kelly was charged with murder, the prosecution was seeking capital punishment, bail was set at *ten million dollars*, and Bernard found himself working with an incompetent lawyer and paying for an entire floor of luxury suites at the Pendrite.

Then came the start of an epic video game tournament, and unable to concentrate, he was losing.

But no more. Bernard proved the "evidence" produced by Cannecare Automation's "revolutionary" technology had been faked, that Kelly had been framed. The case was thrown out of court, even if the judge hearing it had left a bitter image in their minds. Yes, Bernard's work here was done.

Now, as quickly as a taxi could drive him to Sea-Tac Airport, as quickly as a plane could fly him down the coast, Bernard was heading to his oceanfront studio south of San Francisco, where he would hide from the world and focus on his tournament.

Bernard Walker was the three-time world champion of *Woeful WasteWorld*; he had no intention of losing this year.

🎮 🎮 🎮

Kelly.

Freed from house arrest Kelly's first impulse was to go shopping, and the first thing she bought was a pair of capris—dark jeans that stretched down just past her knees.

The second was a pair of sandals that in no way obstructed the view of her ankles.

Kelly Chambers had never been crazy about her legs; they'd always seemed kind of bony at the knees and curvy at the ankles; but today they were the most beautiful sight she could imagine, and she was prominently displaying, nearly *modeling*, to the entire world, her *bare*, bare ankles, sans clothing, sans socks, and—and this was the big one—*sans ankle bracelet*.

Yes, the sky was blue and the sun was shining as Kelly Chambers paraded down Third Avenue bearing a smile bigger even than that first spring grin that Seattleites collectively take on when the sky finally clears after a long winter's drizzle.

In fact her mood was infectious. She caught the eye of every man, and many of the women, she passed, and most of those onlookers wound up a tad happier themselves as a result.

Finally Kelly stopped at a tavern she knew of just up the street from Pike Place Market and took a seat at the bar. Moments later she was sipping a glass of Chardonnay when the five o'clock news appeared on a TV above the bar.

> In the latest twist to the bizarre murder of Randolph Tate, the case against Cannecare's CEO, Kelly Chambers, was thrown out of court today, and Chambers, who had been under house arrest in an area hotel since the murder, was released.

Kelly lifted her glass and toasted the woman, a blonde with a face and smile so perfectly shaped that she appeared computer-generated.

> To recap, Tate hired Chambers to replace him as CEO of Cannecare Automation, so he could focus on the company's technology. The two of them then allegedly became romantically involved, which police believed was a likely motive for his murder.

> The judge hearing the case, though, dismissed it today after it was established that the damning video evidence against Chambers was doctored.

> Police are reopening their investigation and have raided Cannecare's headquarters, where the murder was committed, in search of new evidence.

The bartender was also watching at this point. He turned to Kelly. "I can't believe they let that woman go. You just look at her, you can tell she did it."

"Yeah?" Kelly asked with a grin, sipping.

"Sure. You can tell when someone's lying about something *that big*. They can't hide it in their faces, you know?"

"Is that right?"

"Yeah, it is. I can spot lies when I see 'em. It comes with the job."

"Really?" She drained her glass.

"Yep," he said, for the first time actually focusing on Kelly's face.

"Well, then, I guess you'd better be real fast in getting me another glass of Chardonnay," Kelly informed him, just as the poor guy realized the supposedly very dangerous woman he'd been talking *about* was also the woman he was talking *to*.

Kelly's grin grew as the bartender grabbed her glass and moved readily away.

'Yeah, Kelly Chambers is *back*,' she said to herself. 'And now, ladies and gentlemen, Kelly Chambers is going to *get* the crumb who killed Randolph Tate.'

Herbert Iggid spent a wonderful afternoon at the Seattle Art Museum, but he was beginning to feel pangs of guilt over all the sightseeing when he should have been keeping his eye on Bernard. And Ron O'Brian.

As chief financial officer of Bernard's video game company, OffCide Studios, and also O'Brian's investigations firm, Herb had a responsibility to ensure they spent company funds wisely, and currently both firms were being taken to the cleaners.

Bernard and O'Brian had rented an entire floor at a luxury hotel and with their "team" were running up room service bills that made their five-hundred-dollar-a-night rooms appear reasonable.

A thought that again brought on pangs of guilt, since Herb too decided to stay in an expensive hotel.

So before dinner, he sat in his suite and surveyed his own expenses, then took out pen and paper and made a list of all the expenses Bernard and the others had racked up.

O'Brian said they were working on a test case for SimCide, his investigations firm. But clearly they were going well beyond what would be considered reasonable spending for a test case, and certainly too much OffCide Studios manpower was being used.

What was more, as far as Herbert was concerned, any association with Kelly Chambers was bad for both companies; both stood to take a serious public relations hit when the woman was found guilty, as she surely would be.

Ah, what he would tell the directors: "Both Walker and O'Brian," he would say, "have misappropriated company funds for personal use, and that to help a ruthless murderer."

In a better mood, Herb picked up the phone, dialed room service, and ordered a steak and a bottle of champagne.

Then turned on the five o'clock news.

> . . . today, after consultants for the defense proved the evidence had been doctored, and with all charges dropped, Kelly Chambers was released. We go to our correspondent Nancy Cain in front of the King County Courthouse. Nancy?
>
> Yes, Jenna, there were some big surprises today. It turns out the consultants for Chambers' defense team created—believe it or not—a video game using sensor data from Cannecare Tower, where Randolph Tate was murdered. They used that and video of the game to help prove that the original evidence, a combination of video and security data, had in fact been faked.
>
> So what happens now, Nancy?

Well, it's back to the drawing board for police, who are reopening their investigation. A police spokesman told me earlier that detectives were heading back to Cannecare Tower in search of new evidence.

Do they have any leads?

The spokesman I talked to said, yes, they certainly do, Jenna. He said the faked evidence itself would likely lead them to the killer. And that's where the story gets even more bizarre.

How's that?

Well, the consultants who built the video game around the murder, it turns out that they have been hired by the Seattle Police Department to help sort through the faked evi—

Herbert muted the TV. He muted it because he couldn't believe what he was hearing. He muted it also because he wanted to very quickly call and cancel the expensive room service order he'd just placed.

🎮 🎮 🎮

Back at the Pendrite, O'Brian was waiting by the elevator for Kelly and the others with plans for an evening on the town—his treat.

His test case had not only succeeded, had not only proved the technology, had not only gotten Kelly released; it also earned him his company's first client.

To celebrate, O'Brian was taking the entire group out for dinner.

The game design team—Lester, Eric, Patricia, and Chen Li, their China head—showed up first and chatted for a few minutes, mostly about the sickly look on the judge's face, before Kelly joined them.

"How was your walk?" O'Brian asked as she approached.

"Nice. The first exercise I've had in weeks. Hey, I heard you're working for the police."

"Yeah, isn't that great? Our test case goes on. Paid."

"Yeah, well, listen: I'm in, too. Consider me a volunteer."

"Generally the police are not crazy about suspects, exonerated or otherwise, working on murder investigations."

"Yeah, well, generally I'm not crazy about people murdering my friends, or framing me for a capital crime. This crumb, whoever it is, is going down."

O'Brian frowned. "Better you're on my side, at least. But it's Bernard we're going to need most, with all the data and other stuff we have to deal with."

A door opened down the hall and the group watched as an oversize shape—Bernard—emerged, laptop bags over both shoulders and pulling a suitcase behind, and waddled down the hall.

"And where is it you're going?" O'Brian asked as Bernard neared.

"San Francisco, as a matter of fact. Or more precisely, my studio in Cliff Shores."

O'Brian scowled. "There's still a murderer out there."

"I did not come to Seattle to find a murderer. I came to Seattle to help Kelly, a task that is fully well complete—and at great inconvenience to me, I might add. Do you realize that zombie Titans have retaken southern Greece? So, I am going to go *back* to my Cliff Shores studio to concentrate on my tournament. There's still a little time left. I have won three years in a row; I shall not let myself get further distracted."

O'Brian pressed: "Remember, as an investor, you stand to make a lot of money if SimCide is successful; and if we can find the killer quickly, we couldn't be off to a better start. This is our first client."

"I am sorry, but—"

"Remember that Hazly guy," Lester threw in. "If you're working for the police, you'll be able to give him all sorts of trouble."

"I have no further interest in Ned Hazly, and I have no further interest in this case. So it is decided: I will allow nothing further to distract me."

As quickly as he said this, as if on cue, a buzz rang out in the hallway. Nearly but not quite all at once, a text alert sounded on all their phones—an event curious enough by itself, spookier the way they each at varying speeds realized what had just happened.

Bernard was the first to move. He turned on his phone and read, silently, the text message that had just arrived.

When finished, he turned his gaze to Les, whose alarmed expression, as he stared at his own screen, confirmed he was reading the same text.

O'Brian then read his aloud:

> You were slick today, very slick. Now, leave Seattle immediately. All of you. By plane, by bus, or by hearse! Your choice. Leave or die!

It was ten a.m. in Beijing and Guo Shangzhen felt not the slightest guilt at sleeping late. He and his colleagues had been working long days, weekends included, and they were getting some time off to make up for it.

Chen Li had them building a strange video game where a woman kills an executive using, using . . .

Again Guo planned to go fishing, and this time he was going to play it smart. He wasn't even turning on a computer, lest someone somewhere had something more for him to do, like making interactive animations of people murdering one another with air conditioners.

He even went so far as to turn off his cellphone. Where he was going, reception would be spotty at best. No one would be expecting him to answer.

Guo got his fishing gear together along with a tall thermos of hot tea and a box lunch he'd bought the night before, and headed out.

In front of the building he found his colleague and fishing buddy waiting in a beat-up old car.

And he nearly sang as he climbed in: "Shouji guandiaole. Woman jintian shi qu diaoyu. (Cellphones shut off. Today we're going fishing.)"

Moments later the two of them were cruising down the road and they would travel a good two kilometers before Guo would realize the car was heading not to the lake but to the office.

🐟 🐟 🐟

"No one touch your phones," O'Brian commanded. "Don't do anything with them—don't touch the screens. Very carefully, bring them in here."

He unlocked Suite 2202 next to the elevator, walked in, and slid an arm across a dining table to clear space. "Carefully set your phones down here, every one of them. And, Bernard?"

"Yes?"

"Do you have another phone handy, one with a decent camera?"

"Of course." Bernard pulled one from a laptop bag.

"OK, I want a picture of every phone with the text messages that just arrived.

"And the police are going to want statements from every one of us. By the look of things, we're going to have to cater in for our celebration dinner tonight. Everyone stays here until the police say we can leave."

"Damn," Bernard said, handing the extra phone to Les and turning to leave.

"Where do you think you're going?" O'Brian asked.

Bernard shot back a resigned expression. "To return my suitcases to my suite, thank you."

"Sorry. We leave everything as is, and we all stay here—until the police tell us otherwise."

"Greece!" Bernard replied. "I used to control everything from England to Greece. And now mutant cows and pigs are taking over. Have you ever seen a mutant fanged pig eat a zombie?"

O'Brian took the extra phone from Lester and dialed 911. As he did he surveyed the room: the group of them crammed in close, stripped of their phones . . .

This wasn't going to be easy.

"Police," he said urgently into the phone.

🐾 🐾 🐾

Within thirty minutes the twenty-second floor of the Pendrite Hotel had transformed from a nearly empty hallway of suites into something more resembling Grand Central Station. Police were everywhere, inspecting, shooting pictures, and taking statements. Officers walked back and forth asking questions, testing windows, and discussing security.

The group remained in Suite 2202 where off to one side, Patricia, Chen, and Eric had taken over a sofa.

Patricia turned to Eric. "And to think, my mom insisted that studying computers and video games was just going to be boring."

"Think of poor Chen Li here," Eric said. "This is his first trip to the U.S."

Patricia smiled. "Yeah, Chen, so what do you think so far?"

"Just like America in the movies."

"I promise, it's not always like this."

"Yeah, sure."

Bernard walked over and slumped into an armchair. "I cannot believe they won't let me set up a laptop. I need to check my game."

The statement was met with silence. All four were suffering from device withdrawal.

O'Brian came over with an officer.

"This is Captain Bellows," he said. "The captain's going to explain our new security procedures."

"Security procedures?" Bernard asked.

"That's correct," the captain said. "We're taking this threat very seriously."

"The only security procedure I need is a ride to the airport."

"We want to keep you around at least until morning. We'll have more questions, and anyway, we don't consider this a safe situation yet."

"Listen to what he has to say," O'Brian insisted.

"First, we've secured the building entrance and this floor. We're going to station an officer in the hallway outside and one in the lobby, as well."

The group listened in silence. Kelly and Lester walked over to join them.

"I understand you booked the entire floor. I want all of you in three or four adjacent rooms. That way there'll be fewer doors for us to watch."

"Does it matter which rooms?" Lester asked.

"Yeah. Choose rooms on this side of the building, the south side. There are fewer tall buildings over here with proximity to the Pendrite."

"What's that mean?" Kelly asked.

"It means fewer places a person could, say, shoot from."

"You think someone's going to try to shoot us?" she asked.

"We don't think anything, so much as make sure every precaution is taken. Oh, and on that note, keep all curtains closed at all times. Make sure every window is covered, and stay away from them. Stay toward the center of any room."

"Wow, I sure feel safer now," Kelly moaned.

"You are safe. We've fully secured the building. That means we checked every room on every floor—not an easy task in a hotel this size, and not too good for the Pendrite's business, either. We also combed the building with bomb-sniffing dogs."

"Bomb-sniffing dogs?" Bernard cried in disbelief. "You really think this . . . person is going to turn to bombs?"

"It's very likely that whoever made this threat is the person who killed Randolph Tate. So we're taking every precaution."

Bernard lifted both eyebrows. "The dangers of an air conditioner murderer."

The detective shot Bernard an angry look, but the rest of the group, O'Brian included, smiled.

🐾 🐾 🐾

That night everyone except Bernard and O'Brian moved into a three-bedroom suite next to 2202, with the help of a couple of rollaway cots. Kelly roomed with Patricia, and Chen set up a cot in the living room.

But all that was pretty much in theory, since the death threat left them spooked, and they sat up together until close to three in the morning, watching movies and playing games.

Only O'Brian and Bernard opted for their own suites, the next two down as the police requested.

Bernard tried to spend time on his tournament, but was unable to concentrate despite the expensive noise-canceling headphones he put on to block out the world. And soon he found himself slipping in and out of slumber, his dreams mingling with fanged farm animals and possessed zombies.

Only O'Brian was able to go straight to sleep. Still, his sleep was far from deep. By instinct he remained close to awake, ready to hop into action should the need arise.

2

"We're not going anywhere," O'Brian told reporters gathered in front of the Pendrite. Many of them showed up early Tuesday morning; a few had spent the night in front, eager to get the early scoop.

"We're staying right here in Seattle until we find out who's behind all this. The police asked for our help, and this is exactly what SimCide Investigations was set up to do." Eric, Lester, and Patricia stood beside him looking equally determined.

"So the death threat doesn't worry you?" one reporter shouted.

"Of course it worries us. It's a death threat. But it's not going to scare us away. Rather the contrary: It's made us more resolute."

"You're not afraid?"

"No. We have excellent police protection, and this is our business. We wouldn't be very good at it if we got scared away every time there was danger."

"Have you taken extra security measures?"

"We have fully ample security. I cannot comment beyond that."

Bernard watched the impromptu press conference on a TV in the hotel lounge. He stood, a laptop bag over each shoulder and a suitcase by his side, next to a police officer who was assigned to drive him to the airport.

Bernard's plan was to head back to Cliff Shores, and the death threat served only to make him, as it had O'Brian, more resolute, just over a different task.

But seeing the crowd of reporters and O'Brian heading out to answer questions, he ducked into the lounge to avoid being seen himself.

Bernard figured he'd find a rear entrance, that's what he'd do. Sneak out the back and be done with Seattle and death threats and murderers.

"So whoever's behind the murder and the attempted framing of Kelly Chambers, that is one person who'd better be afraid," O'Brian stated. "Very afraid."

"How about your staff?" another reporter asked. "Are they scared after the death threat?"

The sight of Patricia, a twenty-year-old girl with short-cropped hair framing a baby face, said a lot as she stepped forward beside O'Brian.

"No. Not at all. There's a creep out there somewhere and we're going to *hunt him down.*"

"Damn, this is *not* making it easy to leave," Bernard mumbled.

"I just checked my phone," the officer said. "The freeway's clear all the way to the airport. You ready to go?"

Bernard glanced at the officer, then back at the TV.

At the press conference outside, he saw Kelly appear next to O'Brian, drawing a barrage of questions from reporters.

Kelly waited until the group quieted down before she began. "Listen, I first want to make a quick statement."

The reporters quieted, reluctantly, but they quieted.

"First, I want to thank Ron O'Brian and his team for proving the Cannecare evidence was faked."

That raised another round of shouted questions. Kelly held up a hand and waited until the noise subsided.

"Second . . . Second, I'm going to stay here with the SimCide team and help out. As Cannecare's CEO until very recently, I know the company and its technology."

More questions, including from a reporter who yelled to ask if Kelly was afraid.

"And third . . ." She waited for quiet. "Third, no, I am not afraid. Some crumb killed my friend, and I'm going to hunt him down like an animal. In fact he'd better hope the police find him before I do."

'Damn, damn, damn, damn . . .' Bernard said to himself. How could he take off now?

". . . felt great to be released," Kelly said. "What was that? Oh, well, the first thing I did was go shopping. After that I went to a tavern and had a cold glass of Chardonnay."

That won much of the group over.

"What? No, I haven't been in contact with either the board or senior management. No, I don't know what condition the company is— What? I believe that Ned Hazly is currently serving as interim CEO. But he's also a person of interest in the case, police say. So, no, it is not a great situation for the company currently."

"Did your attorney, Wilbur Kendeff, play a big role in getting you out?"

"If a nun jumped into traffic to save a baby, Wilbur Kendeff wouldn't be able to get her out of a jaywalking ticket."

That got a murmur.

"What about OffCide Studios CEO Bernard Walker? He's been playing a role in the case, right?"

"Yee-ah! Well, if he weren't, things . . . wouldn't be very good at the moment."

"Will he continue to help with the investigation?"

Kelly's head went down as she spoke: "I don't know."

"You ready to go, Mr. Walker?" the officer repeated.

"Yeesss . . . *damn* . . . it appears in fact that I am. Here, take care of these," he said, handing over the laptop bags and walking—reluctantly but not without a bit of show—toward the main door and the reporters beyond.

Just as it seemed the press conference had reached its logical conclusion, Bernard appeared behind Kelly, O'Brian, and the others.

"Excuse me, are you Bernard Walker?" a reporter asked.

"That is correct."

"And you also received the death threat text?"

"Yes, I guess I am among the privileged in this case."

"Are you going to help with the investigation?"

Bernard's eyes widened at the question as he turned briefly to Kelly, then to O'Brian.

"Yyyeeeaaahhh. It would appear in fact that I am." The frown that defined Bernard's face, embedded deep in the cheeks, could have served as inspiration for a Mayan statue, a medieval painting of suffering in hell, or a moaning Mississippi blues.

🎮 🎮 🎮

Hazly.

Ned Hazly sat before his kitchen TV fuming. He had slept only a few hours during the night, and even that was restless and troubled.

Ned Hazly became interim CEO of Cannecare Automation following the murder of Randolph Tate, whom he co-founded the company with. They were also best friends, at least until their argument over privacy and company products.

Hazly saw a day when Cannecare's technology could be used not only by transit departments and emergency responders but also by police and even the military. He also saw it as a tool companies could use to keep an eye on employees, just as law enforcement could use it to spy on people. He called his new applications Project X, a name no one but Ned understood.

All that was, however, too much for Randolph, whose immense intelligence suddenly shrank, as Ned saw it, when their company's true potential became clear.

In no time at all, Randolph convened the board of directors and drew up a "privacy policy" that prohibited such applications for Cannecare's technology.

Not that that stopped Ned from secret research, and with Tate dead and out of the way, the privacy policy no longer had any meaning.

Things were going pretty well, in fact, until . . .

Those kids. They had caused no end of trouble. Now, seeing them on the morning news speaking like celebrities in front of their hotel, it was more than Ned's sleepy mind could comprehend and accept.

And Chambers! The audacity of that woman, fresh out of house arrest and making threats. And shopping and drinking wine? Who the hell did she think she was?

Bringing Chambers into the company was the dumbest move Randolph had ever made, as far as Ned was concerned.

'This whole thing is *not* over with,' he said to himself, the thought directed at Chambers, and Walker, as well, on the TV before him. 'This is not done. Cannecare will prevail. You challenged Cannecare and our technology, and you're going to regret it.'

But no sooner had he completed the thought than the doorbell rang. He walked over, still in his bathrobe, and opened it to find several police officers outside.

"Mr. Ned Hazly?" one of them asked.

"What's this about? I just climbed out of bed. If this has something to do with the Tate murder, we can talk at my office. Along, I might add, with my attorney."

"You're Ned Hazly?"

"Of course. What's this about?"

"I'm afraid we need to take a look at your computers."

🐾 🐾 🐾

"OK, listen up." O'Brian found himself speaking to a team that seemed far more attentive than normal, and yet there was something in their enthusiasm that drew a red flag, as if to say maybe the group's typically sleepy detachment from reality might have had its advantages.

"This is where we're at: The police are going to concentrate on suspects who, A, had access to the Cannecare engineering center, and, B, had the technical skills to fake the video and sensor sequences. They're pretty sure that either something in the faked sequences or on the suspects' own computers may answer a lot of questions quickly. I think Bernard will agree."

"I personally would like to be one of the people searching those machines," Bernard said.

"Good, because the police want us to help with that. They have their own experts, but after delaying the case for two weeks based on faulty evidence, well . . . let's just say they're anxious to have us—*publicly*—working on the case alongside them. You and Lester go check out the computers, and leave the others here to continue going over the data sets."

Patricia countered: "But we've already proved the evidence was faked."

"Yes, but remember, you went over them asking only if the evidence was faked. So you need to go back over them, this time asking a different set of questions."

"Like who faked them?" Eric asked, again shocking everyone by his interest in something that did not take place on a hand-held device.

"Correct," O'Brian said.

Chen spoke up. "I want to go with Bernard and Lester. I have experience at locating evidence on employees' computers."

Bernard shot him a surprised glare. "You mean to say you check up on your employees?"

"No. But before my team joined OffCide, we had to hide things from our boss all the time. China's like that."

O'Brian smiled. "Ah! That is just the expertise we need."

"Anything for me to do?" Kelly asked, a once-stale question reopened.

And as had happened too often in the past two weeks when Kelly asked it, she was again met by a mass blank stare. But this time she was pleased by the lack of response.

"No? Good, 'cause I don't have an ankle bracelet anymore, and I'm gonna go do a little of my *own* investigating."

"Oh no. Just what is it you plan to do?" O'Brian asked.

"I figure I'll go visit a suspect or two myself."

"You'll do no such thing. This is a police investigation. The police will in no way appreciate your, ah, participation."

"Yeah? Like when you went out to see Gradee after they told you not to? Anyhow, I'm Cannecare's former CEO. I still have a bit of work to do, and that may mean a short visit to . . . say, Ned Hazly. And maybe Brenda Tate, as well."

"And just what do you hope to accomplish?" O'Brian asked. "Remember, one of them is probably a murderer, one who might kill again."

"If nothing else, I'll put the fear of God into Ned, or whoever did this. Don't criminals begin to make mistakes when they're scared? Well, I think it's time to provide a little in the way of utter fear."

"I like that," Patricia jumped in. "I can give you a few ideas."

O'Brian eyed Kelly. "That works in the movies. In real life, it does not. In fact in real life you're more likely to cause additional trouble—or get yourself hurt."

"Yeah, well, I've been under house arrest for two weeks, and I'm ready for a fight."

For Phil Gradee, senior building manager at Cannecare Tower, it was embarrassment on the surface and something far uglier underneath.

Gradee lived in a luxury condo complex that overlooked the water, just north of the city. The units were arranged in a semicircle, their backs facing the bay while their fronts faced in at one another.

The arrangement gave pretty much the entire complex a prime view of the police as they paraded in and out of Gradee's front door at eight a.m.

In the end they took five computers from the Gradee household, two of them Phil's, one his wife's, and the other two his teenage kids'—a son and a daughter.

That's a tough one for a father to explain.

But for the most part it wasn't his home computers that Gradee was worried about, and that was the something underneath.

The police would not find anything on Phil's own computers, or his kids'—except possibly illegally downloaded MP3s or torrented video.

As for computers at the office, though, Phil wasn't so sure. The uncertainty left a sinking feeling in his stomach, one strong enough to make him forget all about having to face his kids.

Gradee had erased every trace of anything worrisome on the computer in his office, but the company servers, the email server . . .

The more he thought about it, the less he cared about what his neighbors saw or thought.

🐾 🐾 🐾

For Ned Hazly it was deep-felt anger.

He sat fuming at the desk in his office, his blood pressure surged—he could feel it. His heart pounded overtime and a feeling of emptiness in his stomach grew to consume both strength and spirit.

His mind was still running over and over the image of police searching his house and confiscating his desktop and laptop computers—"oh, and, sir, we're going to need your phone . . ."

Damn it!

And with the projects he was involved in at Cannecare, he was more than a little concerned over what they would find, a thought that further fueled his blood pressure.

And now the police were here. They were scouring Cannecare Tower, had taken the computer from his office and gone to the PEC to examine the computers there.

If that wasn't bad enough, the police brought with them that . . . that . . . Walker.

The guy had waltzed in and smiled as two officers removed Ned's computer, and he followed them into the PEC.

Hazly decided it was high time to call for legal help, and his blood pressure surged higher still as he remembered he no longer had a cellphone. Picking up his office handset, he dialed Lisa Jenkins.

"This is Lisa," he heard her say.

"Lisa, this is Ned. I need help."

"I understand the police have gone back to Cannecare Tower. Apparently they want to check computers for evidence?"

"Yeah, and they came to *my house* this morning. They took *both* my computers with them. This has gone too damn far. It's time to put a legal foot down and stop all this nonsense."

"Randolph was murdered, Ned. It isn't nonsense."

"I don't care. You are to do everything you can. That Walker's here. He keeps mocking me."

"Yes, Ned, and I do have to recommend that you bring in an attorney. Right away."

"I am, damn it. Why do you think I'm calling?"

"I mean *your own* attorney, Ned. I have a contract with Cannecare. I'm legally obligated to protect the company in every way possible. I can't drop that obligation, and I can't keep it and advise you at the same time."

"Damn it," Hazly shouted at no one in particular.

🐾 🐾 🐾

For Rainer Holstenbeck, it was gratitude.

Cannecare's largest investor, as always, was only too happy to cooperate.

Holstenbeck was a yes man, always working to make everyone happy and make everyone get along.

He was also identified as one of the chosen few at Cannecare who had access to the Prototype Engineering Center, so the police wanted his computers as well.

But as Holstenbeck assured them, his venture capital firm—and the government of Lessenburg, which he ran it for—was only too eager to see the police solve this horrible crime. Certainly the valuation of the startup had diminished considerably because of the murder, and continued uncertainty, he explained, could be . . . what's that idiom? Ah, yes, *the final nail in the coffin.*

So he was very happy to cooperate in any way he could, to help the police in their investigation.

And the police knew Rainer Holstenbeck wasn't a serious suspect anyhow. Two things everyone they questioned had agreed on: (1) Rainer was too nice to murder anyone, and (2) the man was a compete nincompoop, especially when it came to technology. So while he had access to the PEC, he did not have the capacity either to murder Tate or to create the evidence used to frame Chambers.

For Brenda Tate, widow of the late Randolph, it was more fear than anger when police showed up on her doorstep.

The neighbors be damned, she said to herself; she wasn't going to be living among these dweebs much longer anyhow. But the police took her computer and her phone, and there were things on both that she couldn't let them see.

As they were finishing their search, Brenda began mentally listing the things she would need to do to get away.

She'd have to move all the money she could and move it immediately. It wouldn't be as much as she could get her hands on a week or two down the line, but it would have to do. God, they had her computer!

She would have to get far away, too, away from the police, away from that bitch Kelly Chambers who was making threats on the news, and away from blasted Seattle altogether.

Brenda Tate had had enough of Seattle.

And if she had to get back at Chambers and her circus of friends, well, that would be all the more satisfying.

3

Kelly parked down the street from the "Tate Estate," as Randolph called it. It was a name he used sarcastically, since his wife had bought the most stately-looking home they could afford, and then added the tennis court in front and other features that were aimed, most people would notice, more at appearance than convenience.

Patricia offered to come along—had begged—and Kelly finally agreed, and it was Patricia who suggested they park up the street and maybe spy a little before confronting the woman.

It proved to be a valuable choice. Just as they reached the driveway gate, Brenda appeared at the front door—hauling suitcases.

Parked in front was the ninety-thousand-dollar BMW SUV Brenda bought recently, much to Randolph's horror.

The vehicle was half-loaded with boxes and suitcases. Kelly watched as Brenda set two more suitcases in the backseat and went inside, apparently for more.

Again Brenda came out, this time hauling shopping bags that she crammed into the back.

Watching, Kelly took out her phone and found the Tates' landline number.

And she suddenly was extra thankful to have Patricia along.

Brenda's hands were trembling. She had been rushing about the large house packing and boxing things for several hours.

Her priority was value: She packed the expensive paintings and other artwork she had persuaded Randolph to buy over the years, and the jewelry, the designer clothes and shoes, and the antique clocks they'd collected. She even rolled up the Persian rugs, knowing full well how much each had cost.

After the police left, Brenda had driven downtown to a jewelry store and maxed out both of her company cards and two personal ones.

They weren't going to be good much longer anyway, Brenda reflected. Best get whatever was possible out of them.

On her way back, she stopped at a public library to use a computer. She logged into her checking and savings accounts and emptied them, moving money to an account she'd opened in her maiden name. Next she did the same with their investment account, which, while not hefty, was all cash, since she had placed sell orders for their stock and mutual fund investments the day after the murder.

Finally she logged onto FashGoods.com, an Internet wholesale website she used to sell goods she'd bought with company credit, and occasionally buy items that were either knockoffs or likely stolen. She posted a message on a site forum saying all items in her store were on sale, twenty percent off—please contact her if interested in buying.

After returning home, Brenda's aim was to be out of the house by three p.m. so that should the police return she would be long gone and hiding in a place they would never look.

Brenda figured she was well ahead of schedule, and so she froze in surprised terror when the phone rang.

She stared at the handset next to her, her body stiff with fear. Could it be the police?

It rang twice before it reported the caller ID out loud, and when it did, Brenda wondered if a call from the police might be preferable.

"Call from Chambers, Kelly," the phone's automated voice informed her.

"What the hell do you want?" Kelly heard through her cellphone. "I saw they let you out. Big mistake that was."

"Yeah, and now I'm gonna find Randolph's murderer."

"Again, I ask, what the hell do you want?"

"Maybe I could start with where were *you* the night he was murdered?"

"I certainly have no reason to talk to you."

"I know you and Randolph weren't happy."

"What business would that be of yours? Oh, yeah, I forgot: You were *sleeping* with him."

"I was doing no such thing, Brenda."

"Liar. I watched you two sneaking around. I tracked your movements with the Cannecare system."

"We weren't sleeping together. You know what we were doing?"

"Liar!"

"We were eating. Eating and talking. Randolph was lonely. He was *not* a happily married man."

"You're lying . . ."

"You *made* him unhappy. He told me."

"He told you what?"

"He told me how much of a control freak you are."

"Liar."

"He talked about how you spent money like there was no tomorrow."

"*I* spent money? Randolph put his entire inheritance into that stupid company."

"He did it so you would stop spending it."

"Liar. You're a damned liar."

"Yeah, well, I know you were unhappy, too. I know you wanted his money, wanted to live in a mansion, have prominent friends."

"I married the bastard, I invested my life, my education, all for him and Cannecare. I deserved better. I still do."

"And you thought he was having an affair with me."

"I *know* he was."

"So you killed him."

". . . I'm done talking to you, bitch."

"Wait. I have one question. I want to know why you're packing."

"What?" Brenda's voice became soft here, very soft.

"Why are you loading your SUV with boxes and suitcases? Are those rugs tied on top?"

"What? Where the hell are you?"

"I'm out front."

"You . . ." Anger took over. Brenda threw the phone at the wall and ran out the front door.

By the time she emerged, Kelly and Patricia were already out the gate and out of sight.

Brenda searched the front yard, then checked the car—saw that both front tires were flat (That was Patricia's doing).

"Damn it," she shouted. "What the hell did you do?"

A moment later she watched with a fixed stare as Kelly and Patricia drove by—very slowly—in the rented Prius, smiling as they passed.

🐾 🐾 🐾

Bernard figured he'd spend half an hour at the police station checking out confiscated computers before heading back to the Pendrite to spend the rest of the evening on his tournament.

He was being beat not only by the unpredictable play of his leading opponent but also by the lack of time he was putting into the game.

But as for getting out of the police station early, he had no idea what he was in for. The storage area the police set aside for their computer forensics was loaded by the time they arrived. Stacked along several tables were some thirty labeled computers and laptops taken from homes and from the Cannecare building, along with ten or twelve phones.

O'Brian noted discomfort on Bernard's face as he took in the sight.

"This will only take a few hours, right?" O'Brian asserted, not sounding at all like he believed it.

One of the uniformed officers walked over. "You're Ron O'Brian?"

"Yeah."

"Well, welcome to our shop. But we need to finish our inventory before you can get started. It'll take about a half hour more. Would you like some coffee?"

"We could come back tomorrow," Bernard offered.

"We'll wait." O'Brian turned to Bernard. "Remember, we have a murderer out there, one who sent us a death threat."

"Eastern Europe is being overrun by genetically coded attack kittens. *Eastern Europe!*"

"Yeah, well, Seattle's been attacked by a smart building with a military-grade air conditioner. So, where's that coffee?"

Ned Hazly spent a miserable day sitting in his office doing nothing.

There was nothing he could do. He had no computer, no cellphone, and the police were all over the place.

But finally they were gone. They'd taken more computers with them, had even stripped hard drives off the PEC computer. But they were gone. Finally.

Ned walked to his beloved PEC. Surveying the room, he felt violated. Strangers had come in here, that Walker fellow had come in here, in this, *his* room; they had gone through hard drives and files that no one—no one!—was ever allowed to see.

This was all going so badly.

He sat at the console, typed a few commands, and the Video Wall lit up. Another command pulled up the building's main security interface, which showed video of empty hallways, empty offices, an empty spa level, and an empty lobby.

The building was finally cleared and Ned was alone, save for a security guard on the ground floor.

Seated before the console, Ned felt his confidence begin to return, even if only a little. His heart was still beating faster than normal, but he was channeling the rush into anger, rather than fear.

They had gone too far. Walker had gone too far. No one walked into Cannecare Tower like that, no one helped themselves to the PEC—*his* PEC—like that.

They would pay. They would pay dearly, they all would. Ned would make sure of that.

The train of thought was broken by movement in the lobby. Ned enlarged a window showing the building entrance.

Oh God, it was Chambers. And that girl, one of Walker's people. Kelly Chambers here! Here in Cannecare Tower.

He watched, his gaze fixed, as they crossed the lobby and got into one of the elevators. And in another window he watched them inside as Kelly put her hand on the biometric scanner.

Oh God, probably no one had erased her security profile. She was on her way up, and certainly this was where she was headed.

Five minutes later Kelly and Patricia opened the PEC door to find the room vacant.

"No one's here," Patricia stated.

Kelly glanced around and smiled. "Oh, he's here all right. He left the Video Wall on. He saw us coming."

"You think?"

Kelly walked to the console as she studied the security interface on the wall. She typed a couple of commands to get a menu that read: "Recent Activity, Floor 20." Underneath appeared a blueprint schematic of the floor and the words "Past five minutes . . ."

"Ah-hah!" Kelly navigated through a few more commands to pull up a window showing video of Ned Hazly hurrying down a stairwell.

Kelly eyed the interface. "He's already down to the fourteenth floor. Not bad."

"If we take the elevator, we can beat him to the ground level," Patricia said.

"Wait, hang on . . ." As she clicked to another menu, Kelly began to giggle.

"What?" Patricia wasn't following

"Phil— Phil's . . ." She was chuckling too hard to talk. "Phil's . . ."

"Phil? What Phil?"

"Phil Gradee's doors. His damn auto doors. Remember, his invention." Kelly studied the wall a moment, saw Ned Hazly reach the eleventh floor, both on video and a blueprint map. "OK. Watch a second. We've got to do this just right."

Patricia certainly was watching. Whatever Kelly had in mind, judging by her expression, Patricia could see it was going to be fun.

They watched as Hazly continued his journey down the twenty-story stairwell, down to the eighth, then the seventh, then the sixth . . .

"OK, I want to do this while he's between floors. I see here he unlocked all the stairwell doors. See, Ned doesn't carry a passkey, a master key. Here . . . watch."

Just as Hazly got halfway between the fourth and third floors, Kelly hit a command on the keyboard, and a chorus of loud metal clangs echoed through the metal doors, railings, and stairs, from the bottom upward—causing Ned Hazly to spin around in surprise and fall to one knee, grabbing onto a railing to steady himself.

Kelly hit another few keys, and on every one of the twenty floors of the rear stairwell, the doors all by themselves creaked open, slowly for safety as Gradee designed them, but deliberately.

And, quite frankly for Ned Hazly at this particular moment, quite creepily.

The smile on Kelly's face said Disneyland, Hawaii, Christmas, and possibly a little Easter too.

"Phil's magical doors," she announced.

And with a wide-eyed Hazly staring on, the doors halted a quarter of the way open, then slowly, deliberately closed, and once they were shut a loud chorus of metallic clangs echoed menacingly from the bottom of the stairwell to the top as the latches on each of Phil Gradee's twenty-two magical doors closed, locking securely.

Kelly turned to Patricia. "One more thing. How about a quick fire alarm test?" She switched menus and clicked an icon, setting off a blaring siren throughout the building, a pounding that echoed through twenty-two flights of stairs and forced Ned Hazly's blood pressure to spiral as it did.

"Wait," Patricia said. "O'Brian said something about doors unlocking during fire alarms?"

"True. But this is only an alarm test. No doors unlocked, no visit from the fire department."

Kelly and Patricia took in a last enjoyable view of Ned Hazly climbing stairs on the Video Wall.

"Are we going to wait for him?"

"No," Kelly said, "he's scared now. Our work here is done."

4

Mira Martin put special effort into the buffet breakfast Wednesday, knowing the hotel's top managers would be inspecting.

She came in to work two hours early and paid personal attention to every detail so as to present a buffet she could be proud of, a buffet the hotel management could be proud of.

And what a buffet it was!

Again she replaced the mess hall–style tubs with platters—filled with bacon, sausage, scrambled eggs, and country fried potatoes that she had peeled and prepared herself.

The bacon was a special touch. The previous evening she had driven all the way to Olympia, more than an hour to the south, to pick it up at a butcher shop she knew of there. It was extra lean and cut extra thick, and flavored with maple syrup and black pepper.

Back at the Pendrite she supervised as a morning cook carefully fried each slice until it reached the perfect degree of crispness, adding just a touch of sugar along the way to bring out extra flavor.

And while the bacon was cooking, Mira cut fruit: cantaloupe, pineapple, strawberries—how many hotels served *strawberries* with their complimentary breakfasts?

Yes, the buffet was ready for inspection, ready for praise. She had done well, was proud, would be more so shortly when the managers came through and saw the culinary masterpiece that was the Pendrite's buffet breakfast.

This was the sort of presentation that got chefs promoted. This might very well be the one that would get Mira promoted to the dining room kitchen, where, she felt, a chef with her background and training belonged.

Nervous, she kept an eye on everything the early guests did and took. As soon as a platter was even partially depleted, she replenished it; as soon as a tray was disturbed, she jumped in and restored it to artistic perfection.

This buffet was going to retain its fine presentation until *after* seven-thirty, when the managers were due.

Then at seven twenty-eight, two police officers showed up along with two women—Mira was quite sure the older one was the murder suspect she'd seen on TV and knew was staying in the hotel.

And the four of them grabbed several trays each and to Mira's horror began piling food onto plates en masse. They cleared a platter and a half of bacon, heaped sausages and potatoes into bowls, and stacked bread, bagels, and butter wherever it would fit. To that they added an entire fruit platter for good measure, taking most the strawberries with it.

One of the officers meanwhile filled a tray with coffee cups, picked up an entire coffee dispenser, and walked over to join the others.

Mira then watched in disbelief as the four of them carried off half the prepared coffee, one of the toasters, *and more than a third of her carefully prepared food.*

"I hate this place," she shouted as they strolled into the elevator.

"You what?" a voice behind her bellowed.

Mira turned to find the hotel's executive chef and its general manager, inspecting the just-gutted buffet.

🐾 🐾 🐾

"This bacon is fantastic," Bernard commented. "You definitely should have taken more."

"There are other people down there eating too, you know," Kelly said.

The officer next to her jumped in. "Sorry, I gotta agree with him. This bacon's far too good to be polite about."

Suite 2202 had fallen into a shambles as it doubled as a secure breakfast room.

Kelly refilled the officer's coffee.

O'Brian walked over and grabbed a slice of bacon. "Mmm, my doctor would not approve. But he would eat it all the same. Any coffee?"

"Over there," Les said.

"Thanks. You guys going back to the station today?"

"I am afraid that is correct." Bernard stared down at the floor. "I need to have another look at Hazly's computers." Bernard's spirits had sunk to the point that even specially prepared Olympian bacon failed to bolster them.

"You learn anything yet?" Kelly asked.

"As a matter of fact, I have. I learned that people and companies spend entirely too much money on computing power that they clearly do not use."

"I mean anything about the murder."

"Oh, that. Yes and no. I found a few disturbing things on the desktop from Hazly's office. I would have to say that your friend Randolph Tate was quite correct in establishing a privacy policy."

"Really?" Kelly asked. "From Ned Hazly, that does not surprise me. What'd you find?"

"I found some extremely amateurish videos—apparently promotional videos—of Cannecare technology . . . doing things like spying on employees. And there was some weirder stuff, like spying on people walking down the street."

"As I said, Hazly's a creep. Hey, you know, maybe it's time Ned Hazly became the person *spied on*, instead of the *spy*. Hey, Patricia, Chen, you think you could lend me a hand today?"

"Oh God," O'Brian moaned. "What are you going to do this time?"

Before she could answer, O'Brian's phone rang.

"Ron O'Brian here," he said, putting the device to his ear.

He listened a moment. Then: "Have you checked hotels? Yeah. Well, she could have driven as far as California by this time. Yeah, well, thanks for the heads-up. And please let me know if you find anything. Thanks."

O'Brian took a deep breath. "Make Brenda Tate's computer a priority. The police went back out to her place this morning with a warrant for a full search. They found her gone, along with a lot of her belongings."

"So the police are looking for her?" Patricia asked. She and Kelly were smiling.

"Yeah, but if she made a run for it, our investigation just got stalled. She could be pretty far by this time."

"We know how they can find her," Patricia said.

"You know where she went?"

"No, but we can find out using GPS." Patricia's grin widened. "Oh, and, Bernard, I'm going to need a new work phone. Mine sort of got left in a box in the back of Brenda Tate's SUV."

🎮 🎮 🎮

Phil Gradee left for work early Wednesday, got out of the house just as his kids headed to school.

He didn't want to be home alone with his wife.

It was hard enough telling the kids about the police, about their missing computers.

But he had been unable to hide his fear, and his wife knew him too well. As she did whenever she had a complaint, she'd wait until the two of them were home alone to bring it up.

As he navigated rush-hour traffic, Phil thought about Randolph, thought about the unease in his stomach, unease not just from fear but also from guilt.

None of this would have happened if it hadn't been for Kelly and that guy Walker.

Gradee knew that among all the confiscated computer equipment, the police had the evidence they needed; he couldn't do anything about that. There was nothing for him to do but wait.

🎮 🎮 🎮

Kelly was surprised to see the name Rainer Holstenbeck as caller ID when her phone rang.

"Kelly Chambers here," she said, her tone guarded.

"Kelly, Kelly, how are you?" Holstenbeck asked. "I was so glad to hear you were released."

"Well, thank you . . ."

"I never believed for a minute that you could have been involved in Randolph's . . . uh . . ."

"Thank you, Rainer. That's kind of you."

"And so now you are helping the police? I just think that's wonderful, truly wonderful."

"Thanks, Rainer. Ron O'Brian, who helped me, was hired to help the police. And I'm sticking around to help him."

"Have the police learned anything new?"

"I'm probably not really allowed to talk about it. Sorry."

"I'm just asking because, you know, I am very worried about Cannecare. Of course and we need to catch the person who did this to Randolph."

"Right. Still, I shouldn't say anything just now."

"Do you think it could have been Brenda? Or that she was somehow involved? I never did trust that women."

"I really can't say." Holstenbeck suggesting Brenda was involved? Rainer *not trusting* someone? That was something. Rainer Holstenbeck never had a bad word about anyone or anything.

"Well, I just want to say, if there is any way I can help, if there is anything I can do, please let me know. I would of course be only too happy to assist, to assist you, the police, or anyone, yes."

"Thank you, Rainer. You've always been not only a loyal investor in Cannecare, but a friend."

"You'd better have a look at this," the young woman told Hazly.

"Where'd you get that laptop? I thought they took all the computers."

"Not on my floor." Ned recognized the woman. She worked in Accounting, he knew, though he had no idea what her name was.

"What are you showing me?"

"Company credit card accounts. This is our bank's website."

"What the hell are you doing on our bank's website?"

"Paying our bills. That's my job. We log on—that's how we pay bills."

"From our credit accounts?"

"I check our accounts regularly. And we've recently received bills totaling around thirty thousand dollars. I had to make sure they were legitimate charges. Normally I would have gone to Ms. Chambers, but . . . of course . . ."

Of course, and Ned knew the young woman was correct. Randolph had always handled all things financial, had not bothered to hire a chief financial officer.

Then along came Kelly Chambers, who took over practically everything. Ned knew her sudden absence left most finances untended for weeks.

He cleared his throat, leaned forward to study the computer screen, and once he focused, his heart dropped. The list of charges went on and on.

"Our other accounts may have some problems, too," the woman said.

"Other accounts?" A mix of anger and fear in his voice left her afraid to answer. But, voice trembling, she did.

"Yeah . . . cash flow. It looks like the company's nearly broke in terms of cash."

"That can't be."

His intent stare was interrupted by the telephone.

"Show me what you mean. Someone outside will answer that."

"There's no one there. Everyone's taking the day off . . . what, with everything that's going on."

"Damn it! OK, hang on then."

He answered the phone to hear the voice of Kelly Chambers.

"Hi ya, Ned, how's it hanging?"

Hazly still felt pain in his legs from climbing down and then up twenty flights of stairs the previous evening. His face turned red, his hands trembled.

"What the hell do you want?"

"I'll tell you what I want, Ned. I want to find out what security applications you were developing. Security applications that go well beyond the scope of Cannecare's privacy policies. You know what I'm talking about."

"I have no idea *what* you're talking about."

"Yeah, Ned, you do, and I believe both the board of directors and the Seattle police are going to be very interested in learning more. Randolph's privacy policy, I would say, makes for a pretty good motive for murder."

"Damn it," Hazly shouted at the phone.

🦇 🦇 🦇

That afternoon Ned Hazly sat on the back deck at his home in northern Seattle staring into flames. Such a day for barbecuing it would have been, the clear sky and bright sun obscured only by the occasional passing of birds.

Before him a small grill poured out smoke, but it was not from roasting meats or seafoods; it was from burning brochures, early mock-up ad material he grabbed before rushing back to the house.

The brochures explained in detail all the things his Project X (and Y and Z) offered, things that went far beyond the privacy policy and possibly in a few cases the law. Chambers was right; the police would take all that very seriously. So the more of it he burned, the better.

Next to him were several boxes of brochures, and on the table to the side were a bottle of flavored vodka, a glass, and a landline telephone handset from inside the house.

Ned wanted to be reachable if the police *were* looking for him. He needed to be warned, had to be ready. He didn't want to get caught with a . . . smoking gun, or barbecue, as it were.

He threw in another stack of brochures and watched them light as he poured a glass of vodka—his second, both without ice, which he normally added. This was not a time for enjoying drinks; it was a time for steadying nerves.

The shadow of a bird crossed the deck as he added another stack to the fire.

The police could show up soon, and Ned wanted to be rid of the brochures. He tried to think of what other evidence he needed to destroy, if he didn't want everything pointing straight at him as the murderer.

He took a long draw from the vodka, noticed again the shadow over the deck.

This was a big bird, the thought flew through his head. Ned tossed a handful of papers into the fire, then noticed the shadow had stopped. Just stopped.

Looking up, Ned saw . . . saw . . . hovering about thirty feet in the air above his back yard, a . . . a small *drone,* the sort you see on TV. And it had . . . a camera, yes, hanging on it.

"What the—?" he said, jumping up. As soon as he did, the phone rang.

In terror, he reached down and grabbed it, pressed Answer.

"Hey ya, Ned," came the voice of Kelly Chambers. "What's cooking?"

🐦 🐦 🐦

Brenda Tate was in the clear.

She'd driven her ninety-thousand-dollar SUV (after unloading it) to a used-car dealer and traded it for ten grand in cash—not a good deal, but she had to get rid of the thing and money was money.

Next, she took a cab downtown, rode a bus for several blocks, and finally caught another taxi to get back to the tiny apartment she'd rented. Under her maiden name.

And for the first time in two weeks, Brenda relaxed.

She had purchased only the basics in terms of furniture for the apartment, and, sipping a whiskey sour out of a can, she was almost having fun unpacking the things she brought today.

The paintings she stacked against a wall, mentally making a list of their value in the process.

The same went for the rugs. Among them was a Chinese rug she and Randolph bought in Hong Kong. That had always been her favorite; it was so thick it seemed to repel your weight when you walked on it. That one she would keep, and in fact she went ahead and rolled it out in the living room in front of the sofa, possibly a good place to sleep on her first night actually staying in the apartment.

Brenda had begun secretly using her and Randolph's credit cards more than a year earlier, buying items and then selling them online. She would go to outlet malls and pick up heavily discounted brand-name goods and then sell them at a premium—bags, belts, accessories, jewelry, leather goods, electronics . . .

In time she began making purchases on her two company credit cards, as well, and after a while rented the apartment, a place to store her hobby and by then successful business. But given the heavy use of company credit cards, it soon grew into outright embezzling.

Not long after, she found FashGoods, an Internet wholesaler that was offering great deals on knockoffs—Coach, Rolex, and other pricey brands. In no time, they became part of her inventory.

Now, finishing her whiskey sour, she began unpacking the second to the last box. It had her expensive silver, her Vitamix blender—that had to come—and other kitchen items that made the value grade.

Finally she looked down at the ceramic "Karma plate" her sister had given her years earlier, a souvenir bought at a tourist trap somewhere.

"It'll keep you honest," her sister kidded her, and the item always amused Brenda since.

Smiling, she lifted it up and faced it to a light. It had a symbol of some sort in the middle and the word *Karma* across the top.

"Here's to karma, Sis," Brenda said.

As she glanced down to see one further item in the box: a mobile phone.

She picked it up, pressed a button to light the screen, and saw an alert for a text message that read:

> Hey, Brenda, with GPS this phone's been tracking your movements all day. —Kelly Chambers

🎮 🎮 🎮

Image: Ned Hazly standing, phone to ear, staring at the drone in stunned bewilderment, not believing what he was seeing and yet too well understanding just what it was he was looking at—what was in turn *glaring* back at him.

This image, later back in Suite 2202, Patricia was showing to O'Brian. "Check out his expression!"

O'Brian let out a smile but one weak enough to show he in no way approved.

"Anyhow," he said, "it's evident that Hazly's been up to something, possibly illegal and at very least embarrassing. Something, mind you, that he is desperately trying to cover up. Probably his Project X. Whatever's going on, it could link him to Randolph's murder."

"It was Ned," Kelly insisted. "The more I think about it, the surer I am."

"It's too early to say yet. Remember, we have the widow on the run."

"Yeeeaahh . . ." Bernard put in. "However, I believe I know why."

"You found something on her computer?"

"I would say so."

"What, what? What'd you find?"

"Well, it would appear that Brenda Tate has been extremely active in online retail."

"Online retail?" O'Brian asked.

"Yes. On several sites. I found photos of items on her computer, as well as lists with prices and saved Web pages."

"So, like . . . eBay and Amazon?"

"Actually, a majority of her activities have been on a less-legitimate site called *FashGoods*."

"Less legitimate?"

"Shady, at the least."

Eric offered details. "It's a sort of online marketplace for people buying and selling . . . *less-legitimate* merchandise."

"Stolen?" O'Brian asked.

"Oh, it has legitimate stuff. But it's known for stuff that's stolen or pirated, for knockoffs. And everything's guaranteed anonymous. It's all hosted overseas and they report nothing in terms of, say, data to the IRS."

"Interesting . . . Hmm, what kind of *merchandise* are we talking about?"

"Fashion, of all things," Bernard said. "That is the *Fash* in the name. FashGoods."

O'Brian nodded. "That might explain the shopping bags I saw at her house."

He set the iPad with the captured image of Hazly down. "I don't believe it—it keeps getting stranger. We have solid evidence showing two suspects with motives."

"Actually three," came the voice of Lester, the latest to enter the suite.

"Three?"

"Yeah. Phil Gradee."

"Phil?" Kelly exclaimed. "No. That I cannot believe. Phil Gradee wouldn't jaywalk in a ghost town, simply because it was against the rules."

O'Brian considered that. "So you found something on Gradee's computer?"

"No, on a company computer. I found a bunch of deleted files, and when I restored them, I found email from Phil Gradee. Including this one."

"What is it?" Bernard asked.

Lester's voice came back a shade darker, even broke a little. "It was the draft of an email. Only a draft, and it has no address, so we don't know who it was for."

He set a tablet in front of O'Brian and Bernard, showing the message:

> I disabled the air conditioning safety switches. Our cooling systems are powerful enough that if concentrated on one floor or area, they can be extremely dangerous without those switches. Remember, Randolph usually swims on weekends.
>
> Phil

5

Showtime.

A dark figure stands before the console in the Prototype Engineering Center. Beyond the two console screens, the Cannecare Video Wall outlines every detail of the building in a six-foot-high schematic—its doors and elevators and stairwells, its security cameras, its fire systems, its heating and cooling equipment . . .

It's showtime.

Things did not go well with the framing of Kelly Chambers, not after Walker and O'Brian got involved.

But losing is unacceptable. One has to be always one step ahead, because by being one step ahead one can adapt, can revise strategies, can even spin events to one's advantage.

Still, it will be with a taste of *pleasure* that the revised plans are carried out, a sweet taste; for revenge is served best not cold, not bitter, but sweet—nice sugary, syrupy sweet revenge that will kill two birds, well, actually *several* birds, heh-heh, with one stone.

The figure studies the Video Wall, inspects the blueprint of every floor. Everything is in place, is prepared, is ready to roll.

Still, the sight seems so out of place.

It was always schematics of Cannecare Tower on the PEC Video Wall before.

So strange it is now to see instead blueprints of the Pendrite Hotel projected there.

Yes, friends, it is showtime.

🐦 🐦 🐦

Jitters were in store for the twenty-second floor of the Pendrite Wednesday night.

It was after eleven before anyone showed signs of calling it in. The image—three images—of suspects with the technical ability, PEC access, and now evidence of wrongdoing, that was unsettling. One of these three was a murderer, Randolph Tate's murderer, and also a killer who issued their death threat.

Maybe more than one of them. Too much to think about.

O'Brian spent an hour on the phone with homicide detectives going over the evidence, while Kelly and Bernard went window shopping on the Internet, checking out what Brenda Tate had for sale.

Lester and the others, meanwhile, discussed how to add the evidence to their mock video game, and possibly even an entire level where various criminal avatars run around trying to destroy evidence before police avatars come along and find it.

Very important for morale, her own included, Kelly talked several times with the officer on duty in the hall, who assured them he would be there all night and remain in regular contact with the officer posted on the ground floor.

O'Brian was the first to head to his room. Though only two doors down, it was distant enough that his going there demonstrated confidence in their safety.

Bernard followed suit about twenty minutes later, going to his own suite with plans to log onto *Woeful WasteWorld*.

Kelly sipped a glass of Chardonnay and marveled at their surroundings.

The three-bedroom suite they were sharing resembled a refugee camp, but a well-fed group of refugees it was, judging by the empty fast-food bags and room service trays.

Clad in expensive headsets, Lester and Eric sat at the dining table playing *Counter-Strike*. Chen and Patricia meanwhile had settled in the living room in front of a movie.

Kelly finally walked over and sat next to Patricia.

"What's on?"

"It's a horror movie. You scared?"

"By a horror movie?"

"No, the death threat. Your friend's killer."

"Oh. No, and you shouldn't be either." Kelly gulped her wine. "We have a police officer in the hall, Ron two doors down, and another officer in the lobby. And that's not counting hotel security, security cameras . . ."

"I know. But I still feel . . . I don't know."

"And remember, no one could get up here anyhow. The stairwell doors are locked and it takes a key now to get the elevator to come to our floor."

"Yeah." The two of them let their attention fall to the TV, where a young blond woman wearing a white blouse was running around a house frantically locking doors while outside, a crazed maniac armed with a chainsaw tried to break in.

"Want me to turn the channel?" Patricia asked.

"Yeah, please."

A dark figure slips through the Pendrite's lobby unseen by either the midnight front-desk clerk, who is lost in a YouTube video on his cellphone, or the police officer on duty, who is patrolling the business center and dining room off to the back.

Swift and without a sound it is easy to duck into a stairwell, but be careful to stand against the wall so as to stay out of the security camera's view. Then sliding along the cold concrete, slither under the camera and you're in position to reach up with a can of spray paint and *sssshhhh,* the camera no longer sees.

That clears the way to the B1 level, where another camera is similarly disabled.

From there it is but a quick hop down the hall to the elevators, where it is time to get to work, where it is, yes, *showtime.*

With an elevator car locked open, the figure removes a backpack and unloads its contents: a homemade incendiary bomb consisting of chemicals and newspaper; two small cans of gasoline; and, and this is the kicker, a stick of dynamite that, strategically placed, will launch the whole fiery mess a good long distance.

Ah, the wonders of how-to articles on the Internet . . .

All of this the figure arranges in a circle at the center of the elevator, the dynamite placed to the rear.

And after igniting a small fire under it all, the figure has a quick run to the Pendrite's engineering center, which is left empty as the security guard on duty carries out his hourly inspection round.

Showtime.

🔫 🔫 🔫

Seen from across the freeway on Pill Hill, the Pendrite would have spooked onlookers as the entire building all at once fell dark. All lights on all floors in all hallways and throughout the lobby and restaurant simply blinked out, and no emergency lights came on to replace them.

Inside, the blackness was oppressive, it was debilitating. Especially for guests, who had only a short time in the building to get their bearings, for them, movement in the black seemed impossible.

Except on the twenty-second floor, where several laptops defied the sudden power cut and where Lester and Eric were defying normal sleep hours to play *Grand Theft Auto*.

"Hey, dude, the lights went out," Eric moaned.

"Yeah, what's going on?" Lester hopped up and rushed to the door. He opened it to find complete darkness outside.

"Hello?" he yelled out. Down the hall he saw the officer on duty illuminated by a smartphone screen.

"The power's out up here, too," he heard the officer say.

Before Les could do anything more, the fire alarm sounded, an ear-splitting combination of bell and siren echoing in every direction.

Here thinking more or less stopped. Grabbing their phones Eric and Lester shook Kelly, Patricia, and Chen awake, and the group of them hustled into the hallway using their phones as flashlights.

"Down this way," the officer shouted. "The stairwell's here. No elevators during a fire. They won't work anyhow."

"We've gotta get Bernard and Ron," Kelly shouted.

"Bernard!" Patricia yelled out, knocking hard on his door.

O'Brian came out the next door down, strapping his revolver and holster over the undershirt he had been sleeping in. "What the hell's going on?"

"Fire alarm," the officer shouted. "But, hey, the stairwell door won't open. The damn thing won't open."

"Of course it will," O'Brian yelled as he ran over. "They unlock automatically during a fire."

By this time everyone but Patricia had reached the stairwell.

"Bernard!" Patricia's knocking had become pounding.

"Try the far stairwell, around the corner," O'Brian said pointing. The back stairwell was around a bend at the far end from the elevators.

"Bernard's not answering," Patricia yelled.

O'Brian ran toward her. "You get down there. I'll get Bernard."

"This door's locked, too," Kelly shouted from the back stairwell. "Shouldn't we try the elevators?"

"No," the officer insisted. "We can't. Elevators shut down during fire alarms."

Pretty much just as he said this the display above one of the elevators lit up, showing B1 . . . 1 . . . 2 . . .

"Oh yeah?" Patricia yelled, pointing. "Check out the elevator."

A display at the top of the smartphone reports the elevator car's progress: 7 . . . 8 . . . 9 . . .

At the bottom of the screen, a red square outlines the word Ignite.

. . . 12 . . . 13 . . .

"It's moving further up," Kelly yelled. "Maybe it's firefighters."

O'Brian continued to pound on Bernard's door, but by the time the elevator reached the eleventh floor they all were staring, waiting . . . It should have shut down.

"Maybe it is firefighters," he said blankly but didn't believe it.

They stared: 16 . . . 17 . . . 18 . . .

"We're going to find out now," he said quietly.

. . . 20 . . . 21 . . . 22 . . .

A bulb above the elevator lit up to a loud *ding*.

The car's door slid open, pouring out a thick cloud of smoke, smoke so bright they could see it in the near dark.

"Run. Get to the back stairwell," O'Brian screamed out, doing his best to demonstrate the command as he spoke.

Just as he reached the end of the hall, a pounding seismic blast rocked the building . . . and a second later an audible surge of flame roared out the elevator and shot down the hall . . .

🎮 🎮 🎮

Earlier, in an effort not to be disturbed as he logged onto *Woeful WasteWorld*, Bernard had shut himself in his suite's bedroom, opened a laptop on the bed, and put on six-hundred-dollar headphones designed to provide high-resolution audio while blocking *all* outside noise.

But the long hours, the lack of sleep, and the ongoing traumatic events, they took their toll, and soon he found himself alternating between dozing and deep, nearly unconscious sleep—both states defeating his efforts to continue play.

Again it was genetically coded attack kittens, but this time they somehow began to seem . . . cute . . . as the doze set in . . . and the kittens next became . . . *dribble-able*—there was a funny word, you can dribble them—and soon *Woeful WasteWorld* morphed into an entirely new game . . . called *Kitty Catch*, or *Kitty Bounce* something . . .

Then sleep, at last, deep, deep sleep, the sort that nearly paralyzes brain and body alike . . .

🎮 🎮 🎮

Six (still-breathing) bodies knelt more tightly packed than was either comfortable or legally permitted in the small space next to the rear stairwell.

Patricia was in tears. "We gotta get Bernard."

"Any luck with the door?" O'Brian shouted at the officer, who stood behind them trying to slip the latch with a credit card.

"Nope!"

Chen took out a utility knife, opened a fish scaler, the longest blade on it. "Here, try this."

"We gotta get Bernard," Patricia repeated.

O'Brian peered around the corner. "All right, I'm going to try to get back there."

He lifted his undershirt and used the bottom to cover his face with one hand, while holding his phone out as a flashlight with the other. And bending down, he made his way along the smoke-choked hall, but got only two doors down before turning and coming back.

"There are flames in the way. I need a fire extinguisher."

"Hang on!" Lester shouted. "I got an idea." Les had sat down against the wall and was working away at his phone.

Kelly glanced over his shoulder. "You're playing a video game?"

🎮 🎮 🎮

Woeful Waste— . . . Kitty Bounce . . .: And the genetically coded attack kittens morph into fanged sheep, and they do so with a ground-shaking thump, the sort of impact you feel from a pile driver.

"Fanged sheep? That's the best you can do?"—this a distant notion in Bernard's dreaming consciousness, and the kitten-turned-fanged sheep are buzzing suddenly, loudly, so loudly . . .

They really don't appear dangerous, in fact they're kind of cute; moments ago they were kittens. Attack kittens but adorable attack kittens. But they turned into cute fanged sheep.

Suddenly an avatar appears. It is a medieval knight armed with what appear to be rockets for hands.

"Bernard," it shouts, out of breath by the sound of it. "Gotta run. Get up and run. Fire! Get out of there!"

"Uh-huh! Right! Like I'm going to believe that!" the challenge begins to form, as deep slumber floats back into the realm of doze. "I'm finally beating this . . . this fanged-sheep herder . . . and you're going to try to fool me with . . ."

"Bernard, a bomb went off in the elevator! Didn't you hear it?"

Bernard considers the thump, edges his eyes open, notices smoke trickling in under the bedroom door, then the smell . . .

🐏 🐏 🐏

"I got him," Les shouted to O'Brian, and within seconds the piercing din of the alarm was drowned out by a scream of utter terror as Bernard—wearing a bathrobe—came barreling down the hallway, jumping through flame and smoke as quickly as his awkward size and shape allowed.

He was smoking as if on fire himself by the time he jumped down between Lester and Patricia, who had moved to the floor where the smoke was thinner. Before him, Bernard held a cellphone—amazingly, he somehow managed to grab it on his way out.

"What the hell is this?" Bernard shouted, a thoroughly rhetorical question that got an answer anyway.

"There was a bomb in the elevator," O'Brian shouted. "It came up right after the fire alarm went off."

"And the stairwell doors are locked," Lester added. "They won't open."

They looked over at the officer, who had his phone out again. "We're still locked in up here," he shouted into it. "Get up here and help us."

Bernard shouted to O'Brian. "You said doors in buildings like these unlock during fire alarms."

"They're wired to do so, yes. And elevators are supposed to return to the lobby. But look."

Exasperated, O'Brian drew his revolver and moved for the door.

"That's not going to work," the officer said, but moved out of the way as he spoke.

O'Brian aimed. "Everyone back."

He calmly checked his sight and fired four shots into the lock and latch, then stepped forward to try the knob.

"It's not budging. During a fire!"

"What the hell do we do?" Kelly pleaded.

Bernard surveyed the group: an armed Ron O'Brian shooting a stairwell door, a police officer yelling for help into a cellphone, Patricia huddling between Kelly and Lester, tears running down her cheeks . . . and Eric—apparently checking his Facebook.

"Wait a minute," Bernard declared, struggling to stand. "You said the alarm sounded and *then* the elevator came up?"

"Yeah."

"Did anyone try setting off the fire alarm?"

O'Brian stared back. "What the *hell* are you taking about? What do you think *all this* is?"

Bernard made a wry face, walked two feet over to a fire alarm pull station, opened the cover, and carefully jerked down its red lever—and seconds later the stairwell door let out an invigoratingly pronounced *click*, as did the doors on the floors below.

"It unlocked," the officer shouted as he slammed the door open. "Quick, into the stairwell. Everybody, move it!"

As the group hustled into the stairwell, they heard the shouts of guests on the lower stories as they, too, evacuated their floors.

O'Brian held back to usher the others in. As he did, he glanced at Bernard. "What the hell did you do?"

"Simple. I set off the fire alarm."

"But?!" O'Brian raised his hands to indicate the blaring alarm that had a hallway filled with flame and smoke as a backdrop.

"A siren test?" Bernard offered.

A blank expression on his face, O'Brian appraised Bernard a second. Then muttered as he followed Bernard into the stairwell:

"I don't goddamn believe it."

6

The sun peered over Pill Hill that morning to shed much-needed light and warmth on the Pendrite Hotel as a flurry of police, firefighters, and medical personnel hustled about in a well-practiced state of chaos.

Bernard and the group were bused to a café across the street, where a large window offered a view of the ongoing action. Adding a taste of the surreal, a television above the counter droned on with live coverage of the scene, leaving them to assimilate the actual sight across the street and the news video showing on the TV screen.

O'Brian came in and sat at one end of the counter.

"The fire department says we were pretty lucky. It turns out it *was* just a siren test, not an actual fire alarm. That's why the doors were still locked. Someone got into the Pendrite's building-control computer and also shut down the smoke detectors and sprinklers. The only way a real alarm could get set off then was via pull station."

"*Thank you* will be sufficient," Bernard said.

O'Brian didn't argue. "Yeah, I just don't believe it. But the insurance company's not going to be happy. When you pulled the fire alarm, it not only unlocked the doors, it also sent the elevator back to the lobby. Spreading smoke out on every floor along the way, then smoking out the entire ground floor. Our floor had the only serious fire damage, but smoke damage throughout is going to be costly."

"More important, was anyone hurt?" Kelly asked.

"Fortunately only minor injuries, at least from what we know so far. I think one woman broke her ankle on the stairs, and a couple of others are in the hospital with respiratory complaints."

"Do the police have any idea who did this? I can't believe . . . even Ned."

"Too early to say who. Whoever it was apparently spray-painted a couple of security cameras. Anyhow, the police want us all to stay here a couple of hours. They're going to have a lot more questions. Then they're going to escort us a hotel where we can clean up. They'll find someplace safe."

"Safe is good," Bernard put in. "But do make sure they find a hotel with a soda machine." He turned to the window to survey the mess across the street: the lingering smoke, the emergency crews running about, the strings of hoses, the puddles of water and chemicals . . .

"Thank God no one was hurt," Kelly muttered.

Bernard sighed. "Yes, but I do believe that the night manager is going to be quite cross."

Four hours later the group had checked into the Sheetless in Seattle Sleepery, a dive of a motel south of town where they were left to try to come to grips with, first, the all-too-nearly-successful murder attempt, and, second, withdrawal symptoms suffered from leaving the luxury of the Pendrite.

The Sheetless in Seattle was a two-story budget motel last retrofitted, by all appearances, in about 1952. Early January 1952. Cigarette burns on carpets, bathroom sinks, and bathtubs highlighted painful contrast to the luxury suites they had grown accustomed to.

But there were only quiet complaints as the group walked up the outdoor stairs and selected rooms along the upper story. The prospect of showers and food and sleep made the Sheetless in Seattle seem like the Ritz Carlton, at least for the moment. (Of course, they hadn't yet discovered the poor Wi-Fi.)

The Sheetless had been chosen because it was nearly empty (it was not hard to imagine why), and the few existing guests had been moved—salt in the wound—to nicer hotels, free of charge.

The police held the lower floor, held as in holding a fort or position, with squad cars parked along the street and officers patrolling the grounds. Two were also stationed at either end of the second-floor common balcony.

With the motel to themselves, the group each took a room of their own, with the plan of leaving the one nearest the stairwell as a place to meet.

And as planned, they gathered there around five in the afternoon, following showers and naps, and for the second time in a day they found themselves crammed into an uncomfortably small space, this time squeezed together sitting on beds.

Now, the worst effects of a traumatic experience of the sort Bernard and team had just experienced, those effects don't set in right away. No. At first there is simple relief at having survived. Then, slowly, as if stepping out onto a *possibly* frozen stretch of lake, the unconscious part of the brain lets itself first gently sample, then carefully examine, images and scenes embedded in the mind, pictures of what happened, what was seen, heard, smelled, and felt. The darkness, the noise, the scent of smoke so deeply soaked into the lungs that showers were unable to wash it away . . .

It's only then that the utter horror of the experience hits, as the true weight of the situation sets in on the victims . . .

"God, I want my laptop!" Patricia moaned in a tone that sounded like a coyote during Moon Festival.

They were, save for the phones they had grabbed as flashlights, sans technology. No laptops, no tablets, no game consoles . . .

They each sat in a daze, engrossed in their phones, their single possession at the moment. The authorities provided them with a change of clothes, bath kits, and "basic necessities." There was of course some discussion over whether an Xbox constituted a basic necessity, but it was determined it did not.

O'Brian was the last to arrive, and the sight of the whole team packed into a "double" room at the Sheetless was not readily inviting.

"Why the hell is everyone crammed in here?"

"The lounge was closed?" Kelly offered, a forlorn tone.

O'Brian stepped inside, or at least tried to fake it.

"Is everyone OK?"

This, a question he asked of six ragged-looking bombing victims squeezed uncomfortably onto two beds, staring with crazed expressions into phones, and most alarmingly, wearing identical yellow jogging suits—emergency clothing the police had waiting for disaster victims.

The bright yellow group seemed all the more pitiful in contrast to O'Brian, who had somehow gotten them to bring him a suit of sorts, a mismatched sports coat and slacks.

"Listen. I've been talking with the police. There's a federal manhunt out now for all three of our suspects, and guess what: None of them can be found."

"You're kidding," Kelly said. "What about Brenda? Patricia's cellphone trick didn't work?"

"They found where Brenda Tate was staying—a cheap apartment on Capital Hill. But she wasn't there."

"What about Phil Gradee?"

O'Brian hesitated, then: "It seems Phil Gradee didn't come home last night."

"Oh God. That can't be. Phil Gradee couldn't do what . . . what happened last night. Not Phil."

"His disappearance isn't unique among our suspects, so that's not to say he did."

"What about Hazly?" Bernard asked.

"Wasn't at home, wasn't at his office."

Patricia let out a scared giggled. "Is there any way they all three were involved?"

It seemed a silly question, but no one answered. Or laughed.

Kelly glanced out the window. Off to one side of the common balcony, a police officer watched out over the parking lot and a strip mall beyond where Kelly could see shoppers walking about.

Somewhere out there might be Randolph's killer, their would-be killer, stalking, waiting for the opportune moment.

"This is all pretty scary," she commented.

"Don't worry." O'Brian said sternly. "This is no longer a murder investigation. What happened last night was not a case of a possessed elevator. It was a bombing at a major hotel. In the post-9/11 world, that means a federal manhunt utilizing resources and technology they won't even tell us about. I don't think our three suspects are going to remain on the loose very long."

🐾 🐾 🐾

The Gradee household on this afternoon was setting records for the amount of police activity in the neighborhood, at least judging by the stares of shock on residents' faces

It wasn't just computers that were of interest anymore. Police and federal investigators searched the entire house, searched drawers and cupboards, looked under furniture, and checked everywhere with bomb-sniffing dogs.

Gradee's wife and kids sat in the kitchen as investigators went room to room, closet to closet, seeking clues that might help them locate Phil or connect him with the bombing at the Pendrite. Phil's wife didn't know where he was, but she did know one thing: Somewhere at that moment Phil would be plunged in shame at the thought of his family watching as police ransacked their home. Phil's wife knew that.

🐾 🐾 🐾

Ned Hazly's suburban home was equally busy, and, taking on an appropriately suburban flavor, much of the search focused on the barbecue in his back yard. There, a team of white-coated federal agents sifted through ashes in and around the grill.

Clearly someone had been burning something there, something that was neither meat, fish, nor vegetable.

A half-empty vodka bottle, left uncapped on a nearby table, added suspicion to the scene, as did the badly charred landline handset they'd found on top of the barbecue ashes.

🎮 🎮 🎮

The Tate Estate, a property landscaped to grab neighbors' attention, was on this afternoon very much catching the eye of passers-by. Dark, official-looking SUVs, police cruisers, and a couple of fire trucks had crammed into the driveway and along the shoulder of the road. Scattered around the yard, armor-clad police displaying automatic assault rifles stood guard at strategic positions, while uniformed and plainclothes personnel combed the area using bomb-sniffing dogs, as others hauled boxes of items out of the house.

Just beyond the driveway stood a reporter who had slipped through as police marched news trucks and other press back. Now the only journalist in sight of the estate, the woman slipped out her phone and began streaming video of the police activity.

At the TV station she worked for, several excited staff sat in a production room watching her video stream on one of two main monitors. It showed investigators as they scurried about, alone or in small groups, each carrying out its own search while talking into phones and radios, on and on until pretty much all at once everyone across the entire yard, paused—as they listened into phones and radios for a few seconds, then launched back into action, the bulk of them heading around the side of the house and toward the back.

🎮 🎮 🎮

. . . to fight demonstrators in several cities as President Owahi refuses opposition demands to step down.

But first, we have breaking news locally, where police have new information on last night's hotel bombing. We go to our reporter on the spot . . .

"Hey, maybe more news," O'Brian said, pointing at the TV.

> . . . in front of the Pendrite Hotel, and as you can
> see, the scene here is still one of chaos some sixteen
> hours after an explosion rocked the top story of
> the building. We have just learned, police believe
> they know who carried out the bombing, though
> they are not releasing details. They have scheduled
> a press conference . . .

Before the others could digest this, O'Brian was already on his phone and pacing. He quickly became the object of attention as he spoke. "Yes. Yeah? No! I knew that might be, but . . ."

They stared on as he pressed for details.

". . . Sure, I understand. No, and please do, thanks."

As quickly as he hung up, Kelly was begging.

"They know who did it?"

"Yeah." His tone showed a mix of relief and wonderment. "Sit down, Kelly."

"I don't need to sit," Kelly insisted, almost angrily, as she slid her butt onto a bed behind her. "It was Ned?"

"No. Not Ned."

"Well?"

"Listen, we can't tell anyone. The police don't want it out yet . . ."

"Who?"

"It appears it was Brenda Tate."

Kelly rotated around the corner of the bed, bent her head down in her hands.

"I do hope they caught the crazy woman," Bernard said.

"They haven't. She's on the run."

"How do they know it was her?" Kelly asked without turning.

"Bomb-sniffing dogs. They found dynamite in a shed next to her swimming pool."

"But . . ." Things remained unanswered in Kelly's mind. "I can't believe that. I don't understand. What about Randolph? Did she kill Randolph? Do they know?"

"Well . . . They also found blueprints of Cannecare Tower in the shed."

"Blueprints?"

"That's what they told me. Blueprints, apparently, of the building's heating and cooling systems."

O'Brian couldn't think of anything more to say. They eyed each other in silence a moment before Kelly reached over to a dresser where she had set down a glass of wine.

Watching, Bernard calculated: Kelly out of jail, dangerous murderer identified, it all added up to visions of a quick flight back to SFO, where a short drive south and then east would return him to his beloved oceanfront studio in Cliff Shores.

Until he saw Patricia's tears, a few only, but honest to goodness tears, and Bernard did not do well around tears.

"What's wrong?" Kelly asked.

"She's out there. She killed your friend, she tried to kill us, and she could have killed a lot more people at the Pendrite. And she's still out there *because of us.*"

Watching, Bernard calculated: Visions of a quick flight to SFO diminishing . . .

Kelly moved closer. "What do you mean *because of us?*"

"We sent her that text message. If we had just left the phone, with no message, she wouldn't have run. We'd know where she was."

"Nonsense. Nonsense and besides . . . " Kelly paused to sip her wine and wonder, secretly, if Patricia was right. "But besides, we've only started. Now it's time for *us* to do some shopping."

That drew a groan from O'Brian.

"The hell you are. First, no one leaves this hotel." O'Brian made every effort to appear as if he were stepping forward, despite the lack of anywhere forward in the crowded room to step.

"We're under complete lockdown, indefinitely, no exceptions. And even if we weren't, we're done with this thing. It's a bombing. It's federal, it's terrorist-level. That means FBI, CIA, men in black suits with curly wires running to their ears."

Watching, Bernard was no longer dreaming of a flight home.

"Don't worry, Ron. I have no intention of leaving this hotel. What are you, kidding—in *these* clothes?"

The sight of them all in bright yellow mellowed O'Brian's expression.

"Besides," Kelly went on, "God knows where the hell Brenda's run off to—*we* wouldn't find her if the police couldn't. Physically, that is."

"Oookaay . . ."

"No, it'll be Cyber Monday shopping. Patricia, you and I are going *Brenda Tate* shopping—online."

One final time Bernard calculated: Patricia the kid, with red eyes and tears, Kelly Chambers being, well, Kelly Chambers . . .

And frankly, this whole mess was getting tiresome. If a little online shopping could wind it up once and for all, then what the heck?

He stood. "I did say it once before, and I guess I shall have to say it again: If you want to catch a murderer, you had better be willing to do it yourself."

He faced O'Brian, frowned. "We will need some laptops," he stated. "That, along with some decent Wi-Fi, for crying out loud."

🐃 🐃 🐃

Thursday noontime. Brenda Tate's back ached from shoulder to tailbone, her legs were numb and weak with pain, and her hands shook when not glued to the steering wheel. She had, basically, packed up most her belongings twice in a day, that after weeks without a decent night's sleep . . .

Worse, it wasn't over.

Brenda needed to vacate the area quickly. A long drive awaited, one that would cross the mountains eastward along Route 20—the poorest choice of an escape route and thus, and she was betting her freedom on this, one the police would not be watching as closely.

She had rented a step van and hurriedly filled it. With the police knowing where she had run off to, she allotted no time for sentimentality: She triaged the goods she had collected at the apartment in recent months by value only, stuffing the more-valuable items haphazardly into the van.

Next, she got the hell out of the city. Seattle was not safe. But she knew she needed rest, so she sought out a hotel with a business center—she needed Internet access—and grabbed a few hours' sleep.

By seven a.m. Brenda was on the road, along with a pre-paid phone she'd bought, now on the passenger seat beside her. She was using its map app to navigate out of town and occasionally to check her Facebook page and e-mail—anything to calm her nerves.

That she was breaking California's hands-free law, using her phone while driving, truly that didn't disturb her too deeply. She was driving a step van loaded with the proceeds of months of embezzlement, and was being hunted by federal authorities for bombing a hotel.

What, was she going to get a ticket for using her phone behind the wheel? But she knew, of course, that alone could get her pulled over, so she kept the phone out of sight.

As soon as she reached the mountains, Brenda searched for a turnoff, and finally found a small dirt road that seemed to go nowhere. She pulled in and drove down far enough to be out of sight.

Here, she took out a mirror and using regular office scissors cropped off her previously shoulder-length hair, careful as she could be to guide the cuttings out the door.

She fought shaking hands the whole time, but with her hair shortened and covered by a baseball cap, she at least wouldn't be an instant fit to photos and descriptions that passing police most certainly would have.

But her hands still shaking, she decided more sleep was in order, and this was as good a spot as she'd find. Cursing only briefly at the discovery that the seat didn't recline, she fell quickly under.

🐾 🐾 🐾

"FashGoods-dot-com," Lester announced as he pulled up the website.

"What goods?" O'Brian asked.

"FashGoods—F-A-S-H, as in *fashion*. FashGoods-dot-com. It's one of the sites Brenda Tate uses a lot. But this one's a little different."

"How so?"

O'Brian had contacted the Seattle police and explained Kelly and Bernard's plan, and the police went over it with federal authorities. Now the team sat with new computers—and Brenda Tate's— and the Sheetless in Seattle had received a Wi-Fi upgrade courtesy of the city of Seattle.

Lester, Bernard, and Kelly went quickly to work searching Brenda Tate's hard drives and detailing her online retail transactions and correspondence.

"So how is this website different?" O'Brian repeated.

"This is a site that matches up online retailers to buy and sell. Kind of like wholesale for online retail."

"It is entirely likely," Bernard explained, "that Brenda Tate will be monitoring this site, even while she is on the run."

Kelly smiled. "Let's see if we can interest her in some shopping of one sort or another, then."

"Another reason to use this website," Bernard added, "is that it is a startup, and a small operation. It will be far easier to create what will appear to be an established, reliable account, with ratings and everything to back it up."

"Ratings?" O'Brian asked.

"Yes. As with eBay and Amazon, ratings are all-important. Buyers rate sellers, sellers rate buyers . . ." Bernard studied the screen before him and read aloud:

"Best seller ever. High integrity and trustworthy." He turned to Lester. "Why, thank you, Les. You are too kind."

In a haze as she went to sleep, Brenda failed to set the alarm correctly on the new phone—a prepaid LG model she grabbed at a WalMart for twenty bucks. As a result, her planned two-hour nap snored its way into four hours of deep sleep, a slumber that as she awoke hung over her body and mind like several layers of clothes in a swimming pool.

She leaned over to the passenger side floor and pulled out a bottle of ice coffee—*un*iced since she had no cooler—and chugged it down in a vain attempt to wake up enough to drive safely.

Just before pulling out, she used the phone to check the news, which was more terrifying each time she looked. Lastly, she viewed her email. It was mostly spam, along with a notification that her American Express bill was due—*like you can count on me paying that.*

One email, however, one email stood out, something from FashGoods.com.

It didn't look alarming. In fact, if anything it appeared it might be something positive for a change. Brenda loved FashGoods, had made substantial money and quality contacts on the site.

And after weeks of hell, any communication not connected with all the crap going on in her life, that would be a ray of sunshine, a breath of fresh air.

Staring at the subject line, "Inquiry on multiple products in your stock," Brenda was struck by how lonely she had become. An inquiry from a buyer, that was communication, a connection with someone somewhere, someone who wasn't out to get her.

But better concentrate on the drive for the moment.

🐾 🐾 🐾

"Hey, Kelly, help us choose the products this guy supposedly wants to buy."

Patricia was going over the search results on Brenda Tate's FashGoods store with excitement; she was eager to hear what Kelly would choose.

Kelly was just as eager to get started.

"Yeah, let's see . . . I notice several pricey purses here, and—check it out—this one she lists as having twelve in stock. That adds up into the thousands."

"Yeah, and these coats are pricey—you've got a coat like this one, right, Kelly?"

🐾 🐾 🐾

It was dark by the time Brenda made her way down out of the mountains to the east, and with the help of the map app on her phone she located an RV park on a bank of the Okanogan River, where she was able to park for the night for twenty bucks (cash), no ID required.

Given the manhunt begun after the bombing, she needed to lay off using even her maiden name, at least for a while.

Brenda settled into the passenger seat and ate a sandwich as she studied the map on her phone.

It was decision time in terms of escape route. Soon Route 20 would turn east and become a smaller, windier highway. Brenda had to choose between that and continuing north on U.S. Route 97 into Canada.

Canada: What a wonderful idea, but what a bad one.

Canada was not an option. Brenda could not chance going through a border station, not when she was driving a van full of brand-name goods that would instantly shout out to any self-respecting customs agent: "Tax me, tax me!"

Decision made, as the last of the sandwich gave way to a canned whiskey sour, Brenda turned next to her email. She had very little new except for an amusing neighborhood-watch message, which contained a long string of her Seattle neighbors' posts on all the police activity at "that Tate woman's house."

Brenda was about to set the phone, along with her neighbors' scorn, down when she saw again the FashGoods email.

🐾 🐾 🐾

"It is essential we present a deal that Brenda Tate cannot refuse," Bernard explained, as Kelly and Patricia studied the list of items they would offer to buy.

"If we go too high," O'Brian noted, "she'll smell a rat."

"Hey, I'm the one with a shopping background here," Kelly put in, enjoying that for once she had some sort of expertise no one else in the room did. "These prices are good, but not so high they couldn't be marked up again."

Kelly sat between O'Brian and Bernard, a career of police knowledge on one side and, well, Bernard on the other.

"So what do you think?" O'Brian asked.

"I think we should tempt her with quantity," Kelly explained, "but insist that we'll need to fulfill the order right away. If she's trying to liquidate things, she won't be able to resist."

"We'll need a good story."

"I've got one. Brand-name goods like these go for far higher prices in a lot of countries. If you buy them at near-wholesale, you're talking forty to eighty percent markup, depending on the country."

Here Kelly's expertise caught even Bernard's attention.

"Of course, there's the catch—the country," she went on. "It's another country, and that means shipping costs and, worse, tariffs and taxes, and often it's a major pain in the ass just getting a permit to import the items."

O'Brian remained confused. "So how does this plan work?"

"Well, if you just skip the permit in the first place, and along with that skip declaring the imports . . . then that erases those nasty tariffs . . ."

Kelly smiled.

🔫 🔫 🔫

. . . and since the shipping costs are based on space and container, not weight, I have the opportunity to get rock-bottom shipping for a load to Hong Kong.

I'm interested in brand-name purses and accessories. Items must be in stock, since time is of an
essence.

Also hope for discount on quantity, given the size
of the order.

Below are links to items in your store that I am
interested in. Would like to learn if you have more
similar. Hope to hear from you soon.

Cheers,

Pete Sanchez
Proprietor, Pete's Place

A quick scan of the list perked Brenda up more than any can
of whiskey sour could. The array of designer brands represented
probably two-thirds of her inventory . . . and, yeah, the way
things were going, how long did she have to make something
of that anyway?

After the bombing . . . God! . . . driving around with a load
of goods just wasn't smart, and one thing Brenda knew was that
at this time she needed more than ever to be smart.

🐾 🐾 🐾

"We need to send the next email soon," Kelly told Bernard
and O'Brian. "We still haven't pushed her to meet."

O'Brian agreed. "Yeah, chances are, she's running. If she puts
too much distance behind her, she won't want to turn around."

"I see no reason why we—or better, the police—cannot go
to her," Bernard put in.

🐾 🐾 🐾

The next morning, Brenda sat in front of a gas station filling her stomach with coffee and donuts while staring at the map on her phone and again considering her plan.

It was a depressing sight. She did not look forward to another mountain drive of winding roads, and that just to get to Spokane, where she would have to continue running east. If only she could head north . . .

To the north, a ways beyond the Canadian border, was Okanogan Lake and halfway along that the picturesque mountain city of Kelowna, where Brenda's family went several times when she was a kid. Brenda had memories of pine trees, mountains, and the giant, gorgeous lake.

If only it weren't for the pesky border she would have to cross.

Sure, with her cropped hair and a little makeup, she could skirt photos the police would have sent out. But a step van full of expensive, untaxed goods, that would raise the hair on the back of any border guard anywhere's neck.

Clearly the step van full of merchandise was too much of a liability, a giant ball and chain at a time when she needed to run free.

But if she could ditch the van, find a self-storage facility . . .

Brenda remembered the guy on FashGoods. She checked her email and saw a new message.

Dear B.,

I'm afraid the departure date for my container has been moved up. In fact, I have to deliver my part of it by tomorrow night. And unless you can arrange very fast shipping, I will not be able to make my planned purchases at this time.

I am sorry for the inconvenience.

Although I do see on your FashGoods store that you are in Washington State. I am in Olympia, and my shipment departs from Seattle. Is there any chance I could pick up any of the items you may have in stock in person, rather than using delivery?

Either way, I look forward to doing business with you in the future.

Cheers,
Peter Sanchez
Proprietor, Pete's Place

🐾 🐾 🐾

Roughly five hours later Brenda pulled into a strip mall parking lot in Mt. Vernon, a town north of Seattle, as arranged. She was happy she made it back so quickly—back over the mountains she had crossed in the first place. If she could make the sale, ditch the van, store anything left, and find something practical to drive, she could be back to Route 97 soon and with a revised plan, heading north to beautiful Canada.

Brenda had a strange feeling in her stomach, though. This business of meeting a stranger to sell thousands of dollars worth of jewelry and purses—she knew it wasn't the smartest thing a person could do.

Then again, after all the Internet purchases on company credit cards, after the murder, after Kelly Chambers getting loose, after the bombing . . . A strange feeling in Brenda's stomach was really nothing new.

So after parking, she opened a warm bottle of ice coffee, took out her cellphone, and texted Peter Sanchez. He had given her the number in a follow-up email and she saw that it was the same as listed on his FashGoods store. Little signs of validity.

She opened again Pete Sanchez's FashGoods store, saw again numerous positive reviews he'd received. It all checked out; it was what she expected to find.

So it was with a good deal of shock that Brenda noticed suddenly the flashing red and blue lights coming from pretty much every direction, oh, and the roar of a loud helicopter overhead.

In terror, Brenda jumped out of the van and dashed toward the shops behind her—only to see a dozen officers coming out of them, guns drawn, screaming at her to drop to the ground.

🔫 🔫 🔫

"Its over. They have her." O'Brian said this as he ended a call. "They picked her up as planned."

The announcement raised a cheer along the upper balcony of the Sheetless.

"Did she have what we offered to buy?" Kelly asked.

"That and more, apparently. Only she was a little put out, to say the least, to learn that Peter Sanchez was actually a Seattle Police officer."

"Oh my God—that is so good to hear. I am so relieved."

Watching, Bernard, too, was relieved, as images began to form again in his mind of a quick plane ride back home. How often these days did people look forward to flying, after all? You had to stop to appreciate it.

"Yep, it's over," O'Brian repeated. "Or nearly over."

The beginnings of a Stare set in on Bernard's face.

"They'll have questions, both local authorities and federal. Lots of question, possibly for several days. Then we'll be free to head home.

"Though of course we'll have to fly back up here when Brenda Tate's case comes to trial."

7

The following day, Saturday.

> . . . yesterday charged Brenda Tate with the murder of her husband, and they charged her also in connection with the bombing at the Pendrite Hotel. Police say Tate believed her husband was having an affair with CEO Kelly Chambers, whom she allegedly tried to frame for . . .

The group stood around the lobby of the Sheetless in Seattle Sleepery inspecting the slim pickings of its complimentary breakfast, which consisted of two large tubs of cereal, day-old bread, limp brown bananas, and coffee that even O'Brian would turn down.

It was O'Brian they were waiting for, O'Brian and some sort of surprise he had promised.

They were about to receive a well-deserved reward, he explained, for all their work on the SimCide case.

Despite the dismal breakfast offerings, the atmosphere in the room rivaled that of a beach in Hawaii or a ballroom on New Year's Eve. The whole group shared a feeling of mutual well-being, of relief and released tension, now that Tate was locked up and finally it was over. Finally they were safe.

Whatever it was O'Brian had planned, that would only add icing to an already very tasty cake, emotion-wise.

All save for Bernard, that is. Bernard sat in a corner surrounded by luggage. After several hours of questioning the previous evening, the police gave him the green light to head home. In fact, he noted they seemed to be encouraging him to leave.

That's not to say Bernard wasn't relieved, but for him the icing on the cake would be a Big Bad Breakfast Wrap from MoMo's Minimart, up the hill from his Cliff Shores home.

"Are you sure you want to head straight back?" Kelly pushed. "Ron made plans for the whole day. Something he said that is designed just for video game fanatics."

"I am quite sure, thank you. I have very little time left in my tournament. Short of another death threat or bombing, I fully intend to head back to Cliff Shores today, the earlier the better."

Kelly thought Bernard was being selfish, small-minded. But reflecting on how many times he had gone against his self-obsessed nature in the past two weeks on her behalf, she decided she should let it slide.

Their attention was drawn to the front window by a white stretch limo that pulled up outside, whose rear door opened to reveal O'Brian. The limo driver joined him and together the two of them gathered several shopping bags and hauled them into the lobby.

"Surprise," O'Brian announced as he entered.

Kelly spoke first. "What's all this?"

"Reward time." O'Brian had a Santa Claus-like smile in his eyes. "You guys helped the police catch a murderer, and you helped SimCide Investigations solve its first case—what was supposed to be a *test* case. And as a reward, we're going out for a day on the town, courtesy of SimCide—Herbert Iggid be damned. Some of this is what I was planning before the death threat, actually."

Les walked to the door.

"Cool car!"

The limo was a small converted bus, and through the open door he could see disco lights, a wet bar, and several TV screens.

"Yep, we have it for the whole day. And I have big plans, too. First, we're going out for lunch at this steak house I know of. And you know what we're going to do after that?"

"What?" Kelly asked.

"I was thinking, what would be something really special for a rather . . ." He examined the faces around him. ". . . a rather unique group of people."

"Uh-oh, sounds bad," Kelly commented.

"Here." O'Brian reached into one of the shopping bags and pulled out a box.

"Oh my God," Lester exclaimed, reading the box. "The DTX500. That's one of the coolest airsoft guns around. These things are like seven hundred bucks apiece."

"Dude, those things are, like, fully automatic," Eric added.

O'Brian smiled as he handed Eric the box, then took out two more. "Patricia actually gave me the recommendation, though she didn't know it."

"I did?" Patricia asked.

"Yeah. I ordered these before the death threat. There's one for everybody. A little token of thanks from SimCide Investigations. Oh, and also this." He took out a smaller box. "These are real shoulder holsters, like police detectives wear, the kind you see in movies."

"Oh, this is so cool," Eric said, grabbing a box.

"And get this, guys. After lunch, we're off to a firing range. I rented it for the afternoon. The place has obstacle courses, the kind where you run around shooting pop-up targets and try to avoid shooting innocent-pedestrian targets. I thought that might be the kind of thing that would impress you."

"You've got to be kidding," Kelly complained. But she readily accepted the box O'Brian handed her.

"Oh, and one more thing. And this is the most important." O'Brian walked to the front desk, where the clerk handed him two large shopping bags that had been stashed behind the desk. "Windbreakers," O'Brian said, pulling one out.

He unfolded it and held it up. Embroidered on the left breast was the name SimCide Investigations, along with the company logo. After getting a couple of oohs and ahs, O'Brian turned it around to show the back, which read: "The Bluest Skies You've Ever Seen Are in Seattle."

Five minutes later the group had opened their boxes and were trying on the shoulder harnesses.

"You'll note," O'Brian lectured, "these guns have orange caps on the barrels. That identifies them as toys, not real guns. That makes them, well, not exactly safe, but safer. But all the same, do not take them out in public."

"Hey, what about my gun, the one you took at the Pendrite?" Les asked.

O'Brian squinted. "Fortunately during the fire, it was at the shop where I ordered these. They put an orange cap on it for me—for you. Here . . ." O'Brian reached into one of the bags and pulled it out.

"You ruined it," Les complained.

"Can it. I made it safe. Besides, the cap slips right off if needed. *Which* I can't imagine why."

Of the group, only Bernard appeared less than ecstatic. He took the boxes handed to him, but made no move to open them. "These should be quite fun to carry into an airport," was his only comment.

The situation was quite a sight for the front-desk clerk at the Sheetless: a lobby full of boisterous guests arming themselves with pricey airsoft guns in real shoulder holsters.

If he had any idea what the staff at their previous hotel had seen . . .

🔫 🔫 🔫

Mira Martin stood next to Carl Bessite in front of the Pendrite Hotel. Both were simply unable to comprehend the sight before them.

Like most of the hotel's staff, they were told to stay away after the bombing, while the building was made safe even to enter again.

Now, days later, the lobby still looked like a war had played through. Police still wandered amid scattered yellow tape, construction managers with hard hats and clipboards examined damage, as scattered hotel managers and staff stood around shaking their heads in disbelief.

"It was such a beautiful hotel," Bessite said.

"Yes, it was," Mira agreed. "You know, I'm going back to Sweden. Hotels in Stockholm don't have things like this happen."

Her statement would have put a lot of Americans on the defensive, but Bessite simply turned, a confused expression on his face.

"They don't?"

"No. They don't."

"Hmm . . . what's the weather there like this time of year?"

🐾 🐾 🐾

Herbert Iggid had been on an emotional rollercoaster. When he first saw TV footage of the damage at the Pendrite, he was sure OffCide was going to get hit with the bill for building repairs, which would infuriate board members and investors. Walker had wasted company money renting out a whole floor of suites, and now was responsible for destroying whole parts of the hotel, by the look of it. Iggid was excited; he would soon be able to fire Walker, and probably O'Brian too.

But then the media began calling Bernard and his team heroes after the bombing, and that killed Iggid's arguments. Then they helped the police catch Brenda Tate, and now they were even bigger heroes.

How could Iggid go to the boards now and complain about Walker and O'Brian wasting money?

🐾 🐾 🐾

It was a party atmosphere inside the stretch limo, one complete with wet bar and champagne. O'Brian produced chilled glasses from the limo's minifridge and the well-armed group of airsoft warriors quickly were making toasts as they cruised through downtown Seattle.

The limo's three TV screens were blaring various programs—news on one, an anime cartoon on another, and a poker tournament on the third.

Kelly rolled down a window to peer out. It was a gorgeous day, blue sky and sunshine, the kind she once had only heard legends about in Seattle.

Smiling at pedestrians along the sidewalk, she held up her glass in a toast as they passed.

"You're going to love this restaurant," O'Brian boasted. "They grill an excellent steak."

"Sounds wonderful. You should have stressed that to Bernard. He might have joined us."

"Yeah, but I guess I have to feel bad for keeping him here this long. I don't understand how he can take a game so seriously, but one thing you have to say for Bernard, when he's serious, he's serious. Dead serious."

🎮 🎮 🎮

Realizing his own limo wasn't due for another half-hour—the police were no longer offering rides to the airport—Bernard took out one of the laptops he was carrying, recently rescued from the Pendrite, and began cleaning up some of the mess of files he'd copied during the investigation.

He started by deleting hundreds of folders created for their mock video game, then began sorting through stuff copied at the police station.

He examined briefly the files from Brenda Tate's computer and phone, files they used to help the police hunt her down.

He dragged to select, hit the delete key, and, presto, the fixings of a criminal mind embroiled in embezzlement, money laundering, attempted murder, and successful murder—just disappeared from his D drive.

Next he pulled up a directory of files on Phil Gradee. That was a sad case. The police finally found Gradee hiding in the ground-floor engineer's office at Cannecare Tower. During questioning, they learned he'd been sent bogus email, including several messages instructing him to disable safety switches on the building's heating and cooling systems. The email purported to be from Kelly and Randolph Tate, and when Gradee learned of the murder, he blamed himself and figured he'd be charged as an accomplice.

The police and the FBI went easy on him, releasing Phil quickly. But, as Kelly noted, the poor guy still had to return home to his wife, who was likely to not be so forgiving.

It was a sad story, true, but one that Bernard could make disappear with a drag of his mouse and a loud tap on the delete key. Poof, gone.

Finally he pulled up folders taken from Ned Hazly's computers, including several no one ever had time to go through.

🎮 🎮 🎮

Kelly and Ron watched the four kids appraise the menus, two-foot-tall affairs that advertised a surprisingly small number of dishes, all exotic-sounding entrées running thirty-five to forty dollars each plus a set "service fee" of twenty percent.

"I'm guessing they don't get to eat at restaurants like this very often," Kelly commented.

"Well, this is one of those places where you go in shocked at the prices but exit smiling at the result. Also, the steaks are the size of small cows."

Patricia raised her hand to get a waiter's attention.

"What do you need?" Kelly asked.

"Butter. They served this great bread, but no butter to eat it with."

"Use the olive oil," O'Brian said.

"What?"

Kelly jumped in. "The oil in those two bottles. Pour some on your bread plate and then dip the bread."

"Oh," Patricia responded as all four kids began grabbing bread, finally understanding how they were supposed to eat it.

O'Brian smiled. "I swear to God, if that were Bernard, he'd have come up with a cube of butter from somewhere in his coat."

🐗 🐗 🐗

Bernard was intrigued by a folder from Hazly's computers titled "For Holstenbeck." He opened it to find a single file, a video.

He clicked its icon and was surprised to find an animation, a cartoon. The style was crude and simple, with a bare amount of detail on the people and the settings.

Opening a Snickers, Bernard sat back to watch.

A swelling group of virtual protesters gathers in front of a skyscraper in what appears to be downtown Seattle.

To the young protesters their numbers loom large along the narrow street as they prepare to "occupy" an afternoon rush hour and make a bank shareholder meeting as unpleasant as possible.

But to senior banking executives glancing down from forty-eight stories above, the protesters appear tiny as ants—ants as viewed from a magnifying glass on a sunny day.

One of the executives places a laptop next to a window and smiles at his colleagues as a row of wall-mounted screens on one side of the room come to life—one showing a map of the area and others video and graphic diagrams of sensor data from the streets below.

The executive pushes a few keys, and flashing red lines on the map show traffic cutoffs around the city, with traffic lights closing roads and state police shutting down major arteries: Interstate 5 and Highway 99 to the north and south, and I-90 to the east. The crowd can no longer swell, since no new vehicles can approach the area.

"The city of Seattle is effectively shut down," the executive announces.

Now the map and the live video show lines of giant police vans side by side a few blocks to the north and south, their rear doors open and facing the demonstrators. In seconds, partitions block the spaces between the vans and the sidewalks around them.

"As we speak, security software is scouring video taken of the street, locating and pulling still images of faces, images that are then run through a database of known criminals, occupiers, and anarchists," the executive continues.

With the known troublemakers ID'd, a formation of twenty or more small military drones lines up outside the windows, forty-eight stories aboveground. The executives stare on in awe at the evil-looking vehicles. Painted black with red flames on their sides, the four-foot-wide drones are equipped with cameras—and guns.

Then one by one they light out and down toward the street below, each with its own targets, its own lethal designs.

And in seconds the once-confident crowd scatters in chaos as shots ring out seemingly from every direction, and the troublemakers and rabble-rousers are targeted and shot, leaving the others to run into waiting police vans, the only spots offering cover.

Within minutes the street is quiet, is unoccupied save for the lonely, now-unoccupied bodies lying silently about in pools of virtual blood on the narrow avenue.

"Swell day for a shareholder meeting," the executive comments.

A caption floats to the top of the video, reading:

Cannecare Project Z
Sample Citywide Deployment

"Project Z?" Bernard asked, loud enough for the front-desk clerk to hear.

Phil Gradee was still sitting in his car an hour after pulling into his driveway.

About him, the semicircle of luxury condominiums in his complex provided neighbors a prime view of the latest chapter in the Phil Gradee story, a drama that had been filled with massive police and FBI searches and masses of gossip at the mailboxes by the clubhouse.

Today, afternoon dog walkers would notice Phil sitting alone motionless in his car, staring forward, not moving.

The fact was, Phil Gradee did not want in any way to go into his house, did not want to face his wife, did not want his children to see him. For not only did he disable mechanical safety switches that would have shut down Cannecare Tower's super-cooling system before it could kill Randolph, not only did he hide what he did in a fit of shame . . .

Also in his laptop bag he had his "walking papers," as Ned Hazly had called them.

So Phil Gradee would be telling his wife not only how he had been duped into helping Brenda Tate murder Randolph; he'd also be telling her he was unemployed, and right at the moment, Gradee figured, right at the moment, his résumé would not impress. "So why was it that you left your last job?" "Oh, I obeyed some phony emails and inadvertently helped murder our CEO."

What Phil could not see was that inside his own kitchen window, his wife peered out, wondering, worrying, why the man she loved so much, Phil the husband and father, why he was suffering and why he was not, had not been for weeks, telling her what was happening.

Bernard inspected more folders, found one named Project Y Interface Screenshots. He clicked on it, discovered several JPEGs, and opened the first.

It was a screenshot of an interface, the same basic design he had seen in the Cannecare PEC.

At first it didn't make sense, but the details began to speak for themselves.

The interface showed a blueprint of Cannecare Tower, high-lighted by red poison symbols in several locations.

The next JPEG showed just the thirteenth floor, with red symbols all along the hallway.

The one after that showed the same screen with a pop-up box. It read:

> **Element:** Mini Teargas Gun
> **Installation:** Pending
> **Status:** Pending

On the next, yet another box:

> **Element:** Mini Flamethrower
> **Installation:** Complete
> **Status:** Armed

"Armed? A flamethrower? Installation complete?"

🎮 🎮 🎮

It turns out fifteen-ounce steaks, especially ones packing flavor that keeps you eating, are not the ideal meal before an airsoft gun competition at a police training facility.

This lesson O'Brian and Kelly, both veterans of police firing ranges, reflected on as they slid to the ground along one wall and watched the kids run around—the kids didn't seem to have any problem at all—and shoot pop-up targets pretty much indiscriminately, including those painted with women holding babies and children holding dolls.

"I think I ate too much," Kelly complained.

The expression on O'Brian's face revealed ready agreement.

"I sure as hell wish I were that young again," he moaned.

Kelly countered. "You know, I feel I am. After all that's happened, after how scary things got there, I feel like I have a new life in front of me now."

"And well you should. That's a fine way to feel and one you deserve."

"Hey, you should, too. Your career in the private sector just took off. You can go anywhere from here, the way you helped the Seattle PD, even the feds."

"Yeah, but in the end, it wasn't computer forensics that saved the day. In the end it was the reliable nose of a dog that found dynamite."

"*After* Brenda Tate had been well established as a prime suspect, established by your forensics."

O'Brian frowned. "More Bernard's, actually. But it doesn't matter. I'm just happy the whole thing is done with, you're OK, and Brenda Tate is locked up."

"Agreed. Hey, if we survive the afternoon here with the kids, I'll buy you a drink to celebrate."

"You're on. But I may need it as a painkiller."

Element: Mini Gun Turrets
Installation: Complete
Status: Armed

"Come on!" Bernard demanded as he continued searching through "Project Y" JPEGs—explosive discoveries considering they came from one of Hazly's computers.

"Gun turrets in the hallway of an office building? I simply do not believe this. I should certainly *not* want to be an employee sneaking in late in the morning. Herbert Iggid, I have to believe, would love this."

Continuing through the few remaining menu mockups, he found his attention drawn to a submenu screenshot that offered further violent choices, options that turned Bernard's blood first hot—then cold:

Boiler 1: (1) Heat Stun   (2) Heat Kill
Boiler 2: (1) Heat Stun   (2) Heat Kill
Super Cooler 1: (1) Freeze Stun   (2) Freeze Kill
Super Cooler 2: (1) Freeze Stun   (2) Freeze Kill

This from a laptop computer Ned Hazly carried to and from his office each day.

🐾 🐾 🐾

Two days earlier, Thursday morning.

Brenda Tate awoke horrified, images of the previous night floating through her mind.

After finding the cellphone and realizing her long-planned hideaway had been compromised, that the police might arrive any second, Brenda had rushed out and rented the step van. The Internet loot and other items she loaded were worth a couple hundred thousand dollars, she calculated as she stuffed the back.

When finally she drove off at close to eleven at night—not bad timing, considering—she was staring more in the rear-view mirror than at the road ahead, hoping, praying, not to see the flashing lights of police cars coming after her.

But she made it, and while she had only the vague structure of a plan in mind, she knew she would have to execute it as quickly as possible. That plan would take her east over the mountains, but first she needed sleep.

She drove north taking Highway 99, avoiding the main route, I-5. Once she was well clear of Seattle, she started checking hotels to find one with a business center, one that had a computer for guests.

On her third stop, she was successful and checked in, careful to use a debit card for an account opened under her maiden name and with her sister's social security number—a girl's gotta cover her tracks.

It was well after one a.m. when she got to her room, and with the business center closed until five-thirty the next morning,

Brenda opted to grab a few hours' sleep. Sitting on the hotel room bed, she sucked down two canned whisky sours while watching Home Shopping Network.

As exhausted as she was, Brenda still felt she needed something to help her sleep, and canned whiskey sours somehow fit the darkly romantic turns her life had suddenly taken.

But between the physical exertion and stress of a painfully long day, both body and mind plummeted readily into slumber.

When five-fifteen rolled along, she answered a wake-up call but rolled right over and sank back to sleep. Just before six, she roused, slowly at first but finally garnering the resolve to explore the hotel coffee maker.

As she examined the cheap appliance, she flipped on the TV to catch the six o'clock news.

The report that flashed on the screen injected a much-stronger punch than all the caffeine in Seattle could have packed.

> . . . incredible that no one was killed in the bombing, not when you see the condition of the Pendrite Hotel. And police are saying they believe the incident was not a terrorist act, but rather was somehow connected to the recent murder of tech executive Randolph Tate, co-founder of Cannecare Automation.
>
> It appears the bomb was set off in an elevator on the floor where consultants who were investigating the Tate murder were staying.
>
> In connection with the incident, police are trying to locate Tate's wife, Brenda Tate, a person of interest in the case; and also Cannecare co-founder Ned Hazly . . .

"What the hell?" Brenda asked aloud, confused. "A bombing at the Pendrite? Ned?"

Saturday evening.

Ned Hazly sat in his favorite spot at the computer console in the PEC, and the feeling of being back in control offered tremendous relief.

Randolph's murder was behind him, Brenda was behind bars, and the police and the behinds working for Chambers, they would not be back sticking their behinds into places where their bothersome noses did not belong. Ned could get on with salvaging Cannecare, turning it into Cannecare Control instead of Cannecare Automation, by finally implementing security projects that would propel the company, and Ned himself, to profit and to fortune.

Cannecare Tower was empty again, it was his again. In fact, think about that, it really *was* his, *all* his for the first time ever—no Randolph, no Brenda, no Kelly Chambers, no Phil Gradee even, telling him what Cannecare and Cannecare Tower could and could not do. Projects X through Z could all continue at full speed; Ned could even begin testing the experimental installations already completed.

Wow. That would be a first.

He'd been able to install software that could trigger lethal heat and cooling in places, but weapons were much trickier. He'd even been able to block off two and a half floors, making them off limits even to Phil Gradee, by labeling them "Top Secret Systems Research Areas," but *testing* them even the slightest bit was impossible, what, with Randolph and Brenda around.

Wow.

Ned inserted a thumb drive into a port on the console and opened a video file. It was a cheesy promotional video of the type Randolph used to make, but it was the only video footage Ned had of the weapons. He clicked Play and sat back to watch.

"The future of building and site security," a voice nearly sang. *"Modern, high-tech, ultra-light remote weapons that are sleek enough to easily tuck out of sight but powerful enough to stop a minor invasion if needed.*

"Meet Tanaire Defense Systems, the company that is redesigning the way buildings and facilities are secured.

"The Tanaire Weapons Platform uses sophisticated plastics to house barrels, gun chambers, and other components to create a variety of sleek, ultra-light weapons, which while small in size pack the same firepower as their conventional counterparts.

"Their small form factor allows these weapons to be easily hidden and then deployed remotely, allowing a single guard using video surveillance to secure numerous stations—with lethal force if required.

"Based in Silicon Valley, with production and most operations in Tel Aviv, Tanaire's early customers include Israel Defense Forces, the U.S. Navy, and several private companies.

"Let's take a look at the Tanaire Gun Turret, a testament of high-tech weaponry of the twenty-first century . . ."

Ned smiled. He had read about pedestrians who got spooked at the design of their building and chose to walk on the other side of Second Avenue as they passed. Little did those who crept by on this particular day know that the red glow that seemed sometimes to emanate from Cannecare Tower's pointy crown, that glow was never more ominous than now.

🐾 🐾 🐾

A new imaginary video game gleamed in the eyes of Bernard Walker as he continued to study files copied from Ned Hazly's computer.

Scattered about him on the lobby sofa were pizza boxes delivered from two local choices for lunch—one of the boxes half-full, the other half-empty—as well as plastic soda bottles and snack wrappers that accumulated, surprisingly to the front-desk clerk, without Bernard's ever having stood up.

In this new imaginary video game, Bernard pictured his antagonist, the Evil, Pointy Ned Hazly, seated before the PEC's spaceship-style computer console and the Cannecare Video Wall beyond it—bridge of a starship—in command of a tower armed with an array of weaponry, all at Hazly's pointy fingertips as he peered down on a helpless city below.

This might well inspire a video game for OffCide Studios where a player must enter a possessed, evil tower, a building that can see, think, kill . . . and he (or *she*, yes, Patricia and Kelly) must journey through the dark high-rise to the uppermost story, there to confront a cold-hearted (icy cold in this case) villain.

Bernard thought about that. Bernard thought about mutant sheep and possessed zombies and all the defeats going on in the virtual waste world that had been consuming him.

Then thought again about a villain that was not virtual at all, a villain back in charge of an armed tower.

Bernard did not stand for losing, and something deep inside insisted it was more painful to lose in the brick-and-mortar world than in a virtual one. Especially for brick-and-mortar murder victims like Randolph Tate, who would not be respawned.

All this wasn't to say, though, that there wasn't a video game yet to be played.

In fact it dawned on Bernard at that moment, that it might well be time for a proof-of-concept test for *just* such a video game. And if the test were held not in a make-believe game environment but in the brick-and-mortar world, well, that would be all the better to show investors.

Bernard group-texted the team, saying simply: "Emergency, return to Sheetless ASAP."

Then logged onto *Woeful WasteWorld*.

Best play. There'd be no time later.

But in minutes, as Bernard went for a jaunt into zombie-occupied Rheinland . . . he instead drifted slowly but deeply into badly needed Slumberland.

🐾 🐾 🐾

"What the hell's, he . . . sleeping?" O'Brian bellowed as he followed the others into the lobby of the Sheetless.

"It appears he didn't make it to the airport." Kelly ventured.

The anxious group watching, O'Brian edged his way to a motionless Bernard, leaned down, and shook an arm.

Bernard opened an eye slightly, let in varying shades of light, closed it again and thought, half dreaming of a postapocalyptic Rheinland that had . . . 'My God, Ron O'Brian?' . . .

Then started, shook himself awake, and set about a vain pocket search for Pepsi.

"What the hell's going on?" O'Brian demanded. "Are you OK? What's the emergency?"

Bernard located a half-bottle of non-Pepsi on the sofa, one warm enough it was half-empty, not half-full. He sipped, let the liquid wet his throat, and forced his eyes to clear as he made out eager faces . . . imploring him for information.

"You OK? What's the emergency?" Kelly repeated from a distance.

"How come you didn't head back to Cliff Shores?" O'Brian added.

Bernard blinked sad, sad eyes at the question.

"Emergency? What's wrong?" he asked morosely, holding up the Sprite bottle. "Why, do you realize that the soda machine in this establishment does *not* stock Pepsi?"

🐾 🐾 🐾

It was a mix of shock and disbelief that gripped Kelly minutes later when she saw the screenshots, menus whose layout clearly fit Cannecare's automation software.

"I don't goddamn believe it," O'Brian repeated several times, apparently to make sure everyone heard.

"Oh God," Kelly agreed. "But Brenda . . . she's . . . What about the dynamite in her yard?"

Bernard set down a now-empty soda bottle. "I would point out that whoever framed you went to a great deal of trouble to do so. It would be far easier just to drop some dynamite in someone's yard."

"Not if you have to somehow *have* dynamite in the first place."

O'Brian butted in. "Moot point. Whoever set the bomb in the Pendrite had dynamite. Bernard, how sure are you these files came from one of Hazly's computers?"

"Entirely. Groups of manually backed-up files, in folders using the same naming system Hazly used at work and at home. Other subfolders include archived email—also Hazly's."

"But Brenda . . ." Kelly's mind just wasn't wrapping around all this. Brenda Tate was locked up in jail for the bombing, for Randolph's murder. "So you're saying Hazly set off the bomb and also framed Brenda?"

"That would appear to be the case."

"Then we have to get this to the police," Kelly urged.

O'Brian sucked in about ten minutes' air in one breath. "Yeah, we call the police with this now, tell them they were wrong again . . . they're not going to want to talk to us."

"Seriously?"

"Actually, yeah. First they have a suspect—you—with solid evidence and we proved them wrong. Next we help them catch Brenda, help them compile all sorts of evidence on *her*, and then we call to say, whoops? On the basis of a couple of files."

"They have to listen to us."

"Add to that, the files were found *not* on the original machine, sitting documented in an SPD evidence room, but are copies of copies on Bernard Walker's laptop in the lobby of . . ." O'Brian took in the room . . . "of the Sheetless in Seattle Sleepery."

"Yeah," Kelly admitted.

"My guess, they'll invite us down to the station sometime tomorrow, hear what we have to say. Then maybe, maybe, they send someone over to talk to Ned Hazly. Remember, the police have concrete evidence linking Brenda Tate to the Pendrite bombing, evidence that the feds helped them discover."

Bernard stood. "More important, if the police do question him, he could say come back tomorrow when his lawyer's there, and then *un*install weapons he appears to have up currently. He has the building to himself, no police running around, no top executives watching. Ned Hazly is in charge. Sitting up in that room, he has power."

Incredibly, given the mood he just created, Bernard tore open a bag of Doritos, pulled one out, and produced a nacho-themed audio crunch that he in no way tried to conceal.

O'Brian flinched. "Do I get the feeling maybe you have something in mind? If not, you'd be on a plane back to San Francisco."

"It would just happen that I do. Here is the thing. I believe it is safe to assume neither the police nor that arraignment judge will be happy to hear from us. What was the judge's name again?" Bernard grimaced at the memory of bitter jowls.

"Merlson?" O'Brian offered.

"Yes. Merlson. I did get the definite impression that Judge Merlson is not in fact a big fan of technology."

This got a hint of smile from O'Brian and Kelly.

"So what we will need to do is to provide a little brick-and-mortar evidence for the police and for King County's judiciary."

"Oh God," O'Brian moaned. "What do you have in mind this time?"

"Very possibly the next title in the OffCide Murder Mystery series."

"Cool!" Les and Dirk chanted from the back, their blind optimism over what Bernard Walker might be plotting eliciting a very different response from the general confusion in the rest of the room.

"Yes. I scarcely believe the police would fail to return to Cannecare Tower for serious investigation immediately if that building were made to look like the Pendrite Hotel does right currently.

"I believe it is in fact time to test Ned Hazly's Project Y."

Cannecare Tower, a video game forming in Bernard's head:
A dark, evil tower, its pointy red top cutting into the sky.

Within lies horrible certain death for most who dare enter,
and yet the payoff at the apex of this spooky high-rise, the stash
up in the tower's keep so to speak, the prize is so valuable that
no one who learns of it can help but be drawn, sucked in, unable
to resist its pull . . .

As one finds oneself facing off against an evil presence, a
consciousness that watches—from everywhere—*and whose lethal*
weapons—from anywhere—*might at any moment strike.*

Of course the catch, there's always a catch: In the brick-and-
mortar world—unlike video game land—players, when killed, do
not get respawned.

"You know this is a bad idea, right?" O'Brian repeated for
about the fortieth time as Kelly picked up the phone.

"Quiet, now, Ron. You don't want Ned to hear you."

"I think this is too dangerous."

Bernard remained adamant. "We have to get Hazly to go up
there—if he isn't already—and it is essential that he be desperate
and afraid when he does."

"Besides," Kelly added, "our plan will give Phil Gradee a
chance to make up for what happened."

"Yeah, right," O'Brian said in evident disagreement.

With a new Tanaire software installation underway, Ned took
out a small bottle of champagne and a plastic cup he'd brought.

As he watched the installation's progress bar, he poured and sipped.

The police were long gone, so he could restore the PEC systems to the level he had them before: armed and dangerous. Sure, only about a tenth of the weapons he had planned were up and running, but, the weapon-control software reinstalled, Ned would within the hour once again be a man with power at his fingertips. Real and deadly power.

To this he lifted his cup. "To Randolph," Ned said aloud. "And to Cannecare and all it can become, my dear friend."

As if in answer to the toast from beyond, the phone rang, and a brief conversation with Kelly Chambers caused Ned's mood to swing dramatically, as a new set of emotions, marching to a now-audible heartbeat, set in.

🎮 🎮 🎮

Cannecare Tower, the Video Game:

A ruby-red arrow at its top points at the sky, a shimmering gleam in the Seattle skyline's eye. And that's just the brain overlooking, for its lenses lurk throughout, from head to toe, observing, feeling, and, more than anything, waiting, always patient, waiting . . .

For the gamer who bids to enter and climb and try to claim the treasure, to beat the building and conquer the villain at its top . . . a tower fully defended and with seeing eyes . . .

Ah, there's that sticky problem again. Since brick-and-mortar players cannot respawn, perhaps we need to change the programming, to rearrange the rules.

If you can change the very fabric of a video game world with a little programming, why can't you do the same for a brick-and-mortar "reality"?

🎮 🎮 🎮

The taxi driver pretended not to be listening as he inspected the three passengers in his rear-view mirror.

"It's too damn dangerous," O'Brian insisted.

"I am certain it will in fact be perfectly safe, considering we will have a detailed map of everything installed in the building," Bernard explained. "When you know your world, you can beat it."

Bernard was rushing to Northgate Mall before the stores closed. He had made two shopping lists and sent the design team to fill one while he headed out to complete the other.

O'Brian tagged along somewhat in terror to try to talk him out of whatever it was Bernard was planning. Seated beside O'Brian, Kelly wasn't sure whose side she was on.

"How do you know the screenshots you found on Hazly's computer aren't way out of date? There could be more weapons in the building."

"We won't be looking at old screenshots; we'll be looking at the same screen Ned Hazly sees. In fact, we will *decide* what Ned Hazly sees. That's where Phil Gradee comes in."

O'Brian stared down at the car seat. "You're talking about real weapons. Guns, flamethrowers. He could very well try to kill us."

"That happens to be exactly what I expect him to do," Bernard said grandly as the cab driver swerved back into the lane they'd just drifted out of.

🎮 🎮 🎮

Ned simply failed to comprehend.

Freeze Kill? This, a term from Kelly Chambers on the phone? He'd removed that software module the very morning after Randolph's murder, before the police came along. It would not have been found in the police search.

Unless, maybe . . . maybe one of Phil Gradee's insane backup systems had made a copy somewhere. On an external server or hard drive. Phil Gradee lost sleep if his browser plug-ins weren't up-to-date. Lost files at work added to the man's graying hair.

The call: Kelly said she *heard* about Project Z, was coming to inspect personally, would meet Ned in the PEC immediately, and if he couldn't explain, she would go to the police. Immediately.

But that wasn't it. That wasn't what set Ned Hazly into a state of nearly debilitating confusion and panic.

What set Ned Hazly into a state of panic was Kelly's claiming also that Brenda suddenly turned out to have an alibi for the night of the bombing, was going to be released.

You see, originally, the day after Randolph's murder, Ned figured Kelly Chambers had found Project Y, had used it to murder Randolph.

Then it turned out to be Brenda who had found it, had used it to kill Randolph.

But if Brenda hadn't found Project Y and used it to kill Randolph, if Kelly had only just now found it . . .

Muscles just above Ned's nose tightened uncomfortably—it was as if he could *feel* his mind at that very spot grappling with but failing to grasp the meaning of the reality before him, of yet another unexpected turn of events.

So, what . . . if it wasn't Kelly, and it wasn't Brenda, then . . . who?

As if on cue, just as this thought navigated its way through his mind, Ned Hazly heard an overwhelming crash, a collision, a crushing whack so hard, so loud, it somehow failed to make any sound at all . . .

🐾 🐾 🐾

An hour later the group stood in the lobby of the Sheetless as Bernard traced out on a map the routes they would follow on their journeys through Cannecare Tower, to the top, to the evil Ned Hazly in the PEC.

O'Brian had planned to physically stop Bernard from going if needed, until Bernard fully explained his—what could be described only as *high-flying*—plan.

"This blueprint is no different from a map of a video game world," Bernard explained. The blueprint on his tablet showed each floor of Cannecare Tower, along with cute skull-and-crossbones icons indicating where weapons were installed, and other icons showing the locations of sensors and cameras.

"The plan is for us to split up into three teams. Kelly and Patricia's route will climb the rear stairwell, cut across the building on the thirteenth floor, where we know weapons are installed, and then proceed up the side stairs. If they make it. And remember, you have to reach the thirteenth floor within ten minutes."

"You sure you want the two girls going alone?" O'Brian asked.

"That will definitely add theatrical effect."

Kelly frowned on the dramatic. "It has be the thirteenth floor?"

"Where we know some weapons are installed already. It seems somehow appropriate. Theater Ned Hazly–style."

"And remember, we're armed," Patricia teased, opening her windbreaker enough to show the shoulder holster and fully automatic airsoft gun inside.

Ignoring her, Bernard continued. "Next, Lester, Eric, and Chen Li, your route will follow the main stairwell, then switch on the sixteenth floor to the side stairs, which exit the top floor just down the hall from the PEC. It's marked as having weapons installed too. But remember, the stairwells also appear to be armed."

"Right," Lester answered.

O'Brian edged next to Bernard. "And you and I? What do we do again?" He did not project the picture of comfort.

"Ah, well, it so happens I am somewhat adverse to stairs, so you and I will be taking the elevator."

"I should appreciate that, given the colossal steak I had for lunch. You know there's only a small chance all this will come together and work, right?" he asserted.

Bernard smiled. "I fully believe it will. Now, is everybody ready?" he asked the group.

Kelly replied with enough enthusiasm to answer for everyone: "Yeah. Game time."

9

Game time.

It was with a visible air of anxiety, of pent-up frustration that his eyes appraised the room. What a mess the situation was by all appearances, by all considerations.

Kelly Chambers again, those kids again. That former cop and that Bernard Walker.

Kelly threatening Ned Hazly over the phone—he'd heard it. The VOIP system Cannecare used for office phones was easy to tap into. And Chambers could cause a lot of damage if she knew so much about Project Y and Project Z.

Oh well, what's a fellow to do?

Game time. Fingers journeyed out over keyboard and mouse, causing windows to pop open. Directly before him the two console monitors provided command menus while the PEC Video Wall displayed everything that went on anywhere in and around Cannecare Tower, illustrated with video, graphs, maps, and more.

Prominent toward the center a large window showed the lobby, one of the priority spots to monitor.

The lone security guard there, it seemed he might be the only person to survive—that is, if he were smart enough get out before trouble began.

Such a shame what was likely to happen; this might well be his last visit to the Prototype Engineering Center.

Best then again, was it not, while he had the opportunity, best to test the room properly and thoroughly and show all that it could do, all that Cannecare Tower could do—a demonstration of the X, the Y, and the Z, the prize and the payoff of investment he soon would be taking home.

Game time.

Nick, the guard on duty in the lobby, shot a mean face at a drunk who stopped to peer in the glass doors, a mug that sent the man scurrying. It was an expression Nick had perfected. Though he didn't carry a gun, he was still an armed guard, one armed with a scowl that sent would-be trespassers on their way.

Nick hated this post more than any other. His job was, simply stated, to stand around for eight hours, minus a lunch break, and do absolutely nothing other than give the passing riffraff dirty looks to let them know they were unwelcome.

Within ten minutes into a shift, the spine pressed on the lower back, the feet hurt. But no leaning, no slumping was allowed, his sergeant insisted. Nor cellphones nor books nor newspapers.

So on this night as on many others Nick was facing hours of boredom. As always, he thought about his mother's insistence that he find a safer job. On this night, as always, he found himself almost wishing something would happen, that something would break through the monotonous boredom and send a little adrenaline to his aching lower spine.

That was when four people suddenly slammed open the giant glass lobby doors as they rushed in . . .

The figure in the PEC saw the kids burst into the lobby, they were carrying backpacks, the security guard saw them—but then the lobby went black, the whole building seemed to go black.

What?

No electricity alerts were flashing. On a whim he pulled up a camera view from across Second Avenue . . . to see Cannecare Tower from the outside, to see . . . only darkness

It was the video feed itself that was dark. There was no video feed.

But the blueprints and graphs, they were still showing everyone's locations, as measured by Cannecare's newest installation of sensors, a mix of infrared, motion, heat, and sound.

Whatever they were up to, Kelly Chambers' kids appeared to not know what they'd gotten into. They just showed their hand and they were chasing a higher straight with an inside draw.

They would have to be far more clever than that, would have to do more than cut video streams, if they were to, yes, even survive.

Seeing the small champagne bottle on the console, he brushed it aside and replaced it with a pint bottle from his own pocket.

"So Hazly can't see any video?" O'Brian asked.

"Correct." The expression on Gradee's face failed to instill confidence.

"How is that possible?"

"Ned thinks he has control of the building. About six months ago, he set it up so the PEC could take control, which is neither legal nor advisable. We're supposed to always have final control here on the ground floor. For any manner of emergency purposes. But Ned insisted it was only for demonstrations."

"So if Hazly has control up there, how can you shut down his video?"

"It's still hard-wired for control from here—something Ned thought he could work around. You see, he has control, but his control is still routed through here."

"He couldn't have rewired it?"

"Sure. At considerable cost. Also, I may have neglected to tell him I could easily regain control down here."

"You lied?" O'Brian mused in a friendly voice.

"No, though it's possible I may have failed to dampen his enthusiasm."

"Good thinking. Still, you don't look exactly confident."

Gradee put on his best no-confidence face. "I'm not. When Ned told me about setting up control for the PEC, that shook me up. Not exactly best practices. Now you're telling me he has weapons in the building? In areas no one but his people have been allowed into? I don't have any software here that can confirm that. Or control these things if you are correct."

"But you can see Ned's screen in the PEC?"

Gradee pulled a window to the front. "Yes, here. It's a simple remote-desktop system we set up so we could make fixes to the PEC computers from here."

"Yet still you look uncertain."

"I can see what he sees, I can back up his email, I can defrag his hard drive, but I don't have any access to these weapons he supposedly has.

"The only thing we'll be able to do from here is watch him use those weapons."

Nick the guard slipped back several yards as he pulled out his radio.

"Engineering Center, this is the lobby. Do you copy?" He was calling the ground-floor room, where the building's day-to-day operations were managed.

Nothing. He pulled out his work cellphone, which was set also to work like a radio.

"Engineering Center."

Instead of a radio answer, though, the phone instead rang, seemingly in response. The caller ID read Phil Gradee.

"Sir? Yes! This is Nick Kyle on duty in the lobby! A group of kids just ran into the lobby and then back to the stairwells. We better call 911."

"No, Nick, listen. This is Phil Gradee. This is a drill. Those kids are part of an exercise to test Cannecare security systems. You did perfect. So come down to the Engineering room immediately. Please exit from the front of the lobby and walk around the outside of the building down to the Engineering Center."

Nick was confused. He'd heard Phil Gradee the building manager had left the company.

"What? Are you serious?"

"Yes. This building's empty tonight, so Ned Hazly decided to run tests."

"But I should call—"

"Ned's the only other person in the building, and I've got him on speakerphone here. Come on down and join us. I think you'll get a kick out of this."

Confused or not, the prospect of going down to Mr. Gradee's office versus having to confront a bunch of rowdy kids . . .

Meanwhile, across the lobby, Lester shouted to Bernard: "Stairwell doors are unlocked."

"The master key opened them all?"

"Yep."

Everyone nodded as Bernard gestured them to huddle up and listen.

"OK, it is essential that we carry out our assigned tasks very carefully and get them right every step of the way. Let's break up and get started. Head to your respective battle stations, people. Go."

Twenty stories above, the figure heard clearly the exchange; there wasn't a lot that Cannecare Tower's audio sensor system did not pick up.

Forget the video.

Red lights showed the ground-floor doors to all three stairwells had been opened, confirming what he'd heard from the lobby audio. The kids were tracked loosely by dim red lights that brightened when sensors confirmed locations.

After a minute the system showed the intruders making their way up the front and rear stairwells, three lights/people in the main stairs and two in the rear.

But, oh my, how stairwells can be dangerous places!

The figure clicked on an icon and a menu appeared, one labeled Rear Stair. He used an arrow key to select the menu's second option: Freeze Kill, and instantly a blast of near-hurricane winds and frosty air pumped visibly in from vents on every floor.

A few more clicks brought up a menu for the front stairwell, where sensors also reported intruders climbing upward: third floor, fourth floor . . . For this one he chose Heat Kill.

He did the same for the side stairwell, lest anyone enter it.

"How will you die?" the figure inquired aloud. "By cold or by heat, by fire or by ice?"

Phil Gradee sat bewildered in the small ground-floor engineering center. He was perplexed because he really didn't understand what was happening, what it was that Kelly Chambers and her strange friends were doing.

Oh, he understood it had to do with catching Randolph's killer. It was just that these kids seemed to be breaking an awful lot of rules in the process, and some part of Phil's brain was simply unable to process breaking rules as being OK, whatever the circumstances.

A text alert appeared on Gradee's phone. "Push open door, floor 13, rear stair," the message from Kelly read.

Despite deep-felt misgivings, Gradee moved his mouse and complied, and with the aid of a magic self-opening door arm, the thirteenth floor rear stairwell door in Cannecare Tower creaked open.

A blinking red light showed a stairwell breach on floor thirteen, rear stair. The door was set to lock, so the intruders had to be using master keys again.

They were moving fast, too, were running, he could see—had to be to get that far that fast—and to not succumb to the freeze.

He opened floor thirteen's audio feed as he watched two flickering lights enter the hallway. Instantly he recognized the voice of Kelly Chambers.

"Run faster," she shouted.

"I'm running as fast as I can." It was a younger girl's voice, one that like Kelly's rang out in fear.

"Ready on main stair, floor 16. Open door," a new text read, this one from Lester.

Phil didn't like this; it all went against what he'd been taught, what he himself preached. Worse, Phil's magic self-opening doors, his prize achievement, they were being abused, used to break rules. Phil didn't accept that at all.

But he did as instructed, and again one of his famous auto regulators did its magic.

A new red light blinked, showing a security breach from the main stairwell on floor sixteen.

"How is that possible," he said aloud. "They should have fried in that much heat. What the hell are . . ."

Switching on audio for the area, he recognized the voices of the kids who always followed Walker around.

"Are you OK?" one shouted, out of breath.

"No, we have to move quickly. Let's make for the other stairwell!"

On the thirteenth floor Kelly's voice rang out in panic.

"Something's wrong, Patricia," she shouted. "This was a mistake. Call 911! We have to get out of here."

"We need to try the other stairwell. If it's not too late on that one too."

Listening, the figure turned to the Video Wall sensor maps —two of them now—showing the thirteenth floor. A chart next to them registered the different sensor reads confirming Kelly's and Patricia's movements.

"Oh, dear, it is more than too late, Kelly Chambers. For you think that I cannot see you, but my eyes can see in the dark, yes, the dark!"

The sensor maps showed Kelly and Patricia pausing about halfway along the main hall. Moreover, their lights on the maps remained brightened, indicating a reliable sensor lock on their location.

The figure opened a new menu, labeled Floor 13 Weapons, though it offered only the one installed: 1. Central Gun Turret.

"Yes, yes, it is time to show Mr. Walker and his friends that his video games are just that: video games. Mr. Walker should in no way be disrespectful to Cannecare's technology."

Pictures took shape in his mind—Kelly Chambers and the trouble that woman had caused him . . . then her friends and the much worse trouble . . . then the impressively slick little high-tech gun turrets Ned's engineers bought for Project Y.

Tiny steel barrels and chambers set into ultrahard plastic cases, those positioned and aimed on aluminum robotic arms—remotely and with deadly accuracy on either PC or Mac.

"Good job," the figure said to an unmoving Ned Hazly on the floor. "I am grateful you have these running on floor 13."

He turned to the console menus.

"Goodbye, Miss Chambers, and sorry about your little friend there."

With that he clicked the icon that read Ready, causing a section of drywall ceiling to lift and rotate to reveal the high-tech three-barrel turret case that shifted down and rotated to hone in on its target . . . and, after pausing to smile, the figure hit Fire, triggering a barrage of rounds—fast automatic fire—from all three barrels, a salvo that continued as the turret edged left, then right, up and down, systematically ravaging the entire area with shells—shattering glass, destroying furniture, and tearing apart entire sections of wall.

Behind the noise he heard terrified screams.

"Shit!" the girl moaned.

"Duck in here!" Kelly shouted.

"Aaaahhh—God. I can't! Ah, Gggooood. You gotta help me. I'm shot, I got shot. Oh God . . ."

The figure hit Pause, causing the guns to fall silent, and all that could be picked up by the high-tech microphones on the *thirteenth floor of Cannecare Tower was a high-pitch shrieking, a cry of pain. The girl's.*

He smiled, hit Fire again and a second barrage of bullets roared out, tearing up wall and door and cubicle and glass and silencing any and all sound that had remained.

Three voices echoed out along the sixteenth floor.

"Those were shots, that was shooting," Lester yelled.

"Oh God, a few floors down, I think?" Eric was panicked. "That's where, where Patricia and Kelly were crossing. What do we do?"

"We have to help them," Chen Li insisted.

"Hide in here—it's a meeting room or something. I'm calling 911."

Chen was already on his phone dialing Patricia.

"I'm afraid we will not be calling 911 today. I am not quite yet ready to depart."

"Besides, I really, really want to try out the flamethrowers."

Once the three lights settled in one spot—a conference room, as heard on audio—they brightened: again a reliable read on location.

The figure pulled up a weapons menu for the floor, again getting only one choice, but one he felt fully appropriate for the purpose.

With a click of a mouse, he selected it: 1. Flamethrower. He hit Ready and a turret of similar design to the gun case descended from the ceiling and aimed in the kids' direction, its threatening barrels, wide with holes, looming.

He pictured those smart . . . what's that term, smart-aleck kids there, watching this high-tech flame-thrower's eerie movement.

"So you would like to see reality over a video game, Mr. Walker? Very well.

"Say goodbye to a few more of your friends."

He clicked Fire, Whole Area, and a flare of blue-centered flame burst out and down as the turret began a slow rotation to methodically incinerate the entire room—to the sound, at least initially, of three shrieking voices.

After a moment just silence.

O'Brian pressed the button and the elevator door opened.

"Ah, here, the key goes in here."

"And this key gives us control of the elevator?" Bernard asked.

"Yep. All elevators have them. It's what firefighters use."

"Then I believe we should get started. It is high time we pay Ned Hazly a visit."

"Oh my, not the elevator," the figure exclaimed with a chuckle. "In a horror movie where an evil skyscraper is alive, you never, never, ever want to take the elevator."

He watched as the car rose higher and higher on the Video Wall blueprint, both a graphic of the elevator car and a number at the top counting off floors: 4, 5, 6 . . .

"Sadly, the existence of a meddling building manager and an overly powerful city fire department made it impossible to implement any so-called Project Y solutions in the elevators."

"Oh well, perhaps this is one fix that would be more satisfying in fact to make in person."

From inside a case the figure produced a small pistol. Holding it up, he checked the chamber, turned off the safety. Then walking to the PEC door, he began practicing a talk of sorts as he strolled leisurely out and down the hall, all the while keeping a casual but careful eye on the number panel above the elevator, a far-older technology but one more trustworthy than the PEC's in a brick-and-mortar way.

"I am sad to announce," the figure went on aloud, "that your friends could not be here to join us."

The panel showed the car's continued ascent: 8, 9, 10 . . .

"Yes, I am afraid real life is nothing like a video game, Mr. Walker. In real life, when you die, you die."

"OK, we're nearly there," O'Brian said. "Keep your eyes open and be ready to move."

"You don't want to take your revolver out?" Bernard asked.

"It *is* out." O'Brian's husky voice signaled intrigue.

"Well, do be ready to use it. I would not be surprised to find Ned Hazly facing the elevator when we get there."

Standing in front of the elevator, the figure didn't hear the conversation as the audio played behind him in the PEC.

The count continued: 14, 15, 16 . . .

"Yes, yes, indeed, time to show Mr. Bernard Walker what brick-and-mortar death feels like."

. . . 17, 18 . . .

"Yes, yes, considering all the trouble you have caused me, both of you, I would much prefer the pleasure of pulling the trigger personally."

. . . 19, 20.

Planting a mental snapshot of the elevator doors in his mind, the figure aimed his gun dead center, steadied his arm, delighted that he was about to be the last-ever sight Bernard Walker and Ron O'Brian would experience . . . and as the elevator doors crept open, he sighted the two shapes emerging, his finger eagerly squeezing the trigger, and . . . and—

. . . and his jaw spiked down hard as he realized he was aiming at two . . . two, what . . . two drones of some sort?! With phones—cellphones—hanging on string about three feet beneath.

All this leaving an expression of utter shock on his face, an expression of utter shock equaled only by . . .

. . . gasps of complete bewilderment from Bernard and team huddled across Second Avenue as they stood staring at tablet screens mounted on two drone remotes and saw:

Standing before their two drones on the twentieth floor of Cannecare Tower, gun stretched before him, stood not Ned Hazly as expected but Rainer Holstenbeck.

10

Sergeant Peter Sanchez of the Seattle Police Department had gone to bed early. The murder investigation had been hard enough; after the bombing and after the case went federal both in jurisdiction and the media . . . through all that Sanchez had racked up enough overtime pay to get the department written up by the union, as well as an oppressively insistent sleep deficit.

And that was before providence somehow chose *him*, Sergeant Peter Sanchez, to oversee Brenda Tate's arrest.

So it was from a deep, deep slumber that Sanchez was interrupted by the cellphone placed next to his bed.

Cursing, he rolled over to grab it and sat up.

"Sergeant?" came a voice. "I thought you'd want to know. Something's up at that Cannecare place."

"What? What are you talking about?"

"The Cannecare building on Second Avenue. We got calls. There's smoke pouring out near the top. And we've gotten three different reports of possible gunfire."

"Seriously? You got squad cars headed over, right? Called Fire?"

"Yeah, 'course."

"I'm on my way too. Thanks, Hank."

"Rainer?" Kelly ventured in shock.

O'Brian was equally lost. "Could Holstenbeck have been working with Hazly on this whole thing?"

"I can't believe this." Rainer Holstenbeck was the last person Kelly would have suspected.

"Any chance Gradee can get video of the PEC?" O'Brian asked. Kelly quickly got her phone out. "I want to see if Hazly's in there."

"Phil," Kelly shouted into the phone, "Phil, can you reconnect video streams and access video of the PEC?" Then to O'Brian: "He's trying."

Meanwhile the rest of the group—breathing and well but confused—watched in amazement via drone cameras as Holstenbeck fought to comprehend his situation—entertainment enough that they forget their own shock.

"Jesus, I hope you're recording this," Patricia whined at Bernard and Lester. Lester had taken over O'Brian's remote control.

Nick the security guard had followed O'Brian out from Gradee's engineering center to where the group stood across Second Avenue.

"I really don't get any of this," he said. "That's video from drones we're seeing? Inside the building?"

Patricia giggled and pointed at the tablet attached to Bernard's remote. "Yeah, and that guy there, he thought those drones were *us*. That building's thick with all kinds of cameras and sensors, but we halted the video stream."

Nick's blank expression made it clear he did not follow.

"You see, we blacked out his video feed up there, and these drones registered as people as they passed sensors. They have cellphones attached—that's for two reasons. One, to help trick the sensors into showing the drones as the size of people—that's why they hang several feet below. And two, to trick the audio sensors.

See, those phones were broadcasting our voices as the drones traveled through the building. In fact, I'm pretty sure that guy thinks we're all dead." Patricia smiled, then frowned. "Except . . . that guy's not supposed to be there."

Patricia's further explanation only increased the bewilderment on Nick's face.

The conversation was halted by the thundering sound of Bernard's voice as he held up his remote:

"Aah, watch this, this is going to be *fun*."

🐃 🐃 🐃

The thoughts rushing through Holstenbeck's head were intense, were consuming.

'*Drones! The idiots sent drones? What are they . . . But I heard them talking—*' *Here he noted the cellphones hanging on kite string. A very silly sight until he considered it: The devices set on speaker phone could transmit voices, and the string and phones would make the drones register as people would on infrared and motion sensors.*

'*Oh my, the other floors, the girls and those kids. Were they drones? Yes, yes, and then where are Mr. Walker and . . .*'

Here Holstenbeck noticed the cameras attached to the bottom of each drone, with lenses that moved like eyes as they stared back at him.

'*Oh my, no . . . and they're seeing right back at me?*'

All this while he'd held the small pistol out straight, pointed, and it occurred to him that he was providing video proof of his crimes, video evidence of the very sort Cannecare, well, he, had used on Kelly Chambers.

Holstenbeck straightened his aim and fired. The bullet audibly pinged the side of a drone (the one Lester operated) and hit the ceiling beyond—barely fazing the drone in the process.

Next, the second drone wiggled. And spoke.

It spoke!

"*I have to tell you,*" *the drone (actually its phone) said as it hovered before him.* "*It is not at all polite to shoot people. And it is also not polite to shoot drones.*" *He recognized the voice as Bernard Walker's.*

Suddenly the drone lifted up two feet and darted back to the elevators, accompanied by a loud buzzing of blades . . . then steadied briefly before diving for speed and swooping straight at Holstenbeck. Rainer fell to his knees, nearly dropping his pistol and just barely dodging a direct hit.

Swiveling around, he caught sight of it as it turned to a stop and just hung there in mid-air, eight feet off the floor.

Holstenbeck fired three more shots, dinging the drone twice, but to no effect.

He moved to his feet with plans to dart toward the PEC, but Bernard's drone lowered to block his path while Lester's closed in from behind. Holstenbeck panicked again and fired off two rounds, these at Lester's drone, again with no result.

"How dare you!" came Lester's voice from that drone as it turned tail, sped back to the elevator, then turned back to dive at full speed targeting Holstenbeck's chest. Holstenbeck fired off two more rounds as he jumped to the ground.

Seconds later, as he sat up to see where it went, he saw instead Bernard's drone whipping straight into his line of sight, dragging its cellphone along the floor as it flew—a final image as the thing crashed head-on into Holstenbeck's left ear with a stinging blow, then lifted to the ceiling raising the cellphone into the air just above him.

"Bull's-eye!" came Bernard's voice through the phone.

"Right on target," Les shouted. "That should teach him not to shoot at expensive drones."

Kelly, Chen, and Eric, huddled behind Bernard to watch the tablet screen, were cheering as well, a revelry O'Brian had to quench.

"Hey, can it! Gradee's got video of the PEC. Have a look."

The group shifted to Kelly's phone, held out before her.

"This is a video call," she said, "to Gradee in the ground-floor engineering room. He's showing us video of the PEC."

The picture was hard to make out on such a small screen, but the details were quickly disturbing. Curled on the floor next to the console was Ned Hazly, his wrists and ankles bound with duct tape.

Dried blood covered one side of his face and a red puddle was visible on the floor next to him.

"I'm going up there," O'Brian said.

Kelly blocked his way. "No, the police will be here any minute."

"Sorry, we started this. Hazly's in danger and it might be our fault."

"No, all these weapons—that's Hazly's doing. I don't know how Holstenbeck fits into this, but—"

But O'Brian wasn't waiting around to discuss it. He was, rather, moving across the street in a calm, determined walk that many people would term a run.

"Patricia, I'm going with Ron," Kelly shouted as she followed.

"Oh crap," Patricia muttered as she followed Kelly.

Seeing Patricia head across the street, Chen immediately followed, prompting Lester and Eric, and finally Bernard, to go along too.

Left alone on the sidewalk across from a smoking Cannecare Tower, Nick the security guard marveled over how so short a time ago his evening had been so terribly, terribly dull . . .

In his prime, former police chief Ron O'Brian would have reached the twentieth floor before the others even made the lobby. He certainly wouldn't have waited for them: an armed murderer, a fight in progress—this was a case for trained law enforcement personnel only.

But twenty, well, maybe closer to thirty years down the line, he was thankful that the others held the elevator until he caught up. The gigantic steak for lunch and an afternoon of roughhousing at the range—that hadn't sped him up any, either. Only Bernard plopped in behind him.

In fact by the time O'Brian caught his breath well enough to order everyone to wait in the lobby and let the police handle things, the elevator car had already started moving, so he settled instead on instructions to stay the hell behind him.

Moments later when the door opened on the twentieth floor, O'Brian had his revolver out and ready to fire. He ordered the others to remain as close to the left wall as possible while he led the way down the hall to the PEC, gun held before him.

The hallway journey wasn't made to seem any faster by Bernard's mentioning that, no, he wasn't in fact sure whether the twentieth floor had gun turrets and flamethrowers or not, and by the time they reached the PEC door, the design team had crowded loyally behind Bernard, loyal at least in the knowledge that his oversize form would catch any bullets that came their way.

Once there, Kelly rushed to the biometric scanner, offering her hand and iris for ID.

O'Brian halted her. "Hang on. Bernard. Be ready to swing the door open as fast as possible, and everyone else, get back." O'Brian stepped to the center and aimed his weapon just where the door would open. "OK, go ahead, Kelly."

Kelly put her hand on the hand scanner and eye to the eye reader, and as the door let out a powerful click, Bernard tore it open.

Silence. Only Hazly on the floor, struggling vainly to get loose.

O'Brian jumped forward to check the rest of the PEC—it appeared empty—then spun and raced back into the hallway, gun pointing and ready.

"He may have made a run for it," O'Brian declared.

"I'll check the stairwells," Kelly said and rushed into the PEC, where she bent to check Ned quickly before taking to the console.

"Everybody else inside," O'Brian commanded as he ushered them into the safety of the closed-in space, then slammed the door behind. "If that door moves, tell me. Otherwise, we should be safe in here. Kelly, anything?"

"Give me a minute." She was pulling up sensor maps of the stairs.

O'Brian knelt next to Ned Hazly. "Lester, call for an ambulance. I am—"

A voice from behind cut his sentence short: "Better make it several ambulances. Or hearses."

There, emerging from an enclave behind the Video Wall, its hidden door paneled just like the room's walls, was Rainer Holstenbeck, his pistol pointed at O'Brian.

"Drop it," Holstenbeck demanded. "Drop it! Consider what I have done in this building already, and at the Pendrite. Yes, do not think for one minute I would hesitate to add your gravestones to the list. Oh, and in case you're unsure whether this is loaded or whether I am serious . . ." Holstenbeck aimed and fired a shot into Hazly's leg, causing the man to curl up in a semiconscious groan.

The few of the group who were not already situated behind O'Brian physically were there in spirit and carefully stepping in that direction, testing yet again their tolerance for being packed together in tight spaces.

"Drop it!" Holstenbeck repeated.

Letting his revolver hang between two fingers in his left hand, O'Brian slowly lowered it to the floor.

"Don't shoot. Let's not do anything rash. We can work this out."

"No, we cannot work this out, Mr. O'Brian. The trouble you have caused me and the trouble you have caused my country . . . Slide the revolver to me. Now!"

His eyes glued upward the whole while, O'Brian slid the revolver hard across the floor, to just a few feet in front of the man.

Holstenbeck slid it aside with a foot. "Thank you. Now, goodbye, Mr. O'Brian." He straightened his arm to aim at O'Brian's head, clearly preparing to shoot.

"Hey, Rainer," Kelly jumped in to divert. "Rainer! Why'd ya do it? Why'd ya kill Randolph?" She sounded like a rowdy baseball fan taunting an opponent from the stands of Yankee Stadium.

"I did *not* kill Randolph, Miss Chambers. No, no, *you* killed Randolph. You and your privacy concerns.

"If you hadn't come along, Cannecare systems would be deployed already across all of Lessenberg. All the same, they will be soon."

"That's it? You were planning to take the technology back home with you?"

"I assure you, you may speak in the present tense, for I *am* taking it back home with me. In fact, I'll be leaving as soon as I settle a few debts with you. Our capital is beautiful in the springtime."

"So all your Mr. Joviality, your constant everyone's best friend, that was . . . what? An act?"

"I assure you, I am a very likeable person, but I am not quite the silly, bumbling man you knew."

Bernard shifted forward to Kelly's right. "Also, I would point out, he's not the technology-challenged person he pretended to be." Bernard eyed Kelly and O'Brian. "When we met, you will remember, Mr. Holstenbeck needed a computer to show us a video on, and he had run out and *just happened to buy* a two-thousand-dollar Alienware machine. A powerful gaming machine."

"And I can assure *you*," Holstenbeck said, "that, yes, these are slick machines, very slick. Quality. But I buy them for the same reason I buy Rolex. I demand the best. I do not waste time on video games."

Ron edged to his feet, stood up beside Lester.

"OK, and we're going to cooperate in every way," he assured Holstenbeck. "You need money? A car?"

"I need nothing from you, Mr. O'Brian, other than silence." He renewed his aim on O'Brian. "Say goodbye . . ."

Kelly crept further to her right, away from O'Brian, putting her slightly behind the console, then lit out in a full New York tone of voice:

"Hey, Rainer, I'm glad I got to meet the *real* you, ya know? I mean, you *do* know everyone thinks you're a dork, right? My God, your stupid clothes, and your constant chatter about that stupid place you're from. Who the hell cares?!"

Her comments confused Holstenbeck. "What are you . . ."

"Yo, dude," Eric yelled as he stepped beyond Kelly, creating an even wider area for Holstenbeck to guard. "Who cut your hair, anyhow? You look like Peter Pan, you know that?"

Holstenbeck's now-shaking arm stretched before him, wavering on where to aim first.

Bernard moved further to the right. "Oh, and listen, *I would have you know* that your wife's muffins taste like dirt. I have no idea where the woman learned to bake, but I have eaten month-old donuts that tasted fresher."

That one hit a nerve; the gun swung to Bernard.

"This is real life, Mr. Walker, not a game, as poor Ned Hazly said many times. Real life with lethal weapons. Not toys." It was fair to say Holstenbeck had lost all traces of the jovial air he was known for.

Lester, meanwhile, had slipped from a side windbreaker pocket the airsoft gun O'Brian had returned, slid off the orange cap, and lowered it slowly to O'Brian's left shoulder.

Holstenbeck continued: "I am sure that you get shot in your video games often. Today you will learn what getting shot feels like in real life, Mr Walker."

His eye fixed on the barrel's sight. He faced a large, easy target, just one quick wiggle of the right index finger, and—

"Freeze!" O'Brian shouted, holding out Lester's mock .357 Magnum Desert Eagle. "You shoot, I shoot." O'Brian's commanding voice supported the threat.

"Lower it. Now! Lower your weapon. I am a veteran police officer. I *will* shoot."

Holstenbeck's eyes pivoted between Bernard and O'Brian.

"I said, *lower the weapon.*" A surge in O'Brian's right shoulder just above the gun put lead into the command.

Head moving back and forth, Holstenbeck slowly complied, letting his arms drift down so his pistol aimed at the floor. "I do not have time for this," he stated.

"Put the gun on the ground. *Do it.*"

Holstenbeck, with every eye in the room glued onto him, crouched down to set the pistol lightly on the floor and pushed it forward, though not very far. As he straightened back up, smiling around the room, his jovial voice returned: "You know of course I am a cousin of the president of Lessenberg. I have diplomatic immunity, not to mention numerous contacts in your Washington, D.C., and huge wealth at my disposal. This—"

"And I have a .357 Magnum Desert Eagle loaded and aimed straight at your head," O'Brian sternly interrupted, adding oomph to what he knew was actually an *airsoft* Desert Eagle, one possibly loaded with *pink* plastic pellets.

"Put your hands behind your head."

As Holstenbeck complied, he continued to speak, quietly. "I even have friends high up in this city, Mr. O'Brian. I am sure they will want to hear the side of a prominent VC investor in the region, over some"—and here he fixed his eyes on Bernard—"*toy* maker."

He squinted at O'Brian as he sought a belittling insult for the former police chief, as well, some way to compare the bothersome man to a Walker-like *toy maker*.

"And you, you . . . you *meddler*. You can't even—" and here Holstenbeck's eye fell to the gun, saw the roughly three-millimeter hole at the top of its barrel.

Holstenbeck's smile turned violent. "A *toy* gun? A, how do you say it, *BB gun*? A *toy* maker and a *toy* gun? Brilliant!"

Holstenbeck and O'Brian stared at each other, both tense, calculating, as each estimated just who was closer to the real gun on the floor between them.

Clear to both, Holstenbeck had an easy grab—a fast swipe at the floor and he could be pumping shots into O'Brian with two feet of distance for safety.

Nailing a confident eye on O'Brian, Holstenbeck leaned forward toward the gun, smiling, as O'Brian readied for a last-ditch Hail Mary pounce.

The room couldn't have been quieter or stiller. It was game time and game time had everyone's attention locked in and loaded.

But it wasn't Holstenbeck or O'Brian who moved first. It was Bernard.

"Everyone fire!" he bellowed as he whipped out the (fully automatic) airsoft gun from his shoulder holster, and within a split second Kelly, Patricia, Lester, Chen, and Eric followed, flipping open their new company windbreakers to draw their own airsoft guns.

"Aim for the eyes!" Lester shouted.

Before he finished, a barrage of bright yellow, red, and pink pellets was flying into Holstenbeck's eyes, forcing him to lurch back and shield his face with his hands as he screamed.

Seeing the open mouth, Bernard lowered his gun a few centimeters and shouted: "Get the mouth, too!"

Just as instantly, streams of plastic pellets shot into Holstenbeck's mouth and throat, causing him to stumble back farther, choking.

O'Brian meanwhile dove into a roll that despite his age would have impressed any NFL scout—and readily intercepted both his revolver and Holstenbeck's pistol.

Just as quickly, Kelly whipped past O'Brian and lit into Holstenbeck. She grabbed his collar, thrust him back, then spun his large figure around in a circle and smashed him into the Cannecare Video Wall, cracking some seven feet of plastic screen and fully embedding Holstenbeck into the fixture.

As the beaten man stood wobbling before it, she placed her nose just inches from his and spoke, in a low, raspy, accented tone:

"Schmuck!"

11

Sunday evening.

The lobby of the Sheetless in Seattle had been pretty much taken over by Kelly and the group, the hotel's claustrophobic rooms being simply intolerable for prolonged habitation.

The group spread laptops and devices out along the few lobby tables where the Sheetless served what it advertised as "breakfast." Complimentary, though not one to compliment.

Even after several hours' sleep, they were still exhausted, but leftover adrenaline had driven them down to wait for O'Brian, who was due with news from the police.

When he arrived, his spirited expression suggested the news was good.

"It's done," he said. "Holstenbeck's locked up and it looks like he isn't getting out until his trial."

"What about his so-called diplomatic immunity?" Kelly asked sternly.

"Well, it turned out his country and his high-up friends in Washington weren't so supportive when they learned we had detailed evidence, including video at the end, of everything Holstenbeck did last night. Phil Gradee even put together a video-sensor segment like the one Holstenbeck created on you. The video of Holstenbeck shooting Hazly in the leg was particularly effective, I am told."

"Poetic justice."

"Yeah. Also, the police found bomb-making materials at Holstenbeck's condo, the same that they found in Brenda Tate's back yard."

"My God. How's Ned?" Kelly asked.

"In fair condition, I hear."

Lester jumped in. "Any way we can get a copy of those video segments. I want to see the part where he fights the drones."

"The hell with that," Patricia challenged, "I want to see the part where we nail him with our airsoft guns."

O'Brian went on, "Bernard was correct. The condition of Cannecare Tower is evidence that can't be ignored." O'Brian took out his phone. "Here, check this out. They gave me photos of the floors where Holstenbeck was using weapons." He tapped the photo icon and handed his phone to Lester, who quickly had the others gathered around.

"Hey, that's the thirteenth floor?" Patricia asked.

What they saw looked worse than the Pendrite. The floor was covered with broken glass from windows that looked in on offices, the walls had holes, large and small . . . but what stood out the most was a touching sight:

"Oooohhh," Patricia moaned. "My poor drone. He killed it."

"Hey, by the way, we made it further than you did," Lester proclaimed as he flipped though the photos. "Here it is. See, we made it two-thirds the way down the hall on our floor."

In the center of the photograph, they could see the charred remnants of three drones and two phones.

Bernard joined in. "I do have to say, your acting was quite impressive. I shall remember that the next time we need to hire voice actors for a game. Oh, and also the next time you call in to fake sick."

"And Hazly's OK?" Kelly asked.

"Hazly's OK," O'Brian said. "He's going to be in the hospital for a few days, but he's OK."

"What about Brenda?"

"I'm not sure. But I'm guessing they'll hit her with a string of charges for her little Internet business. I don't think she's going anywhere quickly."

The entire room was euphoric, even the front-desk clerk. Kelly was out, they had finally found and caught the correct suspect, *he* was locked away and was going to remain so, and SimCide's team had solved a huge first case.

Bernard was the exception. Oh, he was smiling, but what lit his face was the pleasing image of his oceanfront home in Cliff Shores.

And so O'Brian's voice hit him like a wet blanket.

"And best of all, get this. The prosecutor's office wants to hire SimCide Investigations to help make sense of the evidence. So we have our *second* client. Of course, that means you guys are going to have to stick around here in Seattle for another week or so."

Bernard moaned.

🐾 🐾 🐾

Wednesday evening, three days later.

Kelly entered the Sheetless's lobby to find Eric alone working at one of the tables.

"Where is everyone?"

"Yeah," Lester complained, "here we finally have some real work to do, and everyone's off fooling around."

"Where'd they go?"

"O'Brian's playing tour guide again. He's got Chen, Patricia, and Eric out in a limo—they went to see some sort of *locks* or something."

"How come you didn't go?"

"Work. I have to get an order off to China by tonight."

"An order for what?"

"Our new Murder Mystery video game. It's going to be good, too."

"All right! Nothing sells like a murder mystery game designed after a real murder. Did you come up with a title yet?"

"No," Lester lied. Actually, they had a working title, but it was not one, they felt, that Kelly was going to approve of, seeing as how it was her friend who was murdered.

Les went over in his mind the titles of the first three Murder Mystery video games that OffCide had put out: (1) *The Case of the Cleavered Clerk,* (2) *The Story of the Strewed Starlet,* and (3) *The Ordeal of the Ornamental Ornithologist.*

No, Kelly was not going to like their current working title for game number four in the series: *The Account of the Iced Executive.*

But a game based on a real murder, as Kelly said, that would rule, just as *The Ornamental Ornithologist* ruled a year earlier. It would sell well and chase investors the heck off their backs for six months.

🎮 🎮 🎮

Friday afternoon.

Kelly was surprised to find Bernard gameless in the lobby of the Sheetless. He sat watching video on a tablet while eyeing—with a sulky squint—a donut.

"I thought you'd be finishing up your tournament."

"It's over." His flat tone did not recommend this as a happy announcement.

"Uh-oh."

"Yes. Uh-oh."

"Oh, God, Bernard. I'm so sorry."

"Really?"

"Yeah. I feel responsible. Of course."

"Yes, well, if you would have been content just to rot away in jail, we would not be having this conversation."

"Yeah . . ."

"Yeah . . . but . . . To be honest, I think I would have lost anyway."

This was quite a confession from the Bernard Walker that Kelly knew.

"What happened?"

"I conceded."

"You *what?!*" That was not in any way the Bernard Walker she knew.

"I gave up. Quit. My opponent was winning, so I conceded."

Bernard stared at his tablet, an attempt to avoid the subject. And Kelly's eyes.

"Come on, tell me what happened."

"If you must know . . ." Then, without looking up: "It turned out my opponent deserved to win."

"That doesn't sound like . . . the Bernard I know."

"I am afraid it turns out that I may have . . . may have had my head somewhat in the clouds. You see, this guy was playing in ways I couldn't understand. He was doing things an experienced player would *not* do, and yet they were working."

"How so?"

"He was *winning!*" Bernard said with an exasperated tone. "That's what video games are about."

"Uh, right."

"Anyhow, I began studying his playing habits. One of the things I did, I made lists of the times he logged on and off."

"Yeah?"

"And I realized that during the day he was logging on at about fifty-four minutes after every hour. Pretty regular for an office, so I thought, maybe a school? So I checked his location on the tournament website and saw he was in a town north of Los Angeles. There were no colleges nearby, so I went onto the websites of the two high schools to check bell schedules."

"High schools? What's a bell schedule?"

"A schedule of when the bells ring, when classes begin and end."

"Oh God—you were getting beat by a high schooler?"

". . . No."

"What?"

"Neither of two high schools' times matched up."

Kelly thought about that, went through a moment of confusion, then smiled in delight. "Tell me you didn't get beat by a *middle school* kid."

". . . no." Bernard sort of groaned, and he did not sound like he was trying to clear his name. He turned back to his tablet without further comment.

"So who was it?"

"Elementary."

"As in *elementary, Watson?*"

"No, as in elementary *school*. It turned out to be a grammar school kid, one punk *who*, when he gets older, will be hearing from me again. That I can assure you."

"Oh, God." The smile and shaking head that she greeted this announcement with were fully involuntary. "How the mighty have fallen."

Bernard peered down at Kelly's feet. "It seems to me you recently went from prominent CEO to Wearer of an Ankle Bracelet."

"Yeah."

"Anyhow, I resigned from the tournament and sent the kid a message."

"Wow. I can't believe it."

"Hmpth."

"What'd you say in the message?"

"I told the kid to contact Les for a job. We need kids like that to test games on. In the future he may be helping *make* them."

From Bernard, just that. The man had a bottomless pit of competitiveness, but after a frustrating loss, just that. No anger, no vindictiveness; rather a note offering a job.

Appraising Bernard, Kelly saw here why she had been able to trust this bizarre man to such a degree.

Epilogue

The following Wednesday morning.

Bernard was not normally the first person to arrive for early meeting times, but on this day he was already seated anxiously in the lobby of the Sheetless, bags on the floor next to him.

He more than any of them was ready to depart Seattle and head home. This time it was real.

Kelly, O'Brian, then a short while later the others strolled in and staked out real estate among the tables, to watch the local TV news as they awaited limos that would drive them to the airport.

"Wow, another gorgeous day out," Patricia commented. "But, boy, will it be nice to get home. I can't wait to sleep in my own bed again."

"Right," Eric agreed.

Lester was less enthusiastic. "Yeah, but that means it's also back to the office, to unhappy investors looking down our necks, and . . . and back to the Rule of the Egghead."

"Yeah hey, boss," Patricia moaned at Bernard, "you gotta do something about that guy."

But it was Kelly who responded.

"No, actually, he doesn't."

"What?" Patricia asked.

Bernard mustered the beginnings of a Stare, wasn't sure which direction to send it, but settled finally on Kelly, a stare that demanded the same information.

Kelly smiled. "Well, it turns out Herb Iggid took a real liking to Seattle. In fact, he found a new job here."

"Seriously?" Patricia asked.

"Yep." Kelly turned to Bernard. "He's out of your hair—I arranged it. I *owed* you that."

Bernard nodded in agreement. "Yes, I would say that you did."

O'Brian butted in. "Wait, so who's going to handle the finances at SimCide and OffCide?"

"*I* am."

Bernard's Look of Death transformed to full deployment. "What about the *daydream* you had of running a company yourself? Being a big CEO and all of that?"

"Yeah, well, I'm going to fix that, too. You see, *you and I* are going to become *co*-CEOs at OffCide Studios. And I'll oversee the SimCide finances until we find a new finance person for them."

"*Co*-CEOs?" Bernard spat out. "And just what would that be? I should think not!"

"No? Think again. I handle all the business stuff, like talking to investors and bankers and making sure bills get paid. And that frees you up to oversee the creative side."

"That is completely unaccept—"

"You will never again in your life be asked to make nine a.m. meetings. *Ever.*"

She found herself peering into a somewhat fading Stare of Death . . . and no further response beyond a lingering hatred in Bernard's eyes.

"We'll talk about this later," Bernard said.

"Wow," O'Brian jumped in to break the tension. "Congratulations, then, I guess, Kelly."

"Yeah," Patricia put in. "Our new boss!"

"I do not care for any of this," Bernard insisted.

"You gotta trust me, Bernard. I got you out of trouble a year and a half ago, I cleared up concerns with investors, I even gave you the idea for a successful video game."

Avoiding eye contact with Kelly, Bernard stared at the lobby TV, which was showing news but with the sound off.

"And I worked things out this time too: I got Herbert Iggid off your back."

"The man whom originally *you* hired."

"And got rid of cheaply. I made it so *he* found a new job, so OffCide won't have to pay a severance package."

The silent TV was showing news footage of Cannecare Tower, of the fire and bullet damage inside.

"I took care of everything," Kelly repeated.

Hatred remained in Bernard's eyes. "Yeah? Then how is it that that creep *Ned Hazly* is being left in charge of Cannecare? I fully believe that man is a danger to society."

"I have to agree with Bernard on that one," O'Brian put in. "To do God knows what with that technology? No privacy policies, no ethics. He's still CEO, right?"

All eyes turned to Kelly.

"Yeeaahh . . . well, that's not so much a problem either," she smiled back.

Bernard set down the maple bar he'd been holding, a donut that remained surprisingly untouched in a hand of Bernard Walker for so long a time.

"What do you mean?" he asked.

"Well, you see, the Cannecare board of directors asked me to *assist* them in their search for a *new* CEO, and I told them they needed a *seasoned*, *proven* executive, one with a drive so strong that he—*or she*—never gives up."

It was clear Kelly enjoyed having the upper hand for a change.

"I mean, that's really the only way they have a chance of picking up the pieces at Cannecare."

Bernard's Look of Death softened ever so slightly. "So Hazly *will not* be Cannecare's CEO?"

"No. It turns out Ned's going to continue as C-*T*-O under a *new* chief executive. I found an excellent candidate, too, a leader re*nowned* for tirelessly and even *blindly* enforcing policies, however bothersome they might be . . ."

Kelly grinned. "Yeah, I found the Cannecare board of directors a *great* new boss for my old friend Ned Hazly."

🎮 🎮 🎮

The following morning.

A security guard leans back in an office chair before two computer monitors, each divided into grids of tiny windows displaying video surveillance from throughout the hotel.

Though the guard's attention is devoted more to a game of Angry Birds on his cellphone, the morning activity emerging in the hotel hallways and lower floors is being displayed real-time in some forty squares of video before him.

It's still dark outside when Herbert Iggid wakes up. His suite's thick curtains provide an extra layer of warmth against the wet chill of Elliot Bay's morning air, ensuring a snug night's sleep—something Herb has grown accustomed to in this wonderful city.

Once dressed, he makes his way down to the lobby, where off to one side the hotel's lounge doubles as a breakfast nook, serving gourmet coffees (surprise!), tea (thankfully), custom-fried omelets, and pastries made from scratch.

Herb has tea and a Danish while reading the front page of the Wall Street Journal. As he finishes, he spots morning light shining into the distant end of the lobby, and noting the time is three hours later in Boston, he pulls his cellphone out of an inner coat pocket—careful not to disturb his tie—and dials his mother.

At this point an NSA contractor in Nebraska has her attention turned from a bowl of cereal and a romance novel by an alert on her computer screen: "A telephone call from Seattle has been tagged as coming from a person associated with a recent bombing incident," the alert informs her.

The woman pulls up a window that plays the conversation real-time over a backdrop of collecting waveform.

"Seattle?" she hears the screechy voice of an older woman nearly shout. "Isn't that in Canada?" The speaker's intonation of the name reveals a mix of dislike and of not really knowing where Seattle is. Or Canada, for that matter.

"It's a beautiful city, Mother. And the new job's a real step up. I've been hired as chief executive officer of a tech company that makes smart-building technology."

That left the woman chuckling. "Well, I do hope they wouldn't be making dumb building technology."

The man argues with her for several minutes, managing to convince her that Seattle is in fact not in Canada, and then describes some of this "gorgeous city's endless cultural attractions— museums, glorious weather, walks along the water, world-class restaurants . . ."

As the game of Angry Birds *ends, the guard looks up briefly to see Herb pocket his cellphone and stroll to the front desk.*

Just as he arrives Herb turns to the hotel entrance to take in yet another divine Seattle morning of sunshine and fresh air and everyone smiling everywhere and—

Only to see that it is in fact pounding *down rain outside, this the first hint of any weather whatsoever that Herbert has seen in Seattle.*

He turns to the front-desk clerk.

"How long do you think the rain's going to last?"

Herb sure hopes it won't be all day.

The clerk examines the deluge plummeting down from the oppressive dark clouds outside, and frowns.

"I'd say . . . July. Possibly August."

About the Author

John Sailors lives in the San Francisco Bay Area, where, when not writing or doing mindless proofreading, he plays (and loses) video games with his son, a college student and future game designer. (Of course, he lets him win.)

Attack Kittens

One snowy winter in Connecticut, my mother allowed two pregnant stray cats to have their litters in the loft above our garage, leaving us with a roomful of kittens to find homes for. My mother put a classified ad in the local paper, but got no response. Desperate, she got creative and placed a new ad that read: "Genetically coded attack kittens, free to a good home." Those cats all had homes by the end of the week. Several people called just to praise the ad, including a drunk man who wanted to make sure such cats weren't real.

Also by John Sailors

Flying the Coop:
The Video Game Mystery Novel
(Book I in this series)

Homeownership Disease:
The Saga of Owen Cash

Flying the Coop:
The Video Game Mystery Novel

Book I in the OffCide Gamer Mystery Series: Game designer
Bernard Walker finds his world taken hostage when police fail to
solve a grisly murder. Desperate for the return of his new million-
dollar oceanfront view, he deploys his San Francisco startup's
game-design technology—backed by jalapeño-infused hot dogs from
a local minimart—to hunt down a highly elusive murderer.

Clouded Ambitions:
The Trial and the Tower

Book 2: Video games, airsoft guns, and drones descend on
Seattle's tech industry as Bernard and his team of game designers
head north to help a friend in trouble, deal with a horrific murder,
and wage a desperate battle against new company rules that require
employees to punch in at nine a.m. Nine a.m.!
In the process they test a video game prototype
in the brick-and-mortar world . . . one minor catch being that in
the brick-and-mortar world, players when killed are not respawned.

Homeownership Disease:
The Saga of Owen Cash
Part I, How Not to Buy a House

Welcome to the world of Owen Cash, a man pushed to finally conform with society and pursue his own slice of the Great American Dream: Homeownership. He journeys forth to battle the trials of financial planning (negative amortization—what the hell is that?), house hunting (kids, go slice that family's tires), and mortgage applications (you need an ultrasound of my kidneys?!), all to please family and society and join the ranks of responsible, landed Americans—just at the height of the real estate boom (ka-pow!).

Visit us at:
www.storycrest.com
Facebook.com/StoryCrestPress